# GUARDIANS

## JOSI RUSSELL

Guardians

**FHP**
Future House Publishing

ISBN-10: 0-9966193-8-0 (paperbound)
ISBN-13: 978-0-9966193-8-7 (paperbound)

Developmental editing by Mandi Diaz
Substantive editing by Jenna Parmley
Copy editing by Jenna Parmley
Interior design by Emma Hoggan

# Acknowledgements

For Rick, my husband and my best friend, who walks with me the sometimes difficult path of creativity, who asks the hard questions, and takes care better than anyone I know.

For Max, to whom the world is an adventure, a puzzle, and a quest. I love it more because I've seen it through his eyes.

For Katy, whose brilliance and boldness light my way and lead me through.

For Lisa, whose gentle encouragement has led me through every draft. Since our first stories, she has given me her expertise, her suggestions, and her encouragement in the moments my stories most needed it.

For Jason, who helps me see things anew.

For my nephew, Simon Russell, whose excitement for this story gave me fresh inspiration.

For my parents-in-law, Kim and Marlene Russell, who support us, shelter us, and encourage us in every endeavor.

For my sister, Jacqueline Latham, who dreams with me and has always believed I could reach the stars.

For my editors, Mandi and Jenna, who have spent their days exploring Minea and making it live.

For my dad, Jack Brewer, the hardest worker on this or any planet, who worked hard without becoming hardened.

And for my mom, Carol Brewer, whose love—constant as the sun—has centered my life, guided me, and cheered me to the end of every journey.

# Chapter 1

The bright disk of the planet Lucidus hung in the morning sky. Countless spires of striped karst limestone stretched away toward the horizon, standing like staggered rows of sentinels as far as Ethan could see through the low-lying morning mist.

It was the day of the twice-yearly Lucidus festival, when the planet rose like an open flower above the settlements on Minea. It marked the changing of seasons from rainy winter to flourishing spring, and then, when it returned, from verdant summer to mellow autumn.

To celebrate, Ethan Bryant and his family had come to the tranquil Tiger Mountain Park in the shadow of two striped towers. The park lay at the edge of the largely unexplored labyrinth of peaks known as the Karst Mountains, which stretched North and East of the city of Coriol, their home. Ethan and his wife Aria had brought their four-year-old daughter Polara and her baby brother Rigel to celebrate the coming of spring. The family's walk through the park was made jovial by Polara's running commentary and by Ethan's spontaneous races with his little girl across the wide, grassy valley that lay at the foot of the peaks.

The park was enormous, with three lakes joined by a river strung like a bracelet across its center. Crowds from Coriol surged around Ethan's family, looking for a spot to rest and wait for the perigee of Lucidus, the highlight of the celebration. Having so many people around brought Ethan some apprehension. He had acquired telepathic abilities through his experiences on a planet called Beta Alora, and he cringed at the proximity of all these people and the swirling mix of thoughts they carried with them.

Ethan's telepathy hadn't bothered him while he was in stasis on the way to Minea. In fact, it had probably made his trip less isolating because even in stasis he was connected with the minds of the nearly 4000 other sleeping passengers on his ship. But when he awoke and began his post-stasis life in the buzzing city of Coriol, he found thousands of thoughts invading his mind constantly. The fear, pain, anger, even the joy and contentment experienced by those around him had been overwhelming. Now, striding through the knee-high grass of the park, Ethan reached behind his ear to double-check the small rounded device that Kaia had created. She had been with him through the ordeal on Beta Alora and had gained similar telepathic abilities. She had invented the device—a thought blocker—to relieve the agony of having so many voices in their heads.

The small implant consisted of two parts: one inside and one outside the skull. The device inside the skull sent electrical impulses through the brain, quieting the incessant thoughts of others. The outside part was a small, rounded button that attached with a strong magnet and activated the thought blocker. Ethan took comfort in the thought blocker's secure attachment. He felt Aria slip her hand into his and took comfort also in how she always seemed to sense when he was feeling anxious.

He looked around at the dusty Ynium miners and

refinery workers, at the farm laborers, the colony officers, and the soldiers from Coriol Defense Headquarters. Their thoughts would be lighter on this day, with the festival in the air. On festival days, Minea almost felt like it had looked in the glossy brochures on Earth: a pristine new planet and an easy lifestyle awaiting them there.

But Ethan knew that most days, for most of the colonists, life was far from easy. He had heard their discouragement, their despair, and those were thoughts he would never forget.

"Hey! Caretaker!" Ethan heard the deep voice of Gil Walters, another passenger from his ship. Gil's four children capered around him as he waded through the grass toward Ethan and Aria.

Gil was dressed in the red coveralls of the Saras Company. Judging by the dust on his face and clothes, he was coming from the mine or the refinery. Ethan grinned.

"Did you find some work with Saras?" he tried to keep the excitement out of his voice.

Coriol was a true company town, where the farms, the water plant, the power plant, the hospitals, and the schools were all set up and run by the Saras Company. They owned everything in Coriol except for the spaceport and the Colony Offices. If you wanted to work, you worked for Saras. Gil ducked his head and Ethan was sorry he had asked.

"Not permanent work. Rose is out there doing a day shift now. They need some help hauling explosives out to a new shaft." He laughed. "It isn't that different from waiting tables. The boss calls an order, I get the boxes from the truck and take them to the blasters, then I do it again." Gil had been a professional waiter back on Earth, at one of the finest restaurants in the capitol.

Aria spoke. "I'll bet you did a great job," she said

encouragingly, but Ethan saw her eyes linger for a moment on Gil's scraped hands and arms.

"I was glad to go. The crew boss picked me up at the Saras Employment Office yesterday." Gil skimmed his fingers across his scrapes absentmindedly. "I stand there just about every day, and there are a lot of days I go home without having worked a single hour." He shook his head, then looked Ethan in the eye. "Do you know how many times I've wished that I had gotten into mining back on Earth? I made good money waiting tables back home, but every day at the Employment Office here I stand and listen to them call for blasters and pickmen and tram operators and all I can think about is the years I wasted carrying soup to people."

There was bitterness in his voice, made sharper by the fact that Ethan knew Gil had loved waiting tables. He was a true server, attentive to people's needs, joyous when he could anticipate and fill those needs.

"Waiting tables was important work, too." Ethan tried to fill his voice with reassurance, and Gil shot him a grateful look.

The two families were at the edge of the first lake, and they stopped to look over its wide surface. It was the lowest of the three lakes, and there was a wide swath of marsh at one end. The smell of fish and thick aquatic vegetation made Polara wrinkle her nose and protest, which set off a chorus of exclamations from the Walters kids, too. Ethan gestured up the park, toward the next lake, and the group went on.

Gil had fallen into a thoughtful silence. Finally, he spoke again. "Don't get me wrong. I know why Yynium production is so important."

Ethan nodded and mentally counted the children, who had skipped ahead of them through the crowd.

Aria spoke up, and her voice was a bit wistful. "Rapid

Space Travel for everyone would be an amazing thing. Can you imagine making the trip from Earth in five years instead of fifty?"

Ethan squeezed her hand, glancing down to catch her green eyes. "It's hard to imagine going that fast. The Super-Luminal drives just can't compare to the YEN drives."

"And you've got to have Yynium to have YEN drives," Gil said, his voice weary.

The Minean morning was warming considerably, and Ethan felt sticky in his jacket. He stopped to take it off.

"Hold up, kids!" Ethan called, and the children swung around and trotted back toward their parents.

Removing the jacket was a process, because first Ethan had to slip out of the backpack where Rigel was riding. Aria held it, kissing the baby loudly. Ethan stretched his shoulders, inhaling the sweet scent of aurelia flowers. He traded Aria the jacket for the baby and they started out again. As they waded through the deep grass, Ethan thought about YEN drives. He'd been in meetings at the Colony Offices last week where they had discussed the obstacles still impeding the completion of the RST ships. The main one was the lack of refined Yynium back on Earth.

"Did you see any of the loads going out, Gil? How much Yynium are they pulling out of those mines?" Ethan hadn't been to the mines for a while.

"I don't know. I know they've got three shifts going every day. It's hard work down there, and at the refinery, too. This planet is full of Yynium, but getting it out is a big job."

"Especially without all the new equipment they've developed back on Earth," Ethan said. "In my meetings, I've seen some of the machines they've got, and they save a lot of time."

"No good to us there, though, are they?" Gil laughed. "How is it, talking to people back on Earth in those meetings?"

Ethan thought about that. Because he had been voted into a Governor position in the Colony Offices of Coriol after he'd arrived, Real-Time Communications meetings were a pretty standard part of his life, but most people on Minea would never be in on one. They weren't exciting meetings, mostly for reviewing Saras' activities and coordinating Coriol's interests with the United Earth Government back home.

"It's . . . surreal, sometimes, when I think that these guys in the meeting who are about my age now were actually born almost half a century after me."

Gil shook his head. "That is surreal. Do they think they'll get those machines out here soon?"

"Not soon, but they're working on it. It's just the old trouble that the Yynium is here and the drives are on Earth. Get the two together, and we can start moving things much more quickly. We have all this Yynium here, but not enough RST ships to transport it all back to Earth so more RST ships can be built."

"I think they should create a YEN drive plant here on Minea," Gil said.

"That's in the plans, too. Kaia says the drives are pretty complicated, and pretty delicate, so the plant has to be pretty sophisticated. We're just not quite ready out here on the frontier."

"Is our ship refitted yet?" Aria asked. The empty passenger ships were being rebuilt with the YEN drives that they'd brought along, and a few were even en route with loads of Yynium, but they were still a long way from their destination.

"Almost," Ethan said. A shadow of uneasiness flitted through his mind when he remembered the long years they'd spent on Ship 12-22, and he was glad its return trip would be much quicker. "They have the SL drive replaced with the YEN drive, and they're just finishing remaking the passenger holds into cargo holds."

"Seems like Ynium's the key to everything," Gil said. "I can see why Saras is so crazy about getting it out of the ground."

Ethan felt his jaw tighten. His theory was that Saras was so crazy about Ynium because Ynium meant money. Seven companies, including Saras, did the bulk of the mining on this planet. Each of them had sponsored a settlement, paying to set up city infrastructures and housing, and paying the passengers' fare from Earth on the stasis ships in exchange for their work on Minea.

This was not the Minea that those passengers were promised. Many of them signed their debt papers back on Earth, confident that if they got their free houses, as Saras promised, they would be able to earn enough to pay off their debt to him for their passage quickly. They didn't know how few scrip a day's work in Coriol would pay, or how much the electricity, water, and food would cost. They didn't know that Saras planned to make his scrip back and then some for every passage.

They were almost to the second lake, and Ethan watched Gil's tired steps as he trudged through the grass.

Aria must have noticed, too. "Maybe we'll stop up here," she said.

Gil shot them a grateful look. "Sounds good to me. I just got off from the graveyard shift and thought I'd bring the kids out for the festival. But I'm beat, and I have swing shift later, after Rose gets back."

Ethan cringed, thinking of all the Saras workers who didn't get paid vacation like the Colony Officers did. Taking a day off from the Saras Company meant missing a day's pay, and that wasn't something most of them could afford.

Calling the children back, Ethan and Aria settled a few yards from the edge of the middle lake. Gil waved apologetically as his kids grabbed his hands and pulled him further up the park.

"Happy Lucidus Day!" he said as he looked back.

"You too," Ethan said, hoping the kids would give his friend a chance to rest.

Aria wrapped up some of their picnic lunch and ran lightly after the Walters', tucking the little bundle under Gil's arm with a smile.

Ethan spread a blanket and set Rigel atop it, then he and Polara dug out the rest of the food from the basket. Ethan and Aria had packed all the children's favorite foods: dark bread made from smooth-ground veam grain, sliced green lapin fruit, sweetbean cheese and chocolate, chei fruit candies that Aria made herself, and the special-occasion olona juice that stained their mouths blue.

Ethan handed Rigel a piece of the sweet, firm bread to gnaw on and made a sandwich for himself, slipping a few thin slices of lapin on to add sweetness for contrast with the savory bean cheese.

Polara guzzled her juice, then turned with a smile to her father. "Can we skip rocks, Dada?"

Aria was a few yards away, eating a chunk of chocolate absentmindedly and peering at the leaves on a bush.

"We're going down near the water," he called, and she glanced up and smiled.

Ethan stood and took Polara's hand. She pulled him to the water's edge and they began to hunt skipping stones. He liked the rounded, flat-bottomed pebbles the best, and he picked over the rocky shoreline carefully for the best ones. Polara's priority was size. She grabbed the biggest rocks she could find and lobbed them into the water. She'd thrown five before he skipped his first one.

It was a good throw, though, and his stone sailed across the calm surface, bouncing and leaving behind widening circles wherever it hit. All in all, six skips. Not bad.

An unusual movement in the water caught Ethan's attention. In the ripples left by the skipped stone, some small, smooth, glossy bodies were arcing.

Swimming lizards. Ethan would never get tired of seeing them. Called natare, they were curious and friendly, ranging in color from warm charcoal to pale lavender. The females were speckled, to help them blend into the dappled shadows under the foliage. The males had a ruff around their necks which streamed behind them as they swam after minnows to carry to their nesting mates.

Minean creatures were not the same as Earth's creatures, but many, like the natare, were similar to the animals of Earth. Though some had been catalogued and named, many species were still being discovered. The colonists usually referred to the animals by the names of their closest Earth equivalents, sometimes with a specific quality of the Minean species, like swimming lizards. Even after four years here, the surprising differences in Minean creatures instilled Ethan with wonder.

The natare rode the ripples to the water's edge, reaching their delicate feet forward and climbing out onto the bank. Their eyes were inquisitive, searching. Ethan held out his hand. Three of the little creatures came forward. They knew humans, knew that they liked the taste of the salt that humans carried on their skin.

Soon they were licking his fingers, and Ethan took his hand back and broke off a piece of the sandwich to offer them.

The boldest, a dusty purple male, snatched it and raised his neck ruff toward the others. Ethan watched them back away from the challenge on their webbed feet. But they followed the purple natare. When he wasn't looking, one grabbed a bit of the sandwich from his mouth and dived into the water, swimming rapidly for his mate on her nest a few yards away.

Polara's voice surprised Ethan. "What about that one, Dada?" She said, pointing to the third natare. "He didn't get any."

Ethan offered her the last bite. "Here you go. Share this with him."

The child brightened and took the sandwich. Ethan watched her careful steps as she crept along after the little lizard, calling, "Here swimmer, here swimmer. Come have a sandwich." She was a bold child, a brave one, and he loved seeing her fascination with animals and people. Watching her embrace the world was one of the great joys of his life.

And Rigel—Rigel's quiet thoughtfulness brought him insurmountable peace. Still not talking at almost two, and deeply empathetic, Ri spent most of his time watching others closely. He didn't walk yet, didn't seem to need to move around and explore like Polara always had. The pediatrician had been a little worried about Rigel's lack of speech, but after tests on his ears and cognition, had sent them home telling them not to worry, he would soon be making a racket alongside his sister.

Ethan felt a familiar need to check on his son. Though he didn't have the charge to look after 4000 sleeping passengers anymore, he still heavily felt the responsibility to protect the people he loved, and when he glanced toward the picnic blanket, he saw Rigel looking at him and reaching for his bread. The nearly-two-year-old had knocked it just beyond his own reach. Ethan rose and retrieved it for him.

It was in that second, that small moment when his back was turned, that Polara fell into the lake. He heard the splash, and turned to the spot he'd last seen her. But she was far beyond that. How had she moved so quickly? She was flailing now in the inlet where the tumbling river flowed into the lake. He ran.

Blindly, Ethan charged into the water, fighting its pull against his legs. The river rocks were slick and round, but he barely noticed as his ankles cracked into them. She was being swept by the current. He had to get to her. Suddenly, the bottom dropped away, and Ethan felt his head go under. He swam, hard, and broke the surface just in time to see Polara's small hand reaching horribly toward the sky.

He lunged, grasping at whatever he could. He felt her jumpsuit, soaked and slick, and clenched it, hauling her toward him and up, up toward the air. He went under, but held her above him, relieved to feel her squirming and fighting in his arms. Kicking, he rose above the surface again and gasped, "Polara! It's all right. I've got you. You're all right."

His girl was crying, gasping. He got her to the bank, where helpful hands of onlookers steadied him as he came out. He collapsed on the stones, cradling her in his arms, curling his body protectively around her, and speaking in a low, calming voice, though he didn't feel calm himself.

Her hysterical crying continued. Suddenly, he found himself singing an old Earth lullaby, gentle and low, that had calmed them both during long nights and tense moments. Slowly, he felt his heart rate returning to normal and heard the child's tears subside.

Aria was suddenly beside them, her arms encircling them both. She didn't say anything, just held them, but he heard her fear in her ragged breathing.

Soaked, Ethan carried Polara back to the blanket. He tried

to still the trembling in his arms. He had watched over his family across the stars, and even now his greatest fear was that something would happen to them, something he couldn't stop.

Ethan pulled his eyes from Polara, who was now sipping olona juice, to catch Aria's gaze. His wife was holding Rigel tightly. Her smile was shaky as she looked back at Ethan.

"It's okay," she said. "I'm glad you were so fast."

He nodded, trying to push away the growing dread that had been sparked by Polara's near miss. He tightened his arm around her. She was strong and bright, but still so fragile. He was going to have to guard her more carefully.

Across the park, Ethan heard the chiming of bells. Lucidus was reaching its perigee, the moment when it was closest to Earth, and it hung bright and round in the sky above Tiger Mountain. He pointed it out to Polara as Aria retrieved from their basket the four silver hand bells they'd brought along. Polara, her fear forgotten, stood to ring hers with vigor. Its bright sound joined the others, echoing off the karst peaks as the crowd began to cheer. A few people set off bright fireworks which threw sparks of color into the air around them. Ethan smiled to see Polara, born here as a true Minean, embracing the tradition.

Ethan glanced up at the bright planet and his smile disappeared. A dark smudge appeared and traveled directly across the face of Lucidus. Others had seen it too. The crowd sunk into an uneasy stillness, choking the clamor of the Lucidus bells. Uneasy murmurs arose at the sight of the opaque spot streaking smoothly across the planet.

Ethan felt a surge of fear, an old apprehension.

"It's just an orbital defense sphere," someone said, as the spot dropped off the crisp edge of the planet and the bells began again.

It could be one of the orbital defense spheres. Ethan tried to let that make him feel better.

*** 

Admiral Phillip Reagan paced in his temporary office in Lumina. His windows were open and the office smelled of mud and greenery: spring. It was his fourth Minean spring since they had made him Admiral of the Minean fleet. He'd been promoted after he arrived, when news had broken that he had disagreed with selling Ship 12-22 to the Others of Beta Alora, and now he got to oversee the ships and command the fleet. Well, train the fleet. There hadn't been much commanding necessary in the ever-peaceful skies of Minea.

But something troubling had been seen in those skies this morning. He shouldn't even be here today; the day of the Lucidus festival was a UEG holiday. But something unusual had been spotted, and he wasn't going back to the barracks until he got some answers.

Until then, he was listening to the guitar riffs of an old Earth band. He was glad that he'd had the Caretaker's drive, full of old Earth music and movies, downloaded from the ship on which he'd arrived before it was scrubbed and repurposed. Now, the thumping bass rhythm provided just enough distraction to keep Reagan's thoughts from running away with all the possibilities of what that spot in front of Lucidus could have been.

He had seen it, a shadow on the bright circle that was the planet, at the height of the Lucidus festival this morning. It showed up and moved across just as the bells rang in the city and the cally blossoms were released from the tops of the buildings. He had seen it just for a second, and had known it wasn't the orbital defenses as others speculated. One thing that made him fit for admiralcy here on Minea was his impeccable eye for detail. The orbitals wouldn't have been in the right place to transit Lucidus. The spot wasn't the right shape or size. And he'd never seen anything pass in front of the planet at perigee.

"You seem cool," Sergeant Frank Nile surprised him.

Reagan turned down the music. "Just waiting for the analysis team."

Nile crossed to the window. "Exciting first day down here."

Reagan's laugh was a little bitter. "Yeah."

"So what's your itinerary, Admiral? How long will you be with us here in Lumina?"

Reagan breathed in the light spring air. Everything depended on what the analysis team found. "Well, the original plan was to do all the routine defense checks here in the next two weeks. Your reviews of personnel, equipment, and procedure haven't been done in far too long. But with this new . . . development, I may be heading to Flynn. I've got to make sure we're ready for whatever happens."

Sergeant Nile gestured toward the map of the Minean settlements on the wall. "Maybe we'll get to try out some of our strategies, huh?" His voice was light.

Reagan stood slowly and walked to the map, laying a hand on it. His voice was stern when he said, "Sergeant, I hope you understand that the best military strategy is the one you never have to use."

Reagan ran his fingers across the eight cities spread almost in an X across this part of the planet. He felt the weight of every settlement, of every person in each one. He lingered for a moment on the city that lay at the northwestern corner of the settlements: Coriol, where he lived with his daughter, Kaia. Lumina, the city he was in now, was at the opposite edge of the settlements diagonally: the most southwestern of the cities.

Between them lay the Azure Mountains, a range of folded mountain peaks that divided the continent almost in half.

Nile was at his shoulder, and Reagan saw the man glance from the map out the window, where the peaks of the Azures fringed the sky in the distance. Reagan felt a certain comfort in seeing the mountains. The Azure range was the larger of the two major mountain ranges near the settlements. Much like the Rocky Mountains back on Earth, they had been formed by folding and faulting and they rose from the plains on either side of them to elevations over 6000 meters. The other range was the Karst Mountains out near Coriol, past the Eastern Plains. It had been formed from the dissolution of Minean blue limestone into freestanding towers. It was as dramatic as it was remote and largely unexplored. Reagan had heard that a new vein of Yynium discovered underneath it was causing quite a stir among the companies. Both ranges offered a certain amount of protection to their neighboring cities.

Nile must have been thinking the same thing. "The mountain cities will have a bit more cover than we have out here."

Reagan nodded. "Oculys and Kantara are in the foothills and they have our best surface-to-air missiles. Minville, Sato, and New Alliance are easily defensible from the ground because they've each got the Azures on two sides. But the plains here in Lumina leave us a little exposed." He considered for a moment. "I don't worry about Flynn. It has two advantages: being surrounded by the Azures and being in the center of the settlements."

Both men glanced at Coriol. It was the outlier. To reach it you had to cross the Eastern Plains, and it lay at the edge of the Karst Mountains, which did not have the altitude of the folded mountains, but made up for it in the sheer grandeur of its towers. They would at least offer a place for people to flee if anything happened.

Reagan found himself growing increasingly tense. Coriol looked so isolated up on the corner of the map, so vulnerable. And Kaia was there now, in their blue cottage, alone. These days away from her were hard. Reagan missed her, and he worried about her. Even after four years on the planet with her, he had still not gotten used to the fact that she was older than he was now and that she was slowing down. Reagan feared the day when he would get a call that she'd fallen or that her heart, which had been beating so long now, had stopped doing its work.

These last few years had been like his first years as a new father, when he'd found himself worrying at odd times about the myriad dangers the world posed to his new daughter. Only this time, instead of becoming more able and more independent each day, she was moving in the opposite direction, and the end of his worrying now would be very different from end of his worrying then, when he'd dropped her off for her first day of school.

Reagan shifted, feeling the jagged weight that he'd carried in his chest since the day he'd left the Treaty Cabinet Meeting on Theta Tersica a lifetime ago. It was the weight of the knowledge that he should have stopped the sale of Ship 12-22. He had voted against the plan that had sold the ship to the Others of Beta Alora, and he planted information that he had hoped David McNeal, the original Caretaker of the ship, would find. But he hadn't fought any harder. He had instead climbed on a stasis ship himself and had done no more to stop the atrocity.

He saw now—and had seen the moment he closed his eyes in stasis, and for the next fifty-three years as he slept—that he should have sabotaged the slave ship, should have taken a battleship up and placed it between the Others and the innocents. Should have made it public. Should have stood in front of a microphone and shamed the UEG for their decision. He should have—should have done *something*.

But he hadn't.

He had consoled himself with the decision's seeming necessity and gone to sleep, expecting to awaken with all of it behind him, a blip on the otherwise bright history of humanity's colonization.

Only it wasn't in the past. He lived with the effects of that decision every day as he saw his daughter lose words she had once known and people she had once loved. Kaia had forgotten her mother's name just weeks ago, and her weeping at its loss had broken Reagan's heart.

Reagan pulled his gaze from the window.

Nile fixed him with a piercing look, and Reagan realized he'd been silent a long time.

The sergeant spoke. "Like you say, sir, I hope we won't have to worry about defenses. But just in case, I'll have the troops ready to show you some maneuvers this afternoon if you'd like."

Reagan nodded. "And pull your personnel files, Sergeant. I might as well start the reviews while I wait."

"Yes, sir." Nile crossed to the desk and punched in some codes before leaving the office with a sharp salute to the admiral.

Reagan put a hand impatiently to his head in response, scolding himself for getting distracted. This was not the time for parental regrets. He'd spoken to Kaia on the missive an hour ago, and she was fine today.

What wasn't fine was the strange spot that had crossed Lucidus this morning. Reagan knew what it was, even before the Anomaly Analysis Team walked into his office moments after Nile had left.

"Sir." The team leader, Lesharo, pushed a length of his black hair behind his ear and looked Reagan in the eye. "We've got some answers for you."

Reagan watched Smith, another member of the team, close the office door.

"I'm not going to like them am I, Lesharo?"

The dark man shook his head swiftly. "It's a ship, sir." He pulled a wide photoflat out of an envelope and handed it to Reagan.

Though the image was grainy and sparse on detail, the inky silhouette was sinister and obviously alien.

He tapped a code into his missive. His voice was tight as he spoke. "I'm putting the bases on alert."

# Chapter 2

The day after the festival, Ethan was still trying to shake the shadow in front of Lucidus from his mind. Ethan looked in on Polara as she lay sleeping. He felt a chill in the air and looked around Polara's little room for an extra blanket.

The room was dominated by the beautiful bed he and Aria had bought from Winn, a carpenter who had been in stasis on their ship. Winn, like many others from Ship 12-22, was having a hard time finding use for his special set of skills on Minea, and since Ethan had been voted into the Colony Government and had a steady paycheck, he and Aria tried to help out the other passengers when they could. The bed was made of Minean wood, rich green and coarse-grained. Carved into the headboard were the most beautiful stars Ethan had seen since leaving space.

He pulled a blanket from the dresser and tucked it around Polara. No need to wake her. He slipped out of Polara's room and down the hall to Rigel's room.

Ethan expected to see his son asleep as he peeked into the next room, but the baby was sitting up in his crib, also one of Winn's creations, smiling at his father. Ethan had the uncanny feeling that his arrival was expected.

He slipped in and picked the little boy up. "We're always

the first awake, aren't we, Ri?" he asked. Rigel looked up at him, his eyes as bright as the stars outside his window. Ethan scooped him up and took him to the changing table. The baby lay happily. As Ethan pulled a warm little shirt over Rigel's head and slipped a pair of bright red pants on him, he remembered the nearly Olympic feats it had required to dress Polara when she was this age.

Rigel was different. He lay quietly gazing at his father as he dressed him. It was hard for Ethan to explain how much he enjoyed Rigel's company. After five years as Caretaker of a ship where the other passengers were in stasis, he still felt the need to connect deeply with other humans. Though Rigel was behind in walking and talking, he was brilliant at connection. When he looked at Ethan, it was as if he knew the very depths of Ethan's soul. As Ethan took Rigel downstairs to feed him his breakfast, he sensed the deep calm that the child carried with him.

Aria wandered sleepily into the kitchen and poured herself a cup of the thick gray milk made from sweetbeans, the main crop grown by the Food Production Division of Coriol. Ethan smiled at her.

"Sleep well?"

Aria nodded.

Ethan peered more closely at her, to see if she was telling the truth. Aria, like all the passengers, still dealt with one of the effects of fifty years in stasis: nightmares.

Aria insisted that her dreams during stasis had been mostly pleasant. She had relived, in greater detail than she would have thought possible, her happy childhood. She had flown. She had lived in a castle. She had lived a thousand dream-lives while she slept through the stars.

But there were dark dreams, too—ones she told Ethan

about in the still of night when he had his arms around her and she was safe enough to explore them again. She told him they were dreams of loss and fear, of dark shapes pursuing her through bizarre landscapes.

They were dreams of abandonment, deep loneliness, and hunger, long and aching. These were the dreams that came to her, even now, four years after their awakening. Ethan hated that they snatched her from sleep. Neither of them got enough of it, with small children in the house whose sleep patterns were still erratic. Ethan himself had a few dark dreams while in stasis, but they only plagued him occasionally now.

He slid a hand over hers on the table. "Any bad dreams?"

Aria cast him a bright look that dispelled his worries. "Nope. I just dreamed I grew a field of wheat here. It was so beautiful, golden against the blue soil."

Aria had been a crop geneticist back on Earth, and there she had developed her own strain of wheat. But she hadn't been able to find work here on Minea.

"You should visit Kaia before you go to work," Aria said. "Take her some of the new mugs that Luis dropped off yesterday."

Ethan nodded and checked his missive for the time. He'd better go if he wanted to have time for that.

***

He stopped in at Kaia's cottage, the little crate of mugs under his arm. When she opened the door, her eyes were red and her face rumpled. She'd had a long night. She didn't sleep well, a product of years in the artificial environment of Ship 12-22.

It was still strange to Ethan that his ship had an official title. They'd started referring to it by its launch and dock numbers during all the government proceedings that took place after they'd arrived at Minea, and the title had stuck.

Kaia smiled warmly. "David!" she said.

Ethan blinked, the sting of it hurting him like it always did, and leaned in for a hug, hoping she wouldn't catch herself this time. She was always so embarrassed when she called him the wrong name, and it was happening more and more often lately.

She didn't notice this time, though, and she took the mugs and pulled him into the kitchen for some lalana, the sweet hot morning drink she indulged in every day.

He sipped it, enjoying the creamy, rich flavor. Saras Food Production could do amazing things with a sweetbean.

"What's on your schedule today?" Ethan asked, trying not to notice the slight shaking of her hand as she lifted one of Luis's bright mugs to her lips.

"I think I'll visit the junkyard. I want to pick up a few new parts."

Ethan shook his head quickly, before he could stop himself. "I don't know, Kaia. That place is a deathtrap. If that central pile of junk ever falls . . ."

He could see her annoyance in her eyes, but she teased it away, her voice light as she said, "You're right. Maybe I'll just stay home and knit a shawl instead."

Ethan tried to remain stern, but he couldn't help but chuckle at her twinkling gray eyes. "Hey, I still have that shawl. You're a pretty good knitter."

"I'm a good robot builder, too," Kaia said sternly. "And I will be careful at the junkyard."

Ethan stood and stretched. "I'll stop by again. I guess I'd better get to work for now, though."

She hugged him. He could barely feel her frail form in his arms.

"Have a good day, David." Ethan flinched as he felt her tense. She had realized it this time, and she didn't pull away from the embrace. He knew she didn't want to look him in the eye.

"I'm sorry, Ethan."

He stepped back, searching her face and trying to convey comfort. "Hey, Kaia. It's okay. Really. It's fine."

Her jaw tightened. "It's not fine, Ethan. I'm really scared. What if I'm slipping?" She walked a quick circle around the kitchen, then grasped his hands.

Staring into her desperate eyes, Ethan felt the old ache of regret over what had happened on the ship so many years ago. But it was long done, and no amount of regret now would change it.

"We'll get through," he said. "This is just another of our adventures. We didn't know what we were facing on Beta Alora, or how to get through it. But we figured it out together. We'll figure this out, too. You're not alone."

She squeezed his hands tighter and blurted out, "But, Ethan, what if I forget you? I will be alone."

He looked at her a long moment, wanting to deny it, but knowing it could happen, "Then it will be my job to remember you," he said, embracing her again and wishing, somehow, that he had better words to say.

# Chapter 3

Marcos Saras saw the explosion before he felt it. A flash, and then the rumbling percussion that he'd come to love. Brighter by far than the planet Lucidus that everyone was so excited about yesterday, it meant a new mine shaft, a new vein of glassy Yynium laid bare, and this time, a new bonus.

Marcos never expected to be mining a planet this far from the desert where he was raised. He never expected to be this busy, and he never expected to be this rich.

His mother wouldn't have liked him saying that, but it was true. The first three UEG bonuses he'd won and held for his efficiency in delivering Yynium had made it true. Still, he probably wouldn't say it in front of her.

And the bonus the UEG was offering this time, *if* he could produce the purest sample of Yynium by the end of next month, wasn't just a measly 2.5 percent. It was also a land grant: the whole of the Karst Mountain range that lay outside of his city, and all the Yynium in it. This was an instant monopoly, the ability and permission to extract every grain of Yynium from what his surveyors were suggesting was a deposit richer than any found on Minea so far. But even though it lay closest to his city, the six other companies would be vying for the bonus as well, and if one of them got it, Saras Company would be hamstrung, blocked from expansion under the karst towers.

As he watched the cloud of rubble settle over the opening to the new shaft, he cursed softly. He should have done this last month, then he would already be on his way to being awarded that land grant.

But he had another plan, one that would secure the grant for sure. He would meet with his vice presidents, Veronika and Theo, in an hour and fill them in on it, just as soon as they were back from their daily checks of the districts.

They were vice presidents, but they didn't spend their days in decorated offices attending endless marketing meetings like they had on Earth. Here in the settlements, VPs ended up doing a lot of assistant work. It couldn't be helped. If there was a snag in the production line or a group of disgruntled workers, Marcos had to have someone he could trust take care of it. His assistants and managers didn't have a big enough picture of the whole operation to make decisions, and his VPs had to be out in the districts to get that big picture. Every decision had potentially disastrous consequences and they couldn't be made haphazardly.

His VPs, though, were anything but haphazard. Tall, thin Theo Talbot had been the first in charge of Saras Company on Minea. As soon as Marcos's father had set up the settlement, he'd returned and left Theo to run the whole city. Theo had been here for a dozen years: four with Marcos' father, five running the operation by himself as acting president, and three after Marcos had come. Theo knew the operation in and out. He could tell Marcos the names of every manager across the city—in the Food Production District, the Market District, the Mine, or any of the other districts. He could quote production numbers for the last ten years off the top of his head. He was friendly and got along with people. He had an energetic manner and could talk his way through problems. Marcos could see why his father had picked Theo to man the operation for so many years.

Veronika Eppes was the opposite. She was cold, calculating, and efficient. She didn't let emotion get in her way, and she dealt with people like tiles in a dragonboard game. She knew where they were best used and she placed them there. If they weren't of use, she'd knock them off the board. Marcos had, more than once, relied on her decisiveness. And more than once she'd saved them from the mire of Theo's tendency toward indecision.

They didn't get the long days in their lavish offices that vice presidents got back on Earth, but Marcos tried to keep them supplied with perks. For Veronika that was expensive imported wines, clothes, and jewelry from Earth. She had a particular affinity for rubies. For Theo, a custom hovercar, which he'd be driving as he finished up his rounds right now.

The day was calm, and now Marcos could see the darkness of the new shaft gaping through the settling blue dust. As he watched it, he was distracted by the beeping of an incoming transmission alert from his hovercar. He slid into the back seat and tapped a screen mounted at eye level. The cost of this one luxury, a receiver in his hovercar for Coriol's single Real-Time Communicator back at Saras's Coriol headquarters, would have built his mansion on Ynium Hill twice over. But his parents insisted that he have it so they could keep an eye on him— though their supervision had lessened considerably after he'd earned the company the second bonus. He took that to mean that they were gaining confidence in him.

Marcos's father, Dimitri Saras, was suddenly looking at Marcos from the screen with the level, piercing gaze that was his trademark. There was no greeting. RTC was expensive, and

Dimitri didn't use it longer than necessary.

"Are you receiving this in the hovercar? Where are you?" he demanded. "Why aren't you at the office?"

Marcos chose which question to answer. "I'm overseeing the start of a new shaft. We just blasted."

His father scoffed. "That's not where the president needs to be."

He said *president* with an emphasis Marcos had grown used to. He knew that for his father, the word was more than a title. It was an identity. Dimitri had made that clear in every interstellar interaction they'd had since he left for Minea shortly after Marcos was born. Marcos had grown up in the shadow of the word "president." In fact, Dimitri had sent him to Minea as soon as he walked back into Marcos's life because he wanted his son to be a company president, no matter the cost.

Marcos felt his body tense. He wanted to defend himself, tell his father that he'd been in the office every day for the last three weeks, explain that Theo said that without some field experience he wouldn't make a very good president. But field experience was not something Dimitri valued. Marcos had wanted to go to college, to have the experiences it seemed everyone had there: late nights, final exams, learning about fields other than mining. However, his father had put him on a P5 RST ship anyway, seeing no use in a boy who already had a job spending valuable time exploring useless fields of information.

*People go to college so they can get a job,* he'd said. *You have a job.* And he'd sent Marcos to do it. Now Marcos had been here three years.

"Do you hear me?" Dimitri's voice was edgy.

"I'm sorry. What?"

"I said, you should be at the office. Something big is

happening on your planet, and I've got you a seat in the defense meeting this afternoon. But it's not going to come into the backseat of your hovercar. It's top secret. You need to be there." Dimitri had a way of making every sentence final.

"I'll be there. I'm heading back now." He closed the hovercar door and gestured to his driver. They set off for Saras headquarters.

"This shaft is important, though," he tried to explain.

"Marcos, every shaft is important."

"But—"

"Don't interrupt me. You need to learn delegation. You need to learn division of duties. You need to learn that being president isn't about getting in on all the fun. It's about making sure that all the parts of your organization are fitting together into a functioning machine."

"There's another bonus up," he tried to say.

"I'm aware of the bonus. And I expect you to secure it as you've secured the others." Again, that final tone.

"I will," Marcos said, hearing the cold edge that had crept into his own voice. While he had his father on the line, he jumped at the chance to ask, "Is there a landing date for Serena's ship yet?" The girl he wanted to marry was on her way back to Earth from an Interstellar Study trip, and she should be landing very soon.

Dimitri grunted, closing his eyes in irritation. "Keep your mind on your work, Marcos. I told you I would let you know of any developments. If you haven't heard anything, then there is nothing new."

"I'm just hoping—" Marcos began, but his father broke in, changing the subject.

"Where are your VPs?" Dimitri said. "Theo? Veronika?"

Marcos hated the way he said her name. Even now, eight

years since she'd been put on the P5 with Marcos and they'd both been sent out of the way, Dmitri's voice held a salacity that turned Marcos' stomach. "They're out on daily checks."

"Ah. Well." He could see that Dimitri was disappointed, and he was glad his mother was not on the call. "You'll be at that meeting, Marcos."

"I will," Marcos said again.

"Message me when it's over. I want to know what's discussed." The screen went blank. His father gave no goodbye.

The hovercar stopped at Saras headquarters and Marcos knew he should go right up to his office, but instead he slipped out to the south shop to see what progress Cayle was making on the P5.

The sleek little ship looked out of place in the big shop, surrounded by earthmovers and drill rigs. Cayle tossed him a wave from atop a twenty-foot rockhammer and Marcos felt a ripple of annoyance.

Cayle must have seen it on his face, because he hurried down and rushed into an apology.

"Sorry, boss, but Theo says they need that hammer for the new shaft and if it's not ready by the end of the day, I'll be drivin' it instead of fixin' it."

Marcos never acknowledged apologies. He'd learned that from his mother. Acknowledgment of bad behavior meant its acceptance.

"How long on the ship, Cayle?"

Cayle shook his head slowly. "Well, there's no tellin'. I've got the grunge cleaned out of the engine, mostly, but I still can't get that YEN drive to fire up, and I haven't had time to machine new rods yet. With my regular work, it'll be a while yet."

Marcos briefly considered, as he did every time they had

this conversation, making the ship Cayle's full-time priority, but Cayle was the best mechanic they had, and pulling him off the mine equipment would raise too many questions. He shook his head quickly.

"Keep working on it. And," Marcos glanced around briefly, "keep your mouth shut."

"I always do, boss."

Marcos left the shop, crossed the liftstrip, and walked through the high, glassed-in entryway of Saras headquarters. He stopped to glance at the rows of windows. They were green with little patches of plants growing along the edges. These plants were showing up everywhere in Coriol. Marcos barked at the receptionist to get the cleaning staff in here and make a note to dock them two hours' pay. Perhaps that would get them to take a little more pride in their work. Missing the windows in the front lobby? Sloppy.

He slipped a sweet, hard gar fruit candy in his mouth and hoped his screens were set up in the office. He had an Interstellar Communications System recording coming online, and he'd be expected to get his response to it out within ten minutes after seeing it. And then he had to meet with Veronika and Theo before this RTC meeting his father had gotten him into with the Coriol Defense Committee. Marcos walked a little faster.

The screens were set up, and the ICS recording was just beginning when he sat down in his Earthleather chair in front of the wide windows that looked out over the heart of Coriol, his city.

The recording was routine. It requested comprehensive Yynium output numbers for the last quarter. As he entered the numbers, Veronika opened his office door and leaned in.

"I'm back," she said.

He nodded. "Get Theo and come back in five minutes."

He finished the numbers quickly. It was vital to keep the UEG happy.

Checking the clock, Marcos saw he had just enough time to fill Veronika and Theo in before the Defense Committee meeting. Veronika entered first, and she came behind the desk, as she always did, to lean against it. Veronika had little use for personal space. Marcos leaned back in the chair as Theo came in.

Theo always gave him plenty of space. This time, he gestured the VP forward a bit so he didn't have to shout the plan down the length of the office. It didn't take Marcos long to explain the idea that would win them the land grant bonus. Theo, as usual, was resistant.

"You want to blast a shaft down from our legal land and tunnel under the Karst Mountains? We don't even know for sure what's down there. We only have the core samples, which were illegal, too, by the way. Why would we risk it?" Theo asked, the tone of authority that Marcos hated sneaking into his voice.

Marcos felt Veronika's hand on his shoulder. She had moved behind him, to face Theo. "Because he knows that not doing it is a bigger risk. If someone else gets the grant, then we might as well get on the P5 and go home now. There won't be enough Yynium left to support a third of this city. The veins we're mining are running out right now."

"But don't you see that if we're caught we lose it all anyway?"

Marcos scoffed. "The UEG isn't going to shut us down for a little bad behavior. We'll be fined, sure, but we've got the scrip to cover whatever they can impose. The veins we're in now are so sparse that we're pulling a lot of rock with the Yynium, and it's possible that we're not getting all the rock out when we refine. We're not on Earth, with the best of equipment and plenty of it. This is the frontier, and you know as well as I do that we're making do as best we can. Still, purity is way down, and we can't win that grant with dirty Yynium."

Marcos stood and walked around his desk to where Theo leaned against a cabinet in the corner. Marcos put his hand on the older man's shoulder and felt the jab of bone through his jacket. "I'm not saying we strip the deposit clean. I'm saying that we blast into the center of it, where the cleanest cake is, and refine that for our grant sample. Just slice off a little. Then, we play it fair and square. If we don't win the grant, we destroy the tunnel and tip our hats to the winner. If we do win the grant, we're ready to start production and get the Yynium heading to Earth twice as fast as we could otherwise."

Marcos saw Theo's discomfort, though he wasn't sure if he was squirming because the plan went against his ethics or because he was jealous that his upstart boss had come up with it.

Veronika came out from behind the desk, too. She always seemed to sense the exact moment that Theo was at a tipping point. "This way, we're sure to win. And you, of all people, ought to want to fight for this city. You built it."

Marcos felt the jab of that. If it had been any other moment, he would have called her on it. His father had built this city, and Theo had only tended it those years when Marcos was growing up and traveling in the P5 from Earth with Veronika. But he saw Theo caving and knew that this was not the time.

Theo agreed, in the end, and Marcos began the process of finding a blasting crew that could keep their mouths shut. He had at least one person in mind, someone who had done covert jobs for him before.

\*\*\*

Daniel Rigo held his breath as he walked from the bright Minean morning outside into the dim interior of the mine. He lined up, waiting for the next tram. He glanced at his mother, Marise. Her eyes were weary as she peered at the dark ahead of them. Daniel put a reassuring arm around her shoulders.

"I miss your father," Marise said, so quiet that only he could hear. She leaned her head against his shoulder, and Daniel was glad he'd grown taller than her since they'd come to Minea five years ago. It made him feel better able to protect her and his little sisters, Merelda and Nallie, who were born here on Minea and still small. He was nearly nineteen now, and there was a lot of protecting in his future.

"I miss him too," Daniel said. "He loved the tram ride in and out."

Marise chuckled. "Only time he got to sit down. I'm starting to look forward to it myself."

The Yynium dust wasn't as thick up here near the mine entrance, but Daniel could already taste its lemony tang in the air. He took a quick drink from the water bottle he carried with him—not much, because he'd need it for later. The first tram left and he and Marise stepped a bit closer to the front of the line.

Zella Panderlin, a neighbor of theirs, was standing in line in front of them. Her pale curls, tied up in a bright cloth, stood out in the dark of the mine. She turned and caught his eye, flashing him a smile.

Daniel felt himself look down, embarrassed. He had known Zella since before they'd left Earth. Their fathers had both operated precision scoring machines in the Yynium mines back there. Thorian Rigo had been one of the best scorers in the industry. He'd signed up thinking that working in the mines on Minea would be similar to working in the mines on Earth, but that wasn't the case. The scoring machines, designed back on Earth, couldn't handle the volume of Yynium they were dealing with on Minea. They had burned out quickly, and parts were half a century away.

That left the workers mining Yynium with archaic techniques, using picks and shovels and hammers and chisels. That kind of mining had wasted Thorian's skills. And the wages were much smaller than they were in the mines of Earth, too. It wasn't the Minea that his father was promised.

Still, his parents had been optimistic that if they worked hard they'd catch up soon. But Thorian's death seemed to squash the optimism from Marise. Now, Daniel felt her weary head drooping on his shoulder and glanced down. She was dozing before the long, laborious day ahead.

Daniel had heard that the scoring machines were being redesigned at the heavy machinery plant in Oculys. But the redesign and manufacturing process would take a while, and Daniel wasn't sure that Saras would spring for the new machines, anyway. The company had plenty of workers, for now.

Daniel hoped that the new scoring machines would be completed soon. His mother didn't. She said they'd put everyone out of a job. Still, the comfort of removing Yynium from inside a scoring machine seemed a good alternative to this: hundreds of workers prying and scraping it from the rock every day. Scorers were small units, and two or three could fit in a section of the drift—the horizontal mine tunnels that followed the Yynium veins—at a time. They had precision ore-removal attachments that scored through the Yynium vein and neatly popped out chunks of it into tram cars that hauled it up and out. Scorers had climate controlled cabs with air filters. Back on Earth, his father had never come home with Yynium dust clouding his jacket. Or his lungs.

Daniel didn't know what the displaced workers would do, but there had to be something better than this. The dry cough of dustlung punctuated the air around him, and though most of the miners wore Saras Company–issued masks, they still came home with the sharp taste of Ynium in their mouths and the thick feel of it in their breath.

And now, another strange sickness was plaguing people in Coriol. It started with fatigue, and moved to a fever followed by purple bruises that appeared on peoples' stomachs, arms, necks, and faces, spreading rapidly until they were covered with the plum-colored patches. Daniel hadn't seen any of the sufferers up close, but he'd passed them in the street, and they looked miserable.

Daniel watched Zella step onto the tram, and he and his mother boarded a few cars behind her, flipping the pivoting seats down as they entered. Under his boots, Daniel felt the grit from the ore the car hauled when it wasn't hauling people. He wouldn't mind designing ore trams. He'd make the seats contoured, so people were more comfortable sitting in them.

As the tram began to move, he put an arm around his mother, tucking her head into him, so the wind didn't sting her eyes. He hunched over her, squinting against the wind as the tram picked up speed, and tried not to think of it plummeting down the slope, deeper and deeper under the ground.

He'd put windscreens on the cars, too. But that got him thinking of the design problem that posed. The tram cars carried people into and out of the mine, at the shift changes. When a tram emptied its cargo of people, it went to be filled with Ynium ore that it would carry back up to the surface. The cars had to be able to carry people and then be ready to carry ore. A windscreen, even a metal one that could withstand being banged by chunks of ore, would get in the miners' way as they threw the ore into the cars. And strong metal screens on each car would add too much weight to the tram as a whole. Daniel enjoyed the puzzle of it as he rode. If he ever got the chance, he'd design trams.

Or even better, hovercars. There were only a few in Coriol, besides the round-backed hovercabs, and he loved to watch them skim by. Theo Talbot's was the most beautiful machine he'd ever seen.

A pang of regret filled Daniel. Last year, when Talbot's hovercar had come to building G, where his family lived, he'd been outside, waiting for his father to come home and for his own shift in the mine to start. He remembered watching Talbot unfold himself from the car and stretch before going into the building.

Daniel and Zella and a couple other friends, Pete and Hadib, had gone to check out the car. He remembered walking around it, looking in at the Earthleather seats. He remembered how Zella had taken his hand and pulled him over to see the glowing dashboard and the multiple drop-down screens inside. He remembered the thrill of her hand in his, and the feeling that someday maybe he could design something like this. Even though they had a night shift to work, that cool evening the whole world had stretched before them like an endless sea of opportunities.

Until Talbot strode back to the car and scattered them with the words, "Rigo, you'd better go in. Your mother needs you."

And that had been it. His father wasn't coming home. His mother had to come to work in the mines because his father's contract still needed filling and they still needed to eat. His little sisters were immediately sent to school for the duration of his mother's shifts, and the sea of opportunities rose into a sea of debt that was slowly drowning them all.

***

A sol train ride after Ethan's visit with Kaia he was at the office. He faced his first task of the day: recording the next in a series of tutorials on how to read Xardn. The Colony Offices valued his expertise, and since the trouble with the Others on Beta Alora, there was a new interest in his work with the dead alien language they had spoken.

Several things had changed in the colonization efforts after the Earth Government had sold the 4000 passengers on Ethan's ship to the Others. A new fear of aliens was driving most of the spending back on Earth, and the defense budget had skyrocketed.

When Ethan's tutorial was finished, he had just enough time to grab a bowl of warm, clear sweetbean soup before his meeting with the Coriol Defense Committee. His official title was "Alien Consultant." He wasn't sure if that meant he consulted about aliens or that he was an alien who consulted. Sometimes he certainly felt like the latter. When the Offices wanted a simple answer, it was often hard to sum up the complexity of his experience with aliens, good and bad, into a single, always-true maxim. Sometimes he thought he'd be a better consultant if he had never met any aliens personally.

A Real-Time Communications session was already going when he got there. RTC was one of the things that amazed Ethan. The screen showed a group of people back on Earth, broadcast almost instantaneously through the vast void of space that had taken him half a lifetime to cross. They could never have RTC without Yynium. Even so, it was only available at the Colony Offices and Company Headquarters in each settlement, and at the military base. It wasn't used frivolously.

Marcos Saras was in on the link, too, from his office across Coriol. Hovering beside him, the skeletal Theo Talbot and Veronika Eppes, as always.

Ethan liked to think that he and the other governors were in these meetings to protect the people of Coriol from Saras, but he suspected they were actually there to protect the Ynium and the interests of the UEG. The Colony Offices were present in every settlement and were owned by the United Earth Government.

The president of the United Earth Government was on the screen now, with her Defense Chair and the head of the Earth Security force.

"Though our meetings are often routine," she was saying, "I'm pleased today that I can report to you, as I have to the other settlement defense committees, that construction on the Minean defense fleet is completed." The screen switched to images of the most intimidating ships Ethan had ever seen. Armored and armed, they reminded him of sleek stingrays, with wide, blunt wings and a tapered tailfin.

There were appreciative murmurs around the room, but the president was obviously disappointed by the lack of outright cheering. The committee in Coriol knew that however beautiful the ships, they were still a long way from their destination. The SL-driven ships had taken fifty-three years to bring members of the committee from Earth to Minea, while Saras and his cronies had made the trip in five.

The president went on. "Your fleet is ready, but we don't have enough Ynium to send them. We need more of it than ever before. If our interactions with the Others of Beta Alora have taught us anything, it is that we need defenses."

The president went on. "I have another important piece of information reported by your defensive forces which you need to be aware of." There was a breathless pause. "An alien ship has been spotted orbiting your planet."

Ethan stood and walked quickly across the back of the room, his heart pounding. The spot that had crossed Lucidus. He had known it was not the orbital defenses. He breathed deeply, trying to focus on what the president was saying.

"Though no aggressive action has yet been observed, you need defenses out there. I want you to know we are working hard to get them to you. But it's vital that you maintain your city defenses until your fleet arrives."

Saras spoke up. "Madam President, if I may?"

"Go ahead, Mr. Saras."

"Perhaps you are aware that a rich new deposit of Yynium has been discovered here on Minea?" In the face of aliens, Saras was still thinking about Yynium.

"I'm aware."

Saras's voice had a tone of forced confidence. "I was informed yesterday that permission to mine that deposit— which my surveyors discovered, by the way, and reported faithfully to the Colony Offices, as the protocol directs—"

Ethan scoffed, glancing at his Colony Office colleagues, who showed their disgust by rolling their eyes. Saras would have been more accurate to replace "reported faithfully to the Colony Offices" with "admitted to finding it only after their survey was leaked to the Colony Offices."

"—will be given as a bonus based on production over the next seven weeks."

The president nodded. "That's right."

"That might not be the most prudent choice, given the time constraints and the UEG's desire to get as much Yynium to Earth as quickly as possible." He didn't wait for her to respond. "I have the equipment and manpower to begin work on that deposit within the week, Madam President, and a track record of timely delivery and—" Did Ethan hear a slight hesitation in Saras's voice? "And clean Yynium. If you would simply grant the land to Saras Company now, you'd have your Yynium much more quickly."

The president took a moment to craft her response. "Mr. Saras, I see your point. It could be more beneficial in terms of time to do that. But no new deposits have simply been given to any of the companies, and I'm sure you can see the kind of precedent that might set."

Saras began to speak, but she cut him off. "In addition, Mr. Saras, we are talking about a few weeks to determine the best company to award this deposit to. Though Yynium delivery is certainly time-sensitive, we must be sure that the quality of the Yynium is superior, as well. We want to know that when we place this new deposit into someone's hands, it will arrive to us as pure as possible. Contaminated Yynium from careless mining or hasty milling is at best a waste of time, and at worst a danger. The seven-week period will give all companies the chance to produce for testing the cleanest Yynium possible, ensuring that we grant the deposit to the company which will refine it best. The UEG doesn't need sloppy production and dirty Yynium. We need it as pure as possible."

A look crossed Saras's face. Ethan wasn't sure whether it was anger or fear, but it was gone quickly and he marveled that he had witnessed a rare occurrence: Marcos Saras did not get his way.

At Saras's silence, Veronika stepped in. "You can be assured," she said, "that we will win the grant."

"Best of luck in that endeavor." The president moved on. "Now, while I have you here, I do want to commission your survey teams, Mr. Saras, to provide for us a more extensive survey of the topography above the deposit. We need to know what we are getting into in terms of terrain. Can we count on you to provide for us surveys of at least the first few kilometers above the deposit?"

Saras was still pouting. He was such a powerful man that Ethan sometimes forgot his youth. Barely twenty-eight, he occasionally showed the willfulness of the spoiled child he was. This time it was Theo that stepped in. "That will take our survey crew off more directly profitable exploration, Madam President. If we don't win this grant," at this Veronika shot him a scalding look, "we're going to need to find ourselves more Yynium to mine."

"We'll pay you well for three crews."

Saras countered quickly, as if glad to strike back at her. "We'll give you one."

The president, undisturbed, considered for a moment. "We'll work with that for now. But—" here her voice took on a warning note, "as you have a vested interest in this project, I'd like a Colony Offices Governor to ride along with the survey team and make sure that the correct area is surveyed. Governor Elias, can your Office handle that?"

Though Saras was a private corporation and could say yes or no as they pleased, when the President of the UEG made a request to the Colony Office, the Office said yes.

After the signoffs, the committee relayed the president's request to the head of scheduling at the Office. Ethan had a sneaking suspicion that as the only Governor without a pressing docket of must-dos, he would be the one sent with the survey crew. Actually, he welcomed a break from the office, so when they asked him, he accepted the assignment.

# Chapter 4

Aria stood on Polara's bed so she could reach up near the ceiling. She swiped at the wall and peered at the cloth as she pulled it back. Little fuzzy green plants coated it. They had been growing all over Coriol the past couple of weeks. She folded it and swiped again. As a botanist and crop geneticist, Aria loved plants and hated to eradicate even these, but they were everywhere and were beginning to become a nuisance.

They seemed to grow on any slightly damp surface, and spring on Minea was nothing if not damp. Everywhere was damp, and Aria was finding the little plants on the counters in the kitchen, in the bathtub, and even on the walls in the bedrooms. Was it a mold?

She climbed down from the bed and took the cloth into the bright living room, where golden sunshine streamed in through the windows and bathed her children, playing on the floor.

Polara was crawling around, roaring, much to the delight of her stationary, silent brother, Rigel. He watched her happily, and Aria felt the old pang of worry that he wasn't more mobile and verbal himself.

She shook the thought from her mind and held the cloth in the brightest stream of light. Peering at it, she breathed a sigh of relief. Instead of rhizomes and sporangiophores, she saw the familiar curves of miniscule roots and hypocotyls. Even, here and there, a tiny set of cotyledons on the biggest of the plants. At least it wasn't a mold.

Aria noticed Polara peering up at the green dots on the cloth. "Are those yucky?" the four-year-old asked.

"Kind of," Aria replied, "when they're growing in our house." She crouched down and slid an arm around her daughter. "But look closely, and you can see the little plant parts. See the tiny white roots?" Polara nodded. "And some of them have brand new baby leaves. See?" She pointed to the tiny wings of the bigger plants.

Polara brightened. "They're baby plants? Like Rigel!"

"Yep," Aria said, straightening, "babies like Rigel." She glanced at the clock. "Okay, guys. We've got to get going or the store might not have what we need. Polara, can you get your shoes on?"

As the dark-haired little girl bounced off to find her shoes, Aria tossed the cloth in the sanitizer and gathered her shopping list and her bags. Though Ethan's work in the Colony Offices assured that they had the scrip to get all the groceries they needed, the company store itself had been coming up short on supplies lately. She wanted to be there early today.

Ever since she'd gone two weeks ago and seen the shortage, she couldn't stop thinking about those empty shelves. Where was the food? Saras had seedbanks and rootstock aplenty. They had tens of thousands of acres of terraformed farmland just northwest of the city, and they had all the fertilizer they needed. Where was the food?

Aria grabbed her scrip chain and wallet and the kids and headed to the Market District. The scrip chain was heavy and unwieldy, strung with triangular brass coins punched through the middle with a triangle hole for carrying on the chain. The coins were the only currency in Coriol. They were only good at Saras stores in the city. The stores took no other currency and the coins were useless in any other colony. Save enough of them and you could trade them in for UEG money, but the exchange rate was pretty dismal, and meanwhile, you had to eat.

Catching a hovercab, she settled Polara and Rigel on either side of her on the smooth, cool seat and made sure they could see out the windows. It would be cheaper to take the sol train, but crowding on with groceries and the two children was stressful for Aria. The press of people, the effort of trying to contain Polara's boundless energy, the weight of Rigel in her backpack carrier, and the grocery bags in her arms always had her snappy and strained when she got home. A hovercab was quiet, private, and convenient, especially for grocery shopping. Anyway, they had the scrip and she might as well use it.

Because their ship had been the responsibility of the government instead of any particular corporation, they'd had no debt to work off when they arrived. Aria figured they'd paid for the journey by being sold to the Others, a cruel alien race on the planet Beta Alora, and she didn't feel bad that they didn't owe the Saras company when they got here.

Many of the passengers on their ship had left Coriol immediately to be nearer family or friends in other cities. All of the passengers of Ship 12-22 who had stayed were placed in the only empty neighborhood in Coriol, the newly finished Forest Heights. Forest Heights was on the edge of the city, inconveniently far from the Market District and the Colony Office, but wonderfully near the wooded hills and karst peaks that ringed the city.

They rode in the hovercab through neighborhoods, just like their own, with the little blue cottages Minea was famous for. After the Housing District they entered the Health and Human Services District, with its towering steel hospitals and research labs. As the hovercab pulled past the last of the health buildings, Aria caught a glimpse of the grimy cement tenements where many of the industrial workers lived. The blue-streaked gray buildings were closest to the factories, mills, and the Yynium refinery that crushed and purified Yynium twenty-seven hours a day, 420 days per year. It never closed. The tenements were tall enough to obscure the refinery itself, which Aria knew was there but had never seen.

At last the Market District came into view, with its cheery red and green storefronts. Aria unloaded the kids, shouldering into the backpack that she used to carry Rigel. She gave the cab driver twenty scrip, and headed into the produce store.

She could tell immediately that this was going to be a difficult day. The store was crowded with people, and the produce bins were low. "Hold Mommy's hand," she said sharply to Polara as a woman with Yynium dust on the shoulders of her black dress stormed angrily past them towards the door.

The woman called back over her shoulder. "Don't bother, lady, they're not selling anything. And when they do, nobody will be able to afford it."

Aria looked at the row of barred registers. It was true. The cashiers were standing still as the people waited in line with their groceries.

Stock boys were scurrying around in front of the bins, swapping out the prices on every item. Their red vests bore the Saras triangle across the back. Aria heard a deep, firm voice and turned to see the store manager, Cyril Gaynes, speaking to a man from the refinery.

"I'm sorry for the inconvenience," Gaynes said, although Aria could tell he wasn't, "but our costs have gone up today and we must recalculate the prices before we can sell anything else."

"We have to be back to work in fifteen minutes," the man said, a note of pleading in his voice. "There won't be anything left by the time we get off. Can't you just open the registers and calculate the costs there?"

"I'm sorry, every item has to be marked with the correct label before we scan it through the register. That's the only way the system works."

"The system doesn't work," the man said. Aria heard the despair in his voice and looked away so he wouldn't see her watching the exchange as he turned and left the store. People began filing out after him as they realized they wouldn't make it to work on time if they didn't leave now. Aria pulled Polara to the back of the store as they left.

Soon, only a few people remained. Aria watched as the stock boys marked up item after item. Beans that were one scrip per measure were now two, and apples had doubled as well. The little packets of meat she and Ethan used to add flavor to their stews had gone from four scrip to seven. Now a new worry pricked her mind. She hoped she'd brought enough scrip. The coins were unwieldy, and she tried to only carry as much as she needed for each trip. If prices continued like this, people would be carrying scrip chains so long that they dragged the ground behind them.

She glanced at the other shoppers. There was a man in a Colony Office uniform and a teen who should probably still be in school but whose dusty red coveralls revealed his work in the Yynium mines. Aria knew he'd probably get docked the full day's pay for being late back from his morning break, but he stood stubbornly in front of the registers with a meager armload of rangkor tubers, Minea's native purple potatoes. They were the cheapest food you could buy here, and not terrible as far as nutrition, but Aria longed for her lab back on Earth and the chance to tinker with rangkors, to increase the protein and breed for a thinner, edible skin. So much of the meat was lost peeling them. She gathered a few of them from the bin herself and shifted Rigel in her backpack as she continued around the store.

When she stepped into line behind the young miner and an old woman in a faded green jacket, Aria's basket was a rainbow. It was filled with bananas, berries, dragonfruit, and sahm, the bright green leafy vegetable that would be just like Earth's kale if it didn't taste like carrots. She glanced down to see Polara taking scraping bites out of an apple, so she mentally calculated that into the bill as well.

The registers had opened and she waited, glad that Polara had something to occupy her attention. Waiting in lines could be hard with an active four-year-old, and she wasn't as good as Ethan at coming up with distracting games to play while waiting.

An interruption in the usual flow of the checkout line caught Aria's attention. She glanced up to see the boy with the rangkors arguing with the cashier.

"I DO have enough to buy them," the boy said angrily. "I only picked out what I could afford."

"The prices changed, kid. You can see that." The cashier, another red-vested Saras worker, gestured at the bins.

"When I picked them up they were two scrip each, and that's what I'm paying." The boy slammed a ten scrip piece down on the counter with a clatter. That's why he'd stayed then, because he'd hoped they would honor their first prices.

Gaynes, a big, broad man, stepped quickly down the aisle behind the bars of the register. "The price is fifteen scrip and that's what you'll pay, unless you want to go to jail for shoplifting." His voice reminded Aria of a chained dog.

The boy's shoulders slumped. He looked carefully at the tubers, weighing and evaluating them in his hands before dejectedly sliding two of them to the side of the counter. The cashier took the ten scrip piece off the counter where it lay and Gaynes reached into the register drawer, pulled out the boy's one scrip change, and flipped it through the air between the bars, where it sailed out and landed on the floor. The boy chased it desperately, and Gaynes laughed as he watched the kid walk out the door clutching the coin and the rangkors.

Aria felt her nails digging into her palms. She tried to breathe calmly. The old woman in front of Aria stepped up to the register and set her basket on the scanner.

"Forty-eight scrip," the cashier said.

It appeared that the woman had underestimated her purchases, too. She was flustered as she counted several times. "What should I put back?" she asked. "I've only got forty-two."

"Oh, no," Gaynes's voice was almost kind this time. "You don't need to put anything back," he crooned.

Aria felt immediately on guard. Gaynes wasn't a kind man. He wanted something.

"But I don't have enough," the woman said, confused. "Do I?"

"Well, I think we can probably work something out," Gaynes said. Aria followed his gaze to the woman's frail hand, where she saw an Earthgold ring. So that was it. "We don't usually do trades, you know." Everybody knew. Trades were against the law in any company colony. Only Saras scrip was accepted in Coriol. "You can make up the difference with that." He pointed to her ring.

She looked puzzled, then Aria saw the woman's mouth open slightly in surprise, "Why, why, I don't know . . . My husband gave it to me back on Earth." She spun the ring nervously on her finger.

Aria couldn't stand it. She unclipped her scrip chain and pulled off six scrip. Stepping up to the counter, she laid them beside the woman's hand.

The woman turned her eyes to Aria in gratitude. Aria smiled, then met Gaynes's narrowed eyes. The woman left the store and the cashier scanned Aria's items. Still, Gaynes glared at her through the bars.

The two rangkors still lay on the counter. Without taking her eyes off him, Aria scooped them up and dropped them in her basket.

"Fifty-four scrip," the cashier said. Aria slid three coins to him and narrowed her eyes to match Gaynes's glare. Then she looked away and reached down for her basket.

"This is my store, young lady," Gaynes said as she loaded the produce into her shopping bags.

Aria's eyes flashed as she met his again. "Oh is it, Mr. Gaynes? My husband and I will be having dinner with Mr. Saras the day after tomorrow, and I'll be sure to let him know you said so." The subtle backwards jerk of Gaynes's head showed her she'd landed her blow. She took Polara's hand and walked out of the store. Just at the door, she turned and called, "And thank you so much for the complementary apple."

Aria's heart was thundering as she stepped out into the cool spring morning. She had forgotten all about Polara's apple until she was at the door, and she wouldn't go crawling back to the register to give that krech another scrip.

Polara chattered about the new blossoms on the trees as Aria pulled her quickly down the sidewalk toward the industrial district. Two blocks away from the store she realized the unlikelihood of finding who she was looking for. She turned to walk back to the cab platform when a flash of dusty red caught her eye. She almost ran across the street, pulling Polara with her into a little alleyway between the shoe store and the clothing store.

The young miner looked up in surprise as she approached, then looked away to hide his tear-stained face. Polara pulled away from her mother and ran to him. Aria watched as the little girl gently took his hand and gazed up at him. He didn't pull away, just looked down at her with incredibly sad eyes. Polara, ever empathetic, put his hand to her cheek.

Aria pulled out the two rangkors and held them out to the young man. Briefly, his eyebrows drew together in suspicion, then he broke into a smile.

"Dama," he said quietly, freeing his hand from Polara to take the tubers. "Dama engala."

Aria smiled wonderingly. "You speak a different language?" she asked.

The boy blushed. "Usually only at home."

"It's beautiful," she said. Ethan would be excited to know another old Earth language had survived.

"It means 'thank you,'" he said.

"You're welcome." Ever since Polara and Rigel had come into the world, Aria saw them in everyone's children. She imagined this boy's mother for a moment. She was probably at work in the mines as well, wondering what was keeping him from his shift and worrying what might have happened. "Will you go to work now?"

The boy looked at his watch and his eyes welled up with tears again. He shook his head. "I'll never make it. It's a ten minute walk." He made a disgusted grunt in his throat. "It's my third time being late. They'll dock me a week's pay this time."

Aria called to Polara. "Can you run, little one?" Polara

nodded and Aria called to both her and the young miner. "Come on, then!"

She must have earned his trust, because he followed her without question. Aria looked down the street as they emerged from the alley and ran for a cab platform. She pulled the door open and Polara, sensing her mother's urgency, threw herself in the circular back seat and scooted around to the far side. Aria slung the groceries in on the floor and pulled Rigel's backpack off, clutching him on her lap as she slid in, too.

She barked, "Take us to the mine!"

The boy slipped in and pulled the door closed just as the cab sped off toward the Industrial District.

Aria watched the buildings speed by and glanced at the boy. A hopeful light had crept into his eyes and he was obviously thrilled by the cab ride. He caught her eye.

"Why are you helping me?"

Aria hugged Rigel a little. "Because I hope somebody will help my boy someday, when he needs it," she said. "And because I think you were trying to do some good yourself by standing in that line. Nobody likes rangkor enough to eat that many by himself." She gestured at his armload of tubers.

He smiled, but it was a sad smile. "They're for my family. We won't get any more scrip for three days, and there won't be anything left we can buy after work." He shook his head quickly, agitated. "I can't hear my little sisters cry for food one more night."

His words hit Aria in the stomach. A long-ago feeling twisted her memory. She wished Ethan was here. The mine came into sight through the window of the hovercab.

"Can I ask your name?" the boy said. "Maybe I can pay you back for these someday." He looked hesitantly at her. "And the cab ride," he added hastily as the cab stopped.

"It's Aria Bryant. How about yours?"

The boy spoke quickly. "I'm Daniel Rigo." He jumped out of the cab, running with the last of the stragglers to the gates of the mine.

"Where to now?" the hovercab driver asked.

"Just wait here a second," Aria replied.

She watched as Daniel checked in seconds before the whistle blew, ending the break. He turned and tossed her a wave, smiling broadly. She saw his mouth make the words *dama engala*: thank you.

*\*\*\**

Daniel threw a wave at the kind woman, Aria, in the hovercab, and walked past the foreman into the mine just as the whistle blew. He stopped to stash the rangkors in his mother's lunchbox in her cubby at the mine's mouth, then pulled up his mask as he walked to the check boards. They were wide pieces of smooth green Minean wood, with rows of small nails covering them. On each nail hung a small metal triangle stamped with the words "Saras Co. Mining" and each miner's identification number. The miners called them pit checks because the underground parts of the mine were called the pit and the little tags gave an easy way to see who was underground. He'd reached for his so many times that it was no chore finding it among all the others. He slid it on the clip on his chest and headed to the tram line.

He hated Gaynes. Hated the way he made people grovel. Hated the way he needled people. Hated the way he made everyone feel small.

Daniel's father had been the opposite. Thorian Rigo had been big and made others feel big, too. He had joked with everyone, and when you were talking to him, you were the most important person in the world.

Daniel felt tears slipping out of his stinging eyes and ducked, blaming it on the wind from the tram ride.

Marise was peering at the tram as it hissed to a stop. She put her arms around him for a long moment. He knew how worried she must have been, but she didn't say anything, simply laid a hand on his cheek and turned back to her work.

"I got some rangkors," he said. "Plenty."

Marise hugged him again, spontaneously. "I don't know how. I heard what happened at the market. But you're like your father, Daniel. You always find a way to take care of us." She kissed him quickly and the two found their way to the section of open vein they'd been working on before the break.

Daniel swung the pick and popped out a chunk of Ynium. He'd gotten pretty good at dislodging chunks that weren't too big, because the next step was for his mother to load the chunk into the tram. He hated to see her strain to lift them, and she was furious if he stopped to help her carry one.

A mine was a funny place: loud with the ringing of the picks and the reverberations on the glassy Ynium vein, loud with the crash of the ore being tossed into the trams, loud with the coughing and shuffling of the miners. But all these sounds were dampened by the immense weight of the stone above them, the narrowness of the drift, and the hovering darkness at either end of their work section, past the tall blast lights that stood precariously on their tripod bases. It was as if, at any moment, the clamor of Ynium extraction might be snuffed out like a flickering lamp and all that would remain would be silence.

Some days they talked. Today, though, they worked in silence. Daniel was lost in his memories of the market. He wished he'd punched Gaynes through the bars or that he'd simply taken the rangkor tubers and walked out.

But being locked up wouldn't help his family. He knew that. What made his heart beat faster and his teeth clench as he swung the pick again was that Gaynes knew it too.

The tram on the way out of the mine was always exhilarating. Even after a long day's work, when Daniel's shoulders and back ached, and his hands throbbed from the percussion of steel on stone, he loved the feeling of going up and out of the pit. When, on the last long slope out of the mine, the tram bogged down and slowed, straining under the weight of the miners and the pitch of the track, he always felt a twinge of apprehension. And then, above them, rising like Candidus, the Minean moon, was a patch of sky that brought his heart to his chest every time.

He glanced around to see if the other miners felt it. But most of them had their eyes closed against the wind or were dozing from their exhaustion. Only one other miner was looking. Only one, whose clear blue eyes caught his and shared with him the moment of liberation from the pit: Zella.

\*\*\*

Daniel's mother was chatting with neighbors as they walked home, and they quickly outpaced him, leaving him walking the long road alone in the crowd. That didn't last long, however. He heard a lovely, bright voice next to his shoulder.

"I love coming out of the mine, don't you?" Zella slipped her arm through his as they walked easily together. She was almost his height, and as they walked she reached up and pulled off her bright head covering. Her light curls cascaded down around her shoulders, and Daniel's breath caught in his throat.

"I do." Daniel glanced away, his cheeks coloring. He suspected she knew how he felt—how Pete and Hadib felt, how every guy who knew her felt—about her.

But Zella didn't let on. She took a drink from her water

bottle, and Daniel heard it swish empty as she did so. She shook it. "All out. Good thing it's the end of the day!" He nodded. "Remember how, back on Earth, lemonade was so delicious on a hot summer day?"

Daniel did remember. He had manned many a lemonade stand with his cousins during his childhood. "It was."

Zella leaned close. "I don't think I could drink it without gagging now." She shook her head in disgust. "Too much Yynium-ade."

He knew what she meant. Even with the masks, by the end of the day, the miners' mouths were so coated with the lemony dust that every sip of water tasted like it. He laughed. "Don't say it too loud. Saras'll have us running Yynium-ade stands at the next Lucidus festival."

"Did you see it?" Zella asked, and Daniel tried to pretend she was just talking about Lucidus.

"Yeah. I was lucky to be on the swing shift yesterday, so I got to go out for a minute in the morning and take the little girls. A lady named Joyce in our building even let them use her bells to ring."

"They must have loved that."

"They did." Daniel thought about how they had held the bells in a reverent way, looking at their reflections in the shiny surfaces. He needed to get them back to church, so they could play hand bells once a month. There was so precious little in their life that was beautiful, so little music. He could add a little more by not sleeping in on worship day every month.

He felt a jerk on his arm and looked down. Zella was expectantly waiting for an answer, but he hadn't heard her question.

"I'm sorry. I was thinking about my sisters. What did you say?"

"That's okay. I was just asking if you saw the spot?"

Daniel nodded. "I saw it."

She squeezed his arm. "Tell me about it! I was working the day shift, so I didn't see it!"

The memory of the shadow passed through Daniel's mind. "It was . . ." He tried to think of how to make it sound exciting. "A dark dot. It just, *fshew,*" he shot a pointed finger up and across the sky, then regretted it as he felt the pain in his shoulders, "streaked across Lucidus, then it was gone."

Zella shuddered, an excited little tremble. He admired her enthusiasm, even after a whole day underground. "What do you think it was?"

Daniel shrugged. "Most people say it was a part of the orbital defense system that just so happened to line up this year."

She looked disappointed. "I guess." Then a mischievous spark came into her eyes. "Or maybe it was a spaceship, come to rescue us from the mines."

"Maybe," Daniel said doubtfully.

"Or a meteor," she said. "Did you make a wish?"

Daniel sighed heavily. They were reaching the edge of the Industrial District, and he turned toward their tenement. The dull gray buildings rose around them, blocking out all but small slices of the clear sky.

"I make wishes every day," he said wearily.

They walked in silence a moment, the wave of day shift workers swelling around them as it met the wave of swing shift workers heading out of the city. Soon, the crowd was crushing, and Zella clung tightly to Daniel. It was the first time he'd enjoyed the crowd.

They found building G and she pulled him onto the sidesteps, where they sat and breathed out the last of the day's stress.

"What do you wish for?" she said, softly. "When you're making all those wishes?"

Daniel looked down at her. Zella shone with chalky Yynium dust, grey bits of stone mingled with the sparkling orange Yynium. Her eyes, bright blue as the slices of sky, captured him and he found himself talking.

"I wish my mother didn't have to work. I wish my sisters could stay home with her instead of going to the school. I wish I could design hovercars and work in an office. I wish you—" He stopped.

"Wish I could what?"

He wanted to say that he wished Zella and he could have time to spend together that wasn't rushing to the next shift or dragging home from the last one, but there was too much invitation in the words. He didn't say them, just looked away.

Zella, still clinging to his arm, lifted a hand to his cheek and turned his face to her.

"Daniel, we can be . . ." She paused, searching for the right words. "Together. My parents like you. Your mama likes me. We could, you know, get married and start a life."

Daniel let himself remain in her arms for one second, then pulled gently away, disentangling her hands from his arm and pushing her hand gently away from his face before standing and leaning on the stair railing.

"Zel, I—" How to assuage the hurt in her eyes? "It's not that I don't want to be with you—I do. It's just that, you know, with my mother and my sisters—" He fumbled. "With my dad dying—I don't think I can . . . take care of anyone else right now."

Her eyes flashed and she stood. "That's not what I want, Daniel. I'm not looking for someone to set me up in a life of luxury. Did you ever think I might be asking because I think maybe you could use somebody who would take care of you?" Zella stomped up the stairs and went into the building. He wouldn't see her again tonight.

He was speechless as he watched her go. He hadn't known the depth of her feelings. He took a step, trying to form words, but the dry taste of Yynium dust choked them back.

***

Kaia noticed that something was different about the junkyard as soon as the hovercar dropped her off. She couldn't see the junk from outside the corrugated metal fence that surrounded it. The last time Kaia had visited, and all the times before that, the refuse from the mines and refinery had lain in twisted, tangled lumps. The junker had bulldozed anything and everything into a big pile in the middle, dumping at the edges and bulldozing around it in a big circle, pushing the trash into an uneven heap that folded in on itself and rendered inaccessible the center of the pile, which was where Kaia suspected all the good stuff was.

In fact, the junker had told her that somewhere in the middle the Saras Company had dumped all the old ship parts from the first exploration missions they'd sent to Minea. Kaia would like to get her hands on some of those first drives. She had read about them in the manuals. Called Octagon drives, they held potential in their cores that Kaia felt had been overlooked in the rush to redesign them. All the parts from the old ships were rumored to be in here somewhere. Buried under ever-increasing loads, they'd become nothing more than refuse, dumped in this unused corner of the city behind the spaceport, and covered with concrete rubble, old hovercars, and tangled mining equipment.

But now, as Kaia entered, the junkyard was inviting.

Flowing arcs of piled metal gave way to smooth lines of old boards. The pathways between the towering piles of junk had been neatly swept, and small columns of smooth stones dotted the intersections, offering navigation through the maze. She was here looking for a set of gears and anything she could use for the body of a little robot she was making for Polara and Rigel.

She glanced toward the middle, where the enormous mountain of junk had shrunk considerably. Around it were smaller piles, obviously being reorganized into small groups of similar items. She took a few steps toward it, wondering if any early items had been uncovered, then glanced at her missive to check the time. There was a new message from Aria, seeing if they could move their lunch date back an hour. She swiped it, and sent a yes. Calculating how much time it would take to get back to the housing district, she knew she'd have to see if she could find the old ship stuff next time. She didn't want to be rushed through exploration like that.

Kaia started today's project by sorting through a pile of old sanitizer and disposer parts, stepping over to a pile of light fixtures and a row of broken mining tools. She made a little pile on the blue dirt of possible pieces. In addition to a steel ball, a shiny silver plate, and a bell-shaped copper light shade, she had found several rusty rods and a smooth cylinder of metal. It gleamed next to a rectangle coated with flaking rust and a bright red chip of unbreakable glass. She stepped back to consider which pieces might make the most interesting torso, which might be good for decoration, and which would go best with the tarnished copper cube she had chosen for the head.

She was holding up the cube, positioning it over each piece, when she heard the voice of Yi Zhe.

"Did you find what you were looking for?"

Kaia glanced up. He was one of her passengers, a young man whose dark hair and eyes were especially kind. His wife, Jin Feiyan, and their little son stood behind him. Kaia hadn't seen them for several months, not even at the gatherings of the passengers of Ship 12-22 that she and Ethan tried to have once in a while.

"Yi Zhe!" She leaned in for a friendly hug. "What are you doing here?"

"I work here now. I could find no other work," Yi Zhe said, shaking his head sadly. "My skills seem to be useless here."

Kaia looked around the junkyard. Quiet pervaded the pathways and piles. Similar objects were grouped together, gears over here, ball bearings there, large rusted metal pieces and small rusted metal plates farther down the aisle, and shining chrome pieces reflecting the overall harmony of the place. She'd never seen a junkyard like it. It was a pleasant place. Of course. It had Yi Zhe's fingerprints all over it.

"The change is remarkable." She couldn't help digging a little. "Did you learn anything about the history of the place when they hired you? I've heard some interesting rumors that there are some old ship parts around here."

Yi Zhe looked thoughtful. "A few," he said, "but I think many of them were stolen early on. At first, the junkyard was unmanned, but from what I heard, too many people started carting off Saras's junk and a little junk trade started. The parts weren't being manufactured here yet. When Saras needed something, they had to pay to get their own junk back. So, they hired a junkyard manager. He ran the place for years, but he died a few weeks ago and I got the job."

Yi Zhe glanced down, moving the robot parts on the ground into a staggered diagonal as he spoke.

His wife, Jin Feiyan, broke in, thrusting a wrapped

packet—Yi Zhe's lunch—into his hand. "I told him before we left Earth that there was no use for him here. I told him there was a mistake that he was chosen to come to the colony. What use is there on a mining planet for a master of balance and harmony? None." She scoffed. "If my parents had known he was going to end up a junkyard man, he would never have been my husband." She kicked at the robot parts, scattering them, before gathering her little boy's hand and leaving the junkyard. Kaia got the feeling that she didn't spend any more time here than necessary.

"She's worried," Yi Zhe apologized, leaning down and gathering the parts. "I've been out of work a long time. Just little jobs, here and there. We have the cottage to live in, of course, but buying food and paying for electricity is hard some months."

Kaia nodded.

"And everything I know is unimportant here. No one pays attention to the flow of qi or the balance of their lives."

Kaia thought of the dusty miners, their crowded apartments, the shouting on payday, and the desperate look in the eyes of the women at the market. "Your skills may be more needed than you realize."

"Oh, I realize how important they are," Yi Zhe said, "and how much Coriol needs them. But no one else does. A lot of us from Ship 12-22 are noticing, Kaia," he gestured toward the spaceport towering above them, its elevators shining in the afternoon sun, "our ship was not supposed to get here, and neither were we."

"But—"

"No, think about it. Everyone else who has come to Minea has had work waiting for them when they arrived. They were carefully chosen to fill their roles here and make the society work. Think about your passengers. What is Silas's great gift? Motivational speaking. What, is he going to talk the Yynium out of the ground? And Minz? Who needs a laundry manager when there's a sanitizer in every home?" Yi Zhe's voice was tinged with bitterness, as if his wife had left behind a germ of it and he had become, suddenly, infected.

He sighed heavily and Kaia, still not skilled at interpersonal communication after all her years alone, simply shook her head. She wanted to tell him that he was needed, that they all had important parts to play, but she knew their reality was contradicting that. Many of her passengers had left Coriol, and she didn't know what they were doing, but of those who had stayed, none were doing what they were known for back on Earth. Some had gotten work in the mines or fields; some were starving, scraping by on odd jobs or charity. She'd given some of them scrip herself.

She knew she was lucky that her father had his work in the military. She knew she was lucky that once in a while Saras Company would ask for her skills as an engineering consultant. She knew that she was lucky to have the scrip they brought in. But until that moment in the junkyard, she hadn't realized how lucky she was that her passion, her life's work, was valued by the creators of Coriol. That this allowed her to continue to do it and to contribute in the way she chose to society.

Yi Zhe had rearranged the robot parts on the ground, and when she looked down, she saw exactly the ones she needed. Only one line of parts he had made seemed complete. The round head, the rectangular body, the rods, the shiny plate, and the chip of glass all came together to form in her mind into a perfect little gift for the children.

As she gathered them, Kaia checked her missive again. If she left now, she would have just enough time to swing by the

Employment Office and still make it for lunch. She paid Yi Zhe, thanked him, and reminded him of the importance of his skills. He shrugged off the praise and took the scrip.

Kaia thought about his words all the way home. Were her passengers useless? She thought through the ones who had stayed in Coriol, thinking about their gifts, their contributions back on Earth, catalogued in the applications they had submitted to be considered, which she had read over and over again when she was fighting the loneliness of her journey.

They didn't have a neat slot to fit in when they arrived. There was no movie industry to welcome the actors, no galleries for the artwork of the painters and sculptors, no laundries or newspapers or professional sports leagues where their skills were needed.

Kaia sat heavily on the bench in the sol train station. She called it the "sahl" train, but most people in Coriol pronounced it "soul" train. Though most of them had never heard of the old Earth show that she had watched from the ship's archives, it still always made her smile. She set the bag of robot parts down beside her. She saw now why there had been such an eclectic mix of professions on Ship 12-22. The delegation in charge of appeasing the Alorans had chosen humanity's sacrifice carefully, sending people they didn't need. Her passengers were expendable.

She got off at the next station and switched lines, heading for the Health and Human Services District. Among the hospitals and clinics there was the Saras Employment Office. Though she'd never been there, she knew they knew who she was, and perhaps she could put in a word for her passengers there. Surely there was some work for them, somewhere.

She stretched as she stood on the platform, holding her bag of robot parts. Her aches were getting worse.

When Kaia rounded the edge of the building, she was shocked to see a line of dejected people that stretched around the edge of the Employment Office building. She walked past them and into the reception area. It was filled with people. The three rows of chairs were full, and the rest of the room was choked with people standing up. In the front was a counter with a desk behind it. At the desk, she saw a young man with an unruly shock of jet black hair. He glanced up at her, his feelings indiscernible behind a pair of dark glasses.

"You'll need to fill out a job request and get in line, ma'am," he said.

Just as Kaia was about to answer, three men in dusty red jumpsuits came in the front door. One of them was carrying a stack of coveralls. Another stepped past Kaia and laid a sheet of paper on the desk in front of the kid. He looked it over and then stood up, tapping a microphone.

"Good news, folks. We've got six mining spots available. Disability restricted, health restricted, age restricted." Several people scrambled forward and formed an impatient line at the desk. Kaia stood aside and watched as the kid reviewed each paper.

"I said age restricted," he said to a man whose hand shook slightly as he reached to take the paper back from the kid, who spoke over his microphone again.

"Age restricted, people, means that nobody over fifty-five is fit for these jobs." Kaia watched the shaky man walk back to where he'd been standing against the wall.

Kaia glanced up to see her reflection in the long glass window. There was a woman unfit for a mining job. She looked around the room. Several people her age and younger sat in dejected silence. She wondered how often they came here, how many days they sat and listened to the list of restrictions edging them out of their chance to earn a little scrip.

The press of people barely moved to let the three miners and the six new miners out the propped-open door. As they passed, Kaia caught sight of someone waving at her from just inside the door. It was Chip, one of her passengers, and she had walked right past him. She crossed the room to hug him.

"Chip! How are you?" She regretted the formulaic question the moment it left her lips. She could see how he was: gaunt, weary, hemmed in by the press of the line.

He looked away briefly. "This could be the day," he said with forced cheer. "I was here early, and I've made it in the door."

Kaia shook her head. "What's going on? Why are all these people here? Don't they all," she corrected herself, "*mostly* all have jobs?"

Chip looked around him, catching the eyes of the others in line sympathetically. "They do, but from what they tell me, a lot of their jobs are at a standstill because of these little plants that the city is infested with."

"They're that bad?"

"Some places. The water plant and the mill have whole stations full of them. Usually I come here and pick up a day's work at a time, but the last few days, with so many of the stations down, it's tough to get anything."

"I'm here to see what I can do about that," she said, patting his arm reassuringly.

But when Kaia left the office an hour later, she had changed nothing. Saras's employment specialist was insistent that only "skilled" workers would be utilized. When she listed the skills of her passengers, the man had the audacity to laugh.

"Lady," the specialist had said, "your friends are on the wrong planet."

# Chapter 5

Ethan walked onto the short liftstrip outside the Saras Company's Coriol Headquarters the next morning. He saw the little airship that would fly them over the forest and deep into the Karst Mountains to do the survey the UEG had requested. Saras's survey crew was standing on the strip, waiting for the airship door to open. They were dressed in red jackets marked with the Saras triangle and toting big packs. Ethan could see nine of them and through the window of the craft, the pilot. There were six men and three women outside. One of the women had short, curly gray hair. She gestured to the others as she spoke, herding them toward the craft. By her commanding demeanor and the silver triangle on her jacket, it was obvious that she was in charge.

She glanced at him as he approached. Her eyes narrowed and she put herself between him and her team members, who were entering the craft.

"I'm Maggie Schübling, captain of this crew." She had the rough voice of a miner: the growl of vocal chords worn raw by years of breathing Yynium dust.

Ethan smiled, trying to put her at ease. "I'm Ethan Bryant, the Colony Offices sent me to ride along with you today."

"To keep an eye on us," Schübling said. She chuckled.

"That's backwards. The Colony Officers are the ones that need watching." She dismissed him with a grunt and followed her team onto the craft.

When he climbed aboard, most of them were already sitting and chatting. One seat remained, near the front, beside Schübling. He sat down and she turned immediately and looked him in the eye as the craft lifted.

Though Ethan liked being out of the office, he didn't always like the role of government overseer. Whether he was doing inspections, reports, or observations like this one, he still felt more akin to the workers than to his colleagues in the government, but the refiners and haulers didn't see him as one of them. Judging from the look she was giving him—as if he were a krech, the many-legged Minean cockroach, scuttling across the bathroom floor—neither did this woman.

"We don't need a babysitter, you know."

Ethan nodded. "I know. It's a good excuse for me to get out of my office, though." He meant it to be funny, but he could see from her face she didn't think it was.

"You don't like working in the temperature-controlled, reinforced Colony Offices then?" she asked.

Ethan glanced out the window. As the craft rose above the city, he was again taken aback by the sprawling industrial district. He could see the dust rising from the refinery, and lines of weary workers making their way through the barren streets. She was right. He had nothing to complain about.

"I like my job," he said.

Coriol, like all the settlements on Minea, had been planned and filled very carefully. Every ship they'd intentionally brought here had doctors and teachers and managers and even strong laborers chosen for the contribution they would make to society. It reminded Ethan of the old playground activity of choosing teams. Each company chose, from the available applicants, the people who would give them a competitive edge over the other companies and fill a slot in their workforce. If he hadn't been voted a Governor, he wouldn't even have a job here.

Ethan glanced past the pilot, out the front windscreen, and saw the cottages passing underneath. They were as pretty and as modern as the brochures back on earth had promised, but paying for their utilities and living at the opposite end of the city from their work had been too much for many workers, and they'd moved from the cottages to the cement tenements in the industrial district, leaving room for the passengers of Ship 12-22 in the blue cottages at the edge of town.

Thinking about the tenements crowded, stifling apartments that had originally been built to house the first builders and farmers on Minea made Ethan feel claustrophobic, and he was relieved to see his house as they passed over the edge of the city. It was easy to spot because of all of Aria's plants, which seemed to spill out of the house from the window boxes she had built, and which were growing all over the yard.

The craft was very fast, and small and light. Ethan hoped it would be maneuverable enough in between the karst peaks.

The Karst Mountains were not like the folded mountain range to the west, where most of the other settlements were. Those mountains consisted of large, thick peaks kilometers in diameter. The Karst Mountains were stone towers, jagged and steep, that dropped to valley floors covered in jungle. Vegetation clung to the towers, and their sheer faces made them nearly unscalable.

The captain grunted, pulling his attention away from the scenery. "Don't get in our way today. You can take your location notes when we touch down, but I don't want to see you again until rendezvous." She reached down and pulled a device out of her pack.

It was yellow, with a black screen and the word "Suremap" across the front of it. She tinkered with some dials and pointed it out the window, pressing a button.

Instantly, the scene they were seeing in between the patches of fog appeared on the screen in two-dimensional detail. She pointed it at her feet and pressed the button again. What Ethan assumed to be the land below appeared.

He loved the tools of various trades. When his friend and former passenger, Luis, showed him the tools he used to work clay into plates and cups and platters and bowls, Ethan had itched to become a potter. Now he wanted to get his hands on a Suremap device learn the layout of this new land.

He gazed at the screen. On it Ethan saw a sharp spike of land directly in front of them. As he opened his mouth to shout to the pilot, a towering stone peak suddenly materialized out of the fog and the little survey ship banked sharply to the left. Ethan was thrown sideways against his seat straps, glimpsing for a dizzying moment the thick forested ridge of the karst tower they'd almost clipped.

"Sorry," the pilot said.

"Nice flying," Ethan replied. "Thought that one had our names on it."

The pilot chuckled. "It wasn't as close as it looked. I think we're about there."

The craft set down in a narrow meadow between two of the shrouded blue monuments. Grass grew up to their knees and ringing the field were lush trees and bushes. Ethan fought the urge to lie down and watch the fog rolling through the little valley. If Aria was here, and the children, he could spend the morning that way, but now there was work to be done. Though he was along only to observe, he introduced himself to the crew and then helped two of them, Carlisle and Collins, unload the survey crew's equipment from the ship. Then, as they began to fan out over the meadow, aiming their Suremap devices around them, Ethan quickly jotted down location notes to prove they'd come where the UEG wanted them. He stood watching them until the crew captain glared at him, then he wandered off to let them do their work.

Ethan still loved the taste of early morning air on Minea. It was fragrant, especially here among the karst where white aurelia flowers glowed among the rich greenery. Thick round calpha fruits hung from gravity-defying vines covering the limestone formations. The air was still crisp in the shadows of the towers, and he walked a little slower as he watched the fog shifting between the peaks. He took out his missive and snapped a photo of himself in the meadow, then tried sending it to Aria, but there was no connection out here.

As he left the little meadow, he heard the laughing sound of water and followed it. The grassy meadow gave way to a narrow passage between two of the towers and he pushed his way through the vines that hung down from the massive monuments like a curtain. On the other side he found a small, swift stream. Beside it, nestled between the stream and the tower, was a boulder worn smooth from eons of rain. He settled himself on it and pulled out a nutrition bar.

Chewing, he leaned back against the tower and closed his eyes. The sound of the water was immensely calming, and the silence beyond it welcome. Though he had become used to life with his wife and two small children, and though he'd lived in the bustling city for four years, his time as Caretaker of the stasis ship still affected him. He had been, then, completely alone, and something about those years of isolation had never left him. It was part of why the onslaught of other people's thoughts had been such a shock. If he'd been used to hearing the voices of those around him, perhaps hearing their thoughts wouldn't have been so difficult.

It hadn't helped that at the beginning he'd been swarmed by people so much of the time. They came to praise him, to thank him, to question him. They came at all times of the day and night, and the Caretaker had come to dread the knocks on his door.

They had known he was telepathic. He told everyone who came. Thoughts were sacred, intimate. By hearing them, Ethan could know a person in an instant better than their mother knew them, better than their spouse knew them. Once, after he'd been made governor, the UEG asked if he would gather some intel using his telepathy. Ethan had walked out of the office. He didn't blame them. They saw it as an advantage. But Ethan knew that crossing into the threshold of someone's mind was more than that.

Even when the people of Coriol didn't come to his cottage, the incessant presence of their thoughts was with him. He had increasingly withdrawn from people and had found himself escaping into the forest behind his cottage and clearing his mind in solitude.

Minea was an excellent place for that. Though colonization efforts had continued, there were still only a few million people on the planet. It was simply impossible to get people across the vast reaches of space fast enough to fill the new planet very quickly. And, there were fewer coming. Since Ship 12-22 had originally been diverted from Minea by the hostile aliens, people back on Earth were much more hesitant to undertake the journey.

The vines next to him rustled and Brynn Tucker, a young woman on the team, stepped through. She jumped at the unexpected sight of him, then smiled. "Sorry, sir. I didn't know you were back here."

"Who's back here?" Schübling called as she shouldered through the vines. "Oh," her eyes narrowed, "Bryant."

Ethan sat up. "Just enjoying the quiet."

Schübling eyed him then dismissed him. She waved her hand at Brynn. "We've got two valleys comin' up. You go west with the cousins. Collins and Jade will be with me. We'll rendezvous with Carlisle, Espinoza, and Baker back at the craft when we're done." She stood aside, waiting to relay the instructions to the rest of the group.

Brynn nodded, making her way past the boulder and splashing across the stream, then veering off to the right. Ethan scrambled down to follow her. Schübling didn't want him in her group, and he didn't want to wait on the boulder all day, so he might as well stick with the group going west. Behind him, two other men whose badges read "Ayo Ndaiye" and "Badu Traore," followed him through the stream. They chattered as the group wound their way deeper into the maze.

"Did you go out with her last night?" Traore asked Ndaiye, who was struggling along behind him with his pack of equipment.

"Tonight," Ndaiye said laboriously.

"Ahhh, what you gonna do?"

"The best noodle stew in Coriol," Ndaiye responded.

Traore stopped on the trail and turned around to throw a playful punch. "Cousin, you take her to the cheapest place in town, you won't see that girl anymore," Traore laughed.

"Well, you know a lot about running women off," Ndaiye jabbed back. "Syllia took off after, what, two weeks?"

"Shut up, Ayo." Ethan glanced back to see Traore's sudden sullen expression.

"Sorry, cousin, too far." Ndaiye's voice was warm and apologetic.

Ethan felt for them both trying to date on their meager wages. Scrip was tight. He'd heard things were getting tough for the workers around here. These guys didn't make as much as they would have back on Earth, especially if they were relatively new. The way Ndaiye was struggling with his pack made Ethan suspect he hadn't worked in surveying long. And they were the lucky ones. Surveying was relatively easy and clean work, and not a bad way to pay off what you owed to Saras.

"Ay, Bryant." Ndaiye's thick accent made Ethan's last name sound exotic. "You been out here much?"

Ethan appreciated the man's attempt to include him. "Not this deep. Mostly just out to the parks with my family."

"Nobody been this deep in these mountains but us!" Ndaiye called. "Ahhh, you're in for a treat today! I'm going to find you a big juicy kwai fruit to try!"

Ethan had heard of the kwai fruit. Though common, the kwai plant was not an abundant producer, so it took skill and no small amount of luck to find a fruit. "I hope you can. I've heard they're delicious."

"He's got a good eye for finding them," Traore spoke up. His feelings were seemingly mended and he and Ndaiye picked up their banter again. Ethan glanced up to see the wisps of fog clearing. The wind swept them aside and the peaks appeared at their full height above the little group.

They hiked up and over a little ridge, then down into a pristine valley. Ethan had never seen anything so serene. Around him, the pale blue formations jutted from the ground, draped in greenery. The lake was perfectly still, the peaks reflected in it like frozen kings. Zan birds, their bright blue plumage shimmering, rose and fell on their wide wings as they dipped above the lake, catching insects in the still morning air. Once in a while a tail feather or wingtip would strike the surface of the lake, and then the ripples danced across it in ever-widening circles as beautiful as music.

"Your first time here," Ndaiye said from behind him. "So you have never seen the ghosts."

"What ghosts?" Ethan asked, still transfixed by the birds.

"The ghosts of the lakes. They come at dawn and dusk. We're too late now, we've missed them. I've been in the mountains twice, early in the mornings, and both times I've seen them." Ndaiye looked around. "Traore's terrified of them, but I think they're friendly."

Ethan nodded. He remembered the forms of animals like calterlek and illumbra when he'd seen them through the fog. There really was something ghostlike about them.

Ndaiye went on. "Our people, we have a lot more spiritual teachings than some on Minea," he said. "We know the ghosts are all around us, and sometimes we can see them."

Ethan wanted to ask more questions, but Ndaiye had work to do. Ethan watched him walk away, taking out his Suremap. As the surveyors plotted and measured, Ethan enjoyed the spring sunshine filling the valley. The foliage began to steam in the damp Minean heat. Ethan sought shade. When he crossed out of the morning sun's intensity into the shadow of the peaks, Brynn was just leaving the valley.

"Going over the ridge?" he asked. She nodded, toying with a silver pendant she was wearing.

"These valleys are one of the best things about these trips," she said brightly. Then hefting her pack higher on her shoulders, she said, "I'll see you at rendezvous."

\*\*\*

Aria wondered briefly about Ethan's survey trip today. He'd said they were going deeper into the karst maze than anyone had ever been yet, and while that sounded exciting, it also worried her. Every passenger of Ship 12-22 carried with them a subtle fear of the unknown.

With Ethan out of the city for the day, Aria had the perfect opportunity to go check out the farms northwest of Coriol. He wouldn't be using his Colony Office badge on the dresser, and it would get her into the farm much easier than any story she could concoct. As she reached for it she paused, looking at it for a long moment, weighing the ethics of using it to gain entry into the farm.

She was just going to look around. Anyway, she would have a badge of her own if Saras had hired her when she asked. Maybe they wouldn't be in this mess if they had. She had offered her help to the Saras company years ago, just after Polara was born, when she was frustrated and jittery from attending to the needs of her newborn all day. She had barely admitted to herself how much she wanted to be back in a lab, to have a test crop to attend to, to use for a few hours a week the knowledge she had worked so hard to earn back on Earth. But all the positions in Coriol were filled, she'd been told, by people hand-picked to fill them. Saras had brought their own crop specialists years before and said they had no need of her help. But Aria knew that they needed her. Their specialists knew nothing of the advances that had taken place in the fifty earth years that it had taken them to get here, and they didn't care to learn.

Aria called it "knowledge dilation," the telescoping of new ideas and discoveries that happened when great minds spent fifty-three years in stasis while their colleagues continued to advance in their field back on Earth. Though RTC was available and the specialists here had some access to the new knowledge, many of the advances couldn't be implemented without new equipment, and the equipment in Coriol was still decades behind what Aria had left on Earth. Also the specialists here were defensive of their knowledge and resistant to change the way they did things every time a new ship came in. She understood it on some level. It bothered her, too, that her own knowledge, so groundbreaking here, would probably be found only on dusty bookshelves back on Earth today.

Either way, Saras should have brought her on board. If they wouldn't allow her to help, she'd have to find another way to do so. She pulled on a formal-looking jumpsuit and slipped Ethan's entry badge into her pocket. Pinning her red hair up, she looked in the mirror. Pretty convincing.

She dropped the children at Kaia's, thanking her profusely and promising to be back after lunch, then caught the Water District line on the sol train.

Aria loved the near-silence of the train. She laid her head against the cool glass of the window. It wouldn't be cool much longer. Bright new growth had taken over every tree outside and shoots were pushing themselves through the drying mud. Minean summer, with its sticky heat, was on its way.

Glancing up, Aria was surprised to see the same tiny plants that had invaded her house clinging to the window and roof over her head. She looked around the train and saw them everywhere.

How could they spread like this? Why didn't they grow out in the soil? Where were they coming from?

When the train pulled silently into the station, all she heard was the "click" of the rail stop and the hiss of the doors opening. She stepped out to see the street full of Saras workers, red vests pulled over their clothes.

She followed the flow of them towards the water plant,

glancing at the map as she went. She found herself eavesdropping on two men walking in front of her.

"Four stations shut down yesterday," one of them said. "Guys just standing around for three hours while they cleaned all of the little plants out."

"Wonder how much longer they'll have to fight it," the other man said. "I didn't even get paid the day my station went down." They veered off to enter the Water Treatment Plant on the left, and Aria kept going straight down the street and out of town.

The city fell away behind her as the wide urban street tapered and the sidewalks ended. The narrow road was fringed on either side by broad grasses that grew taller than she was. Trees pushed their way through above the grasses, and the tangled mass of living things pressed in all around her. Soon she came to the gates of the Saras Company's Food Production Division.

The gateman seemed bored. He gave her badge a cursory check, then ushered her in with a sweep of his hand. Taking in the scene quickly, Aria determined that the big building to the right was probably the main office. She walked confidently into the front lobby, where she was met by a harried-looking man rushing out of his office. The plate on his door read "Neko Nasani, Director of Operations."

"I'm sorry," he said nervously, "we don't have anyone from the Colony Offices scheduled for a visit today. I have none of the proper paperwork in order." She half-expected to be summarily tossed out, but again she was pleasantly surprised by how many doors the Colony Offices badge opened. Under the law, the Colony Offices were charged with keeping the corporations in check and making sure that nothing interrupted the flow of Yynium or even threatened to interrupt it. Their ability to sanction a corporation or shut an operation down altogether made them people to be appeased, not antagonized, and this man apparently was used to it.

"It's not official," Aria said calmly. "I'm just here to visit with you a moment about some—" she searched for the right word, "anomalies we're seeing in production."

Nasani's eyes widened. "We're doing everything we can, I assure you. Everything is completely under control."

From the way he was sweating, Aria doubted it. "But you are having some trouble with your deliveries?" she asked pointedly.

"No, no, the deliveries are fine." His shoulders slumped and he waved her into the office. "Won't you please join me in here?" As he closed the door behind them he said, "You can understand that this is a rather delicate issue. Many people's jobs depend on this facility."

"Many people's *lives* depend on this facility, Mr. Nasani."

He sat heavily behind the desk, which was covered with papers, used cups, and, Aria fought the urge to wrinkle her nose, the ubiquitous green plants. He saw her looking at them and rose heavily, digging in a cabinet drawer and procuring a bottle of Zam cleaner, which he used to spray the plants and wipe them off with a used paper towel. He tossed it in the garbage, laughing nervously.

"You can see we don't have any trouble growing things here!" His voice was thick with a forced cheerfulness, but his eyes darted away from hers as he said it.

So there was a problem with the crops then. That was something Aria could help with, if they'd give her the chance.

Nasani had swept most of the garbage and a few of the papers into the trash with the little plants, so when he sat back down Aria found herself less distracted by the desk and more able to focus on what he was saying.

"Look, I'll level with you," he said. "I don't know what this thing is. It's unlike anything I saw back on Earth, and it breaks all the rules I know about growing things here on Minea."

"Can you explain to me what's happening, Mr. Nasani? What is wrong with the plants?"

"How about I show you?"

Saras operated both a traditional and a clean room operation out here. The clean rooms were huge sterile warehouses where everything was controlled, including lighting, temperature, nutrients, and airflow. They were protected from outside toxins by decontamination rooms which all personnel passed through before entering them. While clean rooms were useful for growing leafy greens, tomatoes, beans, and other staples, some plants still didn't produce as well in that environment. The rangkor tubers, corn, Minean squash called zilen, and melons, along with other substantial bearers, were grown out in the vast traditional farm fields behind the clean room building.

Nasani led her to the decontamination room, where she walked slowly under the glow of the lamps that were meant to eradicate any trace bacteria that may be harmful to the plants. She slipped a paper suit over her clothes and paper booties over her shoes and followed the director into the first clean room.

It was massive. Big enough to house three Minean cottages, the clean room was filled with shining metal shelving. Each shelf unit had seven levels, and each level was full of plants. Strawberry plants lined the aisles in trays stacked on the high shelves with under-mounted lighting. Lettuce, peas, and beans grew farther down the row. Each shelf had a bank of grow lights above it and on the bottom of the next shelf, and root trays below the plants where water and nutrients were made available. To Aria the rows upon rows of plants should have been beautiful.

But they weren't healthy plants. She stepped over to check out the strawberry plants on the shelf to her left. They were brown and limp.

Aria examined the leaves—those that hadn't died were covered with brown lesions. The stems were wilted, wasted away below what appeared to have once been healthy strawberries. The berries themselves were shriveled and black.

It seemed indicative of a pesticide or herbicide poisoning, but here in the clean rooms they didn't use either one. There was no reason to. The plants were grown in a sterile environment without exposure to disease, bugs, or even dirt that could introduce toxins. What could be causing this?

The story was the same on every shelf. Fast-moving blight of some kind was sweeping the crops. Aria herself had never trusted these indoor farms. She much preferred the open fields and the soil. Perhaps something in the outdoor portion of the facility would give her a clue.

"Can you take me to the outdoor crops?" she asked Nasani. He nodded, leading her through another decontamination room, where they discarded their old suits and put on new ones before walking through another bright blue light.

But Aria's hopes were wrecked when she saw the condition of the outdoor plants. They had the same symptoms but had contracted the disease in greater numbers. There were whole swaths of dead rangkors, zilen, corn, and melons. The dead corn stalks pointed skyward like accusing fingers. The sight of so much wasted life made Aria sick. She knelt down and ran her hands through the soil. There was nothing obvious that could be causing this.

"I assume you've run soil tests?" she asked.

"Time and again," he assured her. "There is nothing here

that wasn't here two months ago. Nothing that would cause—" Aria heard how his voice caught, "this." He gestured widely with his hand.

She looked at the sky. The light from Minea's sun was just right for these crops. She crumbled the soil in her hands. It was loose and rich, obviously well-mixed. She plucked a zilen leaf, turning it over and over, searching along its hairy veins for eggs or jagged holes that would show the presence of insects.

"You've had these under a microscope?" she asked Nasani.

He nodded. "There's no pests that we can see."

"Are you using pesticides out here? Herbicides for weed control?"

Nasani nodded. "Only HG9 to keep the krech off the crops, and Bronicide for the weeds."

Both were perfectly safe for these crops. She had seen them used for years without a problem. But things could change.

"Have you tried not using them?" Aria asked. "A test patch?"

He nodded, gesturing to an area separated by steel panels. Walking over she could see that the damage was just as extensive. It wasn't the herbicides or pesticides.

The dead leaves rustled against Aria's covered shoes as she followed Nasani back toward the building. The patch around them looked like a waning late-autumn field, not the tumble of spring vibrancy that they should be seeing. They entered and went through the decontamination room, leaving their suits and booties behind as they entered the main lobby.

Aria was so busy turning the puzzle over in her mind that she barely glanced up in time to see Theo Talbot enter the lobby and stop at the front desk.

Theo was well known for his a perfect memory for faces and names. There was no chance he wouldn't recognize her.

She turned abruptly to Nasani.

"I've got to be going. Thank you for your help." She tried not to sound panicky.

"Please tell the Colony Offices that we are doing everything we can. We will figure it out as soon as possible."

Aria felt for the man. He'd be unlikely to keep his job if the blight went on much longer. She thanked him and slipped into the restroom as he walked to meet Theo.

When the sound of their voices faded from the lobby, Aria left the building and headed for Kaia's cottage.

\*\*\*

Kaia liked watching the children. They had become part of her, now, as well as their parents. With her father off evaluating defenses in the southern cities of Minea for the last several months, it grew too quiet around her cottage. She kept busy tinkering with the basic house systems, improving the heat and the cooling and, of course, visiting Coriol Scrap to gather robot materials to entertain the children when they came.

They were playing now with the latest creation. Well, specifically, Polara was playing with it. It was a go-bot, an invention of which Kaia was particularly proud. The whole purpose of the go-bot was to evade capture. Once programmed and turned on, it would careen endlessly around a predefined space and simultaneously entertain and tire out its pursuer. She made the first one when she, herself, became too tired to entertain Polara effectively.

She was slowing down. There was no doubting it and no denying it.

She had visited the doctors about it and finally, after the hundredth time she'd donated her blood to further medical knowledge and save lives, she'd asked the question none of the doctors had ever addressed: "Why have I aged?"

The doctor smiled. "Everyone ages, Ms. Reagan."

Kaia looked away, following the lines of the window blinds with her eyes as she blinked back tears. She reformulated the question. "When I was on Beta Alora, and even afterwards, in the ship, I healed impossibly fast. I thought I would stay . . . young, somehow."

The doctor took off his glasses, cleaning them on his lab coat. "Many people don't realize that healing and aging are two different processes in the body. When we receive wounds and our bodies heal, it is the result of cells rushing to the wound and multiplying rapidly to repair it. Your genetic modifications seem to have made that rapid multiplication remarkably fast. However, unchecked multiplication can cause other problems," he searched for an example, "diseases like cancer, that blight of the twenty-first century. So human cells have natural mechanisms to avoid endless cell division. Each cell can divide well about fifty to seventy times, but then the cell becomes inactive or dies. That is actually what is happening during aging. It's not a wound, an accident that happens and can be repaired, though there is some promising research. Unfortunately, it doesn't appear that your modifications have changed the amount of times your cells can divide. In fact, while your ability to repair your wounds is enhanced, your aging process is actually slightly increased, because each time you heal, you're using up your supply of cells more quickly than the rest of us."

That was three weeks ago, and Kaia was at least glad to have an answer. That changed how she would spend her days. Who wanted to be immortal anyway?

Kaia's body ached as she settled into a chair next to Rigel. Her trip to the junkyard yesterday, and her early-morning tinkering with the go-bot, had left her sapped of energy.

The baby reached for his shoe, which he'd knocked just out of his own reach, and she looked down and tried to speak his name.

But it wasn't there. She started again, "Sweet—" She waited for his name to leap to her tongue, but it was as if she had opened a drawer in her mental filing cabinet and suddenly found it empty. His name was gone. He looked at her quizzically, sensing, she supposed, her distress.

"Sweet baby," she finished, fighting an edge of frustration that was slowly pulling through her chest. She hunted for the name again and found nothing.

The go-bot chimed as Polara finally caught it. Kaia looked up, searching her mind. Polara squealed triumphantly and then dropped to the floor to disassemble and reassemble the bot with the little wrench set strapped to its back.

The baby looked dismayed that the chaos was over. Watching Polara's chaos seemed to be one of his favorite pastimes.

Kaia reached behind her ear and pulled off her thought blocker, rubbing the callus where it belonged. Even it was sore today.

Suddenly, forcefully, a memory of Polara chasing the go-bot a moment ago flared inside Kaia's mind, unbidden. Kaia looked around, confused. Was this some new trick her memory was playing? Boomerang memories?

Another image, of the baby's shoe, laced with a feeling of frustration and intensity, entered her mind. She glanced down. The child was looking up at her.

His name came to her just as the realization dawned. Suddenly, Rigel's struggles made sense. Kaia gazed at the little boy and nodded.

"Ahh," she said softly. "I know now. I know your secret."

She looked into his eyes and thought carefully of a little treasure box, imagining it opening. Inside was a bright stuffed bear like she had as a child back on Earth.

Ri squealed with delight. His longing for the bear washed over Kaia and she felt guilty for showing him something she didn't actually have to give him. She sent him a picture of a cup of milk, and his attention shifted to that. That she could provide. She lifted him, crossing into the kitchen and pouring a cup of sweetbean milk. She twisted a lid on and handed it to him.

"How does your father not know this?" she asked the little boy as he drank.

"Not know what?" Polara asked, tipping her head to one side.

"Rigel has a gift," Kaia said.

"I want a gift!" Polara was up and across the room to the table in a flash.

Kaia gathered the little girl onto her lap. "You have a lot of gifts, too, Polara," she said, and she began to name them.

When Aria arrived that afternoon, Kaia asked her in. Aria was brimming with news of a crop blight. She had used Ethan's badge to inspect the crops at the Saras Food Production Division.

Where did grit like that come from? Kaia wondered. She couldn't imagine the mother of two making the decision, sometime that morning, to knowingly enter a restricted area while pretending to be on official business. Kaia hadn't seen any deception in her eyes when Aria had dropped the kids off this morning.

Kaia felt a pang of worry. If Aria got caught, what was Saras likely to do? There was only a small incarceration building in Coriol, as most real criminals were shipped out to the prison in

Minville, on the other edge of the settlements.

Kaia felt her mind fogging as she tried to pull her focus back to what Aria was saying.

". . . some kind of herbicide, maybe? Or pesticide? Neither make sense, but I just don't have any other ideas." Aria must have sensed that Kaia had something on her mind because she asked, "How was your day with the kids? Did they behave?"

Kaia pulled back to the moment. "Aria, there's something you need to know about Rigel."

Aria's green eyes grew scared. She glanced at the little boy on the rug, assessing that he was all right before catching Kaia's eyes again.

Kaia hurried to reassure her. "Rigel is telepathic, Aria. I've been having rudimentary conversations with him all afternoon."

The fear in her eyes changed to confusion. "What? Are you sure?"

"I am. He can receive and broadcast thoughts. They're pretty simple right now, though."

Aria put her head in her hands. "Oh, no. One more thing they'll mark on his chart."

Kaia took the younger woman's hands in hers, pulling them away from her face gently and looking into Aria's eyes.

"But you see, all those things on his chart are tied into this one."

Aria's face showed confusion.

"See, he doesn't talk because he sends his needs to you telepathically, and you get him his drink or his bread. It's like magic to him. He doesn't need to learn to say 'drink,' he just shows you. And when he wants something he can't reach, he just sends you or Polara to fetch it for him."

Understanding was dawning in Aria's eyes. "So I can hear him?" she asked.

Kaia shrugged. "I'm not sure, exactly. I can hear him clearly, but without telepathy, I'm not sure what it would feel like for you."

Aria listened, trying to clear her mind, but only her own thoughts were in there. "I'm not getting anything."

"He may have to initiate it. Just be aware of it, and tell Ethan when he gets home from the survey trip tonight. Maybe he can start working with—" and then his name was gone again, and Kaia took a quick breath, embarrassed, "with the baby on learning some basic words. I think it will make a real difference." She had covered up the lapse well, she thought, and Aria seemed too lost in this new information to have noticed.

# Chapter 6

Ethan squinted into the dim interior as he climbed onto the craft at the rendezvous. As they lifted off and the late afternoon shadows fell, his thoughts turned to home and the evening that lay ahead with Aria and the children. It had been a pleasant day, but he was ready to go home, anxious to see how his family was doing. He pulled out his missive and typed a message, but there was still no connection. He'd probably be home before the missive connected and the message sent. Especially at the speed this pilot was flying. As they rose, Ethan heard the missive connect and send the photo from this morning and the last message.

The pilot wove in and out of the mountains. Ethan saw Schübling, next to him, pull out her Suremap and take some readings. "Are we takin' a different route home?" she asked, a strange tone in her voice. The Suremap reading did look different from the terrain they had seen this morning.

"I'm just fightin' some strong air currents between these towers," the pilot said. "I'm seeing if we can loop around a different way to have a smoother ride."

Ethan glanced up from the screen just in time to see the tower that clipped the ship and sent it spinning. Metal ripped and screeched as the wing caught on the edge of the karst formation and flipped them upside down. Leaves and branches tore through the broken windows, raking Ethan's face and arms. He didn't breathe—couldn't breathe—as the smoke from the engine surrounded them. He heard one of the men wailing, and Brynn, behind him, screaming. Schübling, beside him, was silent.

The crash lasted only seconds, but time seemed to slow as the ship slid the last fifty yards down the peak and crashed to a stop on its side in the thick foliage. Ethan felt a sharp pain as he turned to see if the survey team was okay. Ndaiye sat in shock, blood streaming from cuts along his face and neck. Carlisle, who appeared unhurt, unbuckled and staggered over, pulling his jacket off and pressing it to Ndaiye's face.

Brynn was quiet and pale. Ethan glanced at the pilot, who had climbed out to see if it was safe to get his passengers out. He seemed unhurt. The other members of the team were stirring, gasping, and regrouping. Still, Schübling lay silent in her seat beside Ethan. He turned to her and put a hand on her shoulder. She didn't stir. Looking up, he saw the pilot walking by outside her shattered window. "Hey," he called to the pilot, "we've got a problem here." But as the pilot turned to look inside, Ethan saw him drop downward, impossibly quickly. The last Ethan saw of him was the terror on his face.

Ethan tried to comprehend what had happened, and then felt the ship began to shift. "Hang on!" Ethan called as the craft slid off into a deep chasm that yawned below.

The craft rolled and plummeted, thudding into rocks with the sound of ripping metal. The light from outside disappeared as the little ship was consumed by a shaft deep enough to fit the entire Colony Offices building in. Carlisle wasn't strapped in, and he flipped forward as they fell and slammed into the wall near Ethan. Ethan reached out and grasped the other man's arm, hoping to stop his wild tumbling, but the moment the ship shifted again and began to nosedive into the dark, Carlisle was torn from Ethan's grasp and thrown past him to the back of the craft.

Ethan braced himself for another impact. It came, and the screeching metal tore away from the side of the ship next to his seat. He had a quick glimpse of stone and darkness before the ship flipped again, freefalling. There were more impacts, more sudden jolts, more tumbling, until Ethan could not tell up from down or the way they'd come from the way they were going.

When the ship stopped falling, there was an immediate, eerie silence, as if the cacophony of sounds had been swallowed up by the immense and unknown dark outside. And then came the anguished sounds of the passengers.

A fine dust rose through the pale glow of the emergency cabin lights. Ethan breathed against white-hot pain in his chest, willing it to abate as he peered outside the craft.

"Breathe," he told himself. "Breathe."

He glanced at Maggie Schübling, and saw her looking back at him. Her face was still as stone, but her eyes were open, and there was pain behind them.

"What is it?" he asked. "Captain Schübling, are you hurt?"

She didn't speak, but her eyes darted down to her right leg, and Ethan looked to see the pilot's seat crumpled over her shin, which was bent at a startling angle. "Okay," he said slowly. "We're gonna get that off."

Ethan looked around. Outside was darkness, ominous and solid. The little craft was tipped slightly onto its side, and he could see the ground pressing through the hole next to him. He reached through the gaping side of the ship and ran his fingers along the ground. Crumbly, sticky dirt coated his fingers like cake crumbs. He hastily wiped them on his pants. He shifted in his seat, carefully at first, then more vigorously. The craft shifted slightly, but seemed to settle in the soft dirt. It was solid. Ethan reached up, pausing to take a sharp breath as he felt a catch in his shoulder, likely caused by being thrown against the harness. He braced against the pitch of the floor and released his safety harness. Turning, he saw others carefully moving around between the scattered seats and wounded survey crew.

Other than Ndaiye's cuts, the cousins seemed to be all right, and they were pulling emergency first aid equipment out of an overhead compartment, passing it to Collins and Jade, who were attending to Carlisle.

Kneeling beside Schübling, Ethan ran a hand down the pilot's seat. Gently, he tried pressing it forward, but it didn't move. He put a shoulder against it and pushed. It wasn't going anywhere. Schübling, still silent, was looking at him with pleading eyes.

Pain in his shoulder and chest made him wince as he lay down in the aisle and peered under the seat. The emergency lights on the floor illuminated the space and he saw some hope. This was an ejection seat, made to release from the floor. He pulled back, glanced up, and saw the lever that would activate the charge and shoot it skyward. That would free her leg. But he paused, leaning in to look carefully at the tangled mess of seat and bone in front of him. It was obvious that the seat had broken her leg. What if the leg was caught on the seat? The ejection would do far more damage. He'd have to come up with something else. She was in shock, and the floor below her was sticky with blood—he'd have to move quickly.

Ethan scrambled underneath the seat, peering through the wires and metal. He saw the rails that the seat sat on and followed them back to the seat's attachment point. Two release clasps shone back at him, holding the seat to its undercarriage on the rails. They were thick metal, but made to flip up and down to secure the seat to the carriage, or in this case, to release it. He reached back and released them both. The seat shifted and Schübling cried out in pain as he grasped it and shoved it forward, off her leg and out the broken windscreen onto the nose of the ship.

He turned his attention to the leg.

"Hey," he called to Ndaiye, "I need an Emedic over here!"

The man turned a bloodied face to him and nodded. "Comin'!" he called. In moments he was beside Ethan with the med kit. Ndaiye helped Schübling lean forward as he stuck an anesthetic patch on her lower back. Ethan watched as the medicine smoothed the pain from Schübling's features.

He pulled the Emedic from the kit. It was an oblong gray box, metal and heavy, much bigger than the one they had at home. Flipping it open he saw the screen and a number of attachments. Ethan pulled out the camera and checked both ends of the connecting cable, then aimed at Schübling's wound. He tried to keep steady and pressed the green "Assess" button.

Immediately, a full internal picture of the broken limb appeared on the screen. It was a bad break. Ethan pressed the yellow "Treat" button. The Emedic's speaker buzzed with its calm voice.

"Please attach the Instasplint at the indicated points." The Emedic directed.

Ethan popped open the compartment that said "Instasplint" and removed two thick, flat, flexible bars. He wrapped them around above and below the break, as shown on the screen.

"Instasplint attached," the Emedic said. "Alignment sequence initiated. Please do not touch the injury." The screen blinked with a barred circle with the wound picture in the middle. The bars went rigid, pressing into the skin, and suddenly moved forcefully away from each other. Ethan winced as the bones cracked into place, the lower leg perfectly straight again. He glanced at Schübling, who only looked impatient.

"Please connect the injection attachment."

Ethan found the attachment labeled "Injection" and plugged it into one of the ports.

"Please insert the injection attachment at the indicated point." The screen lit up with an external photo of the wound and an animation of the injection attachment sliding into the skin just below Schübling's knee. "The green light on the attachment will glow when the correct insertion point is reached."

Ethan drew the attachment across Schübling's leg, glancing at her face to be sure it wasn't hurting her as he did so.

"Keep your eyes on your work," Schübling snapped.

The pain medicine must be working.

Ethan looked back to see the light switch from red to green. He pressed the long, pointed end of the attachment under the skin and felt the pressure of the vein wall release as it entered.

"Delivering inhibitor," the calm Emedic voice said. "Please do not remove the injection attachment from the patient."

Ethan heard a hiss and waited, watching as the flow of blood from the wound stanched.

"Inhibitor delivered. Delivering matrix material." There was a pause. "Matrix material delivered. Delivering bone morphogenetic proteins. Please do not remove the injection attachment from the patient."

Ethan's arm ached, but he held the attachment steady.

"Bone morphogenetic proteins delivered. Delivering time-dilated, enhanced Reagan cells. Please do not remove . . ." Ethan took a sharp breath. Reagan cells were lab-grown cells that had been enhanced with Kaia's altered DNA. They sped up healing exponentially, though it was nothing like the healing in her own body. Delivering large quantities of them to a wound made it possible for the body to begin rebuilding damaged tissue immediately. Though he had known they were used in trauma cases, hearing the Emedic say her name jolted him.

Ethan thought about what Kaia had told him about her condition and felt the old bitterness. It was patently unfair that she healed quickly, but she still couldn't cheat old age.

Schübling's gruff voice cut into Ethan's thoughts. "Get it outta me, already!" she barked.

Ethan looked down to see the Emedic flashing red. "Please remove the injection attachment from the patient." It was repeating. "Please disconnect injection attachment and place it in the injection attachment compartment."

Ethan did so and the compartment slid closed. The sterilization cycle initiated in the compartment.

"Please connect the Sprayshield attachment." Ethan found and connected it, then followed the Emedic's instructions to position it in front of the wound. "Applying Sprayshield," the Emedic declared, and then sprayed a thick, clear gel across the wound which hardened quickly into a transparent cast.

Ethan was glad that when more experienced medical personnel arrived they'd be able to view the injury and check it's healing through the transparent cast. He followed the Emedic's instructions for sterilizing, then used it to treat the scrapes on Ndaiye's face before the other man went to help Traore open a stuck compartment.

He scanned his own shoulder and found nothing broken, simply a lot of bruising. He took a shot of Vein Complex to aid in the healing of the capillaries and turned his attention back to Schübling. "How are you feeling now?"

She shrugged. "Fine. Can't feel anything below my stomach, and I can't get turned around to see my crew. Go check them and give me a report."

What he found was disheartening. Along with the pilot, three others were dead: Carlisle and Espinoza lay in the back of the shuttle, and Baker had been thrown out of the craft during the descent. That left Brynn, Ethan, the cousins Traore and Ndaiye, Schübling, Collins, and Jade. Seven people left. Two of them, Schübling and Ndaiye, hurt pretty badly, and the rest fighting at least shock. Ethan himself felt sick and shaky. He wouldn't be the only one. In fact, he became increasingly worried as he looked at Brynn. Her skin was ashen and she was walking around, agitated. She kept approaching Schübling and then abruptly turning and walking away. He went to her.

"Brynn, why don't you come over and rest a little?" He gestured to a seat in the right side of the craft which had been bent to a nearly horizontal position and had her lie down. He raised her boots to the back of the seat in front of her and Traore brought over a blanket.

"Just rest," Ethan encouraged her. "You're okay." He left her with Traore and went back to report to Schübling.

"Well, just try to make 'em all comfortable," she said. "Search and rescue oughta be here anytime." She lay her head back against the seat and closed her eyes.

# Chapter 7

As the afternoon sun washed the cottage kitchen with gold, Aria—using a cake pan as a seed tray—mixed another handful of dark loam into the blue Minean clay. Minea's famed soil made beautiful houses, but it also bound roots and blocked water. And the seeds here were sub-par. In fact, she suspected genetic tampering, because yields on her test seeds had been lower than expected. She had long felt the need to grow things, but the seeds Saras sold in its gardening section each spring were hardly more than ornamental. She couldn't coax more than a few seedy peppers and some leggy broccoli out of any of them.

But when she'd come back from Kaia's, she'd been encouraged to see a few little shoots curling out of the trays. Some of them were wheat—real Earth wheat, her wheat—and they thrilled her with their brilliant green. She wanted to keep them growing, so she had to try a few more things, like abrading the clay with some more nutrient-rich soil. She'd kept a backyard compost bin going for months, and now the thick organic material was mixing nicely into the native dirt.

The children were both still napping. They must have had an energetic day at Kaia's. Aria needed to wake them and start supper, but she stole a few more minutes to indulge in her passion for growing things.

Aria sifted the last of the new soil into the trays. As she glanced up she saw more of the little plants growing above the kitchen sink.

Inspecting it, she ran her fingers over the soft leaves. These were very young seedlings, some of them just pushing out the cotyledons—the two first leaves. Their bases branched into the webby root system that attached to any smooth, hard surface and leached water from the air.

She remembered Dr. Laar, one of her favorite professors back on Earth, who had studied a group of Chlorophytum plants to see how to increase the effectiveness of the way plants use water. She smiled as she remembered her favorite part of the class: his accent. A small, round man, he slipped words from his native tongue into his sentences in a charming, absentminded way.

*Before planting*, he had said, *you must listen to the taim.*

Taim meant plant in Estonian, Professor Laar's native language. It took her nearly a semester to figure that out. Now, it came back to her as she realized she had started calling the ubiquitous little Minean plant "Taim" in her mind.

A pang of sadness enveloped her as she thought how long Dr. Laar had been dead, back on Earth. It led to thinking of her family. Her parents, long gone, her siblings. She'd have nieces and nephews that were older than she was now. Even they would have children and grandchildren. Generations of her own family that she would never see. She felt a tear sting her eye and blinked it back, refocusing on the bright little plants, glowing in the afternoon sun streaming through the window.

*Listen to the taim.* He had known, as so few seemed to, that plants could tell you what they needed. There were ways of communicating with them. They were not so different than people. They responded to light, to music, to kindness. Aria wondered if it was her imagination that these little plants were straightening now, as she brushed them with her fingertips. They almost seemed to be reaching toward her, like they craved her presence. Perhaps they were a kind of companion plant, like philodendrons back on Earth. Philodendrons seemed made to live where people lived. Their glossy foliage and robust growth as a houseplant always made Aria think that not only were they suited to the same temperatures and humidity levels as people, but more than that, perhaps they somehow enjoyed the company of humans.

Every plant, Aria had found, gave humanity a gift. Perhaps it was shade, like the tall trees in the forest outside her window, or beauty, like the aurelia flowers. Perhaps it was fragrance or medicine, like the herbs she'd been gathering from the forest and experimenting with since coming to Minea. She lifted a heavy chei fruit off the counter and smelled the sweetness of its thick rind. Perhaps, like the fruits and grains, a plant's gift was food.

Maybe the Taim had such a gift to give. Perhaps people could eat them? They looked a little like sprouted sweet beans in miniature. With some encouragement, the Taim growing throughout the house was more than enough to feed a family, and they grew remarkably fast. But to effectively feed people, they'd need to be cultivated. Aria wondered if they'd bear transplanting and growing in trays. She looked at the tray she'd just filled, but the rich soil wasn't what the Taim chose when it began to sprout. Its seedlings liked a hard, bare surface.

A stack of Luis' platters, plates, and bowls lay next to her on the counter. She pulled out the biggest platter and carefully began to lift the Taim roots off the glass of the window. They were sticky and tiny hair-like shafts clung as she pulled them carefully away. She spread the roots across the platter as best she could. The plants lay limply on the colorful ceramic. This may not work.

Carrying the platter out of the kitchen, she set it on the desk in her work room, which she jokingly called her lab. It wasn't much of a lab—really a spare room with a desk and some basic pieces of equipment Ethan had procured for her over the years: a microscope, some tools, and a strong light.

She was tempted to pop a few of the Taim in her mouth just to see how they'd taste, but remembered her training on poisonous plants and decided against it. She went to check on the children, sleeping upstairs. As she climbed she wondered what it would be like not to have food for them in the kitchen downstairs and she felt a little surge of hope that the Taim could help solve Coriol's hunger problem.

As she looked at the tray of plants, she thought about the food shortage. Why wasn't Marcos Saras doing more about it? She had met him plenty of times, had seen the peculiar sadness he carried with him. It was peculiar for the most powerful man in a city, and such a young man at that, to have such a burden. She had seen, also, his lust for Yynium. Perhaps the two were related. He seemed to have no joy in his eyes except when he talked about the Yynium production, how it was increasing due to their innovations, how they would soon have enough Yynium back at Earth to send ship after ship through space using RST.

He was so obsessed with Yynium production that Aria suspected most of the rest of Coriol, and the Saras Company, was run by Marcos Saras' shadows, Theo and Veronika. They were an interesting pair, and she could see why such opposites would be beneficial.

Aria had seen them during parties at the stone and steel

Saras mansion or at the Colony Office parties. They were always there, always next to Saras, always watching the crowd.

Saras had always done underhanded things to keep the inhabitants of Coriol working at peak production, but surely this food shortage wasn't another of his manipulations. He couldn't be that kind of monster. Veronika's cold face flashed in Aria's mind, though, and she knew she was going to have to find out for herself what was causing it. If Saras, or his Vice Presidents, were using it to control the people, then the Colony Offices would have to know about it, and the sooner the better.

*** 

The wrecked ship's lights were going out one by one as the battery died and the wetness got to exposed circuits. The survey team huddled in the damp, waiting for rescue. The light wasn't enough to keep them warm, but it was enough to keep their shock at bay.

"I'm going out to take a look around," Collins called.

"Be careful." Jade's voice was strained, and Ethan thought she might have an internal injury, though she said she was fine.

He couldn't stand being in here any longer. Ever since being the Caretaker of Ship 12-22, Ethan didn't like enclosed places. He much preferred being out in the forest or even in his broad, windowed office in the Colony building in Coriol. "I'll come with you."

The two men stepped gingerly past the torn seats in front of the gaping hole where the hatch used to be. Collins had a flashlight, and it shone across a broad plain of the same brown crumbly dirt Ethan had felt through the side of the ship when they'd first crashed. It was springy and dense when they stepped out onto it, and within a few steps they found themselves sinking a bit.

There was a sharp, acrid smell, and Ethan found himself gagging and coughing as they struggled away from the craft.

A flash of white on the ground caught Ethan's attention. "Collins," he called, "shine that light over here."

The beam fell on the arched skeletal ribcage of a dog-sized creature, half buried in the muddy floor. The bones were stripped of flesh and skin, so Ethan couldn't be sure, but it looked like a wing jutted out from one side. Ethan shuddered. It was a huge, bat-like creature, fallen to the gummy floor and stuck there, leaving only its bones.

He took the light from Collins and shined it above them, but powerful as it was, it was lost in the immensity of the cavern before it reached whatever was up there. Ethan imagined the creatures that must be hanging above them, dog-sized bats, waiting for their nocturnal feeding time. He glanced down with the realization that the sticky, crumbly pile they were walking on was a huge guano field. That explained the smell.

This was the first he had seen of Minean bats, but many species on Minea were like species back on earth. The swimming lizards, though slightly different than lizards back on Earth, had evolved in a similar fashion. This was probably true of bats, as well, he thought to calm himself. Bats on Earth were mostly insect eaters, and even the hunting species back home usually only took the odd bird or snake. These bat-like creatures were—as he always told Polara about other animals— probably more scared of people than people were of them.

But when he stepped off the guano field onto hard, solid stone, he still felt a little relief. Here the great cavern narrowed to a large tunnel, big enough to fly the ship into, if it had been capable of flight—and if there hadn't been enormous stalactites and stalagmites studding the ceiling and floor of the passage. He stopped at the opening and shined the light inside. It looked like a giant shark's mouth, gaping open, with the huge teeth casting shifting shadows in the beam.

Movement caught Ethan's eye. He blinked as what looked like a figure slipped behind one of the giant teeth on his right. Ethan glanced at Collins, but Collins was looking back up the guano field at the craft.

"Did you see that?" Ethan asked.

Collins turned. "What?" He peered into the darkness.

Ethan strode to the big stalagmite and walked around it with the light. There was nothing there. He shone the light farther down the passage, but neither saw nor heard anything.

"Let's go back," he said, annoyed with himself for letting his imagination run away. The dark was beginning to get to him.

*** 

Ethan had paced the aisle of the craft numerous times in the hours since the crash. Now he crossed to the spot in the back where Jade and Collins had just finished stacking the supplies. He tried not to look at the two dead crew members on the floor.

They'd found nine survey packs. Ethan opened one up and sorted through the contents: lengths of rope, a powerful Maxlight flashlight, a pair of gloves, a vest with a round light on each shoulder, a pair of Everwarm coveralls, four Nutriblock bars, three bags of water, a whistle, a Suremap device, a rain poncho, a mirror, a few fuel bricks, and, in this one, half a sandwich, a chocolate nut bar, and an apple left over from Carlisle's lunch.

He felt a shiver run through him. "We probably ought to put these on," he said, holding up the coveralls. The crew was huddled under blankets, but they were beginning to look chilled, too.

Jade started distributing the packs. Lindsey Jade seemed, to Ethan, tough and efficient, a younger version of her captain, without the bitterness. He looked at the crew, watching as they took the packs. Brynn seemed especially glad to extract her coveralls and pull them on.

Ethan climbed into Carlisle's coveralls, then put everything back in the pack before heading to the front of the plane. He leaned out the broken windscreen and peered up at Traore, who was sitting on the nose of the ship, holding aloft his Suremap device.

"Any luck?" Ethan said, quietly so that the others wouldn't hear.

Traore turned to him, and his bright teeth flashed as he grimaced. "Not good news. We've fallen into a 150-meter shaft. It was small at the entrance but it's like a funnel, and it grows wider as it gets deeper. We've bounced away from the opening pretty far. If you look closely, you can see it just there—" he pointed up and to the right. As Ethan squinted, he could make out a tiny pinprick of light—like a star. Outside, the sun would be fading. Night was coming on, and even that light would be gone soon.

"Are they coming for us?"

Traore shook his head. "It's unlikely they'll know where to look. We were kilometers off course when we dropped in here. The ship's signal beacon was crushed, and we're so far down that even if we were right under the entrance, which we're not, they couldn't see us from the air when they flew over. The Suremaps have locators, but the rock above us will block their signals.

"What are our chances of getting out the way we came in?" Ethan knew the answer, but wanted Traore to say it so he wouldn't have to.

Traore simply waved his hand toward the pinprick and shook his head.

Ethan moved back into the plane and sat heavily in the pilot's seat. They couldn't go out, and the cave was dark and full of danger around them. They'd have to stay here.

He turned to the crew.

"We should probably make ourselves comfortable. Eat something. Try to stay warm. Get some sleep if you can."

It seemed strange to be giving the orders. The team probably knew better than he did what surrounded them, but none of them seemed to want to take charge. He wished that their actual leader, Schübling, would wake up and do the directing, but to be fair, she had a shattered leg, so it only seemed right to let her rest. The team was weary, and there was little conversation as they settled in on their packs and tried to sleep.

Ethan made his way back to his seat carefully, not bumping the sleeping Schübling. He leaned back and closed his eyes, grateful for the encompassing warmth of the coveralls. In spite of all the unknowns, he was tired and he felt himself drift off.

\*\*\*

Ethan was awakened by the whoosh and screech of the bats above as they spiraled out of the opening through which the little craft had fallen hours earlier.

And then he heard the scratching, like the sound of wet wood crackling on a fire. It was a muffled, uneven sound. He sat up and it stopped. Glancing around, he saw the rest of the crew still sleeping, except for Collins, who was scrolling through his missive, though Ethan was sure he hadn't gotten any new messages down here. Ethan lay back down in his seat, trying to shake off the uneasiness that was growing within him. As he stilled, he heard the sound again, closer. It was immediately outside the ship, and it was louder. He looked down through the gaping hole and saw the shiny back of a krech—a Minean cockroach—but this one wasn't like the ones he scuttled outside for Aria. Those were size of a coin. This one was as big as his hand, quick and shining. It moved through the dim light and was gone into the darkness again.

Ethan tried to put it out of his mind. Of course there were creatures down here. It was a cave. Creepy things lived in caves. But he'd seen much bigger monsters, and he wasn't going to let a krech, even a really big one, scare him.

But then he heard Collins swear and saw him jump up, shaking his leg. Attached to it, biting through the thick leg of his coveralls, was another huge krech. Another scuttled in through the broken windscreen, and two more followed it. Ethan saw one crawl through the hole near his leg and up onto his pack. With a side claw sharp as a razor, the creature tore at the pack, shredding a three-inch slit through the tough polyweave material. Ethan kicked it off with his foot and snatched the pack, but Carlisle's half-sandwich fell out and the krech was on it instantly. Three more poured through the hole and squabbled over the morsels of bread and meat. Ethan shouldered his pack and Schübling's, then shook her shoulder.

"I think you'd better wake up, Captain," he said.

Schübling opened her eyes groggily, then looked down at the creatures on the floor. "What the—" she pulled her wounded leg away just as the krech reached her boot in search of more food. These krech were scavengers, and in the remains of this little ship they'd found a feast.

Around the craft, Ethan heard the screams of the crew as the krech advanced. He slipped an arm around Schübling and supported her as she stood. Together they hobbled into the aisle. Ethan stepped on a krech and heard it crunch and screech. His boot was slick as he pulled it out of the mess. The other team members were stomping them, too, holding their packs above their heads, but the krech kept coming.

A horrified scream cut through the chaos and Ethan looked to see Brynn throw herself across the bodies of Carlisle and Espinoza. The men were covered in krech. A huge bug crawled onto Brynn's shoulder. Ethan saw it bite, saw the blood seep through her coveralls. She screamed again and batted at it and the others, trying to clear them off the bodies of her friends.

"Get her out of there!" Ethan barked at Collins. More krech were pouring in, clicking excitedly, their antennae moving wildly. They were communicating, calling more of their kind to the ship.

Their slick exoskeletons shone in the dim lights. The sight reminded Ethan of the Others of Beta Alora, of the battle that he'd fought in the stateroom. His heart was beating hard. He was paralyzed with a sudden rush of memories: the crushing weight of Traxoram's mind shackles, the sharp edges of his armor slicing Ethan's hands. Mixed with the memories, an image—the delicate bones of the bat skeleton—flashed through Ethan's mind. These bugs were carnivorous. The image grounded him, pulled him out of his memories and back to the moment. They would all end up that way if they didn't get out of here.

"Let's go!" he yelled. "Come on!"

He was half-dragging Schübling as he charged out the door, slipping on the shiny backs of the krech as he went, struggling against what he now saw was a horrific tide of them pouring down the walls and across the guano field. He ran for the shark's mouth tunnel, stopping only to kick the krech from Schübling's leg, where they swarmed, trying to get to her wound. Ethan glanced back and saw the survey team scrambling across the field behind him.

He led them to the tunnel and wove in between the stalagmites. He didn't have a light and didn't want to stop to dig one from the pack, but the utter darkness of the passage soon had him crashing into the rock formations and both he and Schübling were tripping over the smaller ones. He stopped.

The rest of the crew came up behind him. Collins, dragging a weeping Brynn, had a Maxlight. Ethan took it from him and swung the beam back toward the mouth of the tunnel. Only a few of the krech had strayed to follow them, and Jade crushed them under her boot one by one. Ethan wondered briefly if that would attract more krech.

Schübling must have been thinking the same thing. "Let's get farther away," she said, obvious pain making her voice waver.

Ethan nodded and led the group farther down the tunnel. The solid stalagmites and stalactites around them were oddly comforting after the shifting, living floor they'd crossed. The smooth rounded sides of the stones, marbled from eons of the dripping water that had formed them, caught the light and cast it back to the little group. Just as Ethan was getting used to the cozy tunnel, the stalactites disappeared from the ceiling. When he shone the light up, he saw the high, arching stone of another cavern.

\*\*\*

Aria flinched as she saw a little krech scuttle across the bathroom floor. She squashed it and felt a ripple of frustration. It was past dark, and Ethan wasn't home yet. She tried calling his missive. No answer.

She was anxious to tell him about Rigel, and about the blight. He'd raise an eyebrow that she had used his badge, but he trusted her, and he wasn't the type to judge. Five years alone had given him perspective. It was a wonderful quality in a husband.

She thought of the moment, earlier that afternoon, when she first saw the shoots of her wheat peeking through the dark soil, and grew more impatient for his return. She had so much to tell him.

But late that night, when Ethan's dinner had been put away on one of Luis's beautiful hand-thrown pottery plates, when Aria had checked the new, growing wheat again, and when the children had been bathed and rocked off to sleep, Ethan still wasn't home, and a knock came on her door.

Theo Talbot stood on her doorstep, the porch light casting shadows around his hollow eyes. He told her the shuttle Ethan was in had disappeared in the Karst Mountains without a trace. No signal remained, no trail. They would send out a search party tomorrow, but there was no indication of what had happened to that ship. He was sorry. He had liked Ethan very much. Saras would compensate.

# Chapter 8

Ethan felt the vast darkness expanding around him as the shark's mouth tunnel opened into the middle of the massive cavern. All along the sides, as far as Ethan could see with the Maxlight, stalagmites were standing like silent people watching the little group as they entered. The center was a wide, smooth plain of bare rock.

Schübling let out a gasp of pain. Even though the Emedic treatment sped up her healing considerably, and the splint's special material took the weight and gave her mobility, she was still badly wounded, and she'd been on her feet too long, Ethan realized.

"We need to take a minute to get organized," he said, running the beam behind them onto the floor of the tunnel. No krech. They should be safe here for a while, anyway. He led them to the middle of the room, and helped Schübling lower herself to the ground. Brynn's weeping had stopped, but her sniffles gave the group a somber feeling.

Collins sat with his arm around her, and Traore sat on her other side, digging in his pack. Everyone but Brynn had made it out with their packs. That was lucky, Ethan thought, because he doubted they'd go back to get any. Though it seemed the krech spent their days up on the walls and it would probably be safe enough to go back in a few hours, the way they had swarmed made him think there wouldn't be much left anyway.

Jade pulled out her vest. "We oughta put these on. It was hard to see back there at the back." She was zipping up the bright red vest over her coveralls. She tapped the round lights on the front of the vest. A pale white light immediately glowed from her shoulders and illuminated the stone directly in front of her. As the others put theirs on, their faces were lost to Ethan in the glare of their shoulder lights, but the cumulative effect was cheery.

Ndaiye spoke up. "And we've got the Maxlights, too." He switched on his big flashlight, setting it up on the stone floor in front of him while he used the Emedic to administer another treatment for the gashes on his face.

Ethan dug in his pack and pulled out his own Maxlight, handing the other one back to Collins, who was helping Brynn with her vest.

"We should conserve the lights." Schübling said gruffly, struggling with the zipper on her vest. She seemed a bit more like herself. "The shoulder ones will last a long time, but the big ones will run outta juice. Jade, Traore, take one Maxlight and do a sweep of the room for any of those bugs, then turn it off. We can't waste the batteries."

The two didn't seem to mind rising and walking together into the dark. The familiarity of taking orders from their boss seemed to calm them. Ethan watched them as they circled the huge room in a spot of light. From where he was, he couldn't see any krech on the walls. It was just smooth, pale stone all around them.

Next to the stalactites, the people looked small. Here and there they went behind a column, where the stalactites from the ceiling had joined with the stalagmites on the floor, and lit it up from behind with their flashlight. The stone spikes they passed looked like spectators, ready to watch the little group of people who'd been thrust onto the stage in the middle of the room. Apparently Ethan wasn't the only one who thought so.

"This reminds me of the stadium Traore and I used to go to back on Earth to watch soccer," Ndaiye said. "Our families would spend a whole Saturday there, watching. Just like these guys are watching us." He gestured to the spikes. Cupping his hands around his mouth, he yelled, "GOOOOAL!" The place was so big that it took a heartbeat for the echo to bounce back.

"GOOOOAL!" Traore's thin voice answered his cousin from the far side of the room.

Ndaiye's bright smile glowed in the half-light.

Brynn spoke, her voice muffled in Collins's shoulder. "They don't look scary, though." Ethan could see just her eyes over the shoulder lights. She was peering past Collins at the spikes nearest them.

"No," Collins agreed. "They remind me of soldiers. Just, I don't know, standing guard and protecting this place."

"And us," Brynn said.

"And us," Collins assured her.

Schübling gestured to Ethan. "Give me my pack. Thanks for carrying it." She looked him in the eye. "And me."

Ethan nodded. Rough as she was, he liked Schübling. She was sincere, unpretentious. You always knew where you stood with her, and she wasn't going to pretend. After a little getting used to, it was refreshing. He suspected she was one of the few people whose thoughts really matched their words.

Ethan began to feel cold seeping into his legs and hands, through his coveralls and gloves, wherever his body was in contact with the stone. He stood and walked around the group. "We're going to have to be careful not to get too chilled," he said.

Brynn looked up from Collins' shoulder has he came by. "Did you turn on your Everwarms?"

"Turn them on?"

"There's a control inside the zipper on your chest. They're heated coveralls." She tapped just beside her shoulder light.

Ethan located the zipper and the control. He clicked the button up and immediately felt soothing warmth encompass him. He let out an involuntary sigh.

Ndaiye and Brynn laughed.

"I remember my first pair of Everwarms. I got them on a survey job a couple years ago in the Rainy Outback. We were soaked for three days, then a supply drop delivered a pair for each of us. It was like being wrapped in my mama's arms!"

Brynn fiddled with her necklace as she spoke up. "I got mine last winter. That's one thing I like about working for Saras. They have the best gear."

"Unless you work in the mines," Collins said.

"Or the refinery," Ndaiye agreed solemnly.

Ethan heard long experience in the voices of the men. He'd heard about the backbreaking labor and the long days in Saras's Yynium operation.

"You spent some time there?" Ethan questioned.

"Five years," Collins said, "in the Saras mine just outside of Coriol." Brynn sat up and Collins shifted away, leaning back and looking up at the ceiling. "Hardest work of my life. Worst part was, they didn't pay you enough to make it so you could go anywhere else. And there wasn't time for management training or anything, with twelve- or fourteen-hour workdays. It's a real dead-end job."

"How did you get on this survey crew?" Ethan asked.

"Same as everyone," Collins answered, gesturing to

Schübling. "The Captain requested me."

Ethan, surprised, turned his attention to Schübling. "Really?"

"I came here with a survey crew early on. When Coriol was all laid out, they didn't have work for us, so we went to work in the mines," Schübling answered. "Worked there for eleven years without complaining." She shot a meaningful look at her crew, obviously disapproving of their dislike for the work. "When Saras started expanding the mines, they called the surveyors back out. I'd seen Carlisle and Baker working their tails off at the refinery. Espinoza ran the accounts at the mine and I needed somebody good with numbers. I'd worked with Collins and Jade and Traore. And Traore told me about his fantastic cousin who worked at the refinery." She scoffed, shooting an annoyed look in Ndaiye's direction, and he laughed. "I got to pick a team, and for some reason I picked this bunch." The warmth in her voice revealed her affection for them, though Ethan was sure she wouldn't have admitted it.

"And just to have it out in the open," Brynn said, "she got stuck with me because my father is a friend of Mr. Saras." Ethan could tell Brynn wanted Schübling to toss her a compliment, maybe about how glad she was to have her or how it had worked out fine, but Schübling didn't work that way.

"Saras doesn't have any friends," Schübling said instead. There was a long, awkward silence.

"Well, I'm glad to have you on the team," Collins said after a moment.

"I'm getting some sleep," Schübling cranked up her coveralls and laid down on her pack. Ethan glanced over in time to see Brynn shoot a scalding look at her boss.

Ethan watched the group get comfortable. He waited until Jade and Traore got back and reported that there was nothing but rock in the cavern before he stretched out on the smooth floor and looked up at the tall stone sentinels.

The new morning would be breaking over Coriol. Aria would know, now, that something was wrong. The Colony office may have called her. There would be people searching. But he faced the fact that Traore was right: it would be next to impossible for anyone to guess where they'd gone.

He heard the even breathing of the crew around him and felt a little wave of apprehension at being, again, the only one awake. Until he heard Schübling's voice, low and calm. "I want to get these people out of here, Bryant, and I'm gonna need your help to do it."

Again, her directness surprised him. He fumbled for words, on the brink of telling her that he knew how she felt, that he'd been Caretaker of 4000 sleeping people once, and that getting them to safety had been the best accomplishment of his life. Although Minea felt a bit less safe now, since the shadow had crossed Lucidus.

"Well?" Schübling's voice scratched across the rock to him. "Are you gonna help me or not?"

"I'll help you, Captain."

"I'm not your Captain. My name's Maggie."

Ethan smiled in the darkness, but tried not to let the sound of it creep into his voice. "I'll help you, Maggie."

***

On his way to the mill, Marcos read the morning security report with little interest. As expected, the orbital defenses were up and running, and there should be no problem keeping out the orbiting ship.

Along with basic orbital defense system, the UEG maintained an air-and-ground force in the city of Flynn, several hundred kilometers from Coriol. In addition, each company was required to keep city defenses and a private security force in their cities. Saras was no exception, and their security force could be seen practicing maneuvers and sighting in their weapons at the defense complex past the power plant.

It was probably overkill, Marcos thought as they drove past the complex. The likelihood of these aliens wanting anything on Minea was small, especially after the extensive negotiations humans had undergone to take possession of the planet.

Marcos was pleased about the outcome of his meeting with Veronika and Theo. He was not as pleased about the outcome of the defense committee meeting.

Why could there be no whole victories in life? It was always a victory and a defeat, paired, or two defeats and a victory. Never a simple, pure victory.

The hovercar stopped at the mill and Marcos gathered his things. He glanced at Veronika as she got out of the car. She'd been distant lately, and he felt that there was something he was missing. Something that she wanted him to do that he wasn't doing. He tried to think it through as they walked into the mill.

Dusty workers passed him on either side, their narrowed eyes a giveaway that they had something to say to him. He was startled to see how many of them had developed the mysterious purple bruising, and he stepped a little more quickly past them, pulling his elbows in to his sides so he didn't brush against the workers.

Veronika handed him a mask as she opened the door to the main refining floor. They walked out on a catwalk, peering down at the heart of Coriol's economy.

The loads of gray-blue stone streaked with bright orange Yynium came in a steady stream on the conveyors at one end of the room. They were coming from the sorting room, and before that, the loading docks. They reached the first workers, who stood ready with a resonating chisel and tapped each chunk along its Ynium fracture, leaving the small silver chisel embedded in the rock, which continued down the belt. By the time the chunks reached the third station, the chisels had cracked them wide, leaving the vein of Ynium bare and exposed on either side of the split.

Workers at the third station rotated up to grab a chunk of rock and step to a picking station, where the thickest of the Ynium was scraped and picked out of the stone, then dropped onto fine mesh baskets on another conveyor, which carried the Ynium to the finishing room. The chunks went back on the original conveyor and down to the crushers.

Marcos saw the crusher feeders, powder-covered men and women, tossing chunks of rock into the chewing jaws of the crusher. He saw them strain, saw their hands and arms dangerously close to the first blades, and thought only that they were going awfully slow today. From where he was he could see the purple bruising on their faces and necks. He tightened his mask.

The crusher churned the powdered rock out into a huge, swirling tank of water, where the heavy Ynium dust fell through grates at the bottom and the rock settled atop it like a layered cake. A scraper pulled continually back and forth across the Ynium layer, mixing it into the water and allowing it to flow out over the cascading tangerine waterfall through the straining conveyor.

There the water passed through and the Ynium dust moved on through the dryers, huge furnaces that blew the damp dust dry on the screens, and into the finishing room.

The workers at the next station removed the screens, caked

with the dried dust from the conveyor, and twisted them over the gaping chasm of the finishing drum. On the other side of the open-topped drum, workers gathered the baskets with the picked Yynium and dumped it in as well.

The Yynium was churned and crushed in the bottom of the hopper, coming out a uniform, fine powder, which sifted into molds on a moving conveyor below. The molds went through a heater to meld the powder together, then through a press from which the bricks of Yynium, proudly stamped with the Saras triangle, finally emerged as a useful product.

All in all, a third of the population of Coriol worked in this building. The rest worked in the Saras manufacturing factories nearby, or the Saras farms to the north or the Saras construction company or the Saras markets or the Saras Mines or the Saras hospitals.

Marcos continued down the walkway, half-listening to Nolan, the floor manager, citing the day's production statistics. Marcos had been right: the workers were slow today. Production was down about three percent below normal. He felt the familiar anxiety creep up on him. Whenever anything threatened Yynium production, it threatened the possibility of getting Serena here. A hard knot twisted in his chest. He reprimanded Nolan and reminded him that he could be replaced.

"But, Mr. Saras," Nolan's eyes were wide, "it's not my fault. And it's not really their fault. A lot of them are sick."

"Then why am I paying all these doctors? Get the workers to them."

"They've been. The doctors don't know what is causing it."

Marcos glanced at Veronika. "We'll have to see if we can encourage them to figure it out."

# Chapter 9

Aria was at the Saras liftstrip as morning broke. She felt hollow. She argued with a guard until Theo pulled up to the gate in his fancy hovercar.

"Aria," he said kindly, "what are you doing here?"

She and Ethan had known Theo since they arrived on Minea. He had been in charge of Saras Company then, until Marcos Saras had arrived and taken over.

She heard the pleading in her own voice as she said, "You said there would be a search party going out this morning. I want to go along."

Theo seemed to consider for a moment, then waved her into the car. She shot a smug look at the guard as she slid in on the Earthleather seats. She had seen a few examples of the rougher, almost pebbly Minean leather, made from the large herbivores here on the planet, but she'd only seen it in Flynn, Minea's capitol city, which had been established longer and had a lot that Coriol didn't have. These seats were smooth and supple, cool to the touch on this already sticky morning. She leaned her head back on the refreshing surface gratefully. She quizzed Theo as he drove her directly onto the liftstrip.

"I know it was a survey trip. Where were they?"

"Well, we're not sure. They were supposed to be pretty deep

in the Karst Mountains, and our last transmission from them was from the survey site, but we sent out some preliminary fly-over searches last night and didn't see any trace of them there. We also didn't pick up any of their beacons, which is highly unusual." He glanced at her with an apologetic half-smile.

"Where will the search parties be going today?"

"They're ground crews, so they'll be going over the survey site."

"Where did the crash happen?" The questions had been running through her mind all night, and now they poured out, one after another.

Theo grimaced slightly and hesitated. Was he keeping something from her or was he just trying to speak delicately?

"To be honest, we're not sure. We know where they were supposed to be traveling, but we're not finding them there."

"Didn't they have a tracker on the ship?"

"No. It was a shuttle craft, not meant for long hauls. There's a signal beacon that is activated in event of an emergency, but not a continuous signal. There's no sign of the signal beacon."

They were sitting on the liftstrip now, and Aria could see the search team loading the last of their gear from the ground into the search ship. She imagined Ethan, stepping onto just such a craft, this time yesterday.

"Will they search the whole route?"

Theo looked at her. "Honestly, Aria, I don't know. The search crew chief seems pretty sure after his passes last night that they aren't out there. We know their planned route, but we don't know at what point they diverged from it, or even if they did."

"What do you mean, if they did? If they didn't, we would see them, or evidence of them, somewhere along that route, right?"

Theo's eyebrows drew together. Aria could tell that he wasn't used to delivering unpleasant news. "They disappeared so completely, Aria, it's almost like they were snatched right out of the air. We're not sure they're out there. They could have been—" he squirmed, "taken."

Aria heard the panic in her own voice. "Taken?"

"It happened before, with the Others from Beta Alora. They took people right from Minea without any trace. Did Ethan tell you that there is a ship orbiting the planet?"

Aria nodded. They had seen the spot on Lucidus at the festival, and he had told her when he came home from the defense committee meeting what it was.

"It's definitely alien. The defense forces have hailed it, but it hasn't responded. It is just hanging out there in space, and we don't know what the aliens want, or why they're here, or what they're capable of."

"You think aliens took this ship?" Aria was incredulous, "but why? What would they want with a survey crew?"

Theo shrugged, and Aria noticed the weariness in his face for the first time, "We just don't know. You need to understand, Aria, that they just disappeared, and there's not a lot of hope that we'll find them." Theo shifted uncomfortably in his seat. "Especially if there's nothing out there today."

Aria grasped his arm. "What do you mean? Why 'especially'?"

Theo ducked his head and untangled his arm. "This is the only rescue mission, Aria. Unless there's some encouraging evidence, they won't go out again."

Anger flooded Aria, and with it a bitter taste filled her mouth. She opened the door, stepping quickly onto the liftstrip. "Then I'll look for him myself." She slammed the hovercar door as hard as she could, sealing Theo in his comfortable insulated world, and turned to board the ship.

The search team followed the route that the ship had been scheduled to take in and out of the mountains and touched down in a pristine valley. They spread out, giving Aria a sketch of the terrain. She hiked the places that the surveyors were supposed to map, wondering if Ethan had gone with them or stayed near the ship. She looked behind every boulder and climbed as high as she could on the peaks, expecting any moment to see a ship's wing or a broken tree that would point her to him.

When the search team gathered back at the ship that evening, she heard them radio back to Saras Company Headquarters that there was no evidence of the craft or the crew.

As the sun dropped to the horizon, Aria stood on the edge of the meadow where the picture, maybe the last picture, of Ethan was taken. She looked at the meadow, at the rising peaks around her, and called his name.

\*\*\*

That night, when Saras sent the box of scrip that was supposed to be "compensation" for the loss of her husband, Aria knew they really weren't going to look for him. She sat at the table and sketched out a plan. She would start with the survey site and she would search until she knew what happened to him. But Ethan had been deep in the mountains, and she couldn't get there without a ship. So she called Kaia, who called Admiral Reagan, who got her one.

\*\*\*

Ethan was sore and aching when he rose from the hard ground. They had slept, on and off, the whole day and some of the night. Now, only the light of Brynn's shoulder lights illuminated his sleeping companions, and he felt again the great loneliness that had found him when he was Caretaker. He knew he would carry it with him all his life, that it would always find him again in moments like this.

The only time he had been without it was when he was with his family in their little cottage or exploring with them. He tapped his shoulder lights on and wandered around the cavern. The thought struck him that this would have been a great adventure if they'd embarked on it intentionally.

The stalagmites stood in uneven rows around the edge of the room. As he walked, he felt the floor rising under him. Behind the stalagmites, he saw an opening.

Walking to the tunnel, Ethan noticed, with renewed hope, that it rose at a sharp incline. That seemed a good plan. If they could get up closer to the surface, the Suremap devices might have a chance of working. It was even possible that they may find a diagonal shaft that could lead them straight out. He returned to the group and waited with increasing impatience for them to awaken.

When Maggie awoke, he told her about the tunnel.

"Seems like as good a plan as any," she said, with her usual lack of enthusiasm. But Ethan didn't let it discourage him. He wanted out of this dungeon.

Maggie didn't wait around for her crew to wake up. Her bold voice rang through the cavern. "Up and at 'em, team," she called. "Time to get out of here."

The cousins complained the loudest, but even they rose and shouldered into their packs.

*** 

They followed the tunnel for hours, with only one short break where they each ate a nutrition bar and started eagerly off again.

After the initial incline, the way evened out and was relatively flat and smooth. Now, for the last fifty meters or more, the tunnel had been climbing steadily. It felt like they were rising out of the nightmare. The group buzzed with anticipation, and Ethan even heard a couple of jokes behind him as he helped Maggie up the slope.

She had fared all right at the beginning, but the climb began to take a toll. A hundred meters later she was really struggling. And she wasn't the only one. The angle of the slope had increased, and the stone was smooth and slick under their boots. They climbed for nearly an hour and their enthusiasm waned in direct proportion to the slope of the tunnel.

Suddenly, Ethan saw a change in the darkness in front of them. Involuntarily, he quickened his steps toward what looked like the top of the slope. It definitely looked lighter ahead.

But as he crested the slope, he realized that the light was his own, the Maxlight's beam reflected back to them from the blank wall of a dead end. For a moment, he didn't know what to think. His mind refused to register that the climb had been for nothing.

Maggie swore, then called back to the others, "Don't bother. We've hit a wall."

Their disappointment echoed through the tunnel. The full reality of the cave began to sink in. There was no way to know for sure if they were going the right way, no way to tell what was at the end of any tunnel they chose. The time they'd spent on this one was a complete waste.

They headed back to the stadium in subdued silence.

If going up was difficult for Maggie on her broken leg, going back down was much worse. Ethan felt her tense against every impact.

"We can stop, Maggie, and give you some rest," he said.

"It's not gonna help. It'll hurt if I go down now, it'll hurt if I go down later." She gripped his arm hard as he tried to brace her against the decline.

Ethan opened his mouth to argue, but just then she pitched sideways and fell hard on the stone, sliding several feet in front of him on the slick floor before scrambling to a stop, bracing with her good leg against the side of the sloping tunnel.

An involuntary cry of pain escaped her. It seemed, to Ethan, so much worse coming from someone who was unused to making them. He clambered down to her, pulling the bright light out of his pack and inspecting her covered wound through the clear Sprayshield. It had been healing well, but now it was seeping blood, turning the transparent dressing an opaque ruby color.

Traore and Ndaiye scrambled up beside them. "It's no good, Captain. You're gonna have to stay off of that." Ndaiye's voice was commanding, a change from his usual jocularity.

"I don't see how that's gonna work," Maggie argued. "You can't carry me, and you're not gonna leave me down here to be krech food." Her voice was stubborn, but Ethan sensed a real fear behind it.

"We won't leave you, Cap," Traore said soothingly. "Just give us a minute to see if we can figure out a way to get you through here easier. Promise that you'll wait here while we check the medical pack."

When they'd convinced her, the two of them disappeared into the darkness, leaving Ethan and Maggie sitting silent on the smooth rock.

"They'll be back soon." Ethan said, trying to be reassuring.

"Maybe," she said gruffly. "It's hard to tell how long things take down here."

Ethan thought a moment. "That's true. It's weird to be in

the dark all the time. Like now, it's midmorning out there, and I feel like it's the dead of night."

"It's always the dead of night here."

Ethan nodded.

"Gonna lose that tan pretty fast," Maggie said, "now that we're mole-people."

Ethan blinked, looking down at the backs of his hands, sticking out of the sleeves of the Everwarms. He was tanned, he supposed, from spending every possible moment out in the forest meadows behind the cottage. It seemed strange that he would be, after all those years on Ship 12-22.

"I'm used to that. When I was Caretaker, I spent five years under artificial lights. I got pale as stone."

Maggie grunted. "If that happens again, you'll fit right in down here."

Ethan looked around. The Maxlight lit up a small portion of the tunnel: a smooth circle of stone encompassing them. "We're not going to be down here that long. We'll get out."

Maggie didn't turn toward him, but he heard the desperation in her voice. "I hope you're right, Caretaker."

The last word hung in the still cave air. Ethan switched off the Maxlight to conserve its battery and listened for the sounds of their crewmen returning, but he heard nothing. Unlike the forests, where a distant bird cry or the scurrying of a small creature was always audible, here only a great silence pressed down on them. They sat waiting.

\*\*\*

Ethan was nearly panicking when the cousins returned. The time they'd been gone was unbearable in the quiet. Ndaiye used the Emedic to re-splint Maggie's leg. They also pulled a foldable stretcher from the medical pack, which they quickly assembled amid Maggie's protests.

Though maneuvering while holding the stretcher behind him was difficult, it wasn't impossible, and Ethan thought it may even be easier than trying to help her hobble down the slope had been. Ethan breathed a sigh of relief when he saw, ahead, the last turn before the tunnel opened out into the Stadium.

Only it wasn't the last one. Rounding the turn, he saw another; a sharp elbow in the passage that he didn't remember coming through when they went up.

It was so sharp, in fact, that they had a bit of trouble getting the stretcher through it.

"You'd better not drop me," Maggie growled, oblivious to Ethan's growing dread. Suddenly, the tunnel narrowed and the roof slanted sharply down. They found themselves staring at another dead end.

"We've made a wrong turn," Ethan said, trying to keep his voice even. "We'll have to backtrack."

The cousins traded off with Ethan, making the grueling climb back out much easier. A few meters back they saw a tunnel smoothly joining the small dead end they'd just come from.

"Here's where we must have gotten off track," Ndaiye said cheerily. "The Stadium is just down there."

But what they found just down there was yet another dead end. This tunnel ended in an outcropping of greenish flowstone. Ethan realized that instead of one tunnel that led up and out, they had wandered into a complex of spurs and tunnels that could go on for kilometers. There was no way to know which one would lead to the Stadium and which would lead to another dead end.

Panicked, they turned the stretcher around and nearly ran

back up the slope, hunting frantically for any sign of the tunnel they'd originally come from.

"Go to the left!" Traore urged. Ethan complied.

"Are we supposed to be going up or down?" Ndaiye asked, trying to get his bearings.

There was an uncomfortable silence before Ethan spoke up. "I'm not sure," he said, hitching the stretcher up a little higher.

"You mean to tell me that you guys got us lost when we were fifty meters from the rest of the crew?" Maggie said, disbelieving. "Some surveyors you are. You're supposed to have some sense of direction."

"Not underground," Traore reminded her. "We signed on as topside surveyors. You were supposed to get us OUT of the mines, remember?"

Maggie, for once, didn't reply. Ethan glanced back to see her digging in her pack, which she held on her stomach. She came out with a notebook and pen and went to work on what looked like a map of the tunnels.

They came to a fork and took another tunnel. Ethan had a good feeling about it. It seemed familiar.

When their lights fell on the green flowstone at the dead end of the tunnel, he knew why.

"We're going in circles!" He said explosively.

"You'd better leave some breadcrumbs then," Maggie instructed, "something to show we've been down this tunnel already."

Ethan carefully set his end of the stretcher on the ground. Traore did the same. Each of them rifled through their packs, but all they came up with were the nutrition bars, and Maggie refused to let them use those.

"I didn't mean literal breadcrumbs, you hobos. You never

know when you're gonna need food. You can't waste it like that."

"We could use our ropes, string them behind us as we go," Ethan suggested, but Maggie refused again.

"Rope is too valuable too. Think of something else."

Ethan kicked at one of the hanging points of the green flowstone formation. It broke off easily. He picked it up. Long and thick, it was about three inches in diameter and tapered at the end where it had dripped for centuries. It was like a giant pencil. He tested it against the cavern wall. It left a broad white streak.

"How about this?" he asked.

"Now you're talking." Maggie seemed proud of him.

They backtracked, keeping a close eye on the point where the tunnels joined and marking a big X on the walls of the tunnels they found leading to dead ends.

In all, Ethan counted sixteen dead-end tunnels. Their sloped floors coupled with the extra strain of carrying Maggie tired the men quickly. Ethan's mind spun with the realization that they had passed another day since leaving the stadium, and he had no idea when or if these tunnels would ever lead them back there.

Soon they came to a passageway where all the tunnels were marked, and Ethan felt the old press of frustration. "We've been down every tunnel."

"Then it has to be back the way we came."

The warren of tunnels wove together and crossed, entangled like a pile of snakes. Sometimes they were going up, sometimes down, sometimes an angling tunnel cut across another open passage and they had to decide whether to follow the original one or embark down the new opening. Ethan came to a point when he couldn't even remember what the last turn looked like, much less the original tunnel that led out of the stadium.

His arms and back ached from carrying the stretcher. His mind spun from the endless maze of tunnels and from the dark and mixing shadows.

As they tried yet another tunnel, Ethan froze. Far away, he heard the sound of his name.

"Do you hear that?"

The rest of the small party stilled to listen, too, then excitement shone on their faces.

"I hear it! They're looking for us!"

"We're here!" They began to shout, calling with all their energy.

The voices responded, louder and more enthusiastically. Ethan recognized them as Collins and Brynn and held still, trying to determine where they were coming from.

Unfortunately, the tunnels caught the voices and tossed them around in a game of keep-away. He heard them one moment from the tunnel on the left, the next from the one behind them. Just when he was giving up hope, a light flickered in the tunnel just ahead.

"Here!" he yelled. "Collins! Over here!" Ethan nearly ran toward the light, sliding on the downward sloping floor and fighting for balance as he hauled the stretcher behind him.

And then he was looking into the bright beam of a Maxlight. Collins reached out a hand and called, "They're here! We got 'em!"

\*\*\*

They took a long rest back in the stadium. None of them were eager to rush out into the darkness again. As they sat on the stone floor, surrounded again by the sentinel formations around the room, the crew worked to map the parts of the cave they'd seen so far. The keyhole entrance, the crash site, the guano field, the Shark's Mouth tunnel, the Stadium. Ethan, Traore, and Ndaiye pitched in what they could remember of the maze they'd just come from, with an occasional comment from Maggie. Her contributions were sometimes helpful and sometimes simply commentary on their incompetence.

Ethan didn't care. He was glad to be out of the tunnels and sitting among the little group in the big open cavern.

It was obvious that this wasn't the kind of place that you simply picked a direction and walked out of. They were going to have to come up with some kind of coordinated plan just to survive, much less give themselves any hope of actually getting out. Ethan said so.

Ndaiye had multiple ideas. "Maybe we could go back to that high point and chip through the roof until we got to the surface? Maybe we could find an underground river and follow it? Maybe we could go back to the shaft we came down and climb out?"

"Good ideas" Ethan reined him in, "let's look at them one at a time, though."

"What do you mean *good ideas*?" Jade's voice was challenging. "The surface is hundreds of feet up. And how do we know where to chip? And what do we have to chip with? An underground river could as easily go farther into the cave as go out, and there's no way our scrawny ropes will be long or strong enough to get us out the shaft, even if we had the strength to climb it, which I doubt any of us has."

"Hey," Ndaiye teased, "speak for yourself." He flexed his biceps exaggeratedly in the dim light. Ethan admired his ability to take Jade's stinging criticism without offense.

Jade ignored him. "The only thing to do is to investigate every tunnel we come to on a case by case basis. We can try to guess what we'll find, but caves are notoriously unpredictable."

Collins spoke up. "What about air flow? We could try to feel if there is any air coming in from anywhere."

Maggie spoke up. "That's a good idea. Air would be a giveaway."

"Okay, then, we search for air. Then we follow it." Ethan liked having a plan, even if it was only a partial one. "And from now on we don't take the whole team into a place until we know it's leading somewhere." He glanced at Maggie's leg, swollen from the strain she had put on it earlier. "We'll send a forward team to navigate the possibilities, then they'll come back and lead the rest of us."

There were murmurs of approval.

Collins cleared his throat. "Listen, I've got to—I need to tell you all something."

"We know you love us, man." Ndaiye threw an arm around Collins, but Collins ducked out of it.

"I'm serious, Ayo." The tone of his voice quieted them. He looked around. "I don't—I'm not really supposed to say anything. But I think you should know that we really need to get out of here."

Maggie was watching him with narrowed eyes. "That's not news, kid. What are you really trying to say?"

"Listen, I don't know exactly how far off course we are, or where this cave is in relation to the Ynium deposit, but I do know that in a few days Saras is going to start blasting new tunnels in under here, to that deposit. It wouldn't matter if the pilot hadn't changed course, but when we crashed, we were headed right to the area near Saras's land. He's starting there and coming under the Karst Mountains. If we're still down here," he trailed off, then spoke with intensity, "we may be buried alive, or worse."

There was general uneasiness. Jade spoke, her voice rough and accusing. "How do you know this?"

Collins ducked his head. "I got an extra 500 scrip to come on this trip and erase your Suremaps to delay getting the topography reports to the UEG. I got about half of them done throughout the day while we were out there, and I was going to do the rest when we got back to the warehouse."

A stunned silence settled over the group. Finally, Maggie spoke.

"Bet you won't fall for somethin' like that again."

Ethan was surprised at her leniency. He saw Collins flash her a grateful smile. They all understood the power of Saras and the pull of scrip.

# Chapter 10

Reagan leaned back in his chair. Four days ago, he'd placed the bases on alert. Since then, the alien ship had continued slowly orbiting Minea, lazily arcing around the planet in what Reagan thought was either a search pattern or a systematic analysis of the planet's defenses. He kept his eyes on the screen, where he had a real-time view of the craft circling his planet.

The top and bottom of the enormous armored rig were like two metal bowls, and there was vertical plating between them to make a wide bridge in the middle. The ship could be used, Reagan guessed, for transport or for war. There were certainly enough guns mounted around the top and bottom to make it a serious threat. There was no indication of the size or shape of the aliens inside.

He wanted to give the order that would trigger the unmanned orbital defenses to fire on it and blast it off his screen. But there were protocols for this, he reminded himself. Watch and wait was the first stage. Being on a planet in an intergalactic society was like living on a city street. You couldn't go blasting everyone who drove by, not if you didn't want more trouble showing up.

So, he was watching. Every day. And he was waiting. This morning, they had moved to the second stage: making contact.

They had tried hailing the ship on the usual frequencies, but there had been no answer. It simply looped around the planet over and over, sometimes changing position, but coming no closer to the surface and making no aggressive moves. As far as he knew, its passengers could be on a vacation, watching Minea like humans watched the sea. There was no need for panic yet.

But Reagan admitted that the ship was unnerving. More so because he had seen the footage of the Aloran ship that had appeared decades ago and transported humans off the planet.

He reminded himself of the fact that the Aloran ship came before the orbital defense system they had now and before the Minean fleet he was in charge of.

He pulled his eyes from the easy sweep of the new alien ship around the planet and looked out the window. On the liftstrip outside sat *Champion*, one of the six battleships that made up the bulk of the Minean fleet. It was his best warship, and he had brought it here to Lumina from Flynn, the central settlement and the only one controlled completely by the UEG instead of a corporation. He'd left two battleships there in Flynn and covered the other three corners of the Minean settlements by stationing the remaining battleships in Minville, Sato and Coriol. The battleships were a motley assortment, ranging from dated to cutting edge. All were on high alert, ready to make battle any moment if necessary. Each city had two Colony Defense ships as well, smaller craft that belonged to the companies. They were part of his fleet and all were on standby, with full crews at the ready.

Reagan again thought briefly about transferring to Flynn to be nearer the central UEG headquarters, but his routine checks here in Lumina had suddenly taken on a new urgency, and he wanted to finish them before anything happened. He wanted to know that the defenses were ready to engage, even way out here.

So he was staying in Lumina, completing his checks. For now he would wait, continue to hail the alien ship, and try to remain calm. He was still calmer than the UEG back on Earth. He'd reported the ship to them and they were nearly panicking. Ironic, he thought, since they weren't the ones right under the thing. So far, only a few people here on Minea knew what had crossed in front of Lucidus. If word got out that there was an alien ship above the planet he was not certain he could keep everyone else here calm.

***

Galo rubbed one set of his hands together, trying to focus. An irritating buzz kept leaping through one of his communications lines, breaking his train of thought. It was unlike anything he'd heard before. His first assistant thought it might be magnetic resistance causing feedback on the line. Finally, Galo switched that line off, quieting the buzz so he could concentrate on the few ships he had left and where they were supposed to be this cycle. It was challenging keeping track of his shipments while orbiting the little blue planet and searching for the life signs of the escaped Vala.

Too many of Galo's merchant ships swayed in their docks back near his home world, useless. They should be flung across the galaxy, delivering goods, but without the Vala, they would go nowhere. Though a few Vala remained, most of them were gone, slipped out through a faulty cell door on this very ship.

This was the Cliprig, his headquarters. He lived here, did all his business from here. He cursed himself for keeping so many of the Vala in one place: the slave quarters here on the Cliprig. But this was the base ship, and he could transfer them to his fleet ships as needed so easily from here. It had seemed like the most efficient process.

He tried to comfort himself: There were still twenty-five Vala children, which meant twenty-five working ships. Customers were still coming, but soon they would be hearing that the Asgre were not delivering on time. Galo cursed and paced the bridge of the Cliprig, clasping and unclasping his two sets of hands in a rhythmic pattern. His shipments were late, his customers angry. He could no longer pretend that there was nothing amiss.

He would find them. They were somewhere on this planet and he would find them and set right his fleet.

He checked his panels. Today's major shipment was being delivered to the Salchor: a shipload of diamond drives that they'd been too patient on already. The Salchor were not known for their patience. He glanced out the window of his office. His assistants, Kal and Uumbor, were joking near the far wall.

Galo walked to the door and barked them, "What have you been doing? We have no time to waste! Get back to your consoles and get the Salchor their diamond drives!"

Customers came to them because things needed to get from one place to another quickly, and space was huge. Luckily, their ships could travel about it with ease.

At least they could before the Vala had escaped and crippled half his fleet. He needed at least one Vala child per ship, and in his most profitable days he'd had two per ship. Vala could move multiple ships at a time, but only to the same place they were physically going. It did him no good to have fifty ships and twenty-five possible destinations. He needed the flexibility of sending each ship to a separate location.

Galo knew the customers wouldn't wait. He was scrambling to fill all his orders with the limited number of ships he had. For the tenth time today, he cursed the Vala. Though they made it possible for his ships to travel faster than any other merchants, they were trouble and they always had been.

He was the best shipper and the best haggler in the known universe. When something needed to be delivered, he was the one people called.

He thought of the call that had brought him here, to this far corner of the galaxy. It was several cycles ago back at his home world, Ondyne II. He had been on the Cliprig, pacing and cursing the escaped Vala when his attention was drawn to an incoming transmission.

Galo had connected to it and immediately Nissot had appeared on the screen. Nissot was of the Fel race, small and stupid. Galo had worked with them before. Their loads were big, they fought to pay little, and they were always changing their minds mid-shipment. Galo reached for the button to hang up the call, but the other creature's voice stopped him.

"From what I've heard, you're in no position to hang up on me," the translator warbled. Galo hesitated. "You'll need loyal customers like us," Nissot said, his voice low and wheedling. "I know others who are not even calling you right now, because they can't afford to have their shipments delayed."

*Delayed.* The word made Galo sick. To some it meant a minor inconvenience. To him it meant angry customers and thousands of lost rhu. It meant apologizing and pleading and promising. It meant lost respect. He hated *delayed*.

Galo pulled his attention back to the grainy picture on the screen. Nissot was continuing, "We have two tanks of qeltra to deliver to Calfa V," the Fel said, "and we are willing to pay 20,000 rhu to get it there."

"20,000 rhu? That is easily a 30,000 load. I couldn't possibly do it for less."

Nissot shook his head. "Well, I am sorry to hear that. I

suppose we'll have to go with someone else. I had heard that your operation was struggling. I'll pass on the information that you're doing fine and are not interested in retaining customers."

Galo saw Nissot reach for the button to terminate their connection. He felt the old surge of challenge that made him love his work.

"Wait," he said. Nissan's hand paused midair and he peered at Galo.

Galo's mind turned over the possibilities. Two months ago he could have sent a windcraft to make this run. But he had only three working windcraft at present: too few to spare one all the way to Calfa V for 20,000 rhu. Without the Vala, his ships were barely faster than light, and it would take decades.

But, Galo thought as he checked his screens, he had a skybarge passing the Fel home world in two days, traveling to a planet within a day's journey from the Calfa system. If there was room for the tanks on that ship, it would make that journey slightly more profitable and keep a customer happy.

"I may be able to do it," Galo said, consciously calming his desperation and putting on a smile, "because you are an important customer." Nissot straightened almost imperceptibly. "I could get them there within twenty-two cycles for—" He tapped his desk thoughtfully, "for twenty-five."

There was a pause, then Nissot caved. "All right. But they have to be kept below the ice point for the entire journey or they will spoil."

That wasn't a problem—the skybarge had an ice hull room for that exact reason—but Galo saw another thousand rhu in the deal for the special request, and tacked on yet another thousand for the trouble of checking a negative ice point shipment every six hours. Almost without trying, he'd worked it up to 27,000 rhu.

There was a reason he was the best shipper in the universe.

He reached for the disconnect button, but Nissot spoke again. "Your enterprise is . . . struggling, Galo."

Galo tensed, wishing he had charged Nissot 28,000. "There is no reason for concern."

Nissot made the Fel sound of amusement, a gurgling that caused Galo to think of strangulation. "The pod of Vala I saw many cycles ago would suggest otherwise."

Galo fixed his gaze on the screen. He spoke slowly. "What did you say?"

Nissot was enjoying this. "I said, as you are the only Vala master in existence, the free-traveling pod of Vala I saw would suggest that either you have become suddenly diplomatic and released them or that they have escaped you. I doubt it's the former."

Galo's mind hummed with fury and frustration. "Where did you see them? When?"

Nissot threw his limbs wide in mock surprise. "This information is valuable to you? You wish to know where I saw them?"

Galo bit back the urge to curse. The fact that the Fel hadn't bothered to contact him when he saw them didn't matter now. "I would be most grateful to know, Nissot. Most grateful."

"How grateful? Grateful enough to take my shipment for—" Nissot considered quickly, "23,000?"

Galo would have agreed to much lower. He had to get the Vala back. He closed his first set of eyelids and swept a hand across his face, fingers fluttering: an Asgre sign of respect. He did feel respect. Nissot was driving a good bargain.

"Yes. 23,000 if you can tell me where you saw them."

Nissot leaned back, growing smaller on the screen. "I can do even better. I can tell you where I saw them drop out of their sleeping state."

Galo gripped the edge of the console, desperate to know. If the Vala had dropped out of their sleeping state, they would still be near the place Nissot had seen them. There was a recuperative time after they traveled during which they could not use their gift. His voice was strange to him as he heard himself croak, "Where?"

Nissot gurgled again. "An inconsequential planet called Minea. A little colony of some species or another. Your Vala were heading straight for it. I'd guess they'll find it much more comfortable than your Ondyne II or your slave quarters."

"Do you have coordinates?" Galo clasped all his hands behind his back to keep them from shaking with excitement.

"Sending them now," Nissot said, his voice smug. Galo knew he would brag about how he had skinned 4,000 rhu off the greatest shipper in the universe. As Galo punched in the coordinates, though, and felt the Cliprig begin to shudder into warp speed, he didn't care. Once he had the Vala back, he'd have his reputation restored soon enough.

By the time he disconnected the transmission, Galo had been well on his way here, to the inconsequential planet Nissot had called Minea.

And now, orbiting the planet, Galo felt his frustration spike again. Though he hadn't seen them yet, they couldn't have gotten far. They had to be here somewhere, and Galo would find them.

# Chapter 11

The forward team consisted of Ethan, Collins, and Ndaiye. They began by inspecting the tunnel next to the Shark's Mouth and then moving clockwise around the Stadium, checking behind the stalagmites for yawning black holes that might lead them out. At each, they stopped and walked a few feet inside, focusing and trying to feel any air circulating.

Ethan felt it now, the stillness of the cave. Its air was damp and cool. It tasted of dirt and minerals. At every new opening he willed the air to move, a breeze to move past them, but every one held the same static gloom.

It was nearly noon when they sat down near one of the gaps to rest and eat a few bites of nutrition bar. Only Ethan had brought his pack. He was carrying food and water for Collins and Ndaiye, so he pulled out their bars, tossing them each one.

They'd worked their way halfway around the huge room, and when Ethan looked across the center of it, he could see the rest of the crew eating, too. Ethan sat down and leaned against the outer wall next to Ndaiye. Collins settled himself at the base of one of the stalagmites across from them. Ethan saw Collins's hands silhouetted against the glow of his shoulder lights. They were trembling violently.

"Are you okay?" he asked. "You're shaking."

Collins looked up in surprise, then stuck his hands in his pockets. "I'm fine." Then, glancing back toward the group, he amended, "Actually, I'm freezin'."

The coveralls had been doing such a good job keeping him warm that Ethan had forgotten how really chilly it was down here. The rudimentary thermometer on his pack read twelve and a half degrees Celsius—much too cold to be comfortable for long.

"Turn up your Everwarms," Ndaiye said.

"They're dead."

"What?"

"They're dead. I woke up this morning and the batteries were out." There was a defensive edge in his voice. "They're solar powered, you know. They're all going to go dead if we don't get out of here pretty soon."

Ethan could tell that Collins had let this go too long. They were going to have to get him warmed up. He pulled a small fuel brick out of his pack and broke a piece off. He laid the piece on the floor by Collins.

"We'll let this burn a few minutes, just to get you a little warmed up."

Collins, whose shoulders were now shaking as well, nodded.

The fuel brick started and let off a warm glow. Collins looked at Ethan gratefully and scooted close to it, holding out his hands.

Chewing on the salty nutrition bar, Ethan wondered how long the heat brick would burn, how many bricks they had altogether, and how long it would be until the warmth of his own coveralls faded.

Sharp smoke from the burning brick snapped Ethan from his thoughts. It burned in his throat and eyes. The smoke simply hung thick in the still air of the cave. Ndaiye, coughing, stood and moved away.

Ethan realized their mistake. Without breezes to blow the smoke away, they were condemned to sit enshrouded in it. Collins, choking, stood too and stomped out the brick, grinding it under his boot until it was nothing more than glowing red powder. The smoke continued to hang in the cavern, reaching out toward the little group they'd left and continuing lazily around the edges of the room.

Suddenly, Ndaiye's voice rang through the cavern. "Look! Look!" he called, pointing excitedly. Ethan followed his gesture and saw, with wonder, the cloud of smoke moving. It drifted toward a wide vertical crack about fifteen meters ahead of them. Lazily, the smoke nosed into the crack like a living thing and slipped out of sight. Overcome with excitement, Ethan ran toward the crack and inside. The passage behind it was wide enough for the three of them to walk side by side. All three members of the forward team made their way along it. Collins shone his light up and Ethan could see the smoke creeping along, rolling down the passage in front of them.

The passage itself rose gradually. It was nothing like the steep incline they'd navigated before.

"Maybe it's finding a way out," Ndaiye said, his voice higher-pitched than usual. "Maybe we can follow it right out."

Ethan loved his optimism. Here, in the dark, when anyone could feel hopeless, Ndaiye always had a bright word. The promise of it shone in front of them. They walked faster.

Later, Ethan would look back on that moment and wonder how he could have missed it. He would wonder why he was in the middle instead of on the left, why Collins had been the one to swing his light up at just the moment that the cave opened underneath him.

Ethan saw the light swing crazily to the side, was blinded

by it for a moment, and heard a heart-stopping cry of surprise. He turned fast, just in time to catch one last glimpse of Collins as he plummeted down a narrow vertical shaft.

Two breaths later, Ethan heard a sound that would haunt him. He lay on his stomach and shone the light down the shaft. Pressing the button that kicked extra light out, he could see that Collins would not be coming back out.

Ethan pulled back from the edge and sat up, gasping. It had been so fast. How could he not have seen it? How could he not have warned Collins?

The bleakness of this place again washed over him. Ndaiye stood against the far wall of the passage, his optimism silent. Ethan didn't look at him, didn't say anything for a long time.

Ethan had never seen so much human death in such a short time. And this cave gave no second chances. People were here one moment and gone the next. There was no going back, no doing it over, no doing it better.

***

The tunnel led to a drab gray chamber, where the smoke leaked out of a cleft in the rock directly above them and no wider than one of Luis's soup bowls. There was, however, a level, smooth passage that exited on the opposite side of the chamber, and Ethan and Ndaiye thought it may connect back somehow to the passage the smoke escaped from. They retrieved the others and brought them to the chamber.

They filed in quiet respect past the shaft that would be Collins's final resting place. Jade had tears glistening on her lashes as she stepped carefully to the other side of the tunnel. She was wearing Collins's pack, and Ethan sensed there was more to her grief than losing a coworker. When they were all safely past the pit, Ethan switched off the light and made his way up the slope behind them, leaving Collins to his rest.

*\*\**

Ethan felt empty as they settled in for sleep. When he came to Coriol he had been cheered as a savior of thousands. They had chanted his name and elected him as a Governor of the Colony Offices. He was lauded as brave and gifted.

But one moment, one thoughtless, distracted moment, had cost a man his life, and Ethan had neither predicted it nor prevented it. How could he be a hero with such blindness?

He was blind here, in every way. As the team switched their shoulder lights off one by one, he felt the darkness closing in around him. He lay back, his own lights still on, seeking comfort in their glow. The usual chatter was absent and the team stilled quickly.

Finally, knowing that every second of light he indulged in now was a second of darkness later, maybe in some far more dangerous circumstance than this, Ethan tapped the shoulder lights of his vest to quell them.

His eyes burned with their afterglow for a heartbeat, two. He shifted his head on his pack, waiting for the pressing, complete darkness that he knew would come.

Instead, emerging from his light-blindness, Ethan saw tiny, bright jewels of light, seemingly suspended in chains from the cave ceiling, like the most delicate of chandeliers. Ethan looked closely and saw tiny worms suspended from the ceiling, weaving straight strings of phosphorescent silk, with hanging jewels of sticky fluid that they used to catch their food.

Their beauty caught Ethan off guard, and the soft sounds of awe from the rest of the team told him they saw them, too. Somehow the gracefulness of the tiny droplets of light soothed. He let the tears come silently, feeling them slip out of the corners of his eyes and race down his temples.

He heard, softly filling the chamber, Ndaiye's deep baritone voice, beginning as a hum, then a gentle ripple of syllables, like falling water: "yangu mtoto, mtoto, ndoto. Itakuwa utulivu mtoto wangu, yangu mtoto, mtoto, ndoto."

A lullaby, in a language Ethan had never heard before. Though the words were unfamiliar, the feeling behind them was not. It was gentle, calming. It was love and comfort.

Somehow, Ethan let Collins go. He let the pilot and Carlisle and Espinoza and Baker go. And he hoped, when it was time, that Aria and the children could let him go.

***

Aria slid down an embankment, following the sound of the river. She had brought the children with her today, and they had loved the ride in the little ship. They'd set down in the clearing and left the ship and its pilot to wait for them while they searched. She'd just completed her second concentric circle around the survey site and was beginning on the third. Because her search had taken her far beyond the usual areas of the Karst Mountains, beyond the edges of the neatly trimmed Tiger Mountain Park, to the valleys and peaks of the inner karst range, she wondered if anyone on Minea knew the mountains better than she did.

Still, Aria had to be continually watchful of the children. Polara was a strong hiker and often in front of Aria, challenging her mother to keep up with her—until the child got distracted by one of the million things that the karst forest had to offer: a butterfly, a flower, a steep peak rising fast from the valley floor.

She took Polara's hand now as the little girl struggled to push through the tall grass. It was becoming thicker, taller, here at the bottom of the embankment. Aria guided Polara behind her, working to stomp the grasses down as best she could to smooth the way for her.

"Come on, Lara, we're going to go this way."

"And find Daddy?" Polara asked directly.

"I hope so." Aria pushed back the sharp sensation of knowing how big this wilderness was and how small, in it, were the three of them.

Rigel rode silently on his mother's back, observing. If she turned her head sharply, she could see his bright blue eyes peering down at her with the aching wisdom he'd seemed to have since he was born. Aria quieted her mind, listening for anything that could be Rigel's thoughts. She'd been listening ever since Kaia had told her of his gift. But she heard nothing that wasn't her own.

"Mama! Mama! Look!" Aria followed Polara's pointing finger and saw, fleeing off to the left in front of them, a white deer-like creature. Its curly fur and sweeping horns made it look strangely cuddly and regal at the same time, like polar bears back home on Earth.

It bounded forward through the long grass, stopping several dozen meters away and turning its head to watch them.

Aria had no name for it, but its majesty took her breath away. There were so many species on this planet, and most of them remained a mystery to humans. On a world where people had come to gather all the Yynium they could as quickly as possible, there was little time for interesting animals. If it wouldn't help make RST more accessible, nobody was interested. Add to their apathy the fact that the karst range remained largely unexplored, and it was likely that she and the children were the first humans ever to see this species.

"What should we call it?" she asked Polara, running through some possibilities in her own head: *Snow Deer, Bryant's*

*Deer, Imperial.*

"Is it a boy one or a girl one?" Polara asked thoughtfully.

"Well, it's hard to tell with some animals here. I'm not sure."

"I think it's a boy and we should call it Chester," Polara responded immediately, then, reconsidering, "or Curly."

Aria laughed for the first time in days. She loved that her children, who lived every moment separately from the next or the last, had the ability to traverse life unburdened by what was to come. Polara was particularly good at that, and Aria found it freeing to be with her, even in the midst of this nightmare. Maybe especially in the midst of it.

She would have liked to observe the new species a while, sit down on a rock and see if it was aggressive or shy, if it had a mate in the area or even a herd. But their course would not lead them near it, and she had too little time and too important a task to bother with wildlife now.

They fought through an especially thick stand of fibrous grass. In fact, Aria noticed, here the usual flexible grass seemed to be interspersed with a dark green, curved-leaf grass as rigid as bamboo. Within a few meters she was unable to push through at all.

She glanced up. The white deer still stood, his large black eyes on them. Poised there, in a beam of sunlight between two karst peaks, he seemed to be waiting for them. Aria altered their course slightly, angling towards the animal. She still held Polara's hand, though her arm was getting weary from being held behind her. She guided Polara in her own footsteps, around stones shrouded in the grass and carefully over the lumps made by bulging roots.

Roughly six meters from where she'd changed course, Aria broke onto a trail. The deer stood on it directly in front of them. The sharp hooves of countless animals had cut out the grasses here and the trail wound in front of them like a ribbon through the sea of green.

Polara pulled her hand free and edged around her mother, skipping ahead down the trail calling, "I'm going to catch Curly!" Aria followed her.

The stag stayed just out of reach, bounding ahead along the trail, which now wound along among a field of the tall curved grass so dense that even Polara wouldn't fit between the stalks. When Aria heard the river turning and rushing away, she tried to leave the trail, to push through the grasses and follow the river as she had planned, but it was futile. Here the stalks of grass grew so unyielding that she couldn't move them. If she wanted to go that way they'd have to be cut. She only had a pocketknife along and the day was going quickly. They'd have to start back in a few hours, and she imagined that she wouldn't make much progress through the field in that amount of time.

So they followed Curly down the trail. It was relatively easy going, and she felt strangely relieved whenever she caught a glimpse of the big animal ahead of them. Above, from their nests on the edges of the karst peaks, Minean parrots and songbirds filled the air with their music, but Aria's encompassing fear for Ethan blocked them out. She found herself watching for any sign of the craft, willing a broken windscreen or strip of fuselage to appear in the jungle of green. But all she saw were the green and growing things of Minea.

They'd been walking about an hour on the path, and Polara's enthusiasm had waned. She was hungry and her feet hurt and she wanted to stop for a rest. Aria peered down the path. Just ahead, two huge karst towers stood like castle gates. The path wound through the only gap between them.

"Let's get to those rocks," she told Polara, "and then we'll take our rest." Polara drooped further, hanging her arms down below her knees and trudging. Aria broke out the secret weapon: "And we'll have some chei when we get there!"

Polara brightened, straightened, and quickened her step. She loved the sweet, gummy candy her mother made from the red chei fruits. Aria kept some handy for occasions such as this.

As the stag reached the gap between the mountains, he bounded up a ridge on the right tower, his climbing impossibly sure and impossibly fast for such a big animal on such a narrow ledge. With one last glance in their direction, he bounded along the ridge and away, his white coat becoming a dot, then a speck, then disappearing altogether by the time they'd reached the towers.

Polara started up the little ridge, fearlessly following him, but Aria called to her, "No, Lara! We're not going up there."

The child obediently, if sullenly, climbed back down.

"Bye, Curly!" Polara's voice was startling in the sudden calm of the forest. Aria noticed, for the first time, that the birds had quieted. An eerie stillness pervaded the trail leading to the towers.

Aria gathered Polara to her and checked the sonic stunner that Ethan liked her to carry when she was in the woods. Silence in wild places was unusual. It often meant the presence of a predator. There were, Aria knew, big cats on Minea. The path suddenly felt constricting. Knowing they could only go forward or back along this narrow strip of cleared ground made her nervous. She hurried along the path, hoping it would open up on the other side of the facing karst formations.

They entered the gap between the towers slowly, walking from the brightness of dappled sunlight into the shadow of the formations. It was cool and damp there, and a relief from hiking through the hot field of grass. The formations were thick, and

Aria couldn't see where they ended. She kept a watchful eye on the limestone above them, searching every ridge for signs of a predator waiting to drop down on them.

When the path widened and golden sun caught them again in its beams, Aria gasped. They were standing in a sheltered cove, ringed around by karst peaks. In its center stood a forest of huge pale maroon plants. They were, Aria supposed, trees, because they had single, woody trunks and clear apical dominance. But they weren't typical. Their long, slender trunks were topped by crowns of soft fluff, like giant dandelion seeds. Long, trailing branches wept down from them, covered in luxurious white flowers.

Their scent was sweet and light, like apple blossoms and vanilla. Aria sunk to the ground, pulling the pack with Rigel in it off her back and getting him out to hold him close. There was no danger, she realized. The creatures were silent because of her and the children. She felt the fear slide from her mind as she breathed the fragrant air and looked up at the tall trees.

For Aria, there was something special, almost holy, about plants. The way they sprung from such small seeds, the way they delighted every sense, and the way they offered their myriad gifts to mankind, filled her with awe. She felt it now, more than she ever had, and as she sat on the ground, marveling at the grove of giants, she pulled her children to her and felt tears sting her eyes.

Polara sat beside her mother, and Aria guessed she sensed the solemnity of the place as well. Aria felt Polara's little hand wriggling into her mother's jacket pocket, discovering and extracting the packet of chei and looking up for permission. Aria smiled down at her. The little girl tore it open and sat contentedly, eating, slipping one of the prized candies into her little brother's mouth as well.

The trees, which had stood still and calm casting a steady pattern of dappled light on Aria's family, began to sway gently in unison. Aria watched, mesmerized, as the trees arched back and forth with increasing intensity, moving in an unseen wind.

And as they moved, Aria saw they released tiny bits of fluff—their seeds—which arced up and over the sides of the karst peaks, on their way to grow for themselves.

She looked at her children. It had always struck her how similar humans and plants were. They needed protection and nurturing when they were small. They needed a safe beginning to grow to their full potential. She and Ethan had worked hard together to give Polara and Rigel that beginning. She didn't want to continue that process without him.

\*\*\*

Polara and Rigel were exhausted by the time the little family hiked back to the ship. Dark was coming on, and the pilot made a comment about leaving without them, but Aria was too tired herself to respond.

She watched the clearing shrink below them as the little craft rose and spun back toward Coriol. He wasn't near here. The crews had searched the first day, and she had searched the last two. There was no sign of him, the ship, or the crew.

Polara cuddled against her, lost in sleep, and Rigel's head was heavy on her shoulder as he drooped in his safeseat on her other side. As she watched the ship move between the towers, she saw, in the fading light, the vast tangled jungle of stone and vegetation below her. At first, she had looked for him behind every stone, sure that she would find him and this nightmare, so much like her stasis dreams, would end. But now she saw this place for what it was: an alien planet with reaches yet unknown to anyone. Ethan was out there somewhere, spending another night away from his home, maybe hurt. Maybe worse.

Though she tried not to cry when she was with the children, Aria didn't stop the tears running down her face. Ethan's absence these long days and nights was growing more real to her, and there was no sign of him in this wild place. What if he didn't return? What if she was left alone to raise their children and to send them into the world? It was not something she thought she could do alone.

She held them tighter, pulling Ethan's image closer in her memory as she did so. She didn't know how to let him go.

# Chapter 12

Marcos skimmed the messages list when it showed up. Every message was marked as viewed.

But something wasn't right. He looked more carefully. The first one that caught his eye was from Serena. "Craters of the Untek backcountry." But she hadn't sent a message about that trip. He remembered distinctly being disappointed when he'd come to the ICS expecting that message and it hadn't been there.

He selected it, but nothing happened. He tried again. Nothing. He scrolled down the list. There were more tantalizing subject lines: "10 Reasons I Love You," and "I'm Scared About the Stasis Trip Home." Then he saw one that chilled him: "Marcos, don't trust . . ." He selected it, knowing that it wouldn't open.

Marcos buzzed in his assistant, Taru. "Where are these other messages?" The man leaned over Marcos' shoulder, smelling of sweat and spices, and peered at the screen, then shook his head, sending his shaggy dark hair spinning around him.

"I don't know, Mr. Saras. They should be here. It looks like someone has been locking them," Taru said apologetically. "I don't have the right permissions to unlock them."

"Who's locking them?"

"I can't tell. Just that it's from an Earth account with Admin permissions."

"Who has those?"

"Just the VPs and up. And Admin Techs, of course."

Marcos couldn't stand it. "So my father has those permissions?"

The tech squirmed. "Yes, sir, of course."

Marcos swore softly. "You can go," he said. He called Veronika into his office.

"My father has been blocking some of my messages," Marcos said, pacing.

Veronika nodded, and Marcos had the uneasy feeling that this wasn't a surprise to her. "From Serena?"

"Mostly. But there are others, too."

"You know he doesn't like you distracted while you're trying to work out here. Maybe they were frivolous messages and he didn't want you to spend your time—"

"Why does he get to decide what's frivolous?" Marcos snapped. He didn't like her taking his father's side, especially when she knew how arbitrary his father could be.

"Because he's the president of Saras Company Intergalactic, and you're only the president of Saras Company Minea," she said bluntly.

*And you're only his ex-mistress*, Marcos thought but didn't say. His father had little room to criticize in the frivolity department.

"I want you to find out how I can get them," he ordered.

"I've got to go do checks in the Health and Human Services Department right now, but when I get back I'll see what I can do." Veronika adjusted her ruby bracelet as she left the office.

As she left, Marcos wondered if she would. He knew, had sensed, what she wanted from this job. She wanted the company, and with it, Coriol. She felt she deserved it as payment for his father's betrayal. He wasn't sure she didn't. But it was him that Dimitri had appointed President, and neither of them could change that.

From the side window of his office, Marcos watched Veronika leave the front gate in the company hovercar before he called Taru back in, gesturing for the assistant to sit down. Taru looked nervous, as he always did when Marcos called him in. It was one of the reasons Marcos didn't call him in much. The other was that Taru had been Theo's assistant before Marcos arrived and Marcos was never sure of his loyalties.

"What would it take for you to get into these messages?" he asked.

Taru considered. "A raise."

Marcos swore. "You'd be willing to break in for a few scrip?" He opened his mouth to fire the man, but the look on Taru's face, one of shock, took the words from him.

"No, no, sir, I was just being funny. Er—I thought I was being funny. I meant that I'd have to get advanced to Admin Tech, which I should be because I'm running the whole Coriol system, and we need one here anyway—" Taru stopped speaking.

"I see," Marcos said. "And, Veronika has to do that? Or Theo?"

"Yes, sir, they can do it. But you have those permissions to advance me as well. I was joking because if I advance I do get a raise."

Marcos leaned back. "How long would it take?"

"Not long. You just have to go into your Admin account and change my status."

Marcos looked at the screen, then back at Taru, gesturing for him to come around the desk.

Taru was a bit sheepish as he indicated the proper steps for Marcos to take.

"I feel like I'm giving myself a promotion," he said, chuckling.

Marcos didn't laugh. He was focused on the messages. "You're an Admin Tech. Congratulations. Now what?"

Taru walked toward the door of the office. "I'll just go update the system and I should be able to unlock those messages shortly. They'll appear on your "new" screen."

Marcos slipped a gar fruit candy in his mouth while he waited. He tasted its tang and felt a certain satisfaction, having handled the problem himself. The one good thing about being on Minea was that his father was too far away to control him. If he wanted something done, he could do it.

He stood and walked around the room, once, twice. It was a wide, deep office, with his desk at one end and a seating area of comfortable Earthleather furniture at the other. Between them was a fireplace for comfort in the rainy winter season. An etched aluminum photograph of his parents hung above it. He made a mental note to have it removed and replaced with a photograph of Serena.

The screen chimed and Marcos tried to slow his steps as he went to check it. There were all the messages. He began with Serena's long-anticipated travelogue about the craters. It was delicious—almost like hearing her voice. She described their ruggedness, their volcanic activity, in vivid detail, and he felt, for the first time in a long time, close to her.

He read the ten reasons she loved him, most of which painted him more generously than he deserved, he realized. He longed to comfort her fears about her stasis trip home, even though she was nearly done with it now. He read all the cheerful messages Serena had sent him and sat for a moment, with his eyes closed, feeling the glow they generated in him.

Finally, Marcos selected the ominous message he couldn't open earlier. It was short, but he froze as he read it.

*Marcos, don't trust Veronika. She doesn't just want Saras Company. She wants you.*

He looked up just as Taru came in. "Sir," he said, ducking his head, "I told you wrong."

Marcos blinked. "What do you mean?"

"The messages were locked from an Earth account, but the account was accessed from Coriol. Your father didn't block them, sir, Ms. Eppes did."

# Chapter 13

Maggie grasped Ethan's shoulder painfully and pulled him down to her eye level. "If you let another of my people die in a stupid accident like that last one, you'll be the next to drop off a cliff," she said, her eyes burning with rage. "I should never have left Collins in the hands of a Colony Office fool."

Ethan wanted to protest, but guilt stopped his words. He simply nodded. She shoved him back and turned away on the stretcher.

It had been so long since he'd seen grief turn to anger. So long since he'd stood face-to-face with that kind of pain. But it wasn't something you forgot. He ached for her and for Collins. The cousins lifted the stretcher. Ndaiye shot Ethan an apologetic look over Maggie's head. Ndaiye, of all of them, understood Collins's death best. He was there. Ethan gave him a wry smile.

Ethan hated to leave the Teardrop Chamber. Above him, the long transparent filaments hung down in perfect parallel. He hoped the worms lived throughout the cave and that he'd see the chandeliers again.

They followed the passage they'd found the day before. A subdued quiet still rested over the group, and no one joked or teased. Three of the crew had their Maxlights on, and the passage was almost unbearably bright. It made Ethan feel better, though, and probably all of them.

Ethan lagged behind, letting Jade lead the way today. Brynn came up beside him.

"She can be pretty harsh," she said quietly.

Ethan, not sure that Maggie couldn't hear them, simply nodded. "It's rough, losing someone," he said.

Brynn walked in silence for a while. "Ethan," she said, "I don't want to complain, but I've got a problem."

He looked at her closely, questioning.

"I'm out of water. Have been for hours. All this walking and the dirt—it's so dry."

This part of the cave was dry and dusty. It was a change from the dampness. Ethan was glad for a problem he could fix. Without stopping, he swung his pack around to the front and rummaged up a bag of water. His last. He handed it to her and got a smile in return.

"Sip it," he said, "don't guzzle or it'll make you sick." She nodded.

They walked on in silence. The tunnel passed on either side in an endless monotony of gray. Ethan held the sparkling chandeliers in his mind, their light and beauty out of place in this dismal passage.

When he traded off with Traore for a turn carrying the stretcher, he half expected Maggie to kick him in the kidneys while they walked, but she didn't, just rode in sullen silence.

"That song you sang last night," he said to Ndaiye, "it was in an Earth language, wasn't it?"

Ndaiye spoke from the other end of the stretcher. "Yes, a very old one."

"Do you speak it?" Ethan had met so few native speakers of other languages. As language standardization became more and more necessary for global commerce, the languages had died.

"I do. A little. My parents and grandparents were tenacious people. They hung on to the scraps and pieces of it that their grandparents had left them."

Ethan nodded. Linguistic enclaves still thrived through such tenacity.

"I'd love to hear more of it someday."

"When we're not trying to die," Maggie interjected.

Her acidity suddenly struck Ethan as funny, and though he knew she was saying it to quiet them, he started to laugh. Ndaiye's laughter exploded behind him. It felt wonderful to laugh at the absurdity of this whole situation. Their laughter ricocheted around the passage, and Ethan heard an annoyed grunt from behind him on the stretcher. He laughed harder.

Jade stopped ahead and held up a hand. They quieted. A distinct ping echoed through the cave ahead. Walking carefully, they continued down the passage. Seconds later, they heard another, followed immediately by another with a slightly different pitch. A long pause, then another ping. As his ears adjusted to the rhythm of the pings, Ethan began to anticipate the next one. He watched Jade walking ahead of him. Her steps fell in syncopation with some of the pings, and he noticed his own were doing the same. Ahead of her, the stone of the tunnel, light grey for the last few hours they'd traveled down it, suddenly darkened. It swallowed the beam of Jade's Maxlight, and she slowed. The passage narrowed here, too, suddenly tapering to a funnel just big enough for a single person to walk through.

"Hold up!" Maggie called, leaning out of the stretcher to peer around Ethan. "Come here," she called, and the team gathered around her. Ethan and Ndaiye set her down and stretched their aching muscles as they turned to listen to her.

"We're gonna have to be more careful," she said pointedly. "This isn't some carved-out, polished-up, metal-backed Yynium mine. No Colony Officers," here she glared at Ethan, "are going through here every day making sure there's nothin' to stub your toe on. This is a wild cave. We've seen enough already to know that there's enough in here to kill us without us throwing stupid into the mix as well. No more charging into caverns blind. No more pretending we're fine if we're not." Her eyes shifted to Brynn, who visibly shrunk from the captain's gaze. "We're gonna have to be smarter."

Ndaiye spoke up. "Then you're gonna let me change that Sprayshield again, right, Captain?" he asked, taking the Emedic out before she could give permission.

Ethan watched over Ndaiye's shoulder. The Emedic was blinking several warnings.

"What's up?"

"Batteries are low," Ndaiye said, "and we're out of Reagan cells and bandages."

"I don't like the sound of that." Ethan said.

"We still have some basics: pain medicine, antiseptic sprays. But," Ndaiye looked up and caught Ethan's eye, "with the batteries going, it's probably better if nobody gets hurt from here on out."

Maggie spoke up. "It's like I said, we're gonna have to be smarter." They nodded their approval. "Now," she said, "I don't like the looks of this next section. It's narrow and it's gonna be slick. I can feel the wet in the air."

Ethan focused. She was right. The humidity had risen again.

"We need to send somebody through there to be sure we don't find another drop off or a krech nest." She gestured at Ethan. "You go first," she barked. "See if it's safe."

He knew what she was doing. He would have to prove himself to her now and maybe every day after. He nodded slowly.

"If you don't die, come back and we'll go in."

Ndaiye started to speak, but Ethan caught his eye. "It's okay," he said, "I want to make sure." And he did. Perhaps redeeming himself to Maggie would help redeem him to himself.

He pulled out his own Maxlight and headed down the passage. Long and smoothly curving, it reminded him of a waterslide. The dark walls cut off the light behind him quickly and he was alone with the ever-nearing pings resounding around him in the narrow tunnel.

When his light fell on a slab of solid rock ahead, Ethan swore. Another dead end. Except . . . a sliver of shadow played at the right edge of the rock face. As he investigated further he found that the passage didn't end, it just made an incredibly sharp turn. Stepping through it reminded him of stepping into the experimentation chamber back on Beta Alora and a shiver ran through him as he stepped quickly around the corner and out of the passage.

Ethan stood in wonder. All around him, jutting ten, twenty, thirty feet into the air, was a chaos of shining white crystals, some of them bigger around than the survey crew's ship had been. They cut across the cavern from floor to ceiling, crisscrossing and tumbling like a broken mirror caught in midair. They were glorious, ghostly and translucent, suspended all around him down through a long arching cavern. The floor was covered with smaller crystals, from two to four feet, covering the ground with jagged edges. Here and there, a pool lay perfectly still, reflecting the jubilation of luminous columns. A ping echoed through the chamber and he saw the ripples of a single drop of water on the surface of one of the pools. Seconds later, another drop fell, again ringing through the crystal cavern like a bell.

"Ethan!" he heard Traore's voice in the tunnel outside. "Ethan! Are you okay?"

It took Ethan a moment to find his voice, and even then it only came in a hoarse whisper.

"I'm all right. It's—it's safe. And it's beautiful!"

Traore responded, "Okay, we're coming."

Ethan didn't return to them. He stood, soaking in the grandeur of the cavern by himself as long as he could. When they shuffled through the narrow entry, Traore first, helping Maggie walk through because the stretcher would never make that turn with her on it, Ethan turned to see the awe on their faces. One by one they entered, standing on the low rock ledge at the edge of the cavern.

No one spoke. Finally, Ndaiye could contain himself no longer. "I've never seen anything like it," he said softly. "Can this be real?"

Ethan leaned down and ran a hand across the nearest crystal, as big around as his own body and three times as long. The mineral was cold and smooth under his hand. "They're real."

Ethan dropped down and sat on the ledge, then lowered himself the three feet to the jagged floor of the cavern. Traore and Brynn followed. Maggie sat on the ledge, but came no further. Ethan saw her watching them intently.

The crystals were solid. The team could climb on them and crawl under them. Traore even grasped the end of a jutting crystal and hung from it. Ethan saw Brynn at the pool, filling her water bags and the one he'd given her earlier. She stumbled as she brought it to him across the uneven floor. Small crystals chimed as they snapped or were kicked across the floor. Ethan couldn't help himself. He gathered some and slipped them in his pack. Everyone took the time to fill their water bags from the cold, clear pools.

He stood in front of the wide face of a vertical crystal. In it he saw his own image reflected in the shiny surface. His shoulder lights illuminated his unshaven face, and his coveralls reminded him of the Caretaker's uniform he'd worn for five long years. He looked different to himself, older, more weary. He was, he supposed, all those things. If he made it back to Aria, he would tell her about this place. He would tell her how the crystals seemed to glow from within when the light touched them, how the light brought out color from the pure white of them. He would tell her how her face came to him at every tough moment, and how he held the children's laughter in his mind like a talisman against the dark of the cave.

Ndaiye and Jade hopped down and did some exploring, too. Ethan watched the whole team, climbing and sliding down the shining spears like children at a playground. That was when he started to get nervous. The loss of Collins was still a shadow in his mind, and as beautiful as this place was, it was no place to stay. The jagged floor would be impossible to sleep on and though most of the big crystals were suspended now, there was no guarantee they would always be. Several of the giants lay on the floor, where they had obviously fallen from their own weight. And the shattered remains of the crystals unfortunate enough to have formed under them were proof enough that a human wouldn't survive being under one if it fell.

Maggie, of course, was thinking that, too. "We've got to keep moving," she called, watching her team. "Let's see if we can find the way out." She stood and Ethan watched as Jade offered to rebuild the stretcher for her. Maggie waved her aside, and began hobbling across the cavern floor. Jade returned the folded stretcher to her pack. He'd have to remember to trade it off with her so she didn't end up carrying the extra weight of it all the time.

The team searched the cavern walls for exit points. Ethan suspected that any way out would be near the back, so he looked around for the largest gaps he could find between the shining fingers of rock and began climbing over and under them, following a dark passageway that ran erratically toward the back of the cave.

It was slow going, and exhausting. Duck down, crawl under, throw an arm over, pull up, climb through. The space between the crystals shifted, and after climbing until he was out of breath he found himself twenty feet above the floor, standing on a gargantuan crystal and looking down at a spectacular spherical crystal structure, which shone dazzlingly bright in the dark of the cave. A shaft of light pierced it from above, illuminating it with vibrant white light. *Sunlight.* Ethan scrambled down to it. Climbing on top of the translucent sphere, he looked up.

The hole was minuscule, no bigger around than Ethan's wrist, and the sun shone directly down it.

He heard a surprised cry behind him and looked to see Brynn scurrying down the huge crystal, calling to the others as she came. "Light! Light! There's light!"

He heard them coming, and stood for a moment with the sun on his face. He stepped back, letting it fall onto his dirty gloves, and held it for a moment, taking in its radiance. He wanted to keep it, put it in his pocket and take it out later, when the cave closed around them again, as he sensed it would. Ethan wanted to taste the sunlight, revel in it, but when Brynn climbed up, he moved to let her feel it on her face.

As he stepped sideways on the sphere, he caught a

movement out of the corner of his eye. He turned to glance at the shining surface of a huge crystal several meters away. For a heartbeat, there in its surface was the reflection of a figure. He squinted, trying to make sense of who it was. He and Brynn were the only ones that it could be reflecting. But when he looked again, the figure was gone, lost in the dizzying crisscross of crystals all around them.

Ethan cleared his head as the rest of the team came. Maggie was last, breathing hard and supported by Traore and Ndaiye. The crazy angles of the crystals could catch reflections in surprising ways. He turned his attention to the team as they each spent a moment in the beam of pure sunlight. But there was no pausing the spin of Minea, and too soon the light was gone. Ethan shone his flashlight up the small hole as far as it would go. He could see no more than a few meters into the rock.

Maggie, resting on a fallen crystal beside the sphere, called out, "I've found something." She pointed.

Ethan turned, half expecting to see the figure again, but she was pointing near the bottom of the sphere on which he was standing. A slender cylinder of rock as long as Ethan's living room back home lay on the ground. Maggie hobbled over and picked up one end, peering at it and running her fingers across it.

"It's a core sample," she said. "The bottom of one, anyway. Sometimes, if they drill more than a hundred meters or so, the tip of the sample breaks off. We won't get out here. We have to keep going. There's at least a hundred meters of stone above us." She peered at the sample, "And," she pointed at the long, orange band that made up most of the cylinder, "looks like a lot of it's Yynium."

Ethan remembered Collins's warning. Saras was coming

after that Yynium. He imagined what would happen in this chamber if charges were set off to reveal the Yynium above it. The weighty, fragile crystals would fall like icicles.

"We need to get out of here," he said.

"No!" The fevered sound of Brynn's voice filled the chamber. "We can't leave it. It's outside. It leads to the surface. We have to go up. We have to get out!" She reached toward the ceiling, her hands clawing at the air.

The team stood silent, seeing their own emotions played out in front of them. But Maggie was right. There was no way they could burrow up through the rock, not if they had the tools, not if they had a month. And they didn't have a month. They had days before Saras started blasting. There was nothing to say, no way to comfort the girl about staying down here, not when they were all feeling the same thing.

She looked around desperately. "Please?" she said. "Please? Can't we get out here?"

Traore threw an arm around her shoulders and spoke softly. "My parents had a saying: 'To run is not necessarily to arrive.'" He looked in her eyes. "We could use all our energy here and still be no closer to the surface. We have to keep going and find a better way out."

Brynn calmed, but sunk into a miserable quiet. She ran her fingers nervously over her silver necklace. The team moved slowly farther down the crystal cavern. Ethan, pushing the figure out if his mind and instead holding onto the image of the sunlight, followed them. The soft clinking of the crystals in his pack was soothing, like chimes in the wind.

*** 

As they traveled, the crystals were fewer. They stopped at the end of the cavern where a huge fallen crystal spanned a chasm so deep, their lights didn't reach the bottom.

Maggie turned, "Well, nothin' here. Let's go back."

"Wait," Jade said, "we can't go back. It will take us days to get back to the Teardrop Chamber. There's an opening right over there. This crystal's as good as a bridge. If we can get across this, we can keep going." Ethan was surprised again at her courage, both to suggest crossing the chasm and to challenge Maggie.

"And how will we do that?" Maggie said. She seemed surprised by the challenge, too.

"We can tie a safety line on and belay while people go across. It's not that bad. We have plenty of rope."

Maggie shot a look at Ethan. "All right. He'll go first. Make sure that crystal doesn't crack when weight gets put on it."

Jade rigged up a safety line and climbed back onto one of the huge crystals to test it. Seeing her dangling from the crystal made Ethan feel both more assured and more terrified.

He didn't want to go first, but his mind kept playing a scenario where he insisted someone else go and then had to watch as the shard of crystal shattered under them and they fell. He couldn't bear to see that. He'd go.

The ropes cut into his armpits and thighs as he pulled himself up onto the end of the shard. He stood, then felt the dizzying effect of seeing the chasm beneath him. No need to show off. He crawled.

As he moved across the gorge, he tried to keep his eyes off the darkness below him. His heart hammered in his chest. He kept his eyes on the crystal. It made a long shimmering path to the other side of the chasm.

"Stop!"

Panicked shouts from behind him snapped him out of his thoughts. He looked up to see a crystal the size of a hovercab plummeting from above. Dropping to his belly, Ethan reached around the narrow bridge, grasping its sides and clenching his teeth. The falling crystal missed him, but glanced off the bridge a meter in front of him, sending a percussion through it that jarred him to his bones.

The pale chunk of crystal grew small as it fell, and he heard it shatter far below at the chasm's bottom. Dust rose around him as he clung to the bridge. When he eased onto his hands and knees again he saw, with horror, stress fractures spider-webbing the crystal bridge.

When Ethan made it across, he belayed the line and waited. He had no idea how sound the bridge was after the blow.

Traore came across first, then Brynn. Ethan felt a ripple of relief when each of them stepped off.

Maggie's crossing was agony to watch. She crawled on her hands and one leg. She reached and pulled, reached and pulled, the broken leg dragging behind her on the broad crystal. As she crawled along the spider-webbed central section, a horrific crack rang through the cavern and she fell onto her stomach as the crystal shifted slightly along a vertical fracture near its midpoint.

She didn't cry out, just clung there, staring straight down into the chasm for a long moment before rising onto her hands and painstakingly crawling forward again.

When she reached the other side, she let them help her down, then barked, "Get it back over! We need to get them across before the whole thing goes down."

Traore tied the harness to the return rope and shouted for them to pull it back.

Moments later, singing filled the cave. Ndaiye was singing himself through his fear. It was a new song, not the lullaby of the Teardrop Chamber, but a bolder, more bracing tune. He made it across.

And then came Jade. She scurried like a mouse, moving quickly and lightly, her small frame hunched.

Just as she reached the midpoint, the crystal gave way beneath her. Ethan heard her cry out, and saw her clinging to the crystal as it fell. He jerked back on the line, shouting, "Let go, Jade! Let go!" Her arms opened and the crystal fell away from her.

He felt her hit the side of the chasm with a chilling thud. Her body was limp on the line when they pulled her up, but she was breathing. She had a three-inch gash where her head had struck the rock, and her eyes were unfocused and open.

Ndaiye, whose instinctive medical knowledge had helped them many times already, slipped a pack under her head. He attached the stitching attachment to the Emedic and used the last of its batteries to stitch the gushing wound. Sliding the Emedic aside, he began to tie strips of cloth around the wound. Ethan remembered they were out of bandages and wondered briefly where they'd come from. Then he saw the ragged material peeking out near the neck of Ndaiye's coveralls. He'd made the makeshift bandages from the soft lining of his own Everwarms.

They sat, watching Jade, for a long time. Ethan felt helpless. Her body moved slightly with her shallow breaths, then she stirred. The crew was around her when she regained consciousness. She seemed disoriented and still sleepy. As they resumed their journey into the cave, Brynn and Ethan walked with her.

# Chapter 14

When Aria heard the knock on the door the next morning, she knew it would be Luis. His rich brown eyes were deeply sorrowful and under one arm he carried a small crate from which his handmade pottery peeked from dry moss like shells at the beach.

"Lo siento," he murmured as he hugged her with his free arm. "I'm so sorry, Aria." He rolled the 'r' in her name slightly.

Aria didn't respond—couldn't respond. She stepped back and gestured that he follow her into the kitchen. He set the crate on the table.

"Do they know what happened?" he asked gently.

Aria shook her head. "They think it could have been some kind of electrical impulse that fried the ship's systems, or even some kind of sabotage. The other corporations are gunning for this land grant, too. The competition is pretty fierce." She sighed heavily, then looked him in the eye. "They even think it could have been some alien ship, snatching them like the Others of Beta Alora did." She hated saying it out loud, couldn't come to believe that Ethan would be subjected to that twice in one lifetime. She shook the thought away. "Either way, it doesn't matter. The fact is that they're missing, and nobody is going to be looking for them."

Luis cursed in his native language. "What? Why wouldn't they look for them?"

"The search costs too much scrip. Too many resources. They say that the survey crew had beacons with them and if the beacons were completely destroyed, which they'd have to be for them to give off no signal, then there's no way the crew could have survived the crash. And Luis, I don't even blame them. I've been out there. It's just jungle as far as you can see. There's *no trace* of them."

"Where are the children?" Luis asked, glancing around. Aria blinked. It was as if her thoughts had frozen.

"They're with Kaia. I—I need to go out again. I need to look for him."

Aria sat in a straight-backed kitchen chair. She felt the tears coming. "I can't leave him out there, Luis. I can't."

"We won't," he promised. "He didn't leave us, and we won't leave him."

"But I don't even know where to look," Aria cried. "I don't even know where to start."

"You come with me today," Luis said, stepping toward the door. "I know some places we can start looking."

"I have a ship," she said, desperately, "but I've searched from the air and I haven't found anything. The trees are so dense you can't see the ground. I keep thinking he could be right underneath us and I still don't know he's there."

Luis shook his head. "We don't need a ship. I go out into the mountains to get my clay and sand. We will take my boat. You can see a lot more from the river."

\*\*\*

Luis's little boat was finely crafted, made out of scrap pieces from Saras shipping crates. "You made this?" Aria said wonderingly.

Luis nodded. "With a little help from Winn the carpenter and Mr. Saras." He tried to smile, but the usual brightness was gone from his face. Aria could see he was as worried as she was.

He helped her into the boat and positioned himself at the back with a long pole, which he used to maneuver them away from the bank and out into the river. The broad expanse of the Mirror River stretched around them, mist rising from it in the pale morning sunlight. Aria pulled her jacket more closely around her. She hated thinking of Ethan spending another night out here. He'd only had a light jacket with him and though spring was here, the nights were still cold. Every time the heat pump had come on in the cottage last night, she had felt more acutely the fear that he was somewhere freezing.

She almost wished that she hadn't left the children at Kaia's for the night. It had been lonely and she'd barely slept. What if they couldn't find him? What if he didn't come home? She pushed the thoughts from her mind. He had to come home. She would not face life on this new planet without him.

Luis poled on, content in the quiet. She didn't feel awkward asking him to help. He and the other passengers of Ship 12-22 were their family now. This was what family did. There were others who'd shown up this morning, after the news bulletins went out. The Karthans, the Syriskis, the Alberts. Jed Albert had promised he would use his reporting skills to gather information about what had happened. It was the only way he knew to help, and Aria appreciated it, even if she felt annoyed at everyone's focus on what had happened.

It didn't matter what had happened. It mattered that they find him and that he come home to her. She tried to focus on the forest around them, going through a list of the landmark names she'd seen on the map: Druid Peak, The Torch, Grand Spire. The names fit the huge towers of rock they were now floating past. They soon passed the named region, though, and the vast unknown range surrounded them.

She watched as the mountains slipped by, one after another, lining up like the teeth of a comb one minute, then jagged and crowded as the thorns on a Minean chrom flower the next as her perspective on the flowing river changed.

She'd know if he was dead, wouldn't she? Feel it somehow? Her mind flicked past that painful possibility and she wished passionately that she was linked, somehow, to his psyche. She wished she, like Kaia, could sense his mind without him speaking.

Suddenly, Aria sat up. "Turn around!" she said urgently.

Luis looked up in surprise, but didn't hesitate to follow her command.

"We have to go get Kaia," Aria explained. "We need to bring her with us!"

***

It took them an hour to retrace their path on the river, and it was midmorning by the time Aria knocked on Kaia's door. She waited, fairly dancing with impatience, but the door didn't open. She knocked again. Nothing. Where could she be? Aria pulled out her missive and called her.

When Kaia finally answered, there was the sound of power tools and Polara's chatter in the background. She was in her shop.

"Kaia, I need you," Aria choked out.

"I'll be right there," Kaia said. When she opened the door, her face was tight with worry.

"What is it?" she asked. "Is there news?"

Polara peeked around Kaia's legs and Aria choked on the words. Her tears came again. Kaia reached out, hugging Aria fiercely.

"I thought, since you can hear his thoughts sometimes, you could come?"

"Of course." Resolve replaced the shock in Kaia's voice. "We're going to find him," she said.

It was time for Polara's school, so they dropped her there and settled Rigel at the Karthan's. Sonya Karthan murmured words of encouragement and sent them a packed lunch to take along, "to keep their strength up."

Soon the three of them were skimming across the river. Kaia placed an arm around Aria's shoulders.

"Now we'll try this, but I may not be able to hear him," she said, "especially if he is wearing his thought blocker."

Aria nodded. If he was wearing his now, he would not be broadcasting his thoughts, and he wouldn't be able to receive Kaia's. Still, it was worth a try.

Kaia reached up and removed hers. Aria always felt awkward and much more conscious of their mental dialogue when she saw them remove the thought blockers.

She watched Kaia. The older woman's short gray hair moved in the breeze as she closed her eyes. Aria consciously tried to clear her mind of thoughts so that Kaia could listen for Ethan.

They glided along the river. When Luis brought the boat to shore, they hiked through the karst forest, all in silence. Aria watched the dense woods around them and watched as Kaia listened.

Finally, after hours, Aria saw Kaia's shoulders slump wearily. She slipped the thought blocker back on, behind her ear.

"I'm sorry," she said, tears shining in her eyes. "I can't hear him."

\*\*\*

Galo paced around the bottom deck of the Cliprig. There must be a clue. Some indication of how to locate the Vala on this planet. Though he knew their recuperation time meant they had to be here somewhere, they had completely disappeared. Eight times this planet had gone around as he orbited, and still his planetary scans were returning nothing. He had lost two contracts that should have been his because he simply did not have enough ships. His ships couldn't travel fast enough without the Vala, and he wouldn't do without his ships. He had not spent his whole life making intergalactic connections and building this fleet one ship at a time to see it all brought to nothing by a sneaky race of fleeing traitors.

Trading across galaxies was tough enough without these kinds of headaches. Between the cost of fuel, the maintenance on the ships, and the cost of tariffs and bribes, Galo was only mildly wealthy, and he wanted to be wildly so. And now half the fleet was at a standstill.

Galo strode out of his office and down to the main deck, making his way to the slave hold, which was guarded by two of his guards. These two mercenaries were his best interrogators.

The heavy door, made from the one metal the Vala could not penetrate, swung hollowly open. Inside the hold, where a thousand Vala should have been, a few pathetic adults hung in the shadows of the room, their luminescent skin shining dully in the dim light.

Galo still held enough Vala to run half his fleet, but other than these few, the rest were on ships, flung out like a net across the galaxies he connected with his shipping lines.

Galo approached one of the creatures, who lay curled miserably on his bunk. He saw the slave stiffen as he approached. "Are you ready to tell me now?"

The Vala didn't respond, which infuriated Galo. "You will

tell me. You will tell me how they escaped and where they've gone. The few of you who are left will have no mercy unless you reveal them."

The Vala remained still and silent.

"I will ask you one more time." Galo sneered. "Where are your friends?"

The Vala, finally responding, began to tremble. Galo had visited them before and he suspected this Vala knew what would happen if he did not comply. Galo raised his weapon, pointing it at the trembling creature.

"I don't know," the Vala sobbed. "They've disappeared. We can no longer hear them! Please—"

Later, Galo regretted it. There were no Vala to spare, but if they were hiding information, they had to know what he was willing to do to get it. He fired the weapon twice and stepped purposefully back toward the door.

"What have you done to work on them?" he asked the interrogators angrily. "At least one of them knows where the others have gone. I told you to find that one."

Before they could respond, Galo strode back into the hold. He stepped into the shadows and hauled out a very old Vala. It was Elencha, a Vala whose usefulness had passed long ago; he was neither capable of moving ships nor producing more children to move them. He had lived a slave in this room ever since Galo had collected the Vala as payment on a past due account when he was first opening his shipping company. The Vala, and their special talent, had revolutionized his business.

"I will ask you the same question." Galo sneered.

"We don't know where they are." Elencha's thready voice bounced throughout the room. Galo leveled the weapon.

"Wait! Wait!" Elencha begged. "I don't know where they are, but when I was young and we traveled, our masters tracked us. We leave a trail, don't you know? You can't see it, but you can track it with sensors. They tracked us then. Always."

Galo lowered the weapon. That was useful information. Perhaps they were finally getting somewhere.

***

The survey crew passed through the opening Jade had spotted on the other side of the crystal bridge. They found themselves looking down across a steep slope slippery with fallen rubble.

Looking up, Ethan could see that the roof of the passage had been crumbling for eons. They would have to keep an eye out to avoid being crushed by the falling rocks. Standing still, he heard the crash of one as it fell somewhere ahead of them in the darkness.

But the slope didn't seem too bad. If they worked their way around the biggest rocks, they could probably traverse it fairly easily. He led the group out onto it, trying to help Jade, who was still a bit unsteady on her feet.

The rocks seemed solid enough until they made it to the center of the slope. Their careful passage was halted by the rumbling percussion of a faraway explosion. Saras. Collins had been right: he was blasting. Tiny rocks began to move under their feet and caused mini-slides everywhere they stepped. Ethan reached for a boulder to brace himself, but the boulder itself sat atop the crushed and slippery rubble, and it began to move.

Like an ocean wave, the rocks began to slide, one after another, one into another. The six members of the team were carried along with them. Jade was swept away from him on the tide of rock. Ethan saw Maggie, and then Traore, go down. The larger rocks knocked them aside like dolls. Ethan fell to his knees, scrambling for purchase among the shifting stones.

He clawed and fought, but the slide carried him until it piled up on itself at the bottom of the slope. He felt their sharp edges through his coveralls, their rough surfaces pulling at him as he slid.

Ethan was trapped, pinned between two huge boulders, and buried up to his waist in the small pebbles around it. His right arm was behind one boulder, extended up and away from him. The pressure on his shoulder blade was incredible, surpassed only by the pain in his hyper-extended elbow. His left arm was free, and he reached around himself and started digging, trying to remove as much of the fine, slick rock beside and behind him as possible.

Around him, he heard the voices of the team.

"Traore!"

"I'm here!"

"Come pull me out! I'm okay, but I'm stuck!"

Brynn's voice. "Captain! Are you all right?"

"My leg's broke and I just went surfing on a pile of rock. I'm not all right. Help me get over there to Jade."

There was the sound of shifting rock and scraping boots. "Jade, can you hear me?"

Jade replied with the same sleepy quality in her voice that she'd had since the crystal bridge. "I'm okay."

Ethan heard the crash of a rock falling from the ceiling somewhere near him. He couldn't turn his head to see how close it had come to crushing him, but he felt the rush of air as it hit, felt it shake the slide and send trickles of pebbles flowing past him.

Ndaiye called out, "I'm free! Who needs help?"

"Over here," Ethan called to him, and both cousins came running. Traore shoved his pack under Ethan's head to support it and they strained against the chunk of rock beside him.

It was no use. More than half of it was buried.

"We'll have to dig," Traore said. They knelt on either side of Ethan, their gloved hands shoving the rock out from around him.

It wasn't unlike being in water, albeit very heavy water. He felt it flow around him, sections giving way in eddies as other parts were cleared. He tried to help with his left hand, but kept running into Ndaiye, who placed a hand on his shoulder and looked him in the eye.

"Be still, my friend," he said, "and let us help you."

***

When they regrouped at the bottom of the slope, they were tattered and filthy, but all alive. The light on Ethan's left shoulder was broken, and he felt the dark more acutely. He also noticed a new chill in the cave. He reached up to crank the heat on in his coveralls and found them dead.

"Mine too." Traore was looking at Ethan. "Back at the Crystal Cavern."

The slide had pushed them into a long, shallow crevice, and the other side was a vast slope of smooth stone. It rose three meters, and Ethan could see they'd have to have get up and let a rope down if Maggie had any hope of scaling it. He started up, but there was no traction and he slid back down. He tried again with the same result. How stupid would it be if they had crossed chasms and outrun krech just to die stuck behind a smooth slope? He kicked at the rock in frustration.

Brynn rose from the rock she was sitting on. "Let me try. I used to climb all the time in the canyons when I was a kid."

"Sure." Ethan stepped back. "I'll stay close to spot you, though." She walked beside the wall, running her hand along it as she went. Ethan walked beside her. She stopped at the steepest section. Ethan brushed his fingers across it, trying to see what had caught her attention. It was slightly rougher than the rest of the wall. He couldn't see it, but he felt it. Brynn reached high and hooked her fingers over a tiny ridge. She put the toe of her boot against the wall and suddenly, with gravity-defying agility, she was climbing.

From Ethan's vantage point, it was as if she was climbing by suction, or magnetism. He could see nothing for her to hold onto. But she somehow found tiny crevices and rough patches enough to scale the face and hoist herself up and over the edge. She sat above them, beaming down on the team.

Ethan grinned up at her. "That was amazing, Brynn. You've got a gift."

"One." She said, her pride evident in her voice. She stood and walked farther up the slope, out of sight.

"The slope is much more gradual up here," she called. "I'm tying off the rope to a stalagmite. Just a second."

Ethan backed up just before the end of the rope whipped down. He took it and pulled hard. It didn't budge. He jumped a little, putting his weight on it. It was solid.

It took the team moments to get up the rock face. Even Maggie, pulling herself hand over hand while pushing with her one good foot, made it up with the help of the rope. At the top they found a gentle, undulating slope leading gradually upward.

The slope turned out to be a dome which led gradually downward on the other side. They passed through a short tunnel, and then into a pod-like chamber, as nondescript as it was colorless. The walls were neither white nor gray and the floor was littered with chunks of rock, but no interesting formations.

Still, the floor was level and there were smooth patches

big enough to lie down in. The strain of the bridge and the rockslide had sapped their strength and Brynn and Jade collapsed gratefully on the smooth floor.

Traore was stomping his feet and blowing his breath into his hands. Ethan felt himself trembling, too. The cold had sunk through the coveralls, and he paced a little to keep his blood circulating.

"Coveralls out?" Maggie asked them. When they nodded, she said, "Mine too."

Ethan marveled at her composure. She revealed nothing without intending to. How long had she been feeling the cold press of the cave? How long would she have gone without telling them?

"This is the most depressing chamber yet," Brynn said sourly. "Did you ever read that old Earth book, *Bleak House*?" That's what this place reminds me of. I'm calling it Bleak House."

"It's just hard to compete with the Crystal Cavern," Ethan responded.

"That may have been the most beautiful thing I've ever seen." The wonder of it still resounded in Traore's voice.

"Not me," Ndaiye countered. "Sara is the most beautiful thing I've ever seen. Especially when she comes in from the Food Production Division and takes her hair down outta her helmet. Mmmmm." He sighed appreciatively.

"That doesn't count," Brynn said. "Of course people are beautiful. What's the most beautiful thing you've seen that's not someone you love?"

Ethan tried to describe the true Alorans, energy beings who he'd met on Beta Alora, and how their bodies shone with every color imaginable. Color somehow seemed so important after these days underground.

"Sorry, Ethan," Jade said, her speech slightly slurred. "I can't see an alien being beautiful. Doesn't seem possible."

Ethan sometimes forgot that most humans had little, if any experience with aliens. He also forgot the human tendency to dislike anything unlike you. He didn't fight for his description. They couldn't know the beauty of the Alorans, the grace of the beings, without experiencing it themselves.

Brynn broke into the awkward silence. "The most beautiful thing I've ever seen is that butterfly we have here that migrates through every autumn: the ellisa sunara. Have you guys seen them? They are about this big," she held her hands out, the size of a dinner plate, "and they're golden. Not just yellow, but metallic gold, with metallic blue under-wings. When they fly, the sun strikes them and sends flashes of light all around."

They were quiet, imagining the light flashing. Ethan wished for a swarm of them now, a kaleidoscope of butterflies to brighten this drab cavern.

"How about you?" Brynn prodded Maggie. "What's the most beautiful thing you've ever seen?"

Maggie was quiet so long that Ethan didn't know if she was going to answer. Finally, she croaked out a single word that settled over them with finality.

"Earth," she said, and it came to Ethan's mind, that last glimpse he'd had of it as McNeal had called him from the observation deck to the passenger hold to be put into stasis. Glowing blue below them as they moved away from it, their home had hung in Ethan's mind and haunted his stasis dreams.

"I miss the ocean," Ndaiye spoke up. "That's my most beautiful thing besides Sara. The way the ocean pulls back and the little seashells dance in the sand as the tide goes out."

Ethan missed the ocean too, now that he thought about it. Minea's oceans were far away from Coriol, and because there were no significant amounts of Yynium near them, there were no settlements, either. He, like most of the colonists, had only seen the vast Minean seas on maps.

"I miss museums," Jade said, shifting uncomfortably. Ethan wondered if she was feeling cold. "And movies." Ethan missed them, too. The new colonies, with their unending work mining and refining Yynium, had no time for producing entertainment. And the Interplanetary Communication System was too overloaded and too expensive to use to transmit anything so frivolous from Earth.

They did have the libraries from the Caretakers' drives on other ships, but most people had no way to play them. Ethan thought of Angela and Manuel, two of his passengers who had been in several movies back on Earth but couldn't find work here on Minea.

"I have some friends putting together a little theater production in Coriol," he said. The statement was met with surprised silence.

"That would be fun," Jade said. "I'd like to go to that."

Brynn poked Jade. "What's the most beautiful thing you've ever seen?" she asked. "You haven't answered yet."

Jade was quiet for a long moment, as if considering something, and then she slowly reached into her pack. She rummaged around and pulled out a small photoflat. Its screen glowed as she activated it. When she turned it around, there was a picture of a pale red cavern with a tiny figure inside. Ethan knew exactly what he was seeing. It was an in-womb photo of a baby.

"When?" Brynn gasped.

Jade held her hand over her belly. "He'll come in about five months."

Even Maggie was hushed.

# Chapter 15

Aria poled the boat up the side river. The sun was hot on her neck and sweat trickled down her back. She was glad the children were with Kaia today. Here, the landscape changed dramatically. The foliage fell away and the gray limestone lay exposed. Between the karst towers was a barren, pockmarked plain, punctuated by petrified stumps and the slant of fallen, broken, stone trees.

Disembarking from the little boat, Aria picked her way between the craters and trunks. She crouched down beside a smooth stone stump and inspected it. As a botanist, she was drawn to the evidence of plant life here.

But as she inspected them, she realized that she had seen these trunks before, when she was with the children in the mountains. These were the same trees they had found in the grove, the ones which had brought her comfort with their swaying.

This had been a grove like that one. The trees, now stone, had been hit with a barrage from above. From the pockmarks, it appeared it had been a meteor shower. She imagined it then, the majestic trees scorched and broken, smoke and fire stripping the vegetation from the underlying limestone. Aria stood and walked in a wide circle, stepping over the fallen trees and around the hollows in the stone beneath. Perhaps the river had risen, too, and covered the area in sediment, because the trees were preserved, perfectly suspended in the moment that their destruction had come. They had just seeded. She saw the open flowers on the ends of their delicate, feathered branches, frozen in ashen stillness.

Perhaps there were even seedlings around. She stood, taking a deep breath of the cool air as she peered past them. At the edge of the circular blast area, she saw what she was looking for. Immature specimens, about half a meter tall. She walked to them. They were lovely, frozen in spiky petrified rows. They had probably grown throughout the grove, but when the meteors fell these small ones had been eradicated in the middle. Here on the edge they hadn't received the full blast. Aria sat on the smooth, bare limestone to look closer.

She leaned down, running a gentle finger over the still plants. Some of the plants, a little further out in the tiny grove, had multiple leaves and she knelt, leaning over and placing a careful palm flat on the ground between the plants to stabilize herself and keep from falling on them. As she did, she pulled her hand back in pain and surprise. The ground between them was sharp with tiny petrified seedlings that had pricked her palm. A few were stuck a little way in her skin, like stone thorns.

Looking at her hand, she ignored the spots of blood to focus on the seedlings. She rolled one across her palm. Aria's eyes widened. It was Taim—the same as the little plants growing in her cottage, on the train, and across Coriol. Those tiny little plants were the seedlings of the huge, swaying trees she had seen in the grove with the children and that had made a grove here before they'd been destroyed by what seemed to be fire from above.

She'd read that Minea was occasionally prone to localized,

destructive meteor showers. Evidence of them existed all over the planet, and she was standing where one had happened.

Aria heard a twig snap behind her and turned in time to see a man angling away from her across the edge of the barren meteor patch. His hair lay in coarse tangles down the back of his tattered jacket, and he ran lightly on boots worn and split with use. He carried a large sack, which bounced across his back as he ran.

"Hey!" Aria called. He glanced back and moved faster. "Wait! I need help!"

At this the man slowed and turned, warily looking across the petrified tree stumps toward her.

"I don't want trouble," he called, his voice creaky. He was, Aria saw now, one of the Evaders, those who had walked away from their debts in the cities and who lived off the land in the Minean wilderness. She had known they were out here, but she'd never seen one.

"No trouble," Aria said, taking careful steps toward him and holding up her hands. "I just need help."

"What're you doin' out here? You work for Saras?" he asked, a jittery tension crossing his features.

She shook her head. "I don't work for Saras." She was, for once, glad of that fact. "My husband disappeared out here. I need help finding him. Have you seen a ship?"

He wasn't running, but he looked like he might. "Your husband work for Saras?"

"No. He doesn't."

This seemed to calm him, and he took a step toward her. "I haven't seen 'im."

Aria realized, suddenly, how much she was hoping he had. Her disappointment must have shown on her face.

"It's wild country," he said apologetically.

Aria nodded. "I'm starting to see that."

The man hesitated, then swung his sack to the ground and rooted around in it. He came up holding a strange yellow fruit, its skin speckled with orange smudges.

She smiled. "A kwai fruit!"

The man seemed pleased. He took a few more steps toward her and held it out. "Take this. I'm sorry about your husband."

Aria took it, smelling its thick, sweet scent. She suddenly realized she was hungry. When had she last eaten?

"How do you eat it?" she asked.

The man removed another from the sack and held it up to demonstrate. Then he bit into it. She heard the snapping sound of the skin and saw the juice trickle into his beard. She held hers to her mouth, breathing in that robust aroma, and took a bite.

She couldn't help but slurp to keep the sweet juice from being wasted. The flesh was firm and tender, and the underlying tang of the fruit countered its remarkable sweetness. Aria laughed a little at her own voraciousness as she finished it off.

She saw him slip the pit from his into one of the pockets of his faded vest and he held out a hand for her pit as well. She handed it to him. "Do you cultivate these?"

He nodded. "I do."

She smiled. "I was a botanist back on Earth. I just grew some Earth wheat in my house back in Coriol."

His eyes widened and he took an involuntary step forward. "Earth wheat? Real Earth wheat?"

She nodded. "It's my own strain. High in protein." She closed her eyes. "I'm dreaming of a loaf of whole wheat bread sometime in the future."

The man looked at her a long moment. Then he spoke gruffly. "I'm Hank," he said, his voice softened by his gray beard. "What's your name?"

She smiled and held out a sticky hand. "Aria."

He shook it and they both chuckled and wiped their hands on their jackets.

"Listen," he said, glancing around, "what would it take to get some of that wheat?"

Aria considered. "I don't have much. I brought some from Earth, you know, to remember it by. I didn't realize there wouldn't really be an exact equivalent here."

"Huh." He made a disgusted sound. "A lot we didn't realize about things here."

She nodded encouragingly, and Hank went on.

"I came here to be a miner. Didn't know they'd make ya use picks and shovels, and that no matter whatcha did they'd never pay you enough to repay them."

Aria grimaced. It was a familiar story.

"You can think what you want," Hank said, "but I walked away from it. Left my key on the table and my red uniform in the closet. Don't take nothin' from nobody anymore. I can make it on my own out here." He hesitated. "Well, mostly. I do a little tradin' to get stuff I want."

"Who do you trade with?" Aria asked.

"Other Evaders, like me." He gestured toward a narrow cut between two peaks. "Headin' to the market now. You can come, if you won't say anything about it back in the city." Saying the words out loud seemed to make him more anxious about that possibility, and he gathered his bag quickly. "Or maybe you'd better not come." He took a quick step away.

"Hank," Aria said, her voice clear and calm. She tried not to let him see how much she wanted to meet others out here, to see if they knew anything about Ethan. Hank turned back toward her, searching her face. "I'm not going to tell anyone.

I'll keep your secret."

His eyes narrowed and he studied her a long moment. "A'right then. Keep up."

It was a challenge keeping up with him. He scrambled between the peaks and through a boulder field. She followed him for what she guessed was about a kilometer before he parted a curtain of hanging vines and entered a brilliant, sunlit valley the size of a warehouse. The sun was directly overhead, and there were twenty or more people in the shade of the vines around the edge, sitting on blankets on the ground. They had a fascinating assortment of items spread around them.

Aria walked through the market in wonder. There were fruits of all different kinds, meat, castoff clothes and camping gear, and even homemade goods like cookies and decorations made from natural or found materials.

She saw their suspicion as she approached, but Hank's reputation seemed secure, because a wave of his hand put most of the other vendors at rest.

He stopped beneath a canopy of leafy vines and reached in his sack, procuring a faded tartan blanket. He laid it out and carefully arranged his fruits—not just the kwai, but also long purple fruits and bright green gourds, red berries and white ones, and two huge orange blossoms dripping with nectar.

"It's as sweet as Earth's honey," he said, holding one toward her. She held out a finger and he let a golden drop fall on it. Putting it in her mouth, she was taken back to the smell of honeysuckle from her childhood and its sweet taste in the air.

"I'm the fruit man," he told her as he turned his attention to his customers. The other vendors descended, trying to convince him how much he needed their goods and trying to downplay his wares as they traded with him.

Aria watched in amazement as they haggled back and

forth, coming to a mutual agreement about what each item was worth. It was so different than the experience of Gaynes's market in Coriol. She admired it.

Finally, as the sun moved past the valley, the Evaders began to pack up. Aria realized she was missing her chance.

"Hold on! Hold on!" She caught up to them and asked about Ethan. No one had seen him, or the ship, but they did talk her out of her jacket and the pocketknife she'd brought along, trading her for several delicious fruits, nuts, and gourds gathered from the forest around them.

Most were kind, as well, telling her not to give up looking, that it was a vast place and he could be alive. Look at them. Some of them had been living out here a long time. Hank had been here twenty years.

Hank helped her carry her produce and find her way back to the boat. There was a gleam in his eye as he said, "Aria, before you leave, I want to know if you'll think of a trade for some of that wheat—just a few grains. I think I could get it to grow."

Aria thought about it. Suddenly, the thought of all this food, sitting out here while people in Coriol were starving, sparked an idea in her.

"I'll work out a trade with you. But it may take a little more than just wheat. Is there anything else you need?" She gestured back toward the market. "Or that they need?"

"Sure, there's a list of stuff we're always on the lookout for." He ran a hand down his beard. "Razors, scissors, knives, ropes, warm clothes, water carriers like bottles and jugs."

A plan was forming. "Is this a good site to meet? Is it safe for you?" she asked.

Hank's eyes darted away toward the forest and she knew he was looking toward his home. He nodded.

"Okay. I'll get you anything you want from the city. But I

need as much fruit as you can give me. And I need you—all of you—to keep an eye out for Ethan."

Hank seemed to consider for a moment, then stuck out a hand. "Deal."

***

Kaia breathed in the sharp scent of Zam as she waited in the hallway for Polara to come out of her classroom. Rigel was sleeping in his stroller, and she pushed it slowly back and forth a little. The school was small, even by Minean standards, and only a fraction of the children in Coriol attended it. Saras had no qualms about employing children over ten years old, and parents needed all the scrip they could get to pay off their heavy debts.

It was a tidy school, though. Even now a Saras cleaning crew was scrubbing the windows at the other end of the hall, scraping at the little green plants, which Aria called Taim. The plants seemed intent on filling up Coriol. The crew, silhouetted against the brightness of the window, looked ominous, somehow. Kaia turned to peer in the open door of Polara's classroom instead, hoping that the little girl didn't see her. She knew that Polara would likely run straight to her without regard for her teacher's discipline plan. She always liked to see Polara learning. She was such a bright, inquisitive child and everything held fascination for her.

Today, though, Kaia saw the little girl sitting at her desk, resting her chin on her crossed arms. She didn't look bored, exactly, or sleepy. Kaia tried to come up with an accurate word to describe Polara's blank expression and slumped shoulders.

*Weak.*

That was the word. Polara looked weak and fragile. Kaia had to stop herself from going to the child. It must have been a grueling day at school. When the teacher dismissed them, Polara gathered her things and smiled broadly when she saw Kaia. There was some comfort in that. And Kaia thought there was a bit more spring in her step as she walked.

Kaia took the child's hand. She never felt so needed and so secure in her own mind as when she was with Polara. The child's enthusiasm had a calming and clarifying effect on her.

She thought as they walked back to her cottage. Polara chattered along and Kaia saw all the mothers coming to pick up their children. It was strange, but Minea was a world without many grandparents. The passenger ships had left the grandparents behind on Earth, stripping away an entire generation from the families who crossed the stars. Kaia was glad that Ethan's children had her and the Admiral. They'd fallen into the grandparent role so easily.

When, four years ago, she and her father had walked into the hospital room and Ethan had brought the newborn Polara to them, both Kaia and the Admiral had seen, in the delicate features of that baby, a brand new start. Their sorrow, their regret, had, for the first time since Kaia arrived, faded into the background, washed out by the hope that Polara brought.

And Polara and Rigel had kept the memories of those hard times at bay ever since.

# Chapter 16

The survey crew used Bleak House as their base for the next several days. Two weeks ago they'd dropped out of the sky, and their equipment was failing steadily. As they explored the tunnels around the dry chamber, the little group moved carefully together in the dim glow of Ndaiye's shoulder lights, trying to preserve their remaining Maxlights while they could. The batteries on the final two pairs of Everwarm coveralls went out within hours of each other.

Something about the conversation they'd shared the first night in Bleak House stayed with them. They couldn't stop talking about Earth. As they settled in after several hours of exploring, Ndaiye was cheering them with tales from his parents' traditional culture.

"Sure," Ndaiye said, "the spirits of people who have died can visit you. And the spirits of people back on Earth can visit Minea, too, when their bodies are sleeping. And you can visit them. Only you think it's a dream when you wake up. And so do they."

Ethan didn't mind that myth. Actually, he liked it. He would like his sister to see Minea, though she'd be over eighty now. And he would like to see her again. It was a comforting thought.

Maggie interrupted the thought, pulling him back into the cave. "If we wanna stay warm, we're gonna have to sleep like sardines," Maggie said. "So I hope nobody's shy."

They put Brynn and Jade in the middle, with Maggie and Traore on either side and Ndaiye and Ethan on the ends. Ethan turned throughout the night to warm his back and his chest alternately. He barely slept. Finally, when he could stand it no more, he laid the packs where he had been to hold some heat near the group and stood, shivering.

There was one direction they hadn't gone yet. He took a Maxlight and went that way. The triangular opening in the far wall was easy to slip through, and Ethan found himself in a chamber that reminded him of the Colony Offices lobby. Several passages opened out of it, which they would need to map.

He went back into the Bleak House chamber and eased the map, pencil, and marking rock out of his pack. He put them in the inner pockets of his coveralls and started down the first tunnel.

After three switchbacks, it dead-ended. Ethan exited and wrote "DEAD END" on the wall inside the tunnel with the marking rock.

He tried the next one. It ran, curving, off down deeper into the cave. Promising, he thought, but it eventually came to another dead end. He was far from the Bleak House chamber, where he'd left the others sleeping, and really alone for the first time since the crash. Ethan wanted to try something, something he hadn't tried in a long time. He had learned to completely suppress most of the alterations made to him on Beta Alora, and this was one he hadn't used since being on that red planet.

But when he'd used it in the past, there were consequences for those around him, and he couldn't try it around the survey crew unless he was sure he could control it.

Ethan stood in front of the wall, his palms in front of him. He tapped into the hopelessness he felt being in the cave, into the fear and anger and loss that this place had brought him. He felt his heart beating hard and fast, adrenaline racing through him. As the energy inside him crested, a beam of it shot out through his extended palms, striking the wall with a deafening sound.

He had a moment to see the damage—a table-sized depression in the solid rock—before the tunnel began caving in. Ethan turned and ran back up the tunnel as the rocks fell behind him and the dust and air rushed past him. Tripping, he flipped over, expecting to be crushed by the collapsing tunnel, but it had fallen and was settling into a wall of rubble.

Ethan lay back on the stone floor. His fear about his power was confirmed. It was useless here. This environment was too unpredictable. Unless he could guarantee the stability of the rock above, he couldn't risk blasting.

He walked back to the lobby outside Bleak House. The avalanche hadn't woken the others, so he jotted a note and left it on the packs. *Looking for our next move. –Ethan.*

Slipping out the triangle exit and glancing toward the now rubble-filled tunnel, Ethan stopped to mark "DEAD END AND FALLING ROCK. DO NOT ENTER!" on the map over the passage he had blasted before starting off down a third passage.

Gray and bland like the rest of this area of the cave, this passage was long and snaking. Tunnels opened up on either side and soon he began seeing flowstone formations jutting from the walls. He glanced up. Strange slabs of suspended rock jig-sawed the ceiling of the passage. Walking on, he lost track of time as he studied the formations' intricacy.

As the formations ended, the passage widened slightly and stopped abruptly. Another dead end. What if they were all dead ends? He shook his head, dreading the trip back up that rock field. And then where would they go? Any of the hundred passages they'd passed could lead them outside or to another dead end like this. Ethan leaned against the wall, trying to think what he'd tell the team when he got back to them. Switching off his light, he laid his head against the cold stone for a moment. Suddenly, an unfamiliar sensation skimmed his face. He swept his hand up instinctively to brush it away, but it remained: a constant, gentle caress. Ethan's heart beat faster. It was air, moving through the cave. Somewhere in this room was an opening for wind to get through. And wind led outside. He switched the light back on and turned his cheek toward the breeze. Shining the light in that direction, he crossed the stony cave floor and followed the breeze around some of the bigger boulders. He felt a breath of relief escape him as he saw it. At the bottom of the far wall gaped a crevice about the size of a bathtub. He knelt beside it and felt the air rushing past him. It felt fresh and bracing.

Ethan took out the marking rock and scratched his initials above the passage. He lay on his belly and crawled into the crevice. It was roomy, roughly squarish, and smoothed by water that had once flowed here. He rolled onto his back and pulled off his gloves, feeling the surface all around with his fingertips. It was dry.

Crawling farther into the gap, he found it tapering slightly to an oblong passageway. As he crawled he was suddenly reminded of exploring the ship's shafts with Kaia. That was a lifetime ago.

He missed her company now. She would have a thousand ideas about how to get these people out of here. She may have even been able to repair the ship so they could have flown out. As the memory of the survey craft returned to him, though, he realized that was wishful thinking. Its twisted wings and the ragged gashes through its sides would have been beyond even her capacity to repair. If there was a way out, this was much more likely to be it.

Ethan felt the thud of rock on his shoulder and realized that the opening had narrowed considerably. Pausing, he shined his light ahead, down along the smooth passage as far as he could see. It grew smaller ahead. Ethan stopped to breathe. Though the last few days had forced him to move past his fear of enclosed spaces, this was extreme. He didn't know if he could force himself to go further into the little passage. He wasn't going to be able to crawl on his hands and knees, and holding the flashlight was going to be tricky.

His breath quickened as he looked down the passageway, shining the light around to reveal a cylinder of smooth gray stone. The breeze flowed past his face, seemingly warmer here. There was a real possibility that this lead somewhere, that getting through it got them closer to getting out. It had to be investigated.

Ethan was no stranger to facing his fears. He held the faces of the crew in his mind for a moment, then he slid the Maxlight into his pocket and tapped the one working shoulder light, telling himself not to panic as he registered how much more shadowy the way was without the flashlight.

He dropped to his belly and slid farther in. After the first few minutes, he found himself fighting the urge to go back. The breath of the cave told him that this passage went somewhere, and if he didn't find out where, he and the surveyors would be at a dead end. If there was any way he could get them out of here, he had to try.

The tunnel constricted more as he crawled. A closing silver fist around him, it was now just inches wider in circumference than he was. His heart began to beat in his throat and he crawled faster. The sides of the narrow passage cut in further, pinning his elbows, forcing him to reach ahead of him to pull himself along. He tried to steady himself with a deep breath, but the breeze he'd felt before had become a rushing wind, catching in his mouth and pulling the air from his lungs.

Gasping, he felt the press of solid rock above and below him and felt his body fill with urgency for oxygen and space and light. He knew the rock's cold indifference, felt its permanence encircling him. He felt heat growing in his chest and tried desperately to control it. An energy pulse now would give him a second of relief but would also bury him under tons of rubble. He had to calm down. He fought for breath, gasping again and again, clawing ahead and feeling the suffocating weight of the cave and the dark closing around him.

And then his hands reached forward and found nothing. The passage opened out. Ethan crawled desperately forward. His dim shoulder light showed him that the tunnel ended in a smooth, white, narrow band of rock, cutting in and ringing the passage. He clawed until his head was through, then felt panic rising as his shoulders caught in the narrow opening. He shifted his shoulders sideways. His chest was still burning for oxygen, so it took every bit of his resolve to push all the air from his lungs and roll his shoulders in so he could wriggle out of the passage.

The expanse of space around him as he emerged into the chamber made him dizzy. He filled his lungs with convulsive breaths as he rolled onto his back. Throwing his arms wide, he lay on the floor, drinking in the feeling of freedom and the taste of the air.

His body was stiff and cold from being in such close contact with the stone for so long, and the effort of the last few meters had him sweating, so he soon found himself shivering. He got up from the floor carefully and flipped on the Maxlight. A burst of color reflecting back at him from the walls shocked his eyes. A huge drapery formation, cascading across the closest wall, glowed vibrant red in the beam of the flashlight. As he ran the light across it, he saw variation in the color and translucence of the stone. In some places it was white, in others almost purple, in others lovely translucent pink. And radiating from it was midsummer warmth.

Ethan pulled off his glove, then reached up and laid a hand against the curtain. It was warm. He moved to the edge and touched the stone cave wall behind it, then pulled his hand away quickly. In some places it was hot. His cold bones pulled the heat in and he sank to the floor, stretching out on the warm ground. He felt himself relax against the stone, letting his mind wander to Aria and the kids. He wondered if they had searched for him, if they were still searching, or if she had given herself to the inevitability of his death and was starting the long road of processing her grief. He switched off the light and indulged in his thoughts of them for a moment.

The warmth made him sleepy, and against his will he drifted off. It felt like days since he had slept.

***

When Ethan awoke, he was comfortable and warm. He imagined for a moment that he was back home in the blue cottage, but the reality hit him and he sat up anxiously, wondering how long he had slept. He pulled out the map, shuddering as he looked back over the last few days laid out on the page. He sketched the chamber where the rest were waiting for him. "Bleak House"

Brynn had called it. He wrote the words above it. He pulled the lines up from it, showing the little incline and the two dead-ends he'd taken, then the ballooning antechamber where he'd found the opening to the tiny tunnel. What to call it? Tunnel of Terror seemed fitting, but a little dark. He thought of the crushing sensation, the constriction of rock around his chest, and scribbled, "Python Pass."

Re-energized, he headed back for the tunnel. He had to get the others here. It was not only their best way out, but a warm, safe place for them to rest. He wanted them warm. He wanted them to have the kind of sleep he'd just had.

The tightest section of the passage was still grueling for Ethan, but knowing that the tunnel opened up and that there was an escape from it calmed the worst of his fears and he made it out the other side. He navigated back through the cave, checking his marks at every intersection, even if he thought he knew the way. As he approached Bleak House, the chamber where he'd left them, he was surprisingly relieved to see the triangle of faint light shining through the entrance. Slipping through the opening, he came face to face with Brynn, who was peering anxiously out the opening. She beamed a smile at him.

"I thought you were gone for good!"

Ethan smiled back, then peered around her. "How's Maggie?"

"I'm fine," the team leader called gruffly from the dim edge of the cavern. "Except they keep making me get up and hobble around."

Ethan's mood had improved dramatically. He walked over to where she and the cousins were crowded together on one of the reflective blankets. "They're keeping you from getting hypothermia. Be nice to them."

Maggie grunted as he sat down on the blanket with them. "Where have you been?" she asked.

"Exploring. And I've found something great."

"Another crystal obstacle course?" Maggie growled. Ethan looked around for Jade. He wanted them all to hear about it. She lay still on the floor where they'd been sleeping. Someone had covered her with the reflective blanket. Ethan went to her and laid a hand on her shoulder to wake her.

Her shoulder was unyielding. Ethan felt sick as he realized that Jade wouldn't be waking up. "She's gone," he said, his voice breaking. He heard a small cry from Brynn.

He slumped back as Ndaiye rushed to the girl, checking her. "Her head injury was worse than we thought."

Without warning, Ethan again felt the energy pulse growing in him. The senselessness of it, the waste, fueled his anger and he felt the heat rising. But the tumbled rocks of the tunnel flashed through his mind and he forced himself to look at the rest of the team. They were still alive. They had a chance to get out of here. He couldn't ruin that by reacting this way. He pressed his palms hard onto the cold stone of the floor and drew in a long, trembling breath.

In the dim glow of the shoulder lights, Ethan looked at the four people huddled around the chamber. It had been over two weeks since they'd seen the sun. Weeks in this tangle of chambers and passages. Weeks—and less—since they'd lost their friends. They were moving toward a dangerous discouragement. He had to give them some hope, had to get them to that warm place to rest and gain strength. But how much to tell them? In the back of his mind, that long dark passage hovered like a stasis nightmare. He knew he was going to have to get them through it.

Ndaiye covered Jade's face with the blanket.

"What do we do?" Brynn asked, her voice broken and pleading.

And then Ndaiye began to sing. No calming lullaby or bracing anthem this time, but a sorrowful, wailing song that rang through the cavern with an aching sincerity. It was in his old Earth language, and it seemed to carry Jade's spirit home.

When the last note of the song ended, Ndaiye and Traore harmonized mournfully as they gathered the packs and helped Maggie and Brynn out of the cavern. Ethan ducked out behind them.

Outside, as the last notes of the cousins' song faded, Ethan saw Maggie. Her shoulders were slumped. She was, as they all were, dangerously weary. She was holding Jade's pack and she slowly removed everything useful—and the photoflat—and divided it among them.

When she turned her eyes to him, Ethan saw no anger. Her grief was, this time, deep sorrow.

For once, Maggie's voice was subdued. "What do we do now?"

Ethan gestured to the group and they followed his flashlight into the third tunnel, leaving the girl's body and the darkness behind them.

The group moved more slowly than usual, each lost in their own thoughts. It took them two hours to reach the antechamber.

"Good news," he said as brightly as he could. "I found where we need to go. Do you feel it? There's a breeze."

He waited.

"I feel it!" Ndaiye's voice brightened with a ripple of excitement. "I feel it!"

"Me too," Brynn said, her eyes kindling with a spark of hope.

"It means there's an opening somewhere. It means air is getting into the cave. I'm hoping we can follow the air and find a way out."

There were murmurs of approval. Ethan opened his mouth to tell them about Python Pass, then his gaze played across their haggard faces and he stopped. They would know soon enough.

He crossed the chamber and they followed. With some apprehension, Ethan showed them the gap they'd be going through. Brynn looked startled, and Ndaiye shook his head, but it was Traore who feared it most. He backed away. "That doesn't look big enough for us." He said, a tremor in his always-steady voice.

Ethan adopted a calm tone. "It's going to be tight, but I've been through, and we can make it." He put his hands on Traore's shoulders and looked into the shadows around his eyes. "It's worth it. On the other side is a thermal chamber. It's like a sauna in there. Traore, it's so warm that you think you're back in your own house in Coriol." He could see Traore fighting to overcome the fear. "You can get through. It's our way home." Ethan said that with more conviction than he felt. In truth, he had no idea if the thermal chamber led anywhere. "I'll be with you. Just follow me."

Traore's gaze shifted between Ethan and the opening. Once. Twice. Ethan saw the moment that Traore's fear of the passage gave way to his desire to get out. Glancing at the others, Ethan saw that the fear had spread among them. If they didn't go now, he wouldn't get them in there.

"Just follow me," Ethan repeated. He dropped down and slid his pack off his shoulders. "I'm going to be honest with you. It gets tight. There won't be any extra room. You're going to have to push your packs in front of you down the passage. Don't panic. Just focus on going the next arm's length, then the next. Just keep moving, and hang on until the passage opens up." He looked at them. "Traore, you follow me. Ndaiye, you come next. Maggie, it's going to be tough for you with that leg—"

Maggie dismissed him. "I'll be fine."

"Brynn, you'll have the easiest time getting through, because you're the smallest. You come through after Maggie. Help her if you can." He faltered, wanting to give them something that would quell their fear in the narrowest part of the passage, something that they could hold onto in the dark. "It will end. It will open up. Keep going. Just trust me."

Ethan's own heart was hammering again. He didn't want to go back in there. He would have done anything to keep from it, but he wanted to go home, and this seemed the most likely way. He pushed his pack in front of him into the opening and crawled inside.

The first few meters were fine. The pack was a new challenge, but he found it gave him something to focus on so he didn't have to think so much about the way the tunnel was closing around him. He heard the sound of Traore's breathing behind him, amplified in the small space. The other man was already breathing erratically. Ethan heard the scraping of Traore's hands and the rasp of his pack against the stone. "You're doing fine. Keep coming."

As the passage narrowed, Ethan willed himself to calm down. It was much worse coming this way. Coming out of the sauna room, the passage began narrow and opened with every meter you crawled, but this direction was the opposite. Just when he thought it could get no smaller, the passage constricted further.

Ethan was well into the tightest part when he heard Traore begin to cry out behind him. The deep voice was muffled by the pack and the stone, but Ethan could tell he was panicking.

He crawled faster, calling out, "We're almost there, Traore. We'll make it. Keep crawling!" Arms outstretched in front of him, Ethan shoved the pack savagely forward, reached ahead, and pulled his body as far as he could. "Keep coming, Traore!"

Again: push, reach, pull. Push, reach, pull. Ethan's own fear of the stone was swallowed up in the drive to get Traore out of there. He felt Traore's pack hit his feet and knew the man was right on his heels.

Traore was wailing, "Get me out! Get me out!"

Finally, Ethan's pack slid away and his arms broke free of the tunnel. He paused, tucking his shoulders quickly and working himself through the last constricting band of rock. He reached back into the tunnel to feel for Traore's pack, but grasped only air.

Now that his own body was out of the way, Traore's voice came to him forcefully. The words had ceased, and the terrified man was now simply screaming. Ethan called to him.

"Traore! Traore! Listen! You're almost there! I'm out. You've got to keep coming."

But the sounds of crawling had stopped and Traore's cries got no closer. He was either stuck or paralyzed with fear. Suddenly scared, Ethan hoped it was the latter.

He could hear Ndaiye shouting at his cousin. "Go, man! I want out of here, too! Go, Traore!"

Ethan dove back into the tunnel, crawling until he felt the pack. He grasped it, then attempted to move backwards. It was much more challenging. He found his feet lacked the grip he'd had with his hands. With Traore's panicked screams landing like blows on his ears, Ethan had to fight to stay calm himself. He wriggled backwards, pulling the pack with him, and made it out again. Tossing the pack aside, he pushed into the tunnel again, crawling as quickly as he could toward the terrified man.

He found Traore thrashing in the tiny space, his hands clawing the sides of the tunnel. He had turned onto his back and his screams filled the small space with deafening volume.

Ethan grabbed for him and shouted, "Ndaiye! Push if you can!"

Locking his hands around Traore's flailing arms, Ethan pulled, trying to work the two of them backwards. But Traore thrashed and clawed at him, wailing. "No! No! I can't! I have to go back! He twisted and contorted, trying to turn in the tunnel. Ethan let go and moved back, trying to shout over the man's cries. He was paralyzed by the knowledge that Traore could wedge his own body in the opening, dooming himself and the three people behind him, leaving Ethan to face the rest of the dark cavern alone. Ethan felt his own panic rising.

And then, clear and bright to his mind came a memory. Polara upon seeing her first yan, the pig-like animals that some people on Minea had domesticated and kept for pets. Polara had been terrified, striking out at the little animal as it approached her. Ethan had pulled her into his arms, stroked her hair, and sang to her an Earth song from his childhood.

Now, in the chaos of the tunnel, Ethan moved forward. Dodging the clawing hands, he reached into the darkness. Traore's head was less than a meter away. Ethan felt the thick hair, the smooth forehead. He put all the gentleness and serenity he could into his touch. Traore seemed to take some comfort. He stilled slightly, though his shoulders still twisted convulsively and his fingers still scraped the stone above him in panic.

Instinctively, Ethan began to hum. Suddenly, the words of the old lullaby he'd heard them sing in the Teardrop Chamber came back to him and he fought for breath to sing, "Yangu mtoto, mtoto, ndoto." His voice was small, lost in the shouting from the others in the tunnel and Traore's fear. He sang a little louder, "itakuwa utulivu mtoto wangu, yangu mtoto, mtoto, ndoto," and felt Traore still as he sang. Both men lay still, Traore listening and Ethan singing softly.

When the song was over, Ethan slid his hand away from Traore's hair and found his arm. "Come with me, Traore. We're gonna get out of here." Traore convulsed, but Ethan felt him trying to move. "You need to turn back over, onto your stomach, if you can." He pulled as Traore slowly righted himself and moved, a painful centimeter at a time, down the tunnel. Ethan heard himself wheezing as he wriggled backwards. The tunnel seemed so much longer as he tried to pull Traore along with him.

When he felt his feet kick free of the tunnel he blurted, "I'm out, Traore! We're almost there! Keep coming."

Ethan worked himself out of Python Pass still holding onto Traore's arms. He reveled in the space and in the leverage he was able to get by bracing against the wall outside the tunnel. He felt Traore slip forward half a meter at a time.

As the light from Ethan's single shoulder light fell on Traore's tear-streaked face, Ethan let go of his arms, but placed a reassuring hand on his head. "You're going to have to wiggle through the end here," he said firmly. "Just tuck your shoulders in and work your way out. You're almost here."

Traore's desperate scramble through the last obstacle of the tunnel revealed his still unsteady state of mind. Ethan lifted him to his feet and Traore rushed several feet away and collapsed near the curtain formation. Seeing him safe, Ethan turned his attention back to the others, still bound in the dark of the tunnel.

They were coming fast. Ndaiye's pack hit the cavern floor

just seconds after Traore was out, and he struggled out after it.

There was a terrible, quiet pause after Ndaiye had settled in the cavern. Ethan leaned into the tunnel, listening. He heard Maggie's labored breathing somewhere ahead. "Are you all right?" he called.

"I'm fine," she snapped. "I'm entitled to a rest once in a while, aren't I?"

Despite the adrenaline still pumping through his veins, Ethan smiled. She was fine. "All right. Do you hear Brynn? Is she okay?"

"She keeps trying to push her pack under my toenails. She must be fine. Now shut up. I can barely breathe enough to move. I'm not gonna lay in here wastin' my oxygen talkin' to you."

"Fair enough." Ethan stood anxiously by the mouth of the tunnel until Maggie, and then Brynn, worn and quiet, emerged from it. Without asking, he led them to the warmest part of the room, where the party spread out and lay on the heated stone, each resting off the last of their fear.

# Chapter 17

For the last several days, Aria had hiked the vast empty range, meeting up with Hank to trade goods and using his tips to find and gather kwai fruits and katellis and sumnas on her own. And looking, always looking, for any sign of Ethan.

The fruits were so abundant in the mountains, and she so enjoyed gathering them, that she found herself with overflowing baskets of them on the table and counters. She had dropped some off at Kaia's, at Luis's, at Silas's and Yi Zhe's, and many of the other passengers of Ship 12-22 who were still in Coriol, but she still had more than she and the children could eat. And the fear that she might never find Ethan was growing, so she fought to find things to keep her busy.

She found herself reaching out more, trying to keep the grief at bay by bringing help or hope to someone. Today, she had come to the industrial district to find Daniel Rigo's family and share with them the delicious fruits she'd gathered.

But now she was lost in the street and growing anxious. The press of people on the street in the baking late afternoon sun made Aria feel claustrophobic. She had brought the stroller, and both Polara and Rigel rode contentedly, unaware of her growing discomfort.

She couldn't wander like this any longer. The crush of

weary workers coming home from work swirled around her like eddies in a stream as she stopped and turned toward the crowd. She stopped several people, but though they were polite, no one knew the Rigos. Just as she was about to give up, she spotted a woman whose hair and face were smudged with the fine dust of the Yynium refinery and whose eyes looked kind.

"Excuse me, my name is Aria Bryant. Do you know where I might find the Rigo family?"

The woman's eyes narrowed. Aria felt a surge of hope. This was not the blank stare she'd received from everyone else. "What do you want with them?"

"I just—" How to explain? "I met their son Daniel the other day and I wanted to give them a gift." She reached under the stroller and produced one of the juicy purple katelli fruits. It was heavy and full in her hands, and the vibrancy of its color was a sharp contrast to the drab and dusty crowd flowing around them.

The woman half-reached for the fruit, then stopped herself. She nodded. "They live in my building. That'll be good for those little 'uns." She gestured. "I'm Joyce. C'mon with me and I'll show you where they live."

They wound through the streets of the industrial district, and the crowd began to thin out. Aria felt the presence of the huge cement buildings on either side of the street like looming giants, gobbling the people a handful at a time until there were only a few dozen left trudging home. The buildings effectively blocked out the horizon and most of the sky, except for a thin long strip of blue running along like a ribbon above them.

"These sure are big buildings," Aria said.

"Not big enough," Joyce said. "Too many people to fit in them all."

"Didn't you get cottages when you came?" Aria asked.

Joyce scoffed. "We got cottages," she said bitterly, "way out on the other side of the city. It took me an hour each way to get to the mill." Joyce shook her head. "I couldn't leave my kids all the way out there for that long. So, we moved in with my brother's family in the G building. That was six years ago. We're still there."

Aria couldn't think what to say. It surprised her that people had moved here because they wanted to, that it wasn't directly the Saras Company making them live here.

"Couldn't you use the sol train?" she asked. "To make the trip to the mill quicker?"

"Fare or food?" Joyce asked, a hard tone in her voice. "Can't have both." She looked up at the towering buildings beside them. "Two families in one apartment gets a little tight." Joyce's eyes were distant. "Even after my husband died, we still don't have enough room."

Aria's stomach twisted. *After my husband died.* Would she be saying that someday? Thoughts of Ethan rushed to her, though she fought them back, as she'd been doing all week.

"I'm sorry about your husband," she managed. "What happened?" As soon as she said it she was sorry, but there was no taking it back.

Joyce didn't seem to take offense. "Dustlung," she said simply. "Although the doctors wouldn't ever admit it. Said he brought a virus with him from Earth. Said the conditions here brought it out of latency. But that's a lie. Tamir was never sick a day in his life on Earth. Worked in the mill for three years and started coughing, day and night. Couldn't stop. I know it was the dust. By the end, he was blue nearly all the time. Couldn't get enough air."

"I'm sorry," Aria said again.

"Not your fault," Joyce said. "Probably what we can all

look forward to."

For the first time, Aria noticed the dry coughs of the people around her. Coming and going, men and women, their occasional explosive breaths punctuated the crowd. And, she noticed, some of them had purple marks on their necks or cheeks.

"What are those marks?" Aria asked Joyce in a low voice.

"Minean fever," Joyce replied, shaking her head sadly.

Aria glanced nervously down at the children. Why had she brought them here? Were these things contagious?

They made a turn into one of the gray doorways. "This is it," said her guide, "you'll find them up on the sixteenth floor. Apartment B. Just above mine." She turned toward a wide electronic bulletin board just inside the door, where people were crowded, reading a scrolling screen. "Guess I'd better see if I have a job tomorrow."

Aria forgot her fears for a moment. "Is there trouble at the mill?"

Joyce reached to the wall, where a thick pad of the little Taim plants was growing, and swiped her hand through it, smearing them in a sweeping crescent shape.

"These've got into the mill," she said disgustedly, wiping her hand on her overalls. "Gummin' up the machinery and spreading like bad news." She gestured at the board, "Management has been sending cleaning crews to the worst spots. But they grow like crazy. Seems like the more people working at a station, the more of these grow."

Aria remembered how she had speculated that the Taim liked to be where people were. A companion plant. Only philodendrons never caused this much trouble.

Joyce was still talking. "You never know if your station is down or not. Gotta check morning and night. No use going out there to stand around. And Saras don't pay if your station is down."

Aria nodded as the woman moved into the crowd. "Good luck, Joyce," she said. Turning away, she remembered the abundance of fruit in the stroller. "Joyce!" she called.

The woman turned back, deep lines around her eyes. Aria bent and gathered four of the slippery fruits from the basket and piled them in the arms of her guide.

Joyce's eyes welled with sudden tears, but she blinked them back. "Thank you," she said simply.

"I'll bring you more next time I gather them," Aria promised. "Thank you for helping me."

It was a long elevator ride up to the sixteenth floor. A suspicious silence hung over the elevator, and the tenants of the building kept shooting uneasy glances toward the woman and the stroller. Yynium dust hung in the air, and the ever-present coughs shook the workers as they rode.

When she finally got out, Aria breathed a sigh of relief. Apartment B was easy to find, and two little girls answered her knock.

"Is your mother home?" Aria asked. "Or your brother Daniel?"

The children ushered their visitors into a stark, drab room with one worn sofa against the far wall and a scattering of bedding piled in a corner. The only bright thing was the detailed drawings covering one wall. They were designs for beautiful hovercars, powerful machinery, and ships with smooth, arcing lines. Daniel's name was written neatly in the corner of each one. Aria had seen enough of Kaia's drawings to know what skilled designs looked like, and she was impressed. She'd have to introduce Daniel to Kaia someday.

The thick, pasty smell of Saras mush, made from the cheap

ground grain known as brakkel, something akin to Earth's oats, filled the apartment. One of the little girls left to get Daniel, and the other one gravitated to Polara, who was playing with the doll Hannah, the doll maker from Ship 12-22, had given her.

"I'm Merelda," the little girl said. "That's my sister Nallie. What's your name?"

"Polara."

"I like your doll."

"Thank you. I like your—" Polara looked around frantically. Aria could see that she was taking in, for the first time, the barren walls, the dirty carpeting, and the grimy windows, which let in a sickly gray light. Polara searched for something to say. "Eyes!" she finished enthusiastically.

The little girl smiled. She did have remarkable eyes. They were blue-gray, nearly violet.

Daniel flashed his broad smile as he came into the room, and his mother rushed past him and unabashedly threw her arms around Aria, murmuring in the same unfamiliar language that Daniel had used when she'd given him the rangkors that day.

"Dama, dama, dama." Though Aria wished Ethan was there to tell her what the language was, there was no mistaking the meaning of the soft words.

"You're welcome," Aria said.

"This is my mother, Marise," Daniel said affectionately.

As the woman released her, Aria bent and retrieved the basket of katelli.

"I gathered these," she said, holding them out, "and I thought you'd like some."

Daniel translated for his mother, who suddenly looked scared. She smiled politely, but shook her head.

Aria was surprised. The children looked at the fruit longingly. They obviously needed it.

"What is it?" she asked. "What's wrong?"

Daniel's mother spoke in her native language again, and Daniel translated for her.

"She says the wild fruits can make people sick."

"Ahh." Aria nodded. The Health and Human Services campaign was still propagating that myth. Their brightly-illustrated posters lined the clinics and showed up on bulletin screens across Coriol, but the premise was so incorrect that Aria had long ago dismissed them. Besides, she suspected the campaign had more to do with the Market District's desire to keep its monopoly on fruit than it did with actual medical facts.

"Oh, don't worry," Aria assured them, "these are perfectly safe." She brought one to her mouth and took a bite.

Daniel's mother waved her arms. "No, no, no, no!" she repeated, rushing to Aria and snatching the fruit. She disappeared into the kitchen and Aria heard the waste disposer activate as she swallowed the bite.

Daniel was apologizing as his mother came back into the room, speaking rapidly. He fought to translate quickly enough.

"She says that the sickness is spreading and we can't take chances and your children are beautiful and they need you and you shouldn't be—" he hesitated and offered his mother another word in their language, but she shook her head.

"Tubba," Marise said obstinately.

Daniel sighed, an apology in his eyes. "That you shouldn't be stupid."

Aria fought a smile. She admired Marise's boldness. But she also longed to see the pale, thin children bite into those juicy fruits. They needed the nutrition. Saras mush was nothing to feed growing children on for long.

"I am a plant scientist," she said. "I know they're safe."

Marise shook her head. She started to speak, but waved an impatient hand and reached for Aria, pulling her toward the door.

"She wants you to come with her," Daniel said helpfully.

"I gathered," Aria said, resisting. "But my children—"

Marise followed her gaze to the stroller and spoke quickly to Daniel. "I'll watch them," he said. "She says don't bring them with you."

Aria hesitated, but her curiosity was piqued, and Polara and Merelda were chattering happily about the doll, so she figured it would be all right to leave them for a moment.

Marise led her down the hall, past apartments 35, 36, 37, and 38. When they arrived at apartment 39, Marise entered without knocking.

A woman, lying on the sofa, turned as they entered. Aria bit her cheek to keep from gasping. Huge purple bruises covered the woman's face, neck, and arms. They were iridescent, ranging from pale lavender to deep violet, fading at the edges to a sickly blue-green. The woman shifted, her face a mask of pain. Fever burned in her eyes. She groaned a greeting to Marise in the Rigo's language, and Marise gestured to her, speaking rapidly. The woman spoke, then looked at Aria, making a gesture of eating and then shaking her head emphatically.

Was it possible that this came from eating the fruits? The thought of the blighted crops at the farm came back to Aria. Could the two be related? Aria felt dizzy. Her shock must have shown on her face, despite her best efforts, because Marise waved to her friend and ushered Aria back to her own apartment.

The encounter had taken less than a minute, but the sight of the woman was burned into Aria's brain. Suddenly, she didn't feel safe. Even more than the cough, she feared this new disease. She stepped quickly to the stroller, assessing her children, a fierce sense of protection welling in her.

Marise was speaking to her, and Daniel's voice brought her his mother's words: "She says that's why you have to listen to the doctors. You have to be smart. Mother's friend was eating berries she found in the park, and a few days later, she started getting the marks. She has another friend with the marks who walked home in the rain last week without an umbrella and got too wet and cold. She thinks those things are . . ." Aria heard the word again, tubba, and knew he was hesitating to speak it. In fact, when he spoke again, he softened it: "Foolish."

Aria was beginning to wonder herself.

"Daniel, are there others with the marks?"

He nodded. "Several people have gotten them lately. I have a friend who has them. He's very sick."

"What are the doctors saying?" Saras employed many doctors, and there were ample health services in the city.

"It seems everyone gets a different answer." So they didn't know either, then. Aria felt a knotting anxiety. She needed to get her children home.

She glanced down as Polara handed her doll to Merelda.

"You keep her," Polara said, "and play with her every day." Aria was proud of her.

Merelda held the doll with reverence. Her sister Nallie stroked its string hair and ran a gentle finger over its painted face.

As Aria pushed the stroller out the door, she heard the little girls calling in unison: "Dama! Dama!"

# Chapter 18

Galo felt an intense darkness threatening to engulf him. Every effort he made was coming to nothing. He had tried to use the new information Elencha had given him to locate the Vala on the little blue planet he'd been circling. He had planned to collect his property and be on his way. He had deliveries to make.

But he was no tracker. It had taken him and his first assistant and scanner specialist, Uumbor, a few cycles just to get the scanning equipment calibrated to detect not only Vala life signs, as he'd been scanning for, but also the unique Vala trail that they left behind while in their sleeping state, which Elencha had revealed to him. To calibrate the equipment, they'd tethered one of his remaining Vala children to the ship and floated her into space, running various scans on her until the sensors could detect the Vala trail with ease.

As they had worked, he'd watched the Vala, so seemingly weak, enter her sleeping state and become fortified against the dangers of space that would kill him in seconds. When they pulled her back in, she awoke unscathed. Such a valuable asset.

But they'd been scanning the planet for many cycles now and even the new scans were returning nothing. Continent after continent he scanned, waiting for the ping of the sensors that would reveal where his slaves had gone. But continent after continent the sensors remained silent.

"Scan this continent for any sign of a Vala trail," Galo demanded. Uumbor conducted the scan.

"Still nothing, sir."

That's when Galo began to worry. He knew they were here. They couldn't have traveled anywhere yet. But what if the Vala had not simply fled? What if they'd been stolen and were now being hidden from him by someone on this planet? Their abilities were valuable beyond measure. Anyone who learned of them would want the Vala for their own.

"Who is living on this planet, and where are they?" he demanded.

Uumbor punched a pattern on his keyboard.

"They are the human race," he said, "uninteresting. Mostly industrial. Class 3."

Galo nodded. That was good. If it came to fighting, they were well-matched, and he would have a slight advantage.

The scan screen showed an outline of the planet. Most of it was dark, but a corner of one continent showed a few red dots: settlements. They were halfway around the planet from Galo's Cliprig. There was no civilization on this side. At least if there was a battle there wouldn't be many of these humans to fight.

Galo opened his fleet communications line. He summoned eight ships and put the rest of his fleet on standby. "Have your Vala ready at all times," he said. "If I summon you, you must be here immediately."

The ships that appeared around him in orbit were his best-armed, but not his most agile. They were mostly skybarges, with two windcraft in case he needed quicker maneuvering.

"I'm going around to those settlements," he told his ships over the communications line. "Stay with me."

Galo was skilled at controlling the big ship, and they were soon hanging in a steady orbit far above the settlements on the other side of the planet. He squinted at the screens and spoke forcefully to Uumbor at the scanner. "Scan for Vala life signs in these settlements."

"I'm not showing any Vala here, either, sir."

Galo emitted a low growl, and took some satisfaction as his subordinates flinched.

"Then we will need to take a closer look," he said.

If they could descend, get closer and make a few passes over the landscape, his scanners may be better able to detect the Vala, or he may be able to see where this race of humans could be hiding them. His success as a shipper had afforded him sophisticated scanning equipment. It would take equally sophisticated technology to shield something from it. And if this race was sophisticated enough to hide the Vala, they were probably sophisticated enough to use them. He might not get his slaves back without a fight.

Galo detested combat, but had done it before to protect his interests, and it was in his interest to reclaim the Vala. The Cliprig was a transport ship, but it was well-armed. He could handle any attacks.

Galo contacted the eight ships which had just arrived above the planet. "Hold in orbit," he said, "and do not advance on the planet. I will go down and begin scans. Stay on alert."

As the Cliprig descended through the exosphere, a pesky orbital defense system moved to interfere, so Galo sent a few well-timed pulses out and the system was disabled. It may not have been so easy with manned defenses, but these were remote controlled and automated. He liked automation, because once he saw the pattern, he saw how to disrupt it. You didn't become the greatest shipper in the universe by not knowing how to deal with orbital defenses.

When the orbital defenses were out of the way, and Galo was sure they posed no threat, he began the descent.

***

Reagan's checks were complete. It had taken over two weeks, and a lot of overhauling, but Lumina was as ready now as Flynn or Coriol. Reagan took some comfort in that as he walked down the liftstrip next to Lumina's chief defensive coordinator, listening to the defense plan as the man gestured at various locations around the base. The days had turned warm here in Lumina, and Reagan wiped beads of sweat off his brow under his hatband. Besides the big battleship standing at the ready in an open hangar on the left side of the liftstrip, the base looked no different than when Reagan had arrived. But it felt different. Reagan had memorized every face, every piece of artillery, every strength and weakness. He had reorganized and rescheduled and though he couldn't see it in the hangars to the left or the operations center to the right, it felt more ordered and safer. Beyond the base, the circular city of Lumina lay like a coin on the plain, and Reagan felt satisfaction knowing that its inhabitants were better protected than they'd been two weeks ago.

Reagan flinched when his missive clamored with news.

The orbital defenses were down. The automated spheres that he had been counting on no longer stood between them and the alien ship. He saw his newly-formed crisis team pouring out of the operations center, heading across the liftstrip toward him.

"Report!" Reagan called as soon as they were in earshot.

"The defenses are down, sir, and it seems that the ship is descending."

"How can they be down?" Reagan growled.

"It appears to have been caused by energy pulses of some kind, sir."

"Weapons?"

"It's unclear. They could be. Or it could have just been energy emissions from their thrusters. We're not sure."

Reagan swore. He couldn't act on that. He had to know for sure if it had been an aggressive move.

"We do know that it only took seconds, sir. The ship swept the orbitals aside like a little Yynium dust in the air. One minute we heard the alarms blaring that the ship was coming closer to the planet, the next the missiles were firing, and the next the orbitals were offline."

This was the problem with remote-controlled defenses. If he'd had men up there, they could have evaluated and responded quickly enough to do some good.

Reagan glanced around, at the wide liftstrip, the offices, the hangars, and tried to recapture the feeling of security he'd had moments ago. The sun was just as bright, the buildings just as solid, but it all seemed more tenuous now, somehow. Mechanics and servicemen moved about the strip, most performing their duties purposefully, some taking a break near the big doors of the hangars. Reagan started to snap at them to get back to work, that something serious had happened, but the sight of a shadow on the liftstrip stopped him.

Reagan tilted his head back and watched as a big ship dropped slowly from the sky like a spider on a string. It was just as he imagined an alien ship would be: an oblong beast spewing plasma exhaust. The ship was squat and dark, made of a tarnished metal that gleamed dully in the afternoon sun. It descended slowly, its exhaust burning red and adding to the heat of the Minean afternoon.

The city lay in stunned silence.

Reagan glanced at the operations center and willed himself to move. Calling on his battle experience, he grappled with his fear and relegated it to a corner of his spinning mind as he strode across the strip. The crisis team followed, and he noted that the other personnel were following protocol and taking shelter in the bunkers.

He entered the wide lobby, walked down the hall past the office that had been his for the past two weeks, and hurried to the communications center.

When he arrived, it was obvious they'd forgotten their situation response training. The room was total chaos. The communications officers were talking, shouting, yelling to each other over the blaring airspace perimeter alarms. Out the window, the dark ship moved slowly down through the sky, growing larger with every passing second.

Regan had never been under alien attack before. He had fought human foes, had fought natural disasters, had fought space itself once, but never an alien force. Only two people he knew had that experience. He spun the dial on his missive and called his daughter.

# Chapter 19

Sitting against the warm wall in the heat of the sauna room, Ethan could see the crew around him, heads on their packs, illuminated by the soft glow of their shoulder lights. Traore's big Maxlight had gone out back in Bleak House, and he'd left it there. The shoulder lights would last longer, but not much. The crew reminded him of his children when a long day had overtired them and drained them of their ever-present energy: sprawled out, sleeping soundly.

Ethan himself had slept again, dreaming, for the first time since the crash, of sunshine and the laughter of his children. Now, as he sat looking over the four surveyors, he pushed back the fear that he would never hear that again.

He breathed deeply and slowly, pulling in the warm air of the chamber. He remembered what his friend Yi Zhe had said about qi, that it runs like water through the world, in and out of people and things, and that one must not block it. One must let it flow.

He let his thoughts flow. Aria's green eyes came to his mind. She would love to see these things, if they were on a vacation instead of buried alive. He ached to talk to her, ached for her company. He longed to hold his children.

Brynn stirred and sat up, pink-cheeked in the glow of the

reflected light off the curtain formation. In fact, the whole room had a pinkish tinge.

Brynn scooted over to him. "That was wonderful, what you did for him. I heard you sing."

Ethan looked at his scuffed boots and deflected the compliment. "How did you even hear me? You were three people away."

"It was a pretty tight fit, and we were pretty still, waiting back there. How did you remember those words?"

"I'm a linguist. Words come easily to me."

He saw her shake her head in the half-light. "That's pretty amazing."

***

The crew napped throughout the day, enjoying the warmth and freedom of the Sauna Room so much that they took off their coveralls and slept atop them to provide some cushioning from the unyielding stone floor of the cave. They were arranged in a loose circle, where they could see each other as they talked about their plans for escape and about what they had waiting for them back home. Restored and warm, they turned festive, and Ndaiye even coaxed a few chuckles out of Maggie. They worked especially hard to cheer Traore. He had not returned to his usual self after the tunnel. He remained quiet and jittery, crying out sometimes in his sleep. When he wasn't sleeping, he sat at the edge of the circle, his back against the warmest wall, and stared down at his hands. Brynn sat beside him now, her hand entwined with his, chattering about her danceball team back on Earth and how they'd taken the championship when she was nine.

Ethan watched for any response from Traore. There was none. Brynn reached around herself and dragged her pack to the middle of the circle. Digging inside, she pulled out a packet of fried, salted bean crisps. She tore them open and poured a few of the crisps onto her hand, then held them in front of Traore. Ethan saw the man's eyes dart up to hers, then he carefully took a few and put them in his mouth.

"Here," Brynn said, passing them around the circle. "Let's have a feast!"

Ethan let the savory, crunchy beans roll around in his mouth for several minutes before swallowing them. After days of dry nutrition bars, they tasted amazing. He passed them to Maggie, who graced him with a rare smile before having some herself. When she passed them along, she dug a package of sweetbean candies out of her pack and shared it around. There was a celebratory feeling, and for the first time in days, Ethan felt his breath come a little easier. When the chewy candies passed from Brynn to Ethan, he held them like a gift.

Ethan wanted to give something, too. He dug in his pack and pulled out the apple. Though a bit bruised, it looked delicious.

"Try this." He handed it to Maggie, who crunched into it and passed it to Ndaiye. The man scooted his makeshift bed closer as she handed it to him, anticipation in his eyes. A hint of a smile played at the corner of Ndaiye's mouth as he tasted it, then laid it gently in his cousin's hand. Traore took a bite, and Ethan saw his eyes close briefly. He passed it to Brynn.

"Mmmmm." Brynn breathed as she savored a taste of the apple, then passed it to Ethan.

He took a bite. He closed his eyes as he reveled in its sweet, tart flavor and bright finish. He glanced around at the others and they were smiling. The five passed the fruit around again and again, taking small bites and making each bite last. They savored each drop of sweet, sticky juice. They even ate the core, spitting the seeds out with little clicks onto the stone floor.

Ethan chewed the last jagged bite of the core and swallowed it, feeling a disappointment that made him think of the time when Polara used all her scrip on candy and cried when it was gone.

From the corner of his eye he saw movement and jumped as he heard a tiny scratching. He looked, expecting the horrible cave krech, but instead caught a glimpse of a small, pink rodent. It snatched one of the apple seeds and scurried back into the arc of darkness surrounding the little group.

"Did you see that?" Ndaiye exclaimed. "It didn't have any eyes!"

"Makes sense," Maggie spoke for the first time since they'd started the apple, "there's no light down here. He doesn't need eyes."

"How did he know the seed was there?"

"He heard it, or smelled it."

"Many animals have heat sensors. Maybe it could feel the seed."

"Here's another one," Brynn said softly as one made its way toward her. Brynn didn't cower from it. In fact, she reached out and picked up a nearby seed, tossing it closer to the little rodent. It snatched the seed, then sat up and chewed it. Soon, several of them had come out to clean up the seeds.

Ethan watched them scamper out into the light, their little noses twitching under the smooth pink skin where their eyes should have been. They didn't move hesitantly, instead scurrying purposefully forward, finding the seeds, and eating them without fear. They had pink pointed ears and seemed aware of any little sound the crew made. Ethan found himself being as still as possible so as not to scare them. He missed living things. The deprivation of the caves made him appreciate all the little things he'd taken for granted above ground.

The little rodents had protruding front teeth and huge claws, but neither looked like they'd be much use for defense. They were comically large, like costume accessories, and Ethan assumed they were great for digging. The room was quiet except for their scratching.

"Have you read the Callitas Chronicles?" Ndaiye asked, referring to a text containing Klaryt myths.

"I have," Ethan said.

Ndaiye scoffed. "You probably read it in the original language."

Ethan had, in fact, and he grinned.

Ndaiye shook his head. "I read a translation, but it was still really interesting." He gestured at the little animals. "These guys remind me of the Xyxos."

"The who?" Maggie demanded, albeit more softly than she usually spoke.

"They were gods, well, not gods, exactly—"

"Demi-gods," Ethan helped out.

"Right. Demi-gods in the afterlife whose job was to usher the dead to their assigned kingdoms. The Callitas thought of the afterlife as a series of various paradises and purgatories arranged in a complex web through the center of their planet, like these caves."

Ethan could see the comparison. "There were judges who made the rulings on where the soul of each person should go, then the Xyxos would lead them through the labyrinth and leave them to their fate. The judges couldn't navigate the underworld. The story goes that after centuries of seeing the terror on the faces of those they were leading to purgatories, the Xyxos ignored the rulings of the judges and took pity on the souls of the damned, leading them to paradises they hadn't earned. When the judges found out, the Xyxos were blinded as a punishment. They could no longer see the faces of their charges, so they were not moved to disobey the rulings of the judges, but the myth says that they knew the passageways and rooms of the underworld so well that they still navigated with ease, even without their sight."

"So we're in purgatory, then?" Maggie spoke up.

There was a moment of uncomfortable silence, then Ndaiye laid back on the warm rock and stretched out. "Nope. This feels more like a paradise to me."

Ethan glanced back at the little rodents. The Xyxos were said to know every corner of the underworld. These creatures certainly seemed to know their way around as well. He wished he could be as confident in the dark as these little Xyxos creatures. As the Maxlights had gone out he couldn't help feeling the dark of the cave closing around them minute by minute like a tightening noose.

A rock clattered somewhere behind them, startling the Xyxos, who froze, then fled, stuffing the last seeds into their cheeks and scampering between and behind the columns, where they disappeared.

Watching them go, Ethan's attention was drawn to the magnificent formations all around the Sauna Room. In addition to the red drapery formation, the far end of the cave had beautiful green splattermite formations: stalagmites that had formed in big leaping droplets that were frozen now in the midst of their action.

And behind them, where the top of the cavern sloped to meet its floor, the roof was covered with brilliant, sparkling white popcorn formations.

Ethan wandered over toward them, inspecting their glistening surfaces. Short and blunt, the bulbs of calcite stuck out along the ceiling and covered the back sides of several of the stalactites and stalagmites. It was beautiful. He followed it up the cave ceiling. About halfway across the room it tapered down to a few knobby protrusions and then stopped altogether. He shone the light along the edge of it. Then something else caught his attention.

But it wasn't possible. Ethan couldn't be seeing what he thought he was seeing. At the top of the cavern, at the very limit of his light, carved into the stone wall, were the curves and cusps of Xardn symbols.

He scrambled closer to them, extending his arm above him to get the best view he could. Xardn, the dead alien language he had spent his life studying, was beautiful wherever it was found, but here, carved into the smooth stone, with the light glancing off the crystalline formations around it, it was especially so.

Ethan squinted, trying to translate. Something was off. Never mind that they were nowhere near the Circinus galaxy and that no record of Xardn-speaking populations existed here on Minea, and never mind that they were hundreds of feet into a cavern where no one should ever have been, there was something wrong with the Xardn sentence he was looking at. There was a symbol he didn't recognize, and the arrangement of the symbols was wrong. As it came to him, he shook his head in disbelief. Ikastn. It was in Ikastn.

Ikastn was a slightly altered form of Xardn. It had been used in the Circinus Galaxy, perhaps still was used, but Ethan had never heard of a modern population of Ikastn speakers.

The real puzzle was what it was doing scratched into the soft limestone of a cave this far from the Circinus Galaxy. And it looked freshly carved. The symbols stood out in pale relief. They weren't worn, as they would have been if the cave's winds and water had scrubbed them for centuries. Someone had been here. Recently.

Ethan swung the light around the room, streaking it across the barren walls. He had felt the breeze so strongly in the tiny tunnel. It had to be coming from this room. He ran the light across the ceiling, fearing a tiny impassable hole like they'd found in the crystal room, but saw nothing. The popcorn caught his attention again and he moved the beam along its sparkling surface, then down where it grew on the backs of the columns.

The backs of the columns. Why didn't the popcorn formations grow uniformly around the column? Could it be like moss on the trees in the forest outside the cottage? The mosses liked the shadiest side of a tree, often the North side, but always the side where evaporation was the slowest.

But here, in the cave, it stood to reason that if the popcorn was growing on one side and not the other, there had to be some difference in the rate of evaporation. The popcorn would grow where the evaporation was quicker. The side where wind dried the stone more quickly. He carefully stepped between the stalagmites and slipped to the back wall of the chamber, where a jagged crack gaped open in the wall behind a huge column. It was easily a meter and a half wide. Ethan flicked the light up. The crevice ran about three meters up, but it grew more narrow as it ran, and at the top looked no wider than a hand's width.

The cool breeze blew out of it onto Ethan's face. He hadn't realized exactly how hot the sauna room was. He shone his light down the corridor, trying to determine if it closed off in a dead end or constricted into another tight squeeze. It appeared to be a uniformly wide crack, and though he couldn't see the end, he felt the breeze distinctly. There must be an outlet. He walked back to the group and told them about it.

"We should stay a bit longer," Traore said guardedly. It was good to hear him speak.

Brynn took his hand, as she had been doing lately, and Ethan saw her look into his eyes. "We have to go sometime, Traore. We have to find our way out."

Traore's gaze dropped down to their clasped hands. His shoulders slumped a bit more. "What if there is no way out? What if we all die down here?"

The room filled with a barren silence. It was the fear that crept around the edges of their minds all the time, ever since they had found themselves in the wrecked ship at the bottom of the shaft. Though no one had said it aloud, they all knew it was a possibility—maybe even a probability. Now, hearing it spoken and feeling the press of the cave all around them, the fear pushed its way to the forefront of their consciousness and hung there in the midst of them, heavy and terrible.

They could not bring themselves to leave the warmth of the cave, could not bring themselves to force Traore out into the cold darkness again. And so they stayed. Another night. Two.

*** 

When Ethan awoke after their third night in the Sauna, his mouth was dry, his cheeks burning, his lips cracking uncomfortably. He was out of water, had been for several hours, and so were the rest of them. They had rationed food, but here in this constantly dripping, weeping, damp place, none of them had thought to limit their water.

It had been over a week since they had filled their water bags in Crystal Springs. The baking heat of the Sauna Room, so welcome when they first came from the chill of the cave, had dehydrated them quickly, and they had awakened from their last sleep parched.

"We need to go," Ethan said, gathering their packs and handing them their discarded coveralls. "We have to find water."

Ndaiye looked up at him. His lips were cracked and Ethan longed to give him a drink. He looked through his pack. No water and precious little food. A single nutrition bar, and maybe two more among the group. The situation was getting more and more desperate.

When he had them all on their feet, he tried to tempt them into the passage. "The cool air feels great in here!" he said with enthusiasm.

Brynn, who had picked up some of Traore's discouragement, replied, "It will be great until we're all freezing again."

Ethan walked on, the truth in her words gnawing at him.

***

Ethan had been gone for over two weeks. Kaia found herself staring out the window aimlessly more often now. She couldn't seem to find the energy to work on bots for the kids, visit the junkyard, or visit her passengers. The last few days all she could manage was losing herself in the battleship manuals the Admiral had brought home for her. Even though she'd been reading them for six months and there was nothing new in them, they were a good distraction and she found that she couldn't put them down.

Ethan couldn't be gone. Not so quickly, without a chance to say goodbye. Not the man she'd mourned for half a century. She looked up from the manual to see a military hovercar pull up. Why would they be coming when her father was in Lumina?

"They do know he's not here, right?" she asked out loud.

But they weren't there, as they usually were, to collect her father. Her missive jingled and the voice on the other end of the line was Admiral Reagan.

"Kaia. We've got an alien situation. I need you in Lumina." His voice was tight with worry.

"I'm coming," she said, and even as her breath came quick with fear of the aliens, she was relieved to have something to distract her from Ethan's disappearance.

# Chapter 20

Aria had spent so many days in the mountains that she had lost her fear of them. They were not, as she had first seen them, waiting to snatch her and her children along with Ethan. They were solid and strong, safe even, compared to the crush of people in the city, so many of whom were ill. And the people were so indifferent to Ethan's loss. At least the peaks seemed to echo her loneliness. She still went out, poling Luis's sleek little boat down the river, and then hiking, sometimes wandering for hours over the landscape looking for a clue about where he'd gone.

She was especially drawn to a section of the river that had a broad, stony bank. In many places, the trees and thick grasses came right to the edge of the river, spilling into the water and blocking hope of passage. But in this section, far beyond the petrified Taim grove, the forest was welcoming. The peaks around it yawned with arches, grottos, caves, and cavities carved by eons of water. Hank had directed her to it as a good place to look. He had a crop of kwai fruit growing nearby and sometimes she saw him as she pulled the boat onto the shore and set off into the forest.

She worried because the children were beginning to show signs of anxiety having both she and Ethan away from them.

Even Kaia was unavailable, staying in the barracks at the base in Lumina, helping her father figure out the alien situation. So Aria took the children with her into the mountains sometimes, and sometimes she took them to their school, and as the days passed and there was no sign of Ethan, sometimes she stayed home playing with them and comforting them in their grief at his loss. She only cried once they were asleep.

She met with her friends from Ship 12-22 often, bringing them fruits and gathering their trade items. Hannah, a skilled doll maker, was one of her favorite people to visit. Today she stopped and offered Hannah a basket of berries.

Hannah handed her two standard dolls, which she tucked into her pack.

"I have something else," Hannah said, "for your friends, you know, with the little girls." Hannah retrieved from a cabinet in her cottage another doll. "Polara told me she gave one of them her doll, so I gave her one just like this when she was here with Kaia the other day. But she said there was another little girl there, in the tenements, so I thought you could give her this."

Aria took the doll carefully from its creator. It was exquisitely made, with delicately stitched hands and a sweetly painted face. Its long dark hair was soft as down, and Aria knew that Daniel's little sister Nallie would love it.

"You are an absolute artisan," she told Hannah. "This is beautiful."

"I wish you could convince the Market District here in the city." Hannah scoffed. "Since your woodsie friends are liking them so much, I took them around to every shop in Coriol and not one will carry them."

"Maybe you should open a little toy shop of your own."

"Saras would never give me any shop space, and he owns it all. Anyway, there's fines for people taking Saras scrip without paying the fee to Saras, and paying the fee to accept it cuts out any profits. A few people come here and they do pay me in scrip, but if he finds out I'm selling them, the fines will be more than I could make on dolls in a lifetime in Coriol. "

"The company town isn't as wonderful as it sounds on paper," Aria agreed.

Hannah went on. "And it's not just that. Saras could make lots of scrip if he'd open up a toy store himself, but he won't ever do it." She lowered her voice conspiratorially. "There's a reason there are no toy stores in Coriol," Hannah said. "Saras doesn't want children playing with toys. Toys won't help get Ynium out of the ground. Toys won't prepare children to be miners and managers of miners. Saras doesn't want any distractions from his main objective."

Aria shook her head. Though Hannah sounded a little extreme, Aria suspected she was right. The few toys Polara and Rigel had came from their friends from the Ship 12-22: the dolls from Hannah, the beautiful wooden animals and finely carved blocks from Winn the carpenter, and the tiny play dishes from Luis. The only things in the Market District made for children were clothes and occasionally books.

Every decision Saras made seemed to tie back to his lust for Ynium. Saras was ruled by Ynium, and Coriol was ruled by Saras.

She hugged Hannah before she left. "I'll take this to Nallie right now," she said. "She's going to love it."

As she rode across town, she looked forward to handing the doll to Nallie. She'd brought berries for them, too.

But when little Merelda opened the door, Aria forgot about the doll in her hands and the anticipation of giving it to Nallie. The child's eyes were red and swollen, as if she'd been crying for days.

Aria leaned down. "What is it?" she asked, gathering the weeping child into her arms. "Merelda, what's wrong?"

Merelda buried her head in Aria's shoulder and spoke in a voice twisted with grief. The single word was muffled, but Aria would have recognized it anywhere. "Mama."

\*\*\*

Aria had never attended a funeral on Coriol. This one was short, held in the evening so that people could get back to their apartments and get some sleep before work tomorrow.

The little all-purpose church was full of Marise's neighbors and other workers at the mine. Reverend Hardy said a few words. There was a song, slow and sad, in Marise's native language, and a dedication of some sort before they took the body away.

Aria looked across at the somber, blank face of the boy she'd helped weeks ago. Daniel was stoic, unnaturally still. He turned his hollow face toward Aria and the emptiness there pulled the air from her lungs.

She glanced away, looking at the mourners as they filed past her on their way home. It was then that she realized how many of them had the flowering purple bruises. Aria involuntarily covered her mouth. As soon as Daniel and his sisters left the church to follow the body, Aria fled, running until she could hold her breath no longer. Standing on the sidewalk, she sucked in great gasping breaths of the fresh air.

# Chapter 21

Brynn had been right. The cold was beginning to seep back into them, maybe even worse for the time they'd spent warm. They'd left the Sauna hours ago, traveling a branching, winding tunnel that required the use of the marking rock. The passage was not wide, but after the Python Pass, Ethan felt he could stand anything as long as he could stretch out his arms. There was little conversation as they tried passage after passage, their thirst growing more and more desperate with each passing hour.

Ethan heard a thud and a scrape. When he turned, Maggie was on the floor. Brynn stepped close to her, but Maggie pushed her away. Ethan went and lifted the captain, his lips splitting as he tried to smile encouragement to her.

"I'm thirsty," she said blearily.

"I know. We'll find something soon." They walked on.

Finally, as they rounded a corner, they saw a sheen on the dead end in front of them. The wall was weeping.

"Water!" Ethan croaked. He set Maggie against the wall and fell against it himself, pressing his mouth to the rough stone. But it was a trickle, and as he scraped his tongue painfully against the wall, he came away with only the barest drops. Frustrated, he stepped back. Pity swelled in him as he saw them all, the rest of his crew, trying to pull life-sustaining water from the stone.

It was then that Ethan saw one more end for them in this labyrinth. If they didn't fall down a shaft or get crushed by a rockslide, if the krech didn't get them and they didn't get trapped, they would survive just to die anyway. They would survive all those horrors just to die of thirst or starvation.

He walked away, unable to watch them. There wasn't enough water there for a Xyxos, much less a person.

As if on cue, a pink flash caught Ethan's attention. It was a Xyxos, darting out nearly to his feet and then back to the edge of the wall. It happened too fast for Ethan to see it clearly, but his attention was diverted by something far more exciting. The Xyxos left little wet footprints, surrounded by puddles, as if it were dripping wet. For it to get that wet there must be a pool around here somewhere.

Ethan called to the others and kept his eyes on the little creature as it scurried along the passageway behind them. Another, dripping Xyxos joined it, and then another. As the crew came up beside him, Ethan helped Ndaiye with Maggie.

They followed the herd of little pink Xyxos. When a split came, the Xyxos seemed to know just which direction to take. Ethan peered ahead of them. What if they were simply getting more and more lost? What if the Xyxos led them to a dead end?

But wasn't that what he had just figured out? That everything down here was a dead end, in one way or another? He let the darkness of the thought play in his mind a moment until a flash of white caught his attention.

Ethan peered ahead of them. At the edge of the light he thought he saw someone. A tall figure slipping around the edge of the next column. But when they arrived at the column, an empty space greeted them. He glanced around. Had anyone else seen it?

He felt something crunch under his boot. At the risk of losing the Xyxos, he paused to pick it up and look at it. It was, impossibly, a chei seed, like the ones Aria had been drying at home. How could it be down here? Excitement choked him as he thought that perhaps they were nearing an exit. More seeds crunched under his boots. Perhaps the Xyxos were dropping them as they ran.

Shining the light ahead of the little herd of Xyxos, Ethan felt a stabbing apprehension as he saw a row of shining seeds stretching before them. The Xyxos weren't dropping the seeds. They were following a trail of them. They weren't leading the survey crew, they were being led themselves.

Ethan stopped abruptly. "Wait," he called to the others. They stopped, nervously glancing ahead as the Xyxos moved into the dark without them. "This may not be safe." Ethan said. "Maybe we shouldn't follow them. I think someone is baiting them, and we could be walking right into a—"

"Hush!" Maggie interrupted him. "Look!"

"But—" Ethan began, but then he saw what she was pointing at. They all saw it.

It couldn't be what they thought it was, what they hoped it was. Ndaiye pulled away and broke into a run. Ethan called after him to be careful, his mouth dry and his voice cracking.

They all ran, more quickly than was prudent, toward the place where their feeble light bounced back to them from the shining reflection of water. A vast underground lake stretched in an enormous cavern. They stumbled to their knees and bellies beside the flat, wide mirror of water that caught the shadowy image of the stalactites on the ceiling and held it in perfect stillness before them.

Ndaiye drank first, his noisy slurping bouncing off the

rocks and his hands, plunging in and lifting the water to his mouth, causing furious ripples across the surface of the lake.

For several minutes, they said nothing, simply drank and dipped their hands and faces in the water, until their cheeks were red with the cold and their fingers came away numb. Ethan didn't think there was anything better than the taste of that cold mineral water. He looked around at the slopes around the lake, covered with slowly flowing, seeping water, drips and streams flowing from small crevasses in the rock, constantly filling the lake. The shimmering water shone back at him and he silently thanked the Xyxos and whoever or whatever had led them here.

Looking down through the clear water, he saw opalescent cave fish pushing lazily along the rock bottom. He glanced over to see Maggie watching them, too. She pulled the cover off her pack. Seconds later she scooped it through the water and pulled it up. In it was a wriggling cave fish, which she grabbed by the tail.

Ethan heard a smack as she knocked it against the rock. It lay limp in her hand and he watched as she put it to her mouth and gingerly pulled the white flesh off the bones with her teeth.

After weeks of limited fare, Ethan shouldn't have been surprised at how delicious the fish looked, but he was. Maggie slurped and peeled and he found himself nearly crazy to get one for himself.

Ethan wasn't the only one. "How did you do that?" Brynn asked, scooting close to where Maggie was feasting.

Maggie scooted away. "Easy," she said between bites. "Just scoop 'em. They're blind. They can't see you coming." Ethan thought her purposeful gaze lingered on Brynn a little longer than necessary, but he forgot about it as he plunged his own makeshift net into the icy water, coming up with a wriggling fish.

The others netted fish, too. Traore accumulated a great pile of them before he started eating. It was a real feast.

Ethan took a bite, trying to pull the skin and flesh off the bone like Maggie had. Even when a sharp, flexible bone poked the inside of his cheek, Ethan hardly slowed. The fish was rich and tender, with the sweetness of meat he barely remembered.

When their hunger was curbed, their thirst was slaked, and their water bags were full again, the crew began to skirt the lake, looking for another passage. It was enormous, and the cavern sometimes closed on it, looking like a dead end. But Brynn slipped through and found, every time, another cavern on the other side of the wall, where the lake continued.

After several of these rooms, Ethan heard an unusual sound. The laughter of running water filled the cave ahead. It took him back to the day this nightmare started, when he'd pushed through the vines seeking solitude. Now, he stayed close to his crew as they moved together towards it.

Traore passed Brynn and slipped around a wall of stone in the direction of the sound. The rest of the crew followed, finding themselves in a small chamber where the water churned through the opening in the wall. Shining their weak lights across the tumbling water, they saw a chute where the cave floor dropped away and the water fell, bright and powerful, out of their view. Ethan, at the rear of the group, was suddenly aware of the damp, slick rock beneath his boots. The seeping water made it slippery and he backed away, images of Python Pass in his mind. What if this led to a funnel, or a flooded chamber where there was no air? He placed a hand on Ndaiye's arm and opened his mouth to offer a warning.

But before he could speak, Traore's arms arched up in a terrible windmill and Ethan saw him slip, falling into the rushing water.

Ndaiye cried out and Maggie clung to him as he tried to get nearer the water. His cousin was gone, down the nearly vertical chute.

"No!" Ethan leaned forward, peering into the gorge. He saw nothing but water and darkness.

And then he heard Traore's voice, small amid the thundering falls.

"Come on!" Traore shouted. "It's safe!"

They all heard him.

"We have to go," Ndaiye said, immediately stripping off his coveralls and outer clothes and stuffing them into his pack, then pulling the waterproof cover over it and securing it. "There's no way to get him back up here, and I'm not leaving him alone down here." The others watched, undecided, while Ndaiye yelled, "Here's my pack!" and tossed it into the torrent.

A second later, Traore called, "Got it!"

Ndaiye sat carefully on the slippery side of the river and launched himself into the swirling water. He slid upright for a moment before disappearing down the hole, calling, "Whoooo!" as if he were at an amusement park.

Ethan saw that there wasn't another choice, unless they wanted to split up. Maggie went next, then Brynn. Ethan's own trip down the chute was surprisingly pleasant, except for the freezing water. Soon they were all on the bank several meters downstream from the chute, trying to dry as quickly as possible and pulling on their clothes with badly shivering hands.

Traore had a new look about him. "That was some ride!" he said, catching Ethan's eye. "I'm glad to be alive!"

"S-some ride." Ethan stuttered, his jaw convulsing as he tried to speak.

"Huddle up!" Maggie commanded. Brynn stepped close

to the older woman, but Maggie hobbled away from her, gathering the rest of them closer and ending up on the other side of the circle from Brynn. Ethan thought Maggie could at least show the girl a little affection. They'd been down here together long enough, been through enough together, that they owed each other something. He threw an arm around Brynn and, on his other side, Ndaiye. The group stood, trying to minimize contact with the cold ground, and talked about the ride down the chute.

Ten minutes later they were no warmer. Ethan knew the dangers of hypothermia. He'd read a lot about it on Ship 12-22, when he was surrounded by the vast, cold vacuum of space. "We have to light a heat brick," he said.

"Not here," Maggie challenged, her teeth chattering so much that Ethan had a hard time understanding her. "We need to see if there's somewhere with a higher ceiling. We'll suffocate if we light it here."

"I can't go much farther," Brynn said pleadingly.

"You'll go as far as you have to," Maggie snapped.

Ethan pulled away from the group, striding down the nearest passageway. It was wide and dark and he sensed it might open up.

When it did, it took his breath away. A cavern covered in sparkling white flowstone arched before him. It was beautiful, a stone cathedral. There was a calm feeling there, a safe and holy feeling.

He shone the light up, but couldn't see the ceiling. He shouted, and though his voice was weak and thready from the cold, he could tell by the reverberation that the room was enormous. Working quickly, he pulled two heat bricks out of his pack with stiff fingers and lit them before going to retrieve the others.

When they all returned, the bricks were glowing cheerfully. Ethan felt the heat reach him as he left the passage. Brynn rushed to the glowing bricks, leaning over them, seemingly oblivious to the smoke billowing up. He was afraid she might climb on top of them. Traore took her shoulders gently and pulled her back, guiding her to sit on the ground near the bricks and stretch her hands toward the heat.

The others came close and huddled around the heat bricks. The ceiling was high and Ethan fanned the smoke up and away from them into the unseen heights of the cavern. Ethan gradually felt the worst of the chill leave him and looked to see the others trembling less as well. He had not reckoned on how the icy water would draw the heat from their bodies, and how difficult it would be to replace. Sitting around the bricks, willing warmth back into his body, the dehydration of the last few days seemed a small price to pay for the radiant heat of the Sauna Room.

"We should also keep moving," Ethan said, standing and swinging his arms back and forth. "That will help keep the blood circulating." He walked in a wide circle, trying not to think about the fact that these heat bricks were their last. Ndaiye stood and walked, too.

"Hey Ethan, look over here! Isn't this an alien language?"

Ethan gazed at the undulating white wall where his friend was pointing. There, dancing across the curves, were more Ikastn symbols. Not just a few more, either. As they walked around the white chamber, they found the symbols etched into nearly every surface. Soon, the whole team was inspecting the cavern.

The symbols were large and small, some simply scratched into the bare rock, some scratched and then painted over with color. Huge epitrochoids arched above them, and smaller ones nestled inside the curves of the larger ones. Around the room, in dizzying variety, were the words of an alien race.

"What do they say, Ethan?" Ndaiye asked with awe in his voice.

Ethan was struggling to decipher them. It was one thing to translate when he had a computer, or even texts to assist him. It was another to try to guess at meaning with unfamiliar syntax and little context.

But one symbol he knew. One symbol seemed to repeat itself over and over.

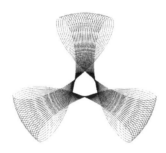

Monster.

Ethan tried desperately to determine the context, reaching into his memory for anything he could remember about Ikastn syntax and pronouns. There were words he recognized: *children, sleep, danger*, but it was like trying to put together the shards of a broken jar. Just when he thought he had two pieces working together, then next slipped out of his hand and broke into two more.

"What's this one?" Ndaiye asked, tracing the delicate lines of the most repeated word.

Ethan bit back the word. Words had power, he knew, and saying *monster* in a place like this, as the light faded and the days grew more desperate, would only introduce an unnecessary fear. He redirected them to the more neutral symbol near his elbow:

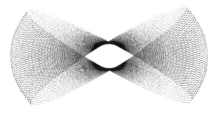

"This one is sleep. I'm not sure what the rest mean. It's a language that came from Xardn, so I can translate some of it, but other words and other rules have been incorporated into it, and I don't know all of them."

He dug in his pack for his missive, hoping it still had enough juice to turn on. He'd been saving its batteries so he could use it as a last-resort light source if necessary, but he needed to capture these symbols. If he did get out of here, he could work to decipher them.

The missive glowed when he switched it on, and he breathed a sigh of relief. Working quickly, he snapped photos of all the symbols that he could adequately illuminate.

"Brynn, stand there so I can see the scale of these," he asked as he pointed the missive at a particularly massive wall of glyphs. "Ndaiye, stand by that one."

The missive's *critical low battery* warning was blinking as he snapped the last few shots. Its screen went dark. Ethan tried not to debate in his mind whether capturing the symbols had been worth wasting the last of the missive's light as he slid it back into the protected pocket in his pack. At least he'd have somewhere to start when he got home. The ever-present echo teased his mind: *If* he got home.

"Who made these?" Maggie asked directly. "Some life form from here on Minea?"

Ethan shrugged. "It's unlikely that they came from here

originally. It's too far from the Circinus Galaxy. And when humans first came to Minea, there were no life forms sufficiently developed to have this kind of language complexity, so I suspect that whoever it is, they've come recently."

Ndaiye was quiet. "I've seen 'em," he said softly.

"What?" Maggie barked.

"I've seen them," he enunciated. "The ghosts at the lake in the mornings."

Ethan remembered standing at the edge of the lake with Ndaiye, a lifetime ago, remembered the man's stories about the ghosts that came just before dawn. Could they be the same beings that made these engravings?

Ethan started to speak up as well, started to say that he'd seen someone at Shark's Mouth and Crystal Springs and that he suspected someone was leading the Xyxos, but the way the figures had simply disappeared and the way that the dark played tricks on them down here made him quiet. He wasn't sure he'd seen anything, and there was no need to add to the growing disquiet he was feeling among them. He had the photos. If he got out, he would decipher what they had to say, and perhaps that would tell him more about who they were and what they were doing on Minea.

***

As the ship descended Galo began to glimpse the planet below. There were huge mountains to the Northeast and broad, flat plains to the west.

The settlement below him lay on the plain, curled in a circle where the tall grasses had been cleared and the land terraformed. Galo cruised slowly over the settlement, then turned the big ship and glided past the settlement again. The scanner's constant low hum grated on him.

He found himself pleasantly intrigued by the settlement. This appeared to be some sort of mining city. He could tell by the extensive infrastructure and the great efforts that were being undertaken that they were obviously producing something of value. To Galo, there were two kinds of beings: customers and potential customers. It occurred to him that perhaps these humans might need a shipper for whatever they were mining. He had the sudden worry that his ship, squat and dark, with its exhaust burning red behind it, might seem ominous and threatening to them. In port cities, where ships came and went all the time, his barges didn't concern anyone, but here it seemed that there were no other beings besides these humans. They wouldn't be accustomed to seeing other crafts and might be more easily frightened than others.

If they had stolen his Vala, then keeping them as customers was unimportant. But if he was misunderstanding what had happened, and this race had nothing to do with the Vala's disappearance, then Galo didn't want to lose their business. He would need to open communications with them and further assess the situation. He engaged his translator.

The Asgre dealt on a constant basis with beings from other worlds and he prided himself on their translator, which gave him the ability to speak to nearly anyone. Though the equipment took up an entire room in each ship, he was thrilled with how the translator worked and how well it worked. When it was engaged, it scanned the area around the target race, which was sometimes just a single ship but in this case was the whole planet, for all communication, written and verbal. Even real-time conversations were scanned and processed, resulting in the translator's nearly perfect knowledge of the language. It took some time, but when the screen lit up showing that the translator was done scanning and processing and was online and operational, he could speak to almost anyone he encountered.

The translator began scanning the communications of the planet and he felt a chill of anticipation as he waited for it to be operational. It began a countdown on the upper edge of the screen. The translator would not be ready for hours. That was longer than Galo wanted to wait. But there was no rushing the technology. To distract himself, he focused on the scanner, still humming, and checked the communications lines. He was surprised to find one switched off.

Switching it back on, he remembered why he'd disabled it. The ship filled with an irritating buzz. It was more frequent now, more urgent. They must be closer to the magnetic field that Uumbor had mentioned. Galo switched it off again, basking in the cessation of the maddening sound.

The city, from above, looked as crosshatched as the moon that orbited Ondyne II, the Asgre home world. Only these striations didn't come from fault lines, they came from the humans' planned streets and buildings. The humans he saw far below were bipedal and bimanual. Galo shook his head. How did creatures function with only two hands?

He noticed two ships rising into the air from what appeared to be a defensive base at the edge of the city. Galo readied basic defenses, just in case. He checked the translator, though he knew it would not be online yet, and he could not yet announce his reason for coming to their city.

Glowing on his screen was the map of the eight human settlements. Galo traced a route up and over the large mountains as he planned the order in which he would scan the cities, ending at the last, an outlying city near the other mountains to the northeast. He would not rush, though. Each city must be thoroughly scanned for Vala life signs and the Vala trail. He could not afford to miss any clue as to their whereabouts.

# Chapter 22

Ethan saw a new weariness in the little group when they left the Flowstone Room. They had staved off hypothermia, but never really warmed up to the point they'd been before the chute. They had eaten their last nutrition bar, split five ways, and the knowledge that the food was gone made Ethan feel more desperate than he had before.

Aided by Kaia's cells, the Instasplint, and the Sprayshield, Maggie was walking better, keeping her balance better, and still barking orders at every turn, but Ethan could see by the weariness in her eyes that even she was almost out of determination.

The arched opening that they chose out of the Flowstone Room led them to a small, narrow passage. Going in first, Ethan found a tangled passageway that curved and looped and ran back and forth in jagged lines for an exhausting distance through the cave. As his shoulder scraped the side, he noticed that the walls in this section didn't catch his coveralls with the same rough scraping as the walls in the rest of the cave. When he shone his one shoulder light onto the walls, he was amazed to see that like opaque orange glass, the smooth walls reflected his light and his image back at him. The passageway was pure Yynium. The crew made their way, single file, through the long winding tunnel, glowing in the reflected light.

When the tunnel opened out, Ethan stopped short. He found himself standing at the brink of a precipice. A narrow ledge led off to his right, up into the dark.

He turned to the others. "Should we go back?" he asked.

They came out of the tangles one by one and lined up on the edge of the yawning chasm. The two remaining shoulder lights penetrated only far enough to see how the rock fell away beneath their feet and left a vast nothingness stretching in front of them.

"Hello!" Ndaiye called. There was, for the first time in weeks, no echo. The emptiness and dark contrasted with the closeness and light of the tangles made Ethan's head spin. He sat down on the ledge and leaned back against the orange Yynium deposit. It felt solid and cool and firm at his back, comforting somehow.

Brynn sat down next to him, gazing fearfully up the little ledge that led up and away.

Traore and Ndaiye started up the path. "I don't want to go back," Ndaiye said. "I want to see where this takes us."

Ethan admired their adventurous spirit. Part of him wanted to go back to the sparkling Flowstone Room and stay in its sanctuary forever. But Maggie was already shuffling after the cousins, and Ethan jumped up to steady her. One wrong step and this could be the last of Maggie.

Brynn followed, if somewhat reluctantly. Ethan watched every step he took. When his foot struck a rock and sent it falling silently into the abyss, he started humming to keep himself occupied.

Suddenly, the cousins' voices filled the air. They were furiously excited about something, and when Ethan reached the top of the sloping ledge, he saw what it was: stars. Reaching in front of them, on the other side of the wide chasm, was an arched opening filled with the night sky.

\*\*\*

Aria didn't see Daniel again for days, even though she made the trek to G building several times. Most often, she found no one home. Once the two little girls answered her knock by calling through the door, but they were home alone and not supposed to open it. She left the fruits outside the door, hoping that they got them.

Finally, when she'd given up on seeing him again, Aria was standing in line to buy the last few pathetic apples and zilen, the squash of Minea. She looked up and saw, through the window, Daniel approaching the market. Before he reached the main front door, though, the young man turned. Aria paid for her purchases quickly and rushed to peer down the alley beside the market. Daniel was emerging into the alley from a back door to the market, a chain heavy with scrip dangling from his hand. He saw Aria on the sidewalk. Daniel ducked his head and looked away before he turned and walked quickly in the opposite direction. When Aria reached the alleyway, Gaynes was standing there, holding a small silver box and smiling smugly. He glanced up, saw her there, and glared, turning and entering a back door into his market.

\*\*\*

Aria wanted to know what Gaynes had been up to. Somehow, he'd gotten to Daniel, and with Marise gone, someone had to watch out for the boy. She thought of an excuse as she strode to the registers.

"I want to see Gaynes," Aria demanded. "You can't sell this produce. It's obviously contaminated." She raised her voice on the last word, just loud enough to make the shoppers near her shift uncomfortably. One woman glanced their direction, then set her basket down and left the store.

The clerk noticed the woman's departure and looked nervously at Aria. She gazed into his eyes, challenging him to deny her request. Though she'd told herself she wouldn't use it again, she flashed the Colony Offices badge out of her pocket just a little.

"Okay," the clerk said, his fear of the Colony Offices warring with his fear of Gaynes. "Come on back." He unbolted the door next to his register and re-barred it after she was through. He led her to Gaynes's empty office, where a broad desk was topped only with a decanter of brown liquid and a glass half full of the same stuff.

The little plants grew up near the ceiling. Aria noted their size. They had been scrubbed away earlier this week and these were fairly new seedlings. She glanced out Gaynes's barred window to the alley. The door next to it must have been the one Gaynes entered from the alley.

"Just, just sit here," the clerk said, indicating a dark, slick chair in front of the desk, "and I'll find him for you." He turned nervously before he left. "Don't touch anything," he said, trying to sound authoritative.

Aria watched him close the door and heard him walk back along the long hallway they'd come down. Well, she was here. She went over what she'd tell Gaynes. The produce was contaminated. People were getting sick. He'd better stop selling it or—or what? Aria was at a loss. Saras's Food Production Division, who was supposed to enforce the food safety rules, was shipping out the shriveled apples and the blighted rangkors.

As she thought about what she'd say to him, Aria's gaze fell on a glass-fronted cabinet behind Gaynes's desk. Inside, behind a large sculpture of a scrip, she could see the edge of the small silver box.

Something made her feel bold. Maybe it was her knowledge that Gaynes was underhanded and shady and didn't deserve the privacy she would have afforded anyone else. Maybe it was her curiosity about what would make Daniel avoid her like he had. What was he involved in? Whatever it was, she slipped behind the desk and retrieved the box. Setting it softly on the desk, Aria glanced nervously at the door. It was still closed. She flipped the little clasps on the box and opened it carefully.

Inside was a small silver object, tapered at one end. There were two more depressions in the lining of the box, shaped exactly to fit two more of these little missile-shaped objects, but they were empty. Whatever they were, this was the only one left. She lifted it out, weighing it in her hand, and turned it over.

Aria heard Gaynes's voice outside in the hallway. Startled, she dropped the little object. It bounced off across the rug. She snapped the box closed and stuck it hurriedly back where she'd found it, closing the cabinet and moving back around the desk. She saw the little silver object on the floor and leaned to scoop it up, then dropped into the chair just as she heard the door open.

Gaynes looked patently annoyed when he saw her. He walked around his desk and sat heavily in the big chair on the other side. "You're not from the Colony Offices."

Aria thought fast. "I never said I was." Then she launched into the offense, standing up and feigning bravery. "You're making people sick, Mr. Gaynes. You have to stop selling these blighted fruits and vegetables."

Gaynes's eyes narrowed as he looked up at her. "I don't force anyone to buy my stuff, lady. Who are you, anyway?"

Aria deflected the question. "Have you seen the people

with the flower bruises, Mr. Gaynes?"

"Get out."

"Are you going to stop?"

"I'm going to call the security force, is what I'm going to do. Get out."

Aria could see he wasn't going to change anything, and as she looked past him she noticed that she hadn't put the silver box all the way behind the scrip statue. It had obviously been moved. She didn't want to know what he'd do if he found she'd been poking through his office while he was away. His heavy hands on top of the desk looked as if he could crack a chunk of Yynium with them, just by squeezing it.

"I'll go, Mr. Gaynes, but think about the stuff you're selling. It's dangerous." Aria spun and walked out the door, forcing herself not to look back down the long hallway towards him. She let herself out the door by the register and controlled her steps, feeling her heart hammering progressively faster until she sank into a cab and gave the driver her address. When she did glance back toward the market, Gaynes was watching her from the window, a puzzled expression on his face.

# Chapter 23

Kaia stood beside her father in front of the Lumina Defense Headquarters, watching as the alien ship moved slowly, methodically, over the circular city, from one side to the other. It cruised, darkening the buildings and people below with its shadow. Kaia felt a surge of apprehension as the Others of Beta Alora flashed through her mind.

But there had, so far, been no aggression other than the disabling of the orbital defenses, and her father said they weren't sure if that was even intentional. The ship just cruised.

Lumina's two company ships were airborne, flying a grid pattern high above the alien ship in case of trouble. Kaia watched the late afternoon sun glancing off them and wondered how much good they would do against the massive alien vessel. She wondered what chance any of their defenses had. Reagan had all the ground troops on alert in all of Minea's settlements, and the battleships stood ready to come to Lumina if needed, but what kind of weapons these aliens had was still mostly a mystery.

Reagan interrupted her thoughts, "What did you do to defend against the Others?"

Kaia thought for a long moment. "We were mostly on the offensive," she said, "trying to make it to the statehouse. But the few times we came up against them face-to-face, I think Ethan mostly tried to strike first. That was the only moment he had an advantage."

Reagan nodded, his eyes clouded with thought. One of the Orbital Defense officers approached.

"Sir, some more information." The man handed Reagan a handheld screen and Kaia saw her father's jaw set.

"What is it?"

Reagan flipped the screen around for her to see. Above their planet, waiting in orbit, were eight more of alien ships. Kaia saw the pieces began to come together in Reagan's mind. He spoke aloud. "This scouting ship, the fleet waiting for an order to move in, this has all the earmarks of an invasion." He straightened his shoulders. The admiral was not about to let that happen.

A chill ran through Kaia. "Why don't we bring all the battleships here?" she asked, wanting as much firepower as possible.

Reagan glanced at the soldiers milling around and gestured her inside the headquarters building. They walked the long hallway to his temporary office. Inside, a screen on his desk was showing the same feed the OD officer had shown him. On it the alien ships hung like spiders against the blackness of space.

Kaia saw her father run a hand across his forehead. He always did that when he was agitated.

"If this is an invasion, and I'm not saying it is, this ship may be a decoy to lure all our defenses down here to the farthest corner of the settlements." He paced, and Kaia pictured the eight settlements, laid out almost like an X across plains and mountains. Reagan continued, "We need battleships in each settlement, in case the other ships make a move. Reagan looked into her eyes.

"We're going to need to revise our defense plan," he said.

\*\*\*

The two small ships that had risen from the base continued to standby for the next several hours as Galo scanned the city. He scanned as close as he dared to, afraid of pushing the defense ships to aggression. But the Vala were not here and had not been here. Though the realization was bitter in his mind, he felt they must be somewhere in these settlements and was eager to move on and attempt to locate them in the next one.

He pulled the Cliprig up and away from the circular city and set a course for the next settlement on his map. Halfway there the translator came online and told him the name of the next city was Oculys. It lay nestled in the foot of the massive folded mountains he saw in the distance, and he watched them grow larger and larger as he approached. At the city's edge, he engaged the translator and opened a communications frequency.

"Humans of—" What was this city's strange name again? He looked at his screen. "Humans of Oculys," he said, using his most convincing voice, "I am Galo of the Asgre, and I have come to retrieve my property."

Galo waited, but no answer came on his comms lines. He was disappointed. He had been looking forward to conversing with them and learning what they knew of his slaves. He wondered if they were just impolitely ignoring him or if they were afraid to respond. Nevertheless, he began his scans of this city, and then of the surrounding mountains. He found nothing, but there were six more settlements, and Galo would visit each one until he found the Vala.

# Chapter 24

Ethan's spinning head was filled with the sounds of the survey crew's cheering. He joined them, hearing his own hoarse voice falling out into the warm night air. Perching in single file on the ridge, the little group sat watching their first glimpse of the outdoors in weeks. Even Brynn's announcement that her shoulder light, one of two that remained, was dead, didn't dampen their spirits. They still had Ndaiye's shoulder light, and they were almost out of the cave.

A clamor drew their attention. They saw hundreds of the big, bat-like creatures spiraling around the opening, dappling the night sky. One of them landed atop the ridge near the group. Before Ethan could stop her, Brynn reached out towards it. She quickly pulled her hand back, though, as spines rose out of the little animal's fur. "It's a porcubat!" Brynn cried. It hissed viciously and launched itself off the edge into the night sky.

Ndaiye was giggling. "A porcubat? I've never heard of that before."

Brynn laughed a little herself. "You know, because it's half bat and half porcupine?"

"I picked up on that. Maybe you should be a zoologist instead of a surveyor."

The path dropped down and around in front of them.

Ethan hoped it led outside. They didn't know if they would be able to see the stars once they descended, though, and they stayed atop the ridge clinging to the sight of them for a long time.

Ndaiye led when they finally started down, the others keeping their eyes on his feeble light. As they progressed, though, Ethan saw they weren't in total darkness. Short, blunt, fluorescing rock formations glowed along the edges of the trail and along the cliff wall, like light posts leading them down the ridge.

He wasn't sure if it was the fluorescing formations or the sight of the outdoors, but something made them bold and they hurried along the knife's edge of the ridge, barely noticing the chasm that fell away beside them. Hope made them giddy. This was the way home. They were nearly out. Ethan felt the sheer exhilaration of being up so high and tasting, for the first time in so long, the fresh outdoor air.

The small ridge sloped down sharply, and they slowed a bit to better navigate it. Ahead of him, without warning, Ethan heard the sickening cry of Ndaiye's fall. Anger washed over him as he scrambled behind Maggie to get to the edge from which his friend had fallen.

The ridge dropped suddenly away, and Ethan leaned over, peering into the darkness below. Ethan sucked in his breath with relief to see his friend only a few meters below, sitting in the glow of their last remaining light. Ethan could see that Ndaiye was holding his arm.

"Everyone be careful. It's a bit of a drop." Ndaiye said, his usually jocular voice strained.

Ethan lay on his belly, wriggling backwards over the edge. He hung his feet over and stretched his arms above him as he lowered himself down. When he dropped the last meter or so, he knew about how far to expect to fall in the darkness before he found the ground again. Once he was down, he helped Maggie, Brynn, and finally Traore as they dropped down one by one. He checked Ndaiye's arm. Though they had little light to diagnose it by, it was assuredly broken.

They dismantled the stretcher from the pack and used the handles as a temporary splint. Ndaiye didn't howl with the pain it must have caused him, but he did hum vigorously.

Brynn's concerned voice cut through the dark. "I can't tell for sure," she said, "but I think this is a dead end."

*Impossible*, Ethan thought, *we saw the outside. We can go home.* He walked over to Brynn, trying to see in the feeble light.

In front of her was a very high wall. Running his hands along the rough stone, Ethan walked in a slow circle and found that Brynn was right. Like so many paths in the cave, following Knife's Edge ridge had led them to a dead end. They were in a pit, shaped like a bowl, probably carved by a long-gone waterfall. Ethan looked backward, up the ridge. It would be hard to get back up to the place they'd dropped down.

Just then, Ndaiye's shoulder light went out, plunging them into total cave darkness.

Ethan swore. "Sit down everyone. Sit down. We can't move around. We won't be able to see where we're going. There could be vertical shafts or drop-offs." He put his head in his hands. There was no way out without light.

It had happened. The dark of the cave had closed around him. He wondered how long a death in this environment would take.

As their eyes adjusted, Ethan saw glowing around the pit a few of the blunt fluorescing formations, like the ones that had lit their way on the Knife's Edge above. Perhaps they could be removed from the wall and used to light their way.

But light their way where? The sides of the pit were smooth and high. There would be no getting out of this one.

Ethan sat heavily on the ground, the cold sinking into his bones. It was over, then. They were out of food and water, and now they were out of light.

Brynn began to cry. "But *I* didn't want to die," she said in the dark.

Hearing her piteous sobs made Ethan's weary soul ache. He stood and slowly moved to kneel beside one of the blunt fluorescent formations. He took out his useless flashlight.

The ringing of metal on stone filled the cavern and stirred up several porcubats that had settled on the sheer faces of the rock. Finally, the formation chipped off and Ethan walked carefully back to the middle of the pit. It was heavy and smooth in his hands.

He set it down, and the five scooted around it miserably. At least it cast a feeble light so they could make out the shapes of each other and know they were not alone.

It seemed particularly unfair that they'd come close enough to breathe the night air only to die this close to the outside.

"Don't cry, Brynn," Ethan said softly.

Ethan glanced up in the direction of the Knife's Edge. He saw the fluorescing formations reaching up and away towards the high point where they had seen the stars. If he was going to die, he would rather die there, with the wind in his face and the sight of the night sky, than here in this dank pit.

Ethan drew in a sharp breath.

There, on the edge of the pit, on the ridge that lead to the Knife's Edge, stood one of the figures he'd been seeing. But this time it didn't disappear.

From what he could tell, it was about the size of a person,

covered with white wrinkly skin that glowed pale in the dark cavern. It had large eyes and it reached a long-fingered hand out to Ethan.

"Look at the ridge," he said quietly to the crew, "but don't panic."

He kept his eyes on the figure. He heard the gasps the moment they saw it, too. They sat still.

At his periphery Ethan saw another, much closer, figure. It was in the pit with them, and when he looked at it, another emerged from the solid rock behind it. Both were carrying blocks which they laid down near the back wall of the pit as more of the figures materialized.

"Dontcrybrynn, dontcrybrynn," they echoed Ethan's words in soft, harmonious voices. "Dontcrybrynn."

More appeared, and more, until the circle of surveyors in the middle was surrounded by the strange white creatures, moving in and out of the rock face, busy stacking the blocks they carried. Startled by their sudden appearance, it took a long time for Ethan to recognize that they were creating a staircase.

As it grew ever higher, so did Ethan's mood. They may get out of here after all.

When the staircase reached up and far out of sight, five of the creatures came forward and took the hands of the humans.

As the long fingers slipped under Ethan's hand, he felt the soft, cool skin of the creature. It raised his hand to its forehead in what Ethan recognized to be a greeting, then, walking carefully, it led him up the blocks. Ethan glanced down as he stepped. He could see from the glassy surface that they were walking on blocks of pure Yynium.

As they climbed with their guides, Ethan watched his steps carefully. The walls of the gap narrowed a bit as they climbed, but the other wall of stone was still plenty far away. It was close enough to see in the pale light of the luminescent formations, but much too far to leap for if he slipped. His guide climbed easily, though, and Ethan saw that these beings weren't as afraid of a fall, and the sudden stop at the bottom, as he was.

Near the middle of the long climb, Ethan felt his strength begin to ebb. He was relieved when, above him several meters, Traore sat down heavily on the staircase to rest. They were all tired, dehydrated, and hungry. Their bodies were at the end of their energy. Carefully, Ethan turned around on the narrow staircase and sat on the slick Yynium blocks, gazing out over the dark chasm.

As he looked, Ethan felt his breath come quickly. Across the abyss was a hanging cavern—a glowing pocket in the stone wall. The inside of the chamber was lit strangely with the luminescent green formations, and around the edges, in shadowy serenity, were the ghosts. Against the walls, small versions of the figures hung sleeping in stretchy, upright cocoons. Their faces were uncovered and serene. Tears streaked out of their closed eyes. Below each one he saw a strange formation that he'd seen nowhere else in the caverns: a loose pile of crystallized droplets, glittering in the feeble light.

Seeing them in vulnerable slumber, his fear of them was erased. He was taken back to Ship 12-22, where he'd watched over his own sleeping loved ones. In their alien faces he saw Aria. He saw the children. He saw, in this strange group of creatures, his family, and he knew he could not give up. Not willingly. He would not sit there in the dark and die. He stood, feeling new strength in his legs. If he fell to his death, if the porcubats lanced him, if the krech overtook him, then he would die knowing that he did not stop. Knowing that they took him down still fighting to get home.

# Chapter 25

Marcos rode the tram in the mine, watching as the spot of light in front of them streaked along the bare gray wall. This drift had been rich with bright orange Yynium two years ago. Now, the hollowed vein gaped beside the tram tracks, kilometers of it. The Yynium was running out in this mine, and what they were getting was low quality.

He shifted uncomfortably. Theo said he had to go into the mines once a month and mingle with his employees, as well as seeing the operation firsthand. But he hated being underground. It was stifling and it reminded him of the heavy years of stasis it had taken him to get here. He hadn't had to spend fifty years in stasis, but five years was enough—too many still—to be asleep.

He thought, suddenly, of Serena, sleeping right now on her way back from Untek, the planet where she'd gone to study. His parents had paid for her trip, under pretense of generosity. Really they had thought he would get to Minea and find someone else. Maybe they'd meant for him to get involved with Veronika, which would, they knew, be good for the company.

But Veronika was not who he wanted. There was no one like Serena. She was honest, sincere. She was enthusiastic about life and about him. Marcos smiled, thinking of their long days together on Earth. They'd met at sixteen, in the city park where he'd gone often to play danceball with his friends. Four years they'd spent together, and when his father returned from Minea one day and told Marcos he was being sent to take over the Coriol operation, Marcos had thought about running away with her. In the end, he couldn't disappoint his parents. They offered her the chance of a lifetime: an Interstellar Study trip to Untek, and promised him that they would send her to him the moment she returned.

But he hadn't known his father then. Dimitri Saras had spent twenty years away from Earth, and back then Marcos still believed in the father he'd imagined. Now he knew the man, and he knew that he'd never send Serena. Dimitri may pay her off when she arrived, or he may simply refuse to see her, but he would not waste a trip on her.

Marcos was going to have to go back and get her himself. As he rode the open tram car deeper down into the mine, the thought of descending back into stasis paralyzed him. He tried to focus on the tram light ahead.

At least he and Serena had not lost too many years. The five years he'd spent on the way were negated by her own Interstellar Study trip, for which she'd spent a little over three years in stasis herself. She had spent two years on Untek while he still slept, writing him every week and scheduling some messages to be delivered while she was traveling home. She started back to Earth about the time he got here, three years ago. He'd been here three years of the eight they'd been apart.

There were no Real-Time Communications on Untek, so he hadn't been able to have a conversation with her in years. Was it even possible that they could have anything in common anymore?

She'd be nearly home now, and he had promised to have

an RST ship waiting to bring her here when she arrived home. How was he to know then, eight Earth years ago, that Ship 12-22 would arrive a year before he arrived at Minea? How was he to know then that the UEG had sold humans to the Others of Beta Alora and that when that ship arrived, with its stories of cruel aliens and humanity's vulnerability, it would spin the UEG into a panic? They had started then snatching up all the Yynium and pouring all their money into a brand new fleet of defense ships and YEN drives to power them all. He had thought personal RST ships would be common by now, or at least that an RST passenger system would be established, but all that was on hold until the UEG could better protect its colonies. And frankly, there wasn't much demand for passenger ships right now. In the wake of the Beta Alora scandal, people weren't rushing to leave Earth.

But the only holdup was Yynium. If they could flood Earth with Yynium, then the defense fleet would have its YEN drives and the private manufacturers of personal RST ships would scoop up the surplus. The more Yynium he mined and the faster he got it to Earth, the sooner Serena could come.

But until then, he felt every day that they were growing further and further apart. Sometimes he looked around Minea for someone as gentle and loving as Serena, and he was convinced that there was no one.

"If all you want is love, why are you leaving?" Her words haunted him, because though he had told her it was all he wanted, he'd known even then that it wasn't true. He had, even before he met her, also wanted approval and success. His father had achieved both.

Marcos wanted, especially, the approval of his parents. But they were critics, used to finding fault. They loved nothing completely, not even each other. Everything, even if it was good, could be better. The attitude had built the Saras Ynium empire and had kept it growing when it was passed on to Marcos, but it took a toll on human relationships.

The tram next to them sped up and switched tracks, veering towards the open car Marcos rode in. He flinched, holding up a hand toward the blinding light, but the tram missed his and disappeared down a side shaft, their paths crossing just a meter or two away from each other. He felt that was how his life had crossed with Serena's—just briefly, for a moment on their home world. And now, they were both holding their breath, waiting for those paths to cross again.

She slept now, and she was still waiting, but he didn't know how long she would wait once she awakened back on Earth. Their life together, the things that bound them—those long rides along the coastline; the way that they felt, together, somehow complete—all those things were fading in the light of the new sun that shone on him.

He brought her to mind and smiled, remembering the way her hair blew around her. The last time he'd seen her they'd been at the beach. The brilliant blue water contrasted with her white dress. Her long dark curls blew around her face, causing her to sweep them into a handful at her neck and hold them there. That was the image he held. He wanted her to know that he was still the same, that he still wanted her here, no matter what doubts had arisen for her in the light of Untek's sun or in the long night of her journey home.

He could have told them no. Could have stayed on Earth or tried going on the Interstellar Study trip with her. They didn't force him to come. Marcos' parents never forced him to do anything. He wished they openly decreed things so that he could openly rebel against them. Instead, they had looked at him his whole life as if, any moment, he would disappoint them, and he had spent his whole life trying not to.

"Marcos? Marcos?" Veronika's voice was raised over the clatter of the tram wheels. She was cutting into his thoughts as she always did when he began to get too melancholy. He wasn't sure whether he was grateful for that or not.

"Hmm?" he looked around.

"Production numbers? An alien ship hovering over Coriol? Any of this making you nervous?"

He snapped back to focus. The gaping veins caught his attention again. "We have to get the new shafts online." Production could not be delayed one more day. He had to get Serena to Coriol to be with him. And the faster the Yynium came out of the ground, the sooner it could be processed and sent back to Earth.

"And what about the alien ship?" Veronika asked, seemingly annoyed. She knew what he was thinking about. It irritated her when he indulged in his childish crush when he should be running the business.

"I'd like to see it up close," Marcos said. "Let's take a drive after we're done here."

The tram finally stopped and the two of them followed the foreman into the deepest part of the drift. Here there was some of the glassy orange Yynium left in the veins, shining along the walls. The picks of the miners rang like bells along the drift as they chipped it out. Heavy dust hung in the beams of their headlamps, and the miners' coughs punctuated the air. Marcos adjusted his mask.

He turned to speak to Veronika, but she'd gone further down the drift. He saw her through the dust, talking to a young miner, probably, Marcos thought, trying to get information on the foreman.

Marcos refocused on the man, trying to ignore the blotchy

purple bruises on the foreman's neck and cheeks. He knew it was impolite to stare, but they were hard to miss.

"Probably a week left in this vein." The foreman's words jolted Marcos's attention away from the marks.

"A week? That's all?"

The foreman nodded. "The veins are tapering off. We're not gettin' a whole lot out now, and even though we're doing our best, it's probably a real job up at the refinery to get much useable Yynium outta the ore we're sending them."

Marcos opened his mouth to reprimand him for his cavalier attitude about the sloppy ore, but a commotion up the drift drew their attention. The foreman ran towards a knot of miners who were gathered around a still figure on the ground.

"Get her in the tram!" he barked, as Marcos approached. On the ground was a woman, her face, neck, and arms a deep plum under the coating of Yynium dust. She was still. Too still.

Marcos looked in panic at the tram. They would have to use it to get her out. He didn't want to ride with her, but it would take an hour to get another one down here.

Suddenly, he felt Veronika's firm hand on his arm. She pulled him toward the tram and into a car as the miners lifted the woman in behind them. He kept his eyes on the light ahead as the tram began its ascent.

*** 

Hours later, Marcos and Veronika rode silently in Marcos's hovercar. He had known the woman wouldn't make it, and by the time they reached the mine entrance, they'd called the coroner instead of the ambulance. Marcos had gone home and showered, but he still felt the grit of the Yynium dust in his eyes and teeth.

They reached the edge of the city, where the ship hovered,

silent and brooding. It looked more ominous through the tinted windows of the hovercar, but Marcos didn't want to roll them down to see it better. Since the food shortage, the workers were growing more hostile. Last week a miner had thrown a rock at Marcos's hovercar. Their unrest was beginning to be a problem.

He pulled out his missive to give Nasani over at the Food Production Division a piece of his mind, but an assistant answered.

"Let me speak to Nasani," he barked at the assistant.

"I'm sorry, sir, you can't."

"What?" his voice trembled with rage. No one told Marcos he couldn't do something, not in his own city.

The line was silent for a moment, then he heard Theo's voice. "Marc, don't yell at the assistants. You can't talk to Nasani because he's dead. Minean fever. I'm out here reorganizing and getting someone new to run the farms," Marcos heard him scoff, "although there's not much use in it. The plants are all dying out here, too."

Marcos turned to Veronika. "Minean fever is out of hand. We need to address it."

She nodded and he spoke to the driver. "Change of plans. Take us to the HHSD main hospital building."

***

At the moment the alien ship had risen and begun to move away from Lumina, Reagan had felt hope. But now, with reports flooding in that the ship had traveled to Oculys and then on to Minville, he saw that it was not leaving his planet yet.

The little situation room in the Lumina Operations Center was thrumming with activity. Reagan was surrounded by comms officers, platoon leaders, and equipment technicians, all focused on their tasks.

Kaia stood across the room, working on a rough schematic of the alien ship. She had already given them several insights into its weapons and speed capabilities. Having her there was comforting on multiple levels. Her expertise was useful, and knowing she was safe there with him allowed him to focus on what was happening in the other settlements without worrying about what was happening to her.

Reagan punched a button on the wide console in the center of the room, replaying footage from Oculys hours ago when the ship had descended there. On the recording, Reagan heard a loud click and the air was filled with the sounds of alien voices. They stilled and a single wheedling voice cut through.

"Humans of Oculys," the voice said, "I am Galo of the Asgre, and I have come to retrieve my property."

Property. What property? Was there something this race had left on the planet? Reagan had aides searching the Minean Treaty documents for any mention of the Asgre, any claim they might have had to the planet before humanity got here.

He didn't remember ever having heard the name before. He stopped the recording and tapped another sequence of keys to listen in on the message the communications center was broadcasting to the ship.

"Galo of the Asgre, you are in restricted airspace. You are requested to relocate to," here the message rattled off a string of coordinates, "where you will find a Special Operations Airspace. Please remain there until communications are established."

Reagan thought the communications officers had done a good job with the message. It was not too aggressive, but commanding enough to encourage compliance. They had received no response, however. Though there was no way to be sure if he was receiving them, all indications were that this Galo seemed to be ignoring their hails. That alone made

Reagan nervous. If the aliens were, as they said, searching for something, why didn't they move to the SOA and allow the humans to work with them peacefully instead of continuing to glide ominously over every city?

Reagan reached for his mug of hot, gray sweetbean drink. Its bittersweet flavor filled his mouth and cleared his mind as he pulled up the live feed from Minville and saw that the big Asgre ship was leaving. It was headed, he knew, to the next settlement.

\*\*\*

It took Galo many sun cycles to search the next four settlements. He had great trepidation as he left the settlement which the translator called "New Alliance" and moved across the Eastern plains to the only city he hadn't inspected: "Coriol."

Approaching, Galo saw the blue soil piled at the mouth of the mining tunnels and the bright orange veins of the humans' sought-after mineral peeking through the bare dirt. He saw wide, flat farms at the top edge of the city and the towering spaceport on the far side. This was the last city. If there were no signs here, his efforts had been in vain. If there were no signs here, he would have to consider seriously the possibility that he would not retrieve the lost Vala. His business would be decimated and he would have to begin rebuilding as best he could.

He settled into the now-familiar scanning pattern over the city. This one was rectangular, with the mine, the industrial buildings, the spaceport, and the jagged peaks of the strange mountains at the four corners. The rest of the city was made up of tall buildings and small blue dwellings just as he had seen in the other settlements.

Galo heard the scanner ping, once and fleetingly. He

rushed to his readouts. It was the slightest of positive scans, but it was more than he'd had yet and his hope soared. No doubt the Vala had been here, perhaps were still here. Galo was disappointed to see that the scanners could not pinpoint the exact location of the trail from this altitude. He thought about descending further, but that was likely to make the humans nervous enough to become hostile, and he couldn't risk that, not when he was this close.

He walked around the bridge, once, twice. A pile of loose garbage overflowing the bin in the corner caught his eye. It was a mess in here. He'd have to get the old Vala in here to clean it up. The jumble made him think of a mess one of his skybarges had made a few cycles before the Vala trouble started. They had accidentally jettisoned a load of cargo. To find it all, Galo had used remote sensors. Perhaps he could send those out and gain a more precise idea of where to search.

His fourth hand trembled with excitement as he extended it to engage the translator. "Humans of Coriol," Galo tried the name, "I have come to retrieve my property."

He waited for a response as he passed over the city. As usual, none came. Galo felt jumpy with irritation and fear. He knew conclusively that the Vala had been here. The humans' silence could suggest that they were hiding the slaves.

Galo contacted his remaining ships, instructing them to join the eight in orbit. He was close. When he found the Vala, he had to have sufficient backup to ensure he could reclaim them. He tensed as he saw the ships begin to appear above the planet. He hated pulling them out of the shipping lanes. Every day here was costing him hundreds of thousands of rhu.

"Uumbor," he barked, and his assistant scuttled to his side. "How many remote sensors do we have on board?"

"Sixteen, sir."

"Can you calibrate them to detect the Vala trail?"

Uumbor considered, then nodded slowly. "Using the settings from the onboard sensors, I should be able to."

"Get to work on them. Let me know when you are finished and we can deploy them."

\*\*\*

When Marcos walked into Dr. Zuma's office, her nervous eyes told him she knew exactly what it was about.

"It's time your people got this thing stopped, Dr. Zuma," Marcos said. Especially with the educated, it helped to be aggressive.

"We're trying, Mr. Saras. This is a complex illness that we haven't seen before. We're on an alien planet, you know, it's pretty impressive that we can even—"

"I'm not impressed," Marcos cut her off. "Have you seen the people? It's starting to look like a horror movie out there."

Zuma seemed to harden. "I've seen them up close, Mr. Saras. It's even more like a horror movie on the inside."

"What do you mean? What is this thing, Zuma?"

"It seems to be related to anemia. For one reason or another, their bodies aren't absorbing iron correctly, in addition to many other nutrients. We've also observed a breakdown in the walls of the capillaries. We're not sure what's causing it, but it is the reason for the bruising."

"Is it a virus? Can a vaccine be made?"

Zuma actually rolled her eyes at him. "Everyone always wants a quick and easy shot to solve every problem," she said, "and honestly, I wish we had one. But we haven't been able to identify it as a virus yet. That doesn't mean it isn't one, just that we don't know how to detect it."

"Then what am I paying you for?" Marcos paced, agitated,

around the room.

"Your scrip doesn't buy us super powers, Mr. Saras." Her voice was acidic.

Marcos stepped closer to her. "I want answers. You'd better be able to show me that you've got doctors on this around the clock."

"Of course we do," Zuma snapped. He saw her hesitate, then she looked him defiantly in the eye. "Do you truly want answers, Mr. Saras? I'll give you answers. Our preliminary findings suggest, Mr. Saras, that something in or near the mines is making these people sick."

Marcos felt himself flinch as if she'd slapped him. He collected himself, sucking in a breath and letting it out very slowly. He met Zuma's gaze.

"That is not a statement you should be tossing around carelessly," he warned. "In fact, I never want to hear it again. The mines have cutting-edge technology to detect hazards. None of them have reported anything out of the ordinary."

"But Mr. Saras, you don't—"

He didn't let her finish. "This is non-negotiable. If you want to remain my head of pathology,—in fact, if you enjoy practicing medicine on Minea at all—I won't ever hear that allegation again." He stepped menacingly toward Zuma. "Keep looking. It's not my mines, Dr. Zuma." It was less an opinion than a command.

She stood still and quiet, and then she spoke. "If I had known back on Earth that the job awaiting me was not medicine but acting and cover-up, I'm not sure I would have come to Minea."

Veronika scoffed, toying with her ruby pendant, and spoke up. "Nobody knew exactly what it would be like here. But it's a long way home, Dr. Zuma. And you probably ought to remember that the other colonies have their own contingents of doctors. If we find it necessary to fire you, you won't have a good reference from Saras company." Veronika leaned in, confidentially. "Regardless of your skills or education, you'll be in the mines or the refineries just like your patients. Your family will be just as hungry, your living conditions just as crowded. You see, every day, where that leads." Veronika swept her hand wide, indicating the floors of people struck with Minean Fever that lay just outside Zuma's office door. "That's not really an option, is it?"

Marcos saw Zuma's defiance crumble. She nodded briefly. Veronika was adept at getting what she wanted. He stepped in to lighten the mood.

"Great," Marcos said. "You'll continue working on a cure, I'm sure. The sooner the better. I'm glad we were able to chat."

Zuma sunk onto the exam table. He knew this was not the adventure she had signed on for. But her job was secure and fulfilling, her house was comfortable, and her groceries were delivered every Thursday without fail. He couldn't allow her to think things here were tougher than they were. Back home she would have had difficult administrators to deal with, too. Back home there would have been mysteries to solve and patients she would lose. He shook her hand and turned toward the door. From the corner of his eye he saw Veronika reach to shake the doctor's hand as well.

When she drew back her hand, Marcos saw she had left Zuma holding a small silver vial. He opened his mouth to ask about it, but Veronika strode past him, out the door, and by the time he had fumbled his mask into place she was halfway down the hall.

When he caught up to her, she looked him in the eye. "Don't ask questions you don't want to know the answers to," she said sharply. "But you always know I'm looking out for Saras Company."

She didn't say, "You know you can trust me," or "You know I'm looking out for you," and Marcos wasn't sure what her answer meant for him, personally. But he did know that plausible deniability went a long way with the UEG, so he bit back his questions.

# Chapter 26

Though the dawn was breaking across the river and Ethan wanted to run as fast as he could out of the cave, he waited at the top of the Yynium staircase to help the crew get out. Brynn and Maggie were the last to come up.

Brynn was walking very close to Maggie. When Ethan reached out to steady the two women, Brynn seemed to trip and lunged savagely forward, toward Maggie. Ethan, knowing Maggie was still too unsteady to catch her, stepped between them, reaching for Brynn. He felt a sharp pain in his side as her weight hit him and figured he must have pulled a muscle. That would make crossing the river and running for home a bit more uncomfortable.

Brynn pulled back from him. He couldn't tell if she was embarrassed that she'd tripped or if she was angry that he'd caught her instead of letting Maggie. But he was glad he did or both women could have fallen back down into the pit. And now they were walking, all five of them, out of the cave and into the growing sunlight of dawn. He reached around and rubbed the sore spot on his ribcage as his eyes played across the surface of the water.

He thought he heard someone call his name.

That's when he saw her. Aria was coming towards him on

a boat, looking like a goddess with the wind in her hair. She jumped out before the boat was all the way to the bank and waded through the river calling his name. He went to her.

He held her without breathing, soaking in her hair against his face, her arms around his chest, her voice repeating, "Ethan, Ethan. You're alive. You're alive." And, lost in the rhythm of her, he closed his eyes and felt himself falling.

\*\*\*

Aria had not known Hank was nearby until he was there beside her, helping the two dark men from the survey crew lift Ethan into the boat.

Aria's head was spinning, and Hank threw an arm around her shoulders. She was enveloped in the pungent aroma of pine and dirt that always accompanied him. "He's likely dehydrated and sunsick. You get him back to the city," Hank said. "He'll be all right."

She looked at the strange man who had taught her so much. She didn't know if she'd see him or the other Evaders again.

"Tell them we found him," she said.

"I will." Hank smiled encouragingly.

"And tell them thank you."

One of the men who'd staggered out of the mine stepped up to take the pole and maneuver them onto the water. Aria waved to direct him down the river, toward home. She was grateful to him as she sat in the bottom of the boat with Ethan's head in her lap. She couldn't believe that he was in her arms, and she was paralyzed by the terror she felt at his collapse. She wished Luis were here, or Kaia. She tried to calm her fears and sent a message to both of them, letting them know he'd been found.

Glancing up, she saw that she was surrounded by strangers.

The little boat was full to capacity with the quiet, weary crew. But they loved Ethan, too. They didn't speak, but she saw it in the way their eyes lingered on Ethan's still form. One of them began to sing, a hopeful, but somber, song in a language Aria had never heard. She hoped Ethan could hear it.

# Chapter 27

Kaia saw from the set of her father's jaw that the Asgre had finally crossed a line. They had gone to Coriol and dropped devices from their ship, scattering them throughout the city. Upon receiving the news, Reagan and Kaia, along with a large contingent of the defense force from Lumina led by Sergeant Nile, boarded *Champion* and went directly to Coriol.

It was the first night they'd spent at home in their cottage. Though Kaia didn't miss the bare walls and thin mattresses of the barracks they'd stayed in at Lumina, the alien ship sweeping over the city robbed even their home of its feeling of security. She got little sleep that night, keeping watch out her bedroom window and listening to her father's snoring in his room downstairs. She was relieved when morning came and they left for the base.

They had a full debriefing that lasted most of the morning. By the time it was done, the devices had been collected from around the city and teams had begun analyzing what they were and what dangers they posed.

As she followed her father into the lab at Coriol Defense Headquarters, Kaia realized she'd left her missive back at the cottage. She didn't use it much, but there was a certain security in having it with her. As they entered the lab she saw a tech team bent over a smooth white table. In the center of the table was a piece of alien tech.

The metal emitted a smoky odor, and Kaia blinked as it stung her eyes.

"What is it?" Reagan barked.

Kaia was guessing a measuring device.

"An instrument of some sort. It was transmitting readings before we disabled it."

She'd been right, then. She smiled a little. "What does it measure?" she asked.

"We don't know yet. Maybe surface radiation, maybe air quality, maybe some element we don't even know about. It's *alien tech.*" Kaia heard the excitement in the technician's voice and couldn't blame him. Reagan heard it, too, and she could tell he was less enamored with the idea.

"Don't forget that we're here to make sure these things aren't going to hurt anyone." He said gruffly. "If you find out what it does, I want to know immediately."

He walked out before they had a chance to answer.

Kaia's head was spinning. She felt a bit weak after all the excitement of the last few days, and the ship above the city set her on edge more than she had anticipated. The summer air hummed with expectancy. Something big was coming. She felt it.

Military personnel flowed around them in the narrow corridor. Many of them had swirling purple bruises on their forearms and necks. They looked afraid. Though she had on her thought blocker and she couldn't hear their minds, those first few months on Coriol came back to her, when she and Ethan were so overwhelmed with the constant thoughts of everyone around them. Now, she felt their presence as an overwhelming weight, hanging above her, waiting to crush her if she were to lose her thought blocker. Her breathing was shallow. She wished for Ethan, wished for his calming presence. He was the only one who really understood her, on every level. But Ethan was gone.

Her father was looking at her strangely. "You'd better get some rest," he said. "You're worn out." She didn't argue. "Go home. Eat something. Sleep a while. I'll let you know if anything important happens."

Kaia looked at him. She looked at the people swarming through the building. She needed to be alone. Nodding, she walked out into the sticky Coriol air to catch a hovercab home.

*** 

Aria watched Ethan for signs of improvement. He had been home almost a full day and there was no change. The doctor had no theories about what was robbing him of his consciousness. Aria could not—would not—believe that she had regained him only to lose him again to this mysterious illness.

She watched as he lay in their bed. Ethan still flinched like he'd been struck when the light fell on his face, so Aria had draped the windows with heavy blankets. The jingle of her missive brought him nightmares. He cried out. So she had stashed the missive in a drawer downstairs after the third time his new friends from the survey crew called to check on him.

When she sat with him she talked to him. She told him about the children, about the plants, about Kaia's departure for Lumina and about the mysterious ship above the city. And she talked about her love for him, because his love was what always pulled her out of her own stasis nightmares.

"I have waited every day to see you come through that door," she said quietly. "Every day, Ethan." She slipped her hand under the heavy press of his unmoving hand. "I don't care how I got you back. It only matters that you're here."

She knew he was still in there. He did respond, sometimes. He tensed whenever she left the room, and she saw the strain of it on his face when she returned.

"I'm here, Ethan," she said quietly. "I'm not leaving. You'll never be alone again."

She smoothed the knots of his dark hair, trying to see through the dark to the familiar lines of his face. She lay beside him and moved closer. Only when she wrapped her arms around him did she feel his body relax. "I'm not going anywhere."

Later, she shaved the curly beard from his face, finding him again beneath its wild tangle. Gently, she removed the thought blocker, sending her thoughts willingly to him, hoping they would reach into the darkness and pull him back.

She washed him, running a warm cloth over his cheeks, over his forehead, over his neck and shoulders, rinsing it again and again as layers of cave dirt came away. It was then that she saw the marks: three pinpricks in a triangle, slightly bruised, hidden on his side just under his elbow. He was covered with strange scrapes, so she wasn't sure what it was about this one that disturbed her so much. She put a bandage over it and reminded herself to ask the doctor about it.

Aria was downstairs when she was startled by frantic pounding on the door. When she opened it, she found Kaia. The message had finally reached her.

"He's home?" Kaia's voice was breathless, unbelieving. Aria nodded.

Kaia didn't hesitate. Aria followed her to Ethan's side.

Aria watched as the frail old woman stroked his hair and his cheek.

"Oh, Ethan." Her words fell as soft as leaves. Aria saw her slip off her thought blocker and felt a surge of hope. But Kaia turned and caught her eye in the dim light, shaking her head softly. Even she couldn't hear him.

They stayed at his side, unmoving, speaking softly to him and to each other, until evening, when the Saras Company doctor arrived to check on him again. Saras was, Aria was sure, less worried about his health than about their liability and Ethan's role in the Colony Offices. Later that evening, Saras also sent a psychiatrist, who had just come from evaluating the members of the survey crew who had been with Ethan.

He said that the strain of the ordeal had fractured their sense of reality. He said they'd had hallucinations in the cave. It was likely, he said, that Ethan was suffering from a breakdown.

But Kaia scoffed at that. "Ethan has been through much more than that," Kaia said, her voice rough with emotion. "Five years in space didn't break him. Genetic manipulation at the hands of aliens didn't break him. What makes you think that a few weeks underground would break him?"

Aria didn't want to say it, but she was afraid he had broken. She heard him last night calling the names of the people whose bodies remained in the cave.

After the doctor left the cottage, she tried to explain it. "They didn't all make it, Kaia. He still feels like the Caretaker— of us, of Coriol, of that survey team—and they didn't all make it. He lost over half of them."

Kaia quieted, but she still clung to Ethan's hand. "He's stronger than this, whatever it is," she finally said.

Kaia stayed another full day, then her missive buzzed. She was needed at the base.

Aria walked her to the door and they embraced. Kaia caught Aria's gaze with her gray eyes. "Take care of him," she said.

Aria closed the door and leaned against it. The weight of

Kaia's words settled on her. She felt her bravery melting and she imagined Ethan on the ship all those years. She imagined him holding all those lives in his hands, going on even though he didn't know if he would ever see her awake again. Now it was her turn to be the caretaker, and she didn't know if she could do it.

# Chapter 28

Reagan had gathered the whole UEG fleet—all six battleships and the smaller company ships—to Coriol. The time to watch and wait was over. He was leaving the company ships to watch Galo's ship above the city and taking his battleships into orbit to assess the rest of the alien fleet. He wanted to see these orbiting ships for himself, and show them that the best of Minea's defenses were not afraid to engage. Perhaps just knowing they were willing to fight would scare the aliens away.

The aliens had never responded directly to their hails. Though they had announced their presence and stated their supposed purpose in each city, they had not complied with requests and had not communicated over the hailing frequency the humans opened for the purpose.

Reagan walked beside his daughter onto *Champion*'s bridge with a strange sense of calm. Though he did not know what was coming and he did not know his enemy, he knew these ships and he knew his troops.

The commander's chair stood empty, waiting for him. He gestured Kaia to a seat near the comms table and noted her buckling in before he hailed the six other ships preparing to launch. Images of their captains appeared like playing cards on his comms screen.

"We're taking these birds up as a unit. I don't know what the Asgre will do, but we don't want them picking us off one by one. We move together until we're in orbit, then, if there's not an immediate threat, we'll group and move to defensive positions. If, as I suspect, we've got an Asgre welcoming party up there, then warp to your safety coordinates and we'll try to come in behind them. We'll rendezvous at 2600."

"How many ships are we facing, commander?" asked Nieman, the relatively new captain of *Vigilant.*

Reagan shook his head. "At last count, fifteen. But they're appearing all over up there. I don't know how many there will be by the time this is over."

The other, more experienced captains kept their mouths shut. They had trained for this, and he felt from them an almost impatient anxiousness to get it started, whatever was going to happen.

Six ships. Nearly fifty times that many lives. He glanced at Kaia. Perhaps bringing her along had been a bad idea. Reagan dismissed that thought and ordered the launch.

Reagan saw them through the observation windows surrounding him as each ship lifted from its secure place on the ground. Five sleek ships around him, rising like steam from the liftstrip. He smiled wryly as he noticed the difference in the captains evident in their ships' ascents. *Unity,* captained by veteran Halo Moscovy, shot straight up, unwavering and putting all she had into the launch. Moscovy didn't wait around for anything, barely even orders.

*Tenacious* went up a couple hundred swift meters at a time, pausing briefly as its captain, Brus Travers, checked the situation before proceeding.

Nieman's ship brought up the rear, cautious if not scared. "Easy *Vigilant,*" Reagan said into his communicator, "don't get panicky."

As they cleared the atmosphere, Reagan saw at least twenty ships, probably more, spread like stars across space outside the atmosphere.

"Insta-Warp us to safety coordinates," Reagan ordered. He didn't know if the Asgre ships would fire, but he wasn't sticking around to find out. He watched his little fleet as they disappeared, then reappeared at the safety coordinates in the shadow on the other side of Minea.

But only five ships, including *Champion*, arrived. Reagan swore as he realized that *Vigilant* was not with them. He heard the buzz of the "shots fired" alarm and punched *Vigilant's* call sign into his locater. The locater screen showed, to his horror, that she was surrounded by four Asgre ships. Nieman was panicking—it wasn't the Asgre, it was *Vigilant* that was firing.

Into his communicator, Reagan barked, "*Vigilant*, cease fire! Repeat, cease fire!" Then, to Captain Daring, his pilot, he hissed, "Get me back over there!"

They warped in above the knot of ships just in time to see the Asgre return fire on *Vigilant*. Reagan whirled in his chair, trying to get a better look at the situation, but their angle was wrong.

"Take us parallel!" he called. As the ship began to move down and behind one of the Asgre's bowl-like vessels, he felt a hit rock *Champion*.

"We're taking fire, sir!" the weapons chief cried, readying the weapons.

"Hold your fire, Brinks! We don't need any more shells flying around out here!" Reagan commanded. Then, "Evasive maneuvers, Daring! Now!"

He felt the ship shift under him and heard the hum of the engines as she warped swiftly around the circle of enemy ships.

He could see *Vigilant* now, as she took volley after volley of explosive projectiles. Though half her armor plating was hanging askew, leaving the delicate engine room circuitry exposed, Nieman wasn't warping out of there. He continued to stream his own missiles at the Asgre ships haphazardly, using up, Reagan could see, his supplies much too quickly.

He tried hailing *Vigilant*. "Vigilant, do you copy?" but all he heard on the comms was the ragged breath of the terrified new captain. He switched tactics. "Nieman, Nieman! Disengage and get out of here!"

All he heard was a shriek and another explosion.

Reagan shook his head. This would be over in minutes, one way or another. "How long to get the electroion magnetic links online?" he asked the engineering chief to his left.

The man looked at him with terrified eyes. "The-the e-links, sir?"

Reagan could see that the chief didn't want to go in there. Neither did he, but there wasn't another choice. "How long?" he demanded.

"Five minutes, sir."

"No good. We have to get in there now."

"There's just not enough power, sir."

Kaia spoke up from her seat at the far side of the room. "Pull the power from the comms reservoir."

Reagan saw the chagrin pass over the engineering chief's face and knew the man had thought of it, too, but didn't want to do it.

"Pull it," he barked.

The engineering chief punched a series of keys. "E-links on line, sir," he said grudgingly.

When Reagan looked back at *Vigilant*, he saw a gaping hole where the engine room used to be. She was blackened and battered and taking more hits every second. On his comms link, Nieman was wailing.

"Get us in there, Daring."

Before Reagan could turn to see if Daring was complying, he felt his head spin with the intense movement of a short-space warp.

They were immediately below *Vigilant.*

"E-links!" he shouted, punching the buttons in front of him to bring the topside cameras online. There he saw the glow as the e-links fired up and he felt the rocking thud as *Champion* became one with *Vigilant.*

"Warp to safety coordinates!" he shouted, feeling the maneuver start before he finished speaking.

His last look at the Asgre ships surrounding them was oddly reassuring. He saw spots of atmosphere venting out of the ships into the void of space. Where *Vigilant'*s erratic shots had made contact, they had scuffed and pierced the plating of the ships.

Perhaps the humans were only outnumbered, not outgunned.

***

When they were safely back in Coriol, Reagan set the *Vigilant* on the landing strip and ordered the e-links shut down. Daring maneuvered his ship sideways and set down beside it. Reagan watched the medical personnel flood onto Vigilant and turned to his engineering chief. "I'll have your dismissal ready by the end of the day. Collect your pay at the office."

The man saluted and left the ship. The next time he looked up, Reagan saw Kaia sitting in the Engineering Chief's seat, dialing some knobs and punching some numbers.

"What are you doing?" he asked, forgetting to erase the

commanding edge in his voice.

"He didn't shut the YEN drive down, sir," she said, looking her father in the eye. "I was taking it off line so it didn't overheat and fracture its frame. YEN drive frames are plentiful on Earth, but mighty hard to find out here."

Though Reagan was weary and the sight of those ships had sunk into his soul, he smiled slightly. His daughter had always had a way of surprising him.

"Looks like *Champion's* got a new engineering chief," he said.

Kaia shook her head, "I don't know," she put a hand to her temple. "I—forget things sometimes. What if I freeze during a critical moment?"

Reagan looked at her. He had always been fiercely proud that she was his daughter. Even now, seeing her lined face and the insecurity in her eyes, he was in awe of her.

"I'm different," she said, "and it scares me."

"Sure you're different." He had crossed to stand beside her, and he leaned against the console, locking her eyes with his. Kaia searched his face as he went on. "I know that some of your memories are fading. But I've seen you studying those manuals. I've seen you building. I think that your engineering knowledge is sharper than it's ever been, even if other things aren't." He paused. "I've heard you talk about technology that's a hundred years old as if you worked with it yesterday. I trust your engineering abilities. Don't abandon everything about yourself just because some things are changing. Of course you're different, Kaia. Aging makes us all different—but it doesn't make us less."

\*\*\*

This planet was beginning to anger Galo. The humans were

defensive and standoffish, carrying on mining the orange mineral and ignoring his attempts to communicate with them. They seemed completely ignorant of common courtesies vital to intergalactic peace, like responding to hails.

This morning they had entered space and fired on his ships, two of which were still filled with cargo. If those shipments got damaged, his reputation would slide even further than the *delays* had caused it to already.

He had forgotten how infuriating it was to deal with young civilizations unused to interacting with other species. Their first response was either total delight or complete fear. This species fell into the second category.

He would have to get more aggressive with the humans. If they wouldn't tell him where the Vala were, he would get out and find them himself.

"Ready the away suits," he barked at Kal and Uumbor. "And get me a team of mercenaries. I'm going out."

# Chapter 29

On the third day of Ethan's illness, Aria brought in her new guitar, crafted by one of their passengers. She sat down next to Ethan's bed, tightening a string here and there, feeling uncharacteristically self-conscious as she began to strum and sing a song that was popular back on Earth before they left, a lifetime ago.

"From the dark
To the light,
You've always made
Ev'rything all right.

Now you're three planets away,
Out of reach, out of sight,
And no matter how hard I try,
It's not all right, tonight.

I'm watchin' for you,
Comin' through the blue—
Come back and then,
My love, never,
Never,
Never leave again."

And, like flowers blooming, Ethan's eyes opened.

Aria dropped the guitar and found herself on her knees beside the bed, Ethan's face in her hands.

"Ethan," she said, as softly as she could, "can you hear me?"

Ethan blinked. She felt a sob welling up and quickly reached down to kiss his forehead.

"I've been waiting for you," she said in a whispered rush, "just weeks. I can't imagine how it was for you—" her voice caught, "all those years."

The muscles around his mouth twitched, just slightly. She could see he was trying to smile. He was coming back to her, and even as she watched, he was gaining strength. She saw it in his eyes.

Aria had only seen him heal once, when he was slicing apples and the blade scored his index finger. Then, it had been so fast she'd almost missed it. The blood had been flowing onto the wooden cutting board, and her eyes found the split in his skin. She had reached for it, instinctively, and watched as it knit itself, one side to the other, paling to scar tissue before her eyes. Ethan had hastily wiped the blood off, and she had taken his hand in hers, running a finger over the smooth wound.

They had not talked about it. It had simply become a part of who he was.

Now, though, she saw his struggle. She saw that his body was healing, but not fast enough for his mind. She saw, in his desperate eyes, him willing his body to mend. His eyes flicked around the room, as if he were trying to orient himself.

Aria drew herself away from him and pulled a corner of the blanket down from the window. The room brightened slightly, and she watched Ethan. He didn't flinch, just laid still with his eyes resting on her.

# Chapter 30

Sitting at the desk, Ethan rubbed the familiar bump of the thought blocker behind his ear and felt the sun streaming in on his face. He was healing quickly, but between being lost in the caves and the strange paralysis, he'd lost weeks of his life. Weeks of Polara's drawings, weeks of holding sweet Rigel to his chest and singing him to sleep. Weeks of laughing with and loving Aria. Weeks of conversations with Kaia.

He heard her voice now, downstairs. She'd come for a quick visit, but she'd have to be back at the base soon. She was the engineering chief on a battleship now, and she was spending a lot of time training. This new alien threat, while not fast-moving, was ominous. He didn't like her being at the front of it, but he saw why the military forces needed her.

Ethan didn't feel like walking downstairs. His legs had the singular numb sensation that came on and off ever since his collapse. Perhaps he could simply read for a few moments until she came.

Where was his missive? When had he had it last? He glanced at his pack, propped in the corner of the room. Reaching over, he hauled it to him and found the missive in the little protected pocket where he'd stored it. It connected to the wireless power and bloomed to life as he pulled it out.

There, on the screen, were the photos he'd taken in the Flowstone Room, with the dazzling white flowstone covering the walls, and the delicate symbols etched into it.

He tapped the computer console on the desk and the monitor and keyboard glowed. He pulled up his Xardn program and entered the symbols he knew, then began on the ones he didn't.

But Ikastn hadn't been studied extensively, and the symbols he found in the program didn't match these.

What was the room filled with these symbols? Was it simply an art gallery? A map? It seemed, most likely, to be a story, based on the words he could decipher. But was it mythology? History? A tourist's guide to the caves of Minea?

What were the strange figures that had helped them out of the cave trying to say?

He loved this about language study. The many ways and the many reasons that populations took the time to write down what they knew fascinated him.

He tried harder. He thought he recognized the phrase, "Sleeping on their (or his or her) journey through the stars."

Perhaps it was about the humans? He continued sketching and typing, puzzling out the possible translations.

One word, a noun, was etched above each entrance to the flowstone room. Ethan entered it into the program, and several related words came up: safety, protection, security, shelter, but none of them were quite right. He had used one very like it before. He reached into the desk drawer and extracted his journal from Ship 12-22. He thumbed to the early years on the ship, when he had written of his desire to get his family to Minea, to a place they would be safe. As he found it, the meaning came to his mind like the tune of a familiar song. He knew this word:

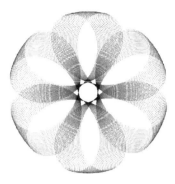

It was *sanctuary*.

The Flowstone Room had felt sacred because it was sacred. It was a place of safety, a sanctuary, for the creatures. But what did they need protection from? And what were all the other symbols?

He was deeply engaged in the search for meaning when he heard Kaia's voice behind him. He turned to see that she had brought him a small flying drone with a tray atop it. It was entirely crafted from junk.

"You can fly this downstairs when you need a drink or a snack and Aria can just send it right up," Kaia said brightly.

Ethan smiled. "I hope to be getting my own snacks soon."

A look of concern crossed Kaia's features, and she changed the subject. "How are you feeling?"

Ethan shrugged. He wanted to say that he was fine, but he had found long ago that it did no good to lie to Kaia. "Just feeling all the time I've wasted."

Kaia nodded. "I know that feeling. The only remedy for it is to stop wasting time."

Ethan laughed. She was right.

"What are you working on here?" she asked, gesturing toward the screen.

"It's a room full of petroglyphs we found while we were underground."

Kaia's eyes widened. "That looks like Xardn!"

"It's Ikastn, a branch language of Xardn. The syntax is different, and there are words I don't recognize, but overall I'm figuring out some of it. And between you and me, I don't like it."

"What is it?"

"There's something off about these. On Earth we often found in petroglyphs what we thought to be histories of various groups, or mythical stories. But these words aren't supporting that interpretation." With Kaia, the strongest person he knew, he felt he could voice his growing dread. "Kaia, what if cave drawings aren't just interesting history? What if they aren't just art or calendars or records of what a group ate and where to find the best hunting?"

Kaia spoke guardedly, as if she didn't want to hear the answer to her next question. "What else would they be?"

"Warnings."

\*\*\*

Ethan was pleased that Kaia had a few hours free after her training session that night. She came by to share dinner with them. Ethan looked at his family: Aria, Kaia, Polara, and Rigel, sitting snugly on Kaia's lap. When they were all together, it felt like home.

He felt much stronger, and to keep his recovery going they'd procured a special meal by sending out to New Alliance for steaks.

"Man, I miss the AAU," Ethan joked, turning the steaks on the backyard grill. The Minean summer evening was pleasant.

Kaia smiled.

"Why can't we have an AAU here?" Aria asked. "It would be wonderful for the hungry Rigo children to have an on-demand food maker. I don't know what they eat over there from day to day."

"It's just not practical on a large scale," Kaia explained. "The amount of energy it takes to reassemble atoms is massive, even when you're only feeding a small number of people. Imagine what it would be like to power one in every home here. It's not such a challenge on a ship, when you have an SL drive two decks away where it can get that kind of power."

Ethan shrugged. "Manual labor it is, then."

Aria went inside to get the plates, and returned with one in each hand.

"Ethan," she said, "I was grabbing Luis's plates, but the HHSD sent out those bulletins yesterday about running everything through the sanitizer before using it." Luis's plates didn't fit in the sanitizer, and the one time they had forced one in, it had exploded. "Shall we just use the old plates for now? They've been through it already."

Ethan nodded. "We probably should. Just don't mention it to Luis if he comes by."

"I'll leave them proudly displayed," she said, turning over the green-glazed dinner plate she was holding. "He makes the most beautiful things. And they grow Taim pretty well, too!" Aria went back inside.

Ethan shot Kaia a questioning glance.

"The little plants growing everywhere," she explained. "She calls them—" Ethan saw that the word had flown from her memory, even though she'd just heard it.

"Taim," he finished for her. Kaia nodded.

"How is your memory, now that you're over at the base?"

Kaia seemed relieved to discuss it. "Actually, my engineering knowledge seems to be mostly intact. I still remember useless diagrams from hundred-year-old Earthships, but my mother's first name disappears all the time. I don't understand it."

"The brain is a complex thing," Ethan said. "Even with all we know, many of the specifics are still a mystery. It can do strange things." He thought of the figures, wondering if he had truly seen them or if they were just the products of his strained mind. "But you've still got your engineering knowledge. That's great for you and for the fleet."

Kaia looked at him conspiratorially. "Actually, there's one piece of engineering terminology that I keep losing, too. I can remember it when I'm not under pressure, but I'm terrified that someday I'm going to have to remember it in an important situation and it won't be there."

"It will."

"Ethan." Her voice was somber, and the sound of it caught at his breath. He stopped and looked at her.

He saw her then, for the first time in a long time. He saw her star-colored hair, the deep creases around her gray eyes. He saw the slight trembling of her hands and he saw a fear behind her eyes that pierced him.

She was looking down at her hands, repeating a phrase. "Angular velocity," she said in a small voice. "Angular velocity."

Ethan reached for her hand. "Something to do with the ship?"

"Yes. How it is moving. I seem to be able to remember it in many contexts, but when I've done the battle simulations it escapes me."

"It will be there, Kaia, when you need it."

She looked at him, those gray eyes doubtful. "I hope so, Ethan." Then, lightening the mood, she squeezed his fingers, "Maybe I'll just have to write it on my hand."

He loved that she could always pull a serious situation back to a cheerful one. Well, almost always. He smiled at her. "How is the alien situation?"

Kaia sighed. "We still can't figure out what the Asgre want."

"The Asgre?"

Kaia glanced at him. "These aliens are called the Asgre. We have heard a few cryptic messages from them. They are here for their property, but we don't know what that is. They won't respond to our communications. Don't tell anyone any of this, by the way. It's all top secret." Ethan pretended to zip his lips, and they smiled at each other, remembering a day long ago.

\*\*\*

Kaia had gone home, the last of the leftovers had been put away, and the Taim had been scrubbed for the last time today. They would be back tomorrow, and the dishes still needed clearing, but Ethan pushed the thought out of his mind and relished the few minutes he and Aria had together alone. The children were asleep. Her head was tipped onto his shoulder, and the contentment he felt was even sweeter contrasted with the terror of the last few weeks. It was all he had wanted, to be home, and even the ominous ship over the city couldn't spoil the moment.

They talked of the last few weeks, of their loneliness, of their moments of despair. Ethan told her about the wonders of the cave, and some of its horrors.

Aria told him about the crop blight, the mysterious Minean Fever, and about her new friends the Rigos and their tragedies. She showed him a photo on her missive of Daniel and his mother and sisters the first day she'd visited them. She told him about how Gaynes had treated the boy, and Ethan promised to report the cruel man to the Colony Offices.

"I don't know what he was thinking!" Aria said. "To be so heartless."

Ethan felt himself tense. He knew. Though he'd never read Gaynes's mind, he'd heard the thoughts of cruel people like him during those first rough months on Minea.

"He sounds like the kind of person whose thoughts are as dark as their actions," he said quietly, and Aria sat up and looked into his eyes.

"Oh, Ethan! Your telepathy! I forgot to tell you!"

"Tell me what?" he reached for her hand, unable to discern if she had something good to tell him or something bad.

"Rigel!" she said, her voice higher than usual. "Kaia says he's telepathic, too!"

Though her eyes were shining with excitement, her words were like blows.

"And it makes sense. That's why he doesn't talk! He just plants his ideas in our heads and we bring him whatever he needs!" He saw why she was so happy. This explained so many of Rigel's worrisome quirks. But Ethan closed his eyes, unable to share her enthusiasm.

He was quiet a long time. When he opened his eyes, Aria was gazing at him quietly.

"I'm sorry," he offered.

She shook her head. "No, I'm sorry. I remember how it was for you." They sat uncomfortably. "But—" she began, "it *is* a gift, Ethan. An amazing one. Maybe with your help, Rigel can . . . grow into it."

Ethan thought about that. He stood to get the dishes off the table and Aria moved to help him.

"I just wish he didn't have to bear it," he said, finally.

"Rigel's strong. They both are. They've gotten so many wonderful qualities from you. This is just one."

Ethan walked into the kitchen. He had to put the dishes directly in the sanitizer because the counters were covered with Luis's pottery and all kinds of fruit. He smiled in spite of himself. "Where did all this come from?"

Aria told him of her time searching in the Karst Mountains, and Ethan loved how she spoke about that wild place with an easy familiarity. Polara, he thought, got her boldness from her mother.

"I made some good friends there: Evaders," she said. "One of them helped me get you in the boat."

Ethan vaguely remembered a bearded man. He was glad people had been there to help her. He would like to thank the man, but even if he saw him now, he didn't think he'd know him well enough to recognize him.

Other memories were clear: the caves, the beings who he thought had helped them. He couldn't have imagined them. He saw them now in his mind with too much detail.

"I need to convince them to stop the blasting," Ethan said. "Those creatures have their families down there. I saw a whole chamber of sleepers. But I talked to Saras on the missive today, and I can't get him to listen to a thing I say. All he wants is Yynium, and he maintains that he is not blasting anywhere near the Karst Mountains, but I don't believe him. I felt the blasting in the caves."

"Well that's no surprise. Yynium is all he has ever wanted." Aria began to load the dishes in her hands into the sanitizer.

"Honey," he said guardedly, "did the doctors think, the last few days, that my illness was some kind of—" he hesitated, "psychotic break?"

Aria paused. "They suggested it, but I don't think it's true. How did you know?"

"Saras mentioned it on the phone today. He thinks the beings we saw were some kind of—" he searched for a word, "hallucinations."

"No one knows what you saw down there except you," she said. "Maybe you should go talk to Saras in person."

\*\*\*

The next day, Ethan stood across the desk from Saras. He clenched his teeth at Saras's stubbornness, reminding himself that he was there to convince Saras to stop blasting until they could figure out who was down there. But he was getting nowhere.

"You have no idea what you're doing," Ethan said.

"Mr. Bryant, I think it's obvious he knows very well what he's doing. Which one of you has a stone and steel house and which one has a free cottage?" Veronika Eppes challenged.

"If you think that cottage, or our life here, came free," Ethan said, venom dripping from every word, "then you know very little about Ship 12-22." He took a deep, steadying breath. "We have a responsibility to avoid hurting others. And we need to find out about them. Why are they here? Where did they come from?"

Ethan saw the sneer on Veronika's face.

"You disagree?"

"We're here to get Yynium, Mr. Bryant. That is our main objective." She laid a hand on Saras's shoulder. Ethan's eyes narrowed.

"I'm not sure that is your main objective, Ms. Eppes." He looked into her startling green eyes. She didn't look away.

Saras slipped a gar fruit candy calmly under his tongue. "Every decision we make has to be considered in light of how it affects the company, Mr. Bryant, because what affects the company affects Coriol, and it affects Earth. What we are doing is vitally important." He looked at Ethan, "Mr. Bryant— may I call you Ethan?" Ethan blinked, waiting for the next manipulation. "Ethan, I know you understand trying to take care of the people you love." There was, almost, a note of sincerity in Saras's voice. "We have to get the fleet here before any other aliens arrive to challenge our claims on this planet."

Ethan sought for words. "But this threat is more real, more present, than the one you think you're preparing for. These beings are here. Now. I can show you what I saw." He reached up, pulling the thought blocker off, steeling himself for their thoughts. But there was nothing in his mind but a strange faint buzzing sound.

Veronika held up a hand. "Don't bother, Mr. Bryant. We're aware of your telepathic abilities, and we've purchased, and improved upon, the thought-shielding technologies developed by the UEG to keep you from using those abilities here."

Ethan listened to the strange buzzing for a second more, then slipped his own blocker back on. He looked Saras in the eye. "I saw these beings. They helped us."

Ethan felt a flicker of sympathy from the man. "I know you believe you saw something down there, Ethan. But you should know that we've done scans, and we haven't detected any significant living beings below the ground level in that area, Mr. Bryant."

Ethan's jaw clenched involuntarily. "Significant? Who decides that? Are you saying that you have detected life there and you're disregarding it?"

Veronika took two steps forward. "Mr. Saras is a very busy man. He's got several appointments this afternoon."

"Answer my question."

Veronika, with that inconceivable unreachability, smiled. Her smile was cold, a stone smile. "Thank you for coming." She walked toward him, steering him toward the door with her presence.

Ethan looked directly into Marcos Saras's eyes. "Are you going ahead with the blasting?"

Saras gazed back, a faraway look in his eyes. "Nine hundred *thousand* tons of Yynium, Ethan. Do you know how many drives that can help build? How many ships we can bring from Earth? How many people?"

"We appreciate your visit," Veronika said, closing the door behind him.

Ethan ran into the other Vice President out in the hall.

"Did you get your questions answered, Mr. Bryant?" the skeletal man asked.

"Not really. Do you want to answer some of them?" Ethan challenged.

Theo shook his head. "Oh, no, tough questions are Veronika's department." He smiled broadly. "But listen, we're going to have a party to celebrate you guys getting back safe. Just a little get-together the day after tomorrow at Saras's. Maybe he'll be in a better mood for answering questions then. I hope you'll come. And bring your family!" Theo walked away, waving cheerfully.

# Chapter 31

The morning sun's rays shone high on the spaceport as Ethan pressed his hands to his temples. Was it possible that there were no figures? That they had found their way out, somehow, on their own and invented the figures? He tried to connect with Ndaiye on his missive, but since the crew had been back to work these last few days, they'd been hard to reach until evenings. Brynn hadn't responded at all. He glanced up as Aria came into the bedroom.

"I want to go back to the cave," he said quietly, hating the words as he spoke them. "I need to see if they are real."

Aria stood beside him, running her fingers through his hair. "Let's go then. Luis says we can use his boat anytime, and I've gotten pretty good at navigating the river."

A few hours later, Ethan watched as Aria skimmed the boat across the water. He smiled when he saw that it was made of Saras shipping crates. She moved it by plunging a long pole down through the water and, when it hit the bottom, pushing the boat forward. When a sandbar came, she navigated around it expertly. The boat scraped the pebbled edge as it passed, and Ethan looked up to see excitement in her eyes. Relaxing, Ethan smiled as he settled in on the small frame seat in the center of the boat.

Ethan soaked in the beauty of the morning sun glinting across the wide expanse of the Mirror River.

"I came out here all the time when I was looking for you," she said, smiling.

"I still can't believe you found me."

Aria seemed lost in her own thoughts as she poled the boat over the glistening surface of the river.

She didn't speak much, and Ethan was glad. He needed to think through what he'd seen. Was it possible that he had simply been overstressed, hungry, and thirsty? Was it possible his mind had created the glistening white beings? Of course there were no ghosts. Of course no one helped them out of that cave.

What was it that the psychologist had said? That his mind had created a construct to embody his ideas so that he could visualize how they could happen? It sounded less plausible to him than ghosts.

He pulled in the fresh Minean air. Ever since the cave, he felt more fully the effects of it, and of sunlight, of brightness and warmth. People walked around in it every day and didn't even notice it. He wondered briefly how long it would be before he went back to thinking that way.

Aria poled the boat aground onto the stony bank. Ahead of them gaped the yawning mouth of the cave exit.

This was it all right. He walked just inside the cave, to where it fell away to the pit.

Ethan paused, closing his eyes, then opening them to peer downwards. Orange shone back at him. Aria squeezed his shoulder as she leaned with him.

"I see it, honey," she said.

The Yynium staircase was still there, block upon block as far as he could see. He wanted to climb down and see if he could see the chamber, but the pit fell sharply below him and he knew it would be foolish to risk it again. He lay on his stomach and reached for the staircase, straining with exertion as he lifted the topmost block of Yynium and pulled it, scraping, backwards onto the surface where he lay at the top of the pit.

He sat, running his hands over it. It wasn't like the jagged chunks of Yynium he'd seen chipped out of the veins in the mines. It was smooth and polished, the corners curved, and perfectly rectangular. It would be impossible to mine it like this. It was as if a fine craftsman had shaped the chunk into a piece of art. And it was grooved on the bottom. When he peered back down he saw matching grooves on the blocks below it. They'd been shaped to lock together.

How could the beings have done it so quickly? How could they have moved in and out of the rock faces as they did? They must have some abilities that allowed them to manipulate minerals.

Aria ran her hands over the block. "It's beautiful," she said, and then, catching his eye. "And you were right."

"I want to wait," he said, "and see if they come out. I think they might look for water at dusk and dawn."

"I brought a lunch," she said brightly. "And the kids are at the Chavez's. I told them we might be back late. We'll just spend the day here."

Ethan nodded. "If I can find them, I can prove to Saras that I'm not crazy," he said.

Aria's eyes were cloudy. "Good idea," she said, "but he's the type that may need to see the beings themselves." She laid a hand on Ethan's shoulder. "Even then, he might not care."

The sound of a blast echoed in the arch of the cave. It was still kilometers away, but the mining was getting closer. Ethan had reported it to the Colony Offices, but Saras was, somehow, still only blasting on his own land, and there was nothing to be done about that.

*** 

Ethan stood at the edge of the cave as night came. He couldn't bring himself to go inside, but he believed that his figures came out at night, just as Ndaiye had said. He nervously tapped the translator on his belt. He hoped he had programmed it correctly.

The clamor of the porcubats surprised him. He had forgotten that they would be spiraling out of the cave to find their supper. They darted through the air, twisting upward in the last scraps of light to pass through the peaks. Even though they were several feet above him, he couldn't help but duck, thinking of their long spikes. Ethan darted away from the cave, back to the river and down along the bank.

"Keep down!" he called to Aria, who was resting on a rock near the boat.

He slowed and then glanced back toward the cave's mouth. That's when he saw them. No longer shadowy figures in the half-light, the rounded, graceful forms moved out into the gathering dusk, walking upright, their musical voices ringing softly through the evening air.

He remained perfectly still, watching as they moved cautiously out, adults with smaller, more childlike creatures, holding their hands.

Their glistening silver-white skin was wrinkled, and Ethan remembered its incredible softness. The creatures moved in family groups to the edge of the river, where they lay down and drank, the drops of water falling from their mouths like jewels.

So he wasn't crazy. He hadn't had a breakdown. They were real, and Saras had to be stopped before they got hurt.

The creatures looked up and saw him, farther down the riverbank, and they rose from the water and walked toward him without fear. Ethan stood still at the water's edge. He reached up and removed the thought blocker.

Aria's clear, warm thoughts washed over him. She wasn't afraid. She was amazed by the beautiful, graceful creatures. Ethan smiled and blinked, searching the voices in his mind.

Amid his own tumbling feelings, he found them. The creatures' thoughts were in no recognizable language. He saw no symbols, heard no words. There was no familiar pattern that he could discern. He knew he had found their thoughts only because there was something strikingly unfamiliar in the known space of his mind. Ethan sucked in a breath at the strangeness of it. Their thoughts were a swirling vortex of experience that he couldn't comprehend. It felt like spinning through a void. He reeled, lost in his own psyche, reaching out and grasping at anything he could find to anchor him.

It came to Ethan just as he began to suffocate under the weight of the alien thoughts. Like a leaf in a stream, one recognizable thing in the twisting maze: love. He felt it among them, felt them radiating it to each other, strengthening each other with it. These creatures loved each other. It was deep and clear and comforting.

Ethan was dizzy. So much of their experience was still too foreign. He put the thought blocker back on with a quick motion and closed his eyes, feeling the silence in his head like a fresh breeze. He took a deep breath.

"I am Ethan," he said, the translator kicking in and issuing a stream of Ikastn words.

One of the fathers stepped up and offered his name. Though the translation wasn't exact, the name sounded like Aemon, and when Ethan tried to pronounce it back, the whole group of them seemed pleased. Aemon took Ethan's hand and touched it briefly to his forehead. The alien's skin was as cool and soft as Ethan remembered from the cave. He watched as the being took Aria's hand as well. She returned the gesture with a smile and a slight nod of her head.

The being spoke again. "We are the Vala."

Ethan was anxious to know how a Circinic-speaking people had made it all the way here. "Is this your home world?"

A sorrowful expression crept into Aemon's eyes. "The Vala have no home world."

That struck Ethan as terribly sad.

"We have been a slave race for as long as our history records," Aemon said, "and have never owned ourselves."

Ethan was grateful for the translator. "Can't you petition for your freedom?"

"No," Aemon replied sadly. "There's no one to whom we can petition. And our masters would never free us. They depend on us."

Aria, next to him, shook her head. "Depend on you, how?"

"They use our children in their ships," Aemon said.

"Use them?" she asked.

Aemon spoke quickly, but the translator buzzed an error. Whatever Aemon was describing, the translator had no words for it. Ethan fiddled with the settings, but "no words found" kept flashing across the screen.

The Vala must have seen the humans' confusion, because he gave up trying to explain exactly what their children could do. He simply reiterated that it was "special" and "valuable" to their masters.

"How did you fall into their hands?" Ethan asked.

"We were given to the Asgre to pay off the debts of our former masters. We do not belong to ourselves, have not since any Vala can remember. If the Asgre find us, we will be placed back into slavery."

Pieces fell together suddenly, and Ethan wondered why he hadn't seen it before. Kaia had let slip the name of the alien race in the dark ships over Coriol: the Asgre. This is what they were looking for.

"The Asgre are here," Ethan said hurriedly. "They have come to Minea."

Aemon glanced at his family. "Then we must go back into the caves," he said.

"Will you be safe there?" Ethan asked.

"We will go to our sanctuary," Aemon gestured to the others, and Ethan felt a thrill that he had translated the word correctly.

"The white room?" he asked, then repeated the word, "sanctuary," in Ikastn.

"That is correct." Aemon gestured to them to follow as the group walked back toward the cave entrance.

"Will you be safe there?" Aria's voice was tense.

"The Asgre cannot detect us in the sanctuary," Aemon said as they walked into the shadow of the cave's arching mouth. "It is lined with a special type of stone which is impenetrable by the Asgre sensors."

"We call it flowstone," Ethan said, his mind filling with the image of the sparkling room.

Aemon nodded. "A fitting name."

"I also saw it in the cavern where your children are sleeping," Ethan said.

"Yes. It makes a shelter for us. We were pleased to discover it on this planet," a shadow crossed Aemon's features and he went on, "though it can also be a danger."

"A danger?" The Vala stood on the wide platform of rock

beside the Yynium staircase. Ethan stayed back from the edge. Aemon lingered, though he kept casting worried glances at the other Vala.

"Yes. We ourselves cannot move through it as we do through other stone. Its properties make it impenetrable to us as well as to the sensors."

Ethan smiled. "So you can travel through stone. That's how you disappeared so completely when I saw you in the caves."

Aemon began to move through the rock as they watched, sinking slowly and serenely into the limestone. "That is correct. Only your flowstone and the metal our Asgre masters use in our cages, shackles, and slave quarters can contain us."

"May we see you again?" Ethan called as Aemon moved into the rock.

"We must come to the lakes and rivers to drink. The minerals in the cave pools are too concentrated for our bodies. We must also have a few moments of sunlight to remain healthy, so we come out in the early morning and early evening. We are here, should you wish to speak to us again."

***

The party was at Saras's stone and steel mansion on Yynium hill. It was a gaudy place, with imported Earthwood and Earthleather everywhere. Just thinking of the resources it had taken to move those extravagances through the stars gave Ethan a tight feeling in his stomach. The children were surprisingly well-behaved. Theo Talbot made a special effort to come and tell Ethan so.

"Your children are delightful," he said, reaching out to brush Rigel's round cheek with the back of his finger. Rigel pulled away.

"Thanks." Ethan actually expected Polara to climb under

the tables or slide down a banister any moment, but she simply leaned against Aria, clasping her mother's hand and casting a blank gaze around the room.

Their early trip out to introduce the children to the Vala this morning must have tired her out. It had been beautiful, seeing her running through the forest and splashing in the river with the Vala children. He wondered if she'd had a nap after Aria had taken her home today. Maybe they should take her home a little early. He blinked and refocused on what Theo was saying.

"I'm sorry I couldn't help you the other day. Veronika can make people feel . . . unwelcome."

Ethan fought a wry chuckle at the understatement, instead taking a quick sip of his drink. "It doesn't matter. We just need to get the blasting stopped around the karst peaks. Is there anything you can do about that?"

Theo contemplated a moment. "Probably not without a very good reason. I've heard you believe there's something down there. Do you have any kind of proof?"

"I've seen what's down there. I could give you proof." This was not the closed-door, no options conversation he'd had with Veronika and Saras. Theo had always seemed much more accommodating, much more likable than his colleagues. Perhaps he could help. "If we weren't in range of Saras's thought blocker, I could show you telepathically exactly what I've seen."

Theo blinked several times, quickly, apprehension showing on his face. "I'm . . . uncomfortable with that idea," he said. "Perhaps you could introduce me to them? I could meet them?" Theo laid a hand on Ethan's arm. "It's the only way I can help."

Ethan tried to consider the implications of showing Theo the Vala. He didn't want to bring more danger to them through his carelessness, but he needed someone on the inside of the

Saras company. Someone who could make decisions.

"Meet me at the docks about an hour before sunrise tomorrow. We'll go up the river."

*\*\**

Theo showed up in a cruising boat fit more for a lavish party than a trip into the wilds. Aria and the children stepped aboard and immediately stationed themselves by a window to watch the river slip by. Aria gave Theo directions as they cruised.

The boat was much more comfortable than the raft made of crates, but Ethan worried that the motor might scare the flighty Vala away. When they were nearing the cave entrance, Ethan said, "Can we quiet it down? I don't know how well they'll respond to the sound."

"Sure thing." Theo cut the big engines, using only a silent sol motor to provide navigation and just enough thrust to move them against the current.

Ethan guided Theo to the little sandbar where he'd been leaving the boat the last few times he'd traveled here. They departed and walked through the jungle. The timing was perfect. Minea was on the brink of waking. The mists hung heavy between the mountains and the sky lightened very gradually as they neared the cave's exit.

Ethan saw the surprise on Theo's face as he saw the Vala. They came to Ethan's family, speaking rapidly. Polara, whose eyes still held that weariness he had noticed the night before at the party, said a few words in Ikastn, and the Vala children cheered her.

Ethan noticed that the children of the Vala avoided Theo. He felt mildly bad for the man as the beautiful Vala children embraced Aria, carried Rigel, and played a game of tag with Polara.

"They will get more used to you," he said.

Theo's eyes were filled with questions. "Where did they come from?" he asked. Then piling more questions on top of the first, "How did they get here?"

Ethan shrugged, "We're still learning about them. The translator isn't very reliable with such an obscure language as Ikastn, and I'm still learning myself, but we know they came fairly recently. Within the last few Minean years."

"But the orbital defense detected no ships until the Asgre," Theo protested.

"They don't use ships. They are able to travel in space without ships."

Theo looked baffled by this. "Why are they here?"

Ethan thought of the dark, ominous Asgre ships. He could not reveal that. Not yet. He still had a hard time fully trusting Theo, or anyone at Saras.

"They are seeking a new home."

"They should continue to seek," Theo said, a carefully controlled tightness in his voice. Had he guessed that the ships above Minea and these beings were connected? Maybe that was okay. Maybe he would help protect the Vala, not only from Saras, but also from the Asgre.

"Will you talk to Saras about the blasting?"

"Why do they want the blasting stopped? Can't they just move to another cave?"

Into Ethan's mind came the picture of the cavern, filled with sleeping Vala.

"Not now. They need to stay here at least a few more weeks."

"What happens in a few weeks?"

"Their sleepers awaken," Ethan said. "The Vala children are depleted, and they are resting. Once they wake up, they can move on if necessary, but I think we should consider letting them stay. They saved us. They're happy here. The planet has the resources they need."

"Daddy! Come and see the fish!" Polara was leaning over the river, her Vala playmates peering into its depths beside her.

"I'll be right back," Ethan said, slipping off the translator and handing it to Theo. He went to see the fish, then chased a froglike creature with the children. When he came back to Theo and Aemon, they were deep in discussion about the caves.

Aemon was describing the white flowstone room where the survey crew had found the symbols carved into the rock. "It is our safe room, our sanctuary." Aemon was saying. Ethan took the translator back, remembering the delicate beauty of that room. It seemed fitting that it was their sanctuary.

The sun was rising higher, and he saw the Vala beginning to gather back together, preparing to go back into the cave. Their shining skin reflected the sun. Aemon stood and bid farewell for the day.

"We must get under cover," he said apologetically, "the sun is difficult for us to bear." He took Ethan's hand and pressed it to his forehead, and then Theo's, before moving back toward the cave.

Ethan heard Theo gasp beside him. He glanced at the man, who held his hand in front of him almost reverently. "Wait!" he called. Aemon paused.

Ethan followed Theo's gaze and saw what had frozen him so completely. Shining in the place his hand had touched the alien was an oval of pure Yynium dust.

Theo's voice was frantic as he reached his other hand toward the translator. Ethan stepped to him and let him speak. "Where did this come from? How did you get it?" He gestured at the Yynium.

"I think they have mineral manipulation abilities," Ethan answered. "They can remove whole blocks of that stuff from the rock."

As he said it, he realized the folly of putting that kind of power in front of the most Ynium-hungry company in the universe.

"Maybe we should go," Ethan said, waving to the children down by the river.

Theo ignored him, walking instead toward Aemon. "Where?" Theo begged. "Let me see."

Aemon gestured to one of the other Vala and spoke softly. She returned with a block of the Ynium from the staircase, which she set on the ground in front of them.

Theo leaned over it, folding his tall frame down to inspect it. He ran a hand across it, looking up at the Vala in wonder.

Ethan saw the opportunity. He remembered what his salesman passenger, Chip, said about convincing people. You had to work through their desires and fears if you wanted to persuade them.

"What would your boss pay for pure Ynium?" Ethan asked quietly. "Ynium that doesn't have to be refined? Ynium that could be shipped out immediately for Earth, and would even be useful in the small amounts you could send on an RST ship? How much?"

He saw the gleam in Theo's eye and remembered what Chip had told him. Make it personal. "And what would he think if you were the one to give it to him?" Ethan asked. He lifted the chunk of Ynium, and Theo's eyes didn't leave it as he rose. "What do you think? Could we work out a deal to protect them if they could provide Saras company with the best Ynium in the universe?"

He held out the block, and Theo took it reverently.

"Can I trust you to talk to Saras?"

Theo caught his eye and held it. "You can."

"Show him this, and I'll answer his questions as best I can."

Theo nodded. As the Vala walked back into the cave, and the children piled into the boat with Aria, Ethan and Theo navigated the stones at the water's edge. Theo, Ethan saw, was shaking, slightly. He must be more excited about the Ynium than Ethan had realized.

Ethan heard Theo slip on the slick stones and turned to see him go down. The block of Ynium fell, too, and fractured into several small pieces.

Theo swore, scrambling to pick them up. Ethan walked over and helped him, gathering chunks of the sharp orange material. He handed some to Theo and slipped some in his own pockets. Polara would like some in her rock collection, and Theo had plenty to show Saras.

*** 

Kaia was with her father on the base when Galo's big Asgre ship moved to the edge of the city and began easing itself to the ground.

"They're coming out." Reagan said, and she heard a mixture of relief and fear in his voice. The moment he knew exactly where the Asgre were going to disembark, he assembled the ground troops. And they moved together, stopping just outside the curve of the last houses on the edge of Coriol, where the ship was landing. Kaia saw her father put himself between the aliens and the humans, and she moved to stand beside him.

The troops behind them were trained Coriol Defense Troops, at the ready. Kaia watched the ship descending through the atmosphere, feeling its heat and breathing the dust it stirred up as it landed. As it neared, she saw something she hadn't noticed before. Below it seemed to be a small suspended cage, half-hidden by the landing gear and tarnished with eons of warp travel. Inside the cage was a small, fragile being. Kaia took two steps forward before she remembered what Ethan had said: "Warnings."

She stopped, waiting.

When it landed, six beings disembarked. Clad in black flexible suits, with masks covering their faces, the Asgre approached.

They had four arms. Kaia shuddered to think of the advantage that would give them in a fight. They were angular, sharp. Kaia thought how much Saras's VP, Theo, looked like them, with his skeletal face and long, gangly arms. She wished he were here so she could compare them.

Kaia was glad to see that they were much smaller than the Others of Beta Alora. Judging by the hiss of the suits, they were not perfectly suited to this atmosphere, either. That could be an advantage.

Reagan stepped forward. He spoke his own language, relying on the translators the Asgre carried with them to convey his message.

"You have not been cleared to land here. I am Admiral Reagan," he said, and Kaia heard his name come out as Ray-gun through the translator. "This is a colony of the United Earth Government. You can't come here and—"

The Asgre at the front of the little pack, whose black suit bore several red bars, stepped forward, bowing slightly and raising a hand courteously. His wheedling voice cut the air and the translator formed the words: "I am Galo, of the Asgre. We do not wish to inconvenience you."

"Why have you not responded to our hails?" Reagan demanded.

The alien took a step back, as if surprised. "We have not received any communications from your planet."

Kaia could see that the response was not what her father had expected.

"We've been sending them for weeks," he replied.

Galo conferred with his companions. He fumbled with a device on his forearm, switching through various frequencies. Finally, he paused.

"Ahhh." The translator brought them his words, "I see. This is my own error." He tapped the control and the humans' message began to play clearly, sounding tinny in the evening air. He listened to it all the way through and then switched it off. "This line came through only as an unintelligible buzzing before my translator was online and I foolishly disabled it." He bowed. "I offer my sincere apologies. We are not here for combat. We are simply here to retrieve our property. When we have gathered them all, we will leave your planet with haste."

"What do you mean? Your property?" Kaia saw Reagan move forward. "We have nothing of yours."

Galo inclined his head and spread his four arms wide, possibly trying to judge Reagan's sincerity. "Then it is your assistance we require. Our slaves have escaped." He gestured at the miserable little being in the cage below his ship. "They are called the Vala, and they are vital for the transport of our ships. I must reclaim them with haste."

Reagan spoke forcefully. "Don't be so hasty. We don't allow slavery here."

"I'll just gather them and take them immediately out of your atmosphere," Galo said smoothly. "And you'll never have to see any of us again." He smiled. "Unless you need something shipped, of course. Then I would ensure its safe arrival by transporting it in my own Cliprig." Galo gestured to his ship.

Kaia watched her father. She knew he was in a difficult position. He disagreed with slavery. The very word tortured him with thoughts of selling Ship 12-22 to the Others. But he also had intergalactic relations to consider. Slavery was commonly practiced among many alien races, and he wasn't likely to change that on this Minean evening. Besides, not allowing them to search for their property could anger the Asgre, and as yet they had shown no aggression except toward *Vigilant*, which had fired on them first. But if they were to become disgruntled and open up their weaponry on the city, it could be disastrous.

"You will let us search for them, surely?" Galo pressed, his voice supplicating.

Reagan turned to his troops. "Stand down," he said, and the soldiers stepped into their at-ease position. Reagan back to Galo. "You have one week," Reagan said. "You can search on this planet for one week, and then you need to leave, whether you have located your—" Kaia heard the hesitation in his voice, "property—or not."

Galo bowed repeatedly. "Thank you, thank you, so much," he said. "We will begin our search this moment so as not to disrupt the lives of our new human friends for any longer than necessary." He switched off his translator, and spoke to the other Asgre. Without the translator, the sound of his voice was grating.

And then Kaia saw them. More ships descending. Five more in all. The black-suited Asgre teams disembarked while the troops stood silently and watched them flow into Coriol.

# Chapter 32

A light rain was falling as the family left their cottage and headed for the sol train. It was quiet and comfortable inside, and Ethan settled Rigel on the seat beside him, pulling the child close and glancing at Polara. Her eyes were half-closed. She hadn't been herself lately.

They had taken her to the doctor, but he had been characteristically unconcerned and sent them home with instructions for more naps. Other than her fatigue, she had shown no signs of the dreaded Minean fever. Still, a somber mood permeated the train.

Bands of Asgre mercenaries were swarming the city. The defense bulletins assured that they were not dangerous to humans who didn't get in their way, but their presence was unnerving. The black-suited figures traveled in packs of five or six, two of them running scanners and the rest of them jingling with the load of manacles and shackles they carried, made from the only metal their slaves could not move through. There was no forgetting that they were here hunting.

Ethan hoped that Theo would value the potential of the Vala partnership and keep quiet. The Asgre had spent three days of their allotted seven. If they could hold out for a few more, the Asgre would leave and the Vala would be safe.

When they arrived at the end of the Water District line, the rain had increased to a downpour. They pulled out their umbrellas and stood to walk to the farm. As Ethan moved to exit the train, he heard Aria's frantic voice calling his name. Ethan saw Polara, usually so active, lying still and listless on the floor of the train. Her shirt was pulled up a bit, and Ethan saw the marks spreading in arching whorls up her stomach. He scooped her up and they caught a hovercab for the hospital.

A nervous young doctor admitted them into an exam room and looked over the bruises.

"It certainly seems to be Minean Fever," the doctor said sadly.

"What can we do?"

The doctor shook his head. "Keep her hydrated, if you can. The vomiting will quickly remove the fluids from her body, then she'll have dehydration as well as the bruising, the weakness, and the fever. You can keep her at home if no more bruises show up, but if they get worse you should bring her back here so we can make her comfortable until—" the man stopped just in time.

"What else?" Ethan knew there was no more to be done, but he pressed for answers anyway.

The young doctor shook his head, and Ethan felt a wave of hopelessness. "That's really all. And I should probably tell you, Mr. Bryant, that your daughter may not make it through this." He adjusted his glasses, cleared his throat, and amended: "Probably won't. We've been seeing the worst of it in kids and the elderly."

Ethan stroked Polara's hair softly. Over half the people he loved were kids and elderly. "I want to see your boss," he said suddenly.

"I'm sorry, Dr. Zuma's gone home for the day."

Dr. Zuma. He should have known. Ethan picked Polara up from the table gently. She stirred slightly and turned into his shoulder as he left the office and caught a hovercab.

\*\*\*

Dr. Zuma's house was one of the stone and steel mansions up on Yynium Hill. Ethan had met her once, when she'd hunted him down at a restaurant near the housing district to sign a Colony Office certificate of clearance. When Ethan had seen her, she seemed distrusting of the blue Minean clay houses and the people who lived in them.

Ethan knocked on the door, expecting one of the Saras household employees to answer, but Dr. Zuma herself opened the door. Her face contorted in annoyance and shock when she saw Ethan and the blanket-wrapped bundle he carried.

"What are you doing here?"

"I need you to take a look at my little girl. She's got Minean fever."

Zuma sneered. "I don't see patients at my house, Mr. Bryant. No matter how well connected their parents are."

"And I don't stamp approvals at dinner in a restaurant," Ethan said pointedly, "but I did." She owed him one, and she knew it.

"I want to know what we can do to stop this," Ethan said. "I want to know what's causing it."

The tick of Zuma's eyes to the right revealed that she was lying to him when she said, "I don't know what's causing it."

"What do the lab reports suggest?" he pressed. "Even if you don't know for sure, you have a guess or two. What could it be?"

Zuma looked at the child and he saw her soften slightly. "We think it's a kind of gas poisoning," she said, and closed the door.

Ethan bit back a curse, glancing down at the child, so limp in his arms. Zuma hadn't told him everything, but at least he had something to go on. He got back in the cab and took Polara home.

Hours later, the little girl lay pale and wheezing, bright purple flowers on her cheeks. They had spread up from her stomach now and covered, in colorful layers, her neck and face. Ethan glanced at Aria. They knew what that meant. Catching another hovercab, they took her to the hospital.

*** 

Aria stared at her little girl, after two days still lying motionless in the hospital bed.

The doctors had treated her as they did all the patients, with Reagan cells and replenishment packs, but the bruising had spread and Polara had sunk deeper into unconsciousness. The chief pathologist had told Ethan that a gas was causing this. What gas would do this? It wasn't unlike carbon monoxide poisoning, but the bruising and the long-term blockage of nutrient absorption didn't fit. Besides, Minea ran on clean energy, and if someone did get carbon monoxide poisoning, they knew what to do about it.

She unzipped the plastic cover over Polara's bed. It seemed to her that the sealed chamber had intensified the effects. Why?

As she walked the hall, she saw the hundreds of people stricken with it. She could find no pattern to the people who became ill and those who did not. Why was she fine and Polara was ill? She suspected Ethan's genetic modifications were protecting him, but why was Rigel free of the marks? And would he stay that way?

***

That evening Ethan came for his shift at Polara's bedside. Aria hugged him, clinging to his strength.

"No one is looking for this gas, that Dr. Zuma mentioned, Ethan," she said. "I'm going to. But I need equipment." She looked into his eyes. "Talk to your surveyor friends. Traore said their equipment is stored in the same warehouse as the equipment of the other agencies. Maybe they could get their hands on an air quality monitor."

"What could we learn that the agencies don't already know? How can we figure out what the experts can't?"

"Ethan, I think they already know what's wrong. They're choosing not to do anything about it."

She could see by the shadow in his eyes that he knew she was right.

"Then let me go," he said. "I don't want you out in the streets tonight, especially not with all the Asgre packs roaming."

Aria looked at him, trying to formulate why she had to go. Her voice was a quiet croak when she spoke again.

"I need to go. I—I can't watch her. I need you to be here if she—" she turned away, tears falling on her shirt.

Behind her, she heard Ethan dialing his missive. He held a quick conversation, then spoke to her. "Traore will meet you at the house with the sensor," he said softly.

An hour later, she crept along, running the sensor in front of her. It had led her across the city and out into the mining district. It glowed yellow, then orange, then, as she approached the mine, a deep blood red. The gas was, unmistakably, coming from the mine.

*** 

Early in the morning, Aria made her way back from the mine and set the sensor next to the front door while she turned the knob. Aria felt resistance when she pushed open the door to her little cottage. Muscling past it, she gasped. The door frame, the walls, the table, were covered with Taim plants. As tall as her fingers, supported by a central stem and spreading into a crown of shining, waxy leaves at the top, they were growing across the cabinets and over the windows. Morning sunshine lit the curtain of plants from behind, turning the living room bright, rich green. Soft surfaces, like the rug and sofa, were clear, but most of the hard surfaces were covered.

She couldn't even fathom the work that lay ahead to clean out all of these plants. They were a mess.

And yet, she thought as she swept some onto the floor to sit on kitchen chair, they were the closest to life she'd felt in weeks. Since the day she had seen Daniel's neighbor covered in bruises, since the day of Marise's funeral, since the day Polara had first begun to act sick, Aria had been surrounded by death and the threat of it. Aria ran a gentle finger over the top of the soft seedlings on the table. They were living, growing, thriving in spite of all the Zam cleaner in Coriol.

She would let them grow for now. She walked into her lab and reached for the microscope. Maybe she should study them, to see what made them grow so well. Perhaps they held a solution to the crippling food shortage that continued to plague Coriol.

On the desk, Aria saw the little silver object she had stolen from Gaynes. Over the last few weeks, she'd thought about trying to return it, but the thought filled her with dread. Instead she'd stashed it here.

She abandoned the idea of the microscope and picked up the little silver object instead. It looked familiar to her. She felt she had seen one before. Perhaps at the Food Production Division? Or the kids' play yard? She couldn't believe she had stolen it. Maybe walking out with that apple weeks ago had started her on a bad path. Polara had enjoyed that apple, though, and every moment of her daughter's joy seemed precious now.

She sat heavily in the chair, and pulled out her missive to check in with Ethan at the hospital. He showed her Polara on the bed, unchanged, and the baby in a playpen nearby.

"Are you all right?" Ethan asked, a hint of fear in his voice. "Your cheeks look a little red."

She made an excuse, not wanting him to know she had only just returned.

"I know where the gas is coming from. And it explains why no one is doing anything about it," she said, looking at Ethan on the screen of the missive. "The mine."

He nodded, as if he had already suspected that. They talked a few more minutes, then he asked her to get a little more rest before she came back to the hospital.

They signed off, and she stayed sitting at the desk. She pushed back the tray of Taim plants she had started what felt like a lifetime ago and pushed the spindly broccoli tray back beside it to give her more room as she examined the little capsule.

It was smooth and small, no longer than her little finger. Upon inspection, the top had a ring and a smooth black band printed with a series of numbers and letters. Carefully, she twisted the top, which came off easily. Out slid a long glass vial filled with a swirling opaque gas. One end of the vial was tapered, the other was topped with three needles in the shape of a triangle.

It was one second's carelessness, as she turned to reach for a flashlight to shine through the gas to get a better view of it, that caused her to drop the vial. She grasped for it, but missed and winced as it hit the desktop and shattered. Instinctively,

Aria threw a hand over her mouth and nose and stood back as the tendrils of gas snaked out of the vial and began to rise. It washed over both trays of plants on the desk and she took a step back, but before it could spread and dissipate into the air near her, Aria watched in wonder as it was pulled toward the flat of Taim as if by magnetism. The gas disappeared and she watched the little plants swaying as their leaves absorbed the gas right in front of her eyes.

Aria stood unmoving as an idea began to form in her mind. The sterile hospital room flashed in her mind. There was no Taim there, and no Taim at the school where Polara had been spending her days. What if this gas was making people sick, and the plants, somehow, had the power to attract it?

She glanced at the common broccoli plants she had been growing next to the Taim tray and drew in a breath. Black lesions that were not there seconds ago covered the leaves. They were exactly like the ones she had seen at the farm. The gas was causing the crop blight as well.

*** 

Galo walked more quickly, striding toward the dark arch of the mine entrance. He watched the humans sidestep, moving out of his way. They were sweating in the morning sun, which was unfathomable to Galo. How could they be uncomfortable in such a temperate climate? Back on Ondyne II they would roast and freeze in a single day. Such fragile creatures.

Six days the Asgre had been on the ground, and only the barest indications of the Vala had been discovered. But now one of the mercenary teams had found signs that the Vala may have been, at one time, in the humans' mines. That made sense, because there were materials that the Vala could not move through, and those materials could also possibly shield them from detection. Perhaps those materials were found naturally underground on this planet. Galo tapped the control panel on his forearm.

"Uumbor!" he summoned his first assistant, who was still on the Cliprig. "Bring the ships to the mouth of the mines, and fill them with mercenaries."

"Yes, sir," Uumbor replied.

As he walked into the dark of the cave and felt his eyes dilating, Galo used his control panel to beam his voice directly to his mercenaries. "Do whatever you have to do to find my Vala."

\*\*\*

When Aria appeared at the hospital carrying the Taim tray, she was stopped at the door.

"You can't bring that in here," the nurse in charge barked. "We spend all day trying to get rid of the stuff."

"Please," Aria pleaded, "my little girl is on the third floor with Minean Fever. I think these plants may help her get well."

The nurse, Aria could tell, had seen a lot of desperate people. Especially, Aria guessed, lately.

"Aw, all right. I guess it's nothin' we haven't had in here before. Just don't take it out of her room."

Aria smiled gratefully and made her way to Polara's room.

Ethan looked surprised when he saw her enter with the tray. "What is that for?" he asked.

Aria didn't feel like explaining. She only wanted to see if it worked. "Help me pull this thing open," she said, struggling one-handed with the thick plastic cover over Polara's bed. Ethan unzipped it and held it open for her. The child was so still. Aria laid the tray next to her pillow, taking a moment to arrange it so that it was solidly positioned. She leaned down and kissed

Polara, then pulled herself out of the cover and re-closed it.

She watched, but nothing happened. Polara turned slightly, tipping her head toward the Taim tray. Her breath stirred the Taim on one end, setting them swaying, gently at first. As each heartbeat ticked by, more Taim in the tray began to move. The long filaments on the tops of the little plants spread out and swept the air in front of Polara's porcelain face.

But that was all. Nothing else changed. The child still lay unaware, her beautiful eyes covered in sleep.

"You can cry, honey." Ethan said softly. She felt her frustration flare again. He slipped an arm around her waist, but she stiffened and stepped out of the curve of his arm. Aria had no more tears. She had no more words, and she was afraid that even her ability to love may have been burned out by the fever of her daughter's illness.

She didn't look at him, but she sensed that it hurt him.

"You go home," she said, trying to make her voice soft. "Get some rest. I'll stay here with them both."

Ethan started to protest, but she saw that the sting of her rejection had wounded him, and he squeezed her hand quickly, then left without speaking.

Aria felt a sting of guilt. She didn't want to lose Ethan, too. She didn't know what she would or could ever do without him. He didn't know what to do, either, and he was scared.

They weren't doctors. They weren't qualified to face this alien illness. All their efforts ended in nothing, and their resolve to try new things was waning. She felt foolish that she had thought plants could solve something so terrible.

Aria picked up Rigel and held him close. He wrapped his thick hands in her hair and laid his head against her chest. She sat with him at Polara's bedside, watching the Taim sway.

For the first time, Aria faced the possibility that Polara

may not wake up. The doctors had been saying it since the beginning, but every time they had begun, Aria had mentally blocked their words, refusing to believe that the child she had carried through the stars would not grow up.

But the blooming bruises covered her everywhere now, and she hadn't awakened for days. Not only was she going, she was going soon. Aria felt Rigel's even breathing. He was asleep. She let the tears come, hot and slick, down her cheeks.

# Chapter 33

Ethan left the hospital fighting hopelessness. The Minean night was warm, and he walked along the street in the Health and Human Services District, abandoned except for a hovercab and a couple of people going in and out of the hospital buildings.

For days he had sat beside that bed, watching Polara's still form. It was agony he remembered from his early years on the ship, when Aria had been in stasis and he'd watched her in her stasis chamber, totally helpless.

As he watched Polara, he had willed her to move, willed her to flutter her eyelids, to cry, to sit up. He remembered when at three months old she had been trying so hard to learn to turn over. He remembered how her determination was evident in her straining shoulders, her flailing legs, her frustrated grunts. Back then, when he had wanted so much to reach out and put a hand under her back to give her a little boost, he had known that doing so would stop her learning how to do it, so he had sat on the floor of the cottage, his hands clasped to keep from reaching over, and willed her to do it. He had sent toward her his best energy.

And these days in the hospital he had done so, his hands clasped again, so hard that now, as he walked along the darkened street, he felt the ache in them. He found himself wishing Polara his own strength, wishing for her whatever it was that kept him from this plague, wishing for her simply the strength to sit up.

But still, all this time, Polara's breath became shallow and ever more silent, and no amount of wishing changed its fading rhythm.

Ethan swore, low and angry. Aria had found the gas. It was coming from the mines. It had to be stopped. If not—his mind choked on the thought—if not to help Polara, then to stop anyone else's child from getting sick.

Ethan turned his steps toward Yynium Hill and walked faster. The HHSD gave way to the manicured lawns of Coriol's elite. Fragrant casien trees blossomed above him, and soft grass grew in the manicured lawns behind tall fences along the road. There were few estates here, but they were expansive. He passed Veronika's estate, Theo's, Governor Elias's estate, and the new one Governor Meck had bought when he'd moved out of the cottages a few weeks ago. And on top he came to the Saras mansion, built by Dimitri Saras before he left Minea and inhabited now by his greedy, grasping son. Ethan shook on the gate and a wary guard stepped out of the little stone guardhouse.

"Where's Marcos Saras?"

The guard glanced at the door of Saras's big house, ten meters away, up the driveway, and Ethan knew the President was home. The guard laid a hand on his holster. "Who's there?"

"Governor Bryant! I need to talk to him!"

At that, the guard looked unsure. "Okay. I'll page him and let him know you're here."

Ethan was surprised when the guard opened the gate and gestured him up to the mansion. He stood outside the door and a cautious Saras appeared on an intercom screen.

"How can I help you, Mr. Bryant?"

"I know about the gas, Saras. I know it's coming from your mines. Shut them down."

Saras's eyes darted nervously to the side. "Mr. Bryant, this sounds like business. Perhaps you could come to the office tomorrow?"

"It's not business, Saras." Ethan felt the heat growing in his chest. He could get in, if he wanted to, could blast the door and drag Saras out. "It's my family. My little girl is—" He thought *dying*, but he couldn't bring the word out. He stopped.

Saras's voice was quieter than usual. "I'm sorry, Ethan."

"Don't be sorry. Stop it."

There was silence for a long moment. Saras seemed to be weighing something. Ethan saw the moment that Yynium came back into Saras's eyes, though. Saw the moment his humanity was lost to his greed. The screen went black.

Ethan pounded on the door until two of Saras's guards dragged him outside the gates and put him on the sidewalk, where he felt the hot tears sliding down his cheeks and turned away, shuffling, broken, down Yynium hill.

***

Marcos switched off the screen. Bryant's child was sick. He heard the man pounding on the door and waited a moment until he heard the scuffle of the guards taking him away.

Saras double-checked the bolt on his door and undressed, wrapping a robe around him to cover the bruising on his belly and chest. He couldn't admit it. They would close the mines. As he lay on his couch, aching for Serena, he closed his eyes against the pain.

She would be landing on Earth any day, expecting to step aboard an RST ship and come to him. But he had failed her.

The personal RST ships weren't available, little Yynium had arrived on Earth, and she would not be here for a long, long time. He knew that may mean never. He spoke, calling the screen up in front of him.

"Messages," Marcos said, "from Serena."

"Messages from Serena," repeated the smarthouse. Her messages appeared on the screen, her words flowing around the pictures she'd sent. He didn't open any single one, just looked at them all en masse and curled into a ball around the pain in his chest. A coughing fit shook him.

Marcos missed Serena with a depth of emptiness he had never known, not even with the hole his father had left when he'd gone off to Minea.

"Show me the camera on the P5," Marcos mumbled, feeling the heat of fever pressing on his temples. The little ship shone dully on the screen in the darkened garage. Its engine compartment still gaped open, the drive removed and laying on a table nearby. If the P5 was operational, he'd leave tomorrow to reach her.

Marcos didn't hear the door unlock or the footsteps. He didn't know how long he'd lain there when he noticed Veronika standing above him.

"We've got a problem," she said. "Get dressed."

She turned to leave, but stopped, her eyes on the screen. "What is that?"

"It's the P5," Marcos heard how his voice slurred and he tried to correct it. "Only it's broken."

Veronika froze. "What do you mean it's broken?" Her voice sounded explosively loud to Marcos.

"Shhh," he scolded, then waved her closer. Part of him was screaming to stop talking, but the fever was blurring his thoughts. He was tired and if he told her maybe she'd go away.

"It's broken because I tried to go home and the dirty Yynium clogged up the drive. Cayle will fix it." He laid his head back and closed his eyes.

Veronika was suddenly in his face, her strong hands grasping the front of his robe and hauling him into a sitting position. He hadn't known she was so strong.

"Dirty Yynium? When? When did this happen?"

"Some months ago." Marcos scrunched up his face, trying to remember.

"Before or after the last shipment, Marcos?" She shook him just when he tried to close his eyes again. "Think Marcos. When?"

"Before. When we got the new filters in the refinery that I guess didn't work so well."

"Did you know this when we shipped?" she demanded.

Marcos nodded. He was beginning to pull out of the haze, and the screaming voice in his head telling him to stop talking was growing louder.

Veronika stared at him for a long, horrible moment. She slipped off the couch and knelt on the floor, running a hand through her long black hair.

"Marcos, this is bad."

Marcos felt the sharp sting of regret sneak in around the edges of the haze. He put his head in his hands.

"I know."

Veronika's head snapped up. "You are an idiot. Why would you hide this?"

Marcos shook his head. His voice sounded more like his own when he said, "We have to keep running the mine to get new Yynium. We have to keep getting paid if we want to buy better equipment. We have to keep shipping."

"Not dirty Yynium. What do you think is going to happen

when that stuff arrives and they put it in the YEN drives?"

"Same thing that happened to the P5? The drives gum up?"

"Maybe," her voice was sharp, "or maybe they overheat and explode and maybe people *die* Marcos." He didn't think that would happen and he could tell she knew he didn't.

"And if it's the ship Serena's on?" Her words drove a knife into his gut, then she twisted it. "And she's the one that gets burnt and hurled into space?"

"Stop it." He stood. The room swayed slightly, but he was regaining control. His anger was overcoming the fever. "It's one shipload. When we get the new vein, we'll have all the clean Yynium we need."

Veronika walked to the window. He knew she was calculating. "I'm sure you faked our report, but how did you get around the Colony Offices purity check?"

Marcos looked her in the eye and Veronika swore softly. "You paid someone off? And you expect them not to talk? Who was it?"

Marcos knew this conversation, knew where it ended. He kept his mouth shut. She started naming governors.

"Elias? Bryant? Mujib? Patten? Meck?" He tightened his mouth to keep from giving it away, but realized his mistake too late.

"Meck then," she said decisively. "I knew something was fishy about that new house." Then, turning from the window, "Does Theo know about this?"

Marcos shook his head and saw her nod, once, satisfied. At least he wasn't always hopeless at lying. She walked a few steps toward him.

"We've got another problem."

"What kind of problem?" he asked.

"We've got an alien problem," she said coldly.

"We've had an alien problem for a while," he said, grimacing as he thought about the black-suited Asgre lurking through the streets on their mysterious hunt.

"But now they're in the mines," Veronika said. She spoke to the house and pulled up the screen with a diagram of the Yynium mines. Four shafts each bore a large red x. His mines. They had already shut down four shafts?

"What are they doing?"

"I don't know, but in these four they have detonated charges, as if they are trying to get further back into the rock. But they're not doing it well. They're moving too fast, and they're sloppy. They've basically destroyed all four shafts."

Four shafts and all the work that it took to build them. Four shafts and the potential for Yynium harvest that they held. Four shafts represented nearly a year's work, and every shaft destroyed set them back months. Marcos's mind was clear now, and fury welled within him. He strode to the wall and punched the communicator. Within moments, Phillip Reagan was before him on the screen.

"Get these creatures out of my mines, Reagan," he snapped. "I've given you the manpower. You've got all the Coriol Defense Troops. What are you waiting for?"

"You don't just charge in and start firing at aliens, Saras. They don't care how much scrip you have. You'd better be sure you know what they can do before you start pushing them around."

"Well, what can they do?"

Reagan's voice was a growl. "Plenty, from the looks of it. I've got analysts figuring out just what kind of weaponry they've got. I should know exactly how we match up soon, but you'd better know I've got *people* to think of before mines."

"You'd better think of my mines, Reagan, or there won't be

any people here to think about."

"We've made a deal, and they've got two days left to get out of here. It'll be better for everyone if we don't engage them before that."

Marcos scoffed. "Made another deal with the aliens, huh Reagan?" Marcos smiled as he saw Reagan's face register the blow. "You've got a good track record with those. Just know that if it comes down to it, I'm not afraid to use my troops."

Reagan started to say something, probably a threat, but Marcos cut the call, his head still pulsing.

Veronika glared at him. "You think it's smart to make the Admiral mad?" She scoffed, then snapped, "I said *get dressed*. We need to get Theo and get this thing figured out." She went back to staring out the window.

As Marcos pulled on his slacks and buttoned his shirt, he looked past her, where he saw the lights of Coriol stretched beneath them, glimmering white all the way to the blue lights of the spaceport on the opposite side of the city. He saw her watching him in the reflection of the glass, and he saw her mouth open in shock as she turned slowly to stare at the bruises covering his torso.

Marcos tried to pull his shirt closed, but it was too late.

"We're going to the hospital," Veronika said sharply. "Right now."

\*\*\*

When Aria opened her eyes in the pale morning light, Rigel was stirring in her arms. Her neck was stiff from sleeping in the chair.

"Mama," Polara's sweet voice called, muffled by the thick cover over her bed, "the plants are dancing."

Aria drew in her breath sharply. Polara was sitting up,

running a gentle finger over the plants. Aria blinked. The plants were twice the size they were last night. And Polara was awake.

Aria's heart beat hard as she jingled Ethan on the missive. When he answered, she saw that he had not gone home. He was in the street near the hospital, unshaven, wrinkled.

"Is she still—with us?" his voice trembled with the question. Aria couldn't speak, just turned the missive towards their little daughter and heard Ethan's cry of surprise as he saw the child looking back at him.

"Go home, Ethan, and bring all the Taim trays you can find. They're in the kitchen and the work room." Aria balanced Rigel on her hip as she slid a hand into the tent with Polara. The touch of her daughter's hand sent joy washing over her.

# Chapter 34

Daniel huddled in the back of the drift with three women and seven men. He hoped that wherever Zella was, she was safe. They switched off their headlights. The aliens that had been combing the city were in the mines now, and their time to find their slaves was up today. In their desperation, they had begun threatening the people in the mines, insisting that their slaves were somewhere below the surface of Coriol and demanding that the miners tell them where. But the Asgre had to leave soon. They were on their way back to the surface now, he'd heard. If the miners could hold out, they might be able to slip out of the mines or wait until the aliens left.

"Don't make a sound," Mullin commanded.

The voices of the Asgre echoed in the dark, muffled by the masks they wore and unintelligible in their rough alien language. They were growing closer on their way out of the mine.

Daniel heard his own breathing and tried to exhale more quietly. He heard the click of a belt against the stone wall and the shush of Illie's uniform against the stone as she tried to ease into a better position for a long-term wait. His own back and legs were burning, and he knew that he'd have to shift soon, too.

He felt bad. Bad that he'd helped Theo and Veronika steal gas samples from the mine. Bad that he'd sold the extra one to Gaynes. His mother would have been ashamed, even if it did earn him almost a thousand extra scrip.

And now Gaynes thought he had cheated him and was threatening his little sisters. Who would be there to protect them from Gaynes if Daniel was killed by aliens today in the mine?

He hadn't cheated Gaynes, but he was far from innocent. He had stolen the samples. He thought a repentant prayer and asked his mother's forgiveness for his foolishness.

Daniel wondered if he should whisper a reminder to the others about the huge blast lights stored back here. They were known for tipping over on their tripod bases even when they were just standing in the drift.

Daniel was amazed at the number of sounds that humans could make when they were as silent as they could possibly be. Tarell's stomach growled loudly, sounding like a great groan in the depths of the mine. Mary's joints cracked as she shifted positions. Carter's labored breathing echoed off the stone around them, even though he held it for as long as he could before inhaling forcefully.

The alien voices drew nearer. Light played on the wall. They'd been lucky twice. If they could avoid this group, they could slip out of the mine and head back to the safety of Coriol.

Daniel's mind went to his sisters. With his mother gone, they needed him more than ever. There was no one, no one on this planet, to whom they could turn if their big brother didn't come home.

Daniel felt, rather than saw, the lamp falling. The rush of air that brushed his cheek preceded a great rattling crash. Splinters of glass grazed his forearm, flying up from the rock floor of the drift.

The voices in front of them quieted and the lights swung out of the main shaft and came towards them. Carter snapped, shouting, "Run!" even though they all realized that there was nowhere to run.

Backed against the end of the drift, Carter ran the only direction he could: toward the coming Asgre mercenary team. He barreled into the first one, knocking them both over and grappling with the alien for a moment, pulling off its mask. A sharp hiss filled the cavern and the creature screeched, clawing at its throat before it grasped the mask and pulled it back on. The light from the helmet had clattered down the drift, where it spun and threw a beam of light up behind the approaching aliens, backlighting them and casting their shadows onto the cowering group of humans at the end of the tunnel.

Daniel saw Carter half-rise as the Asgre raised its weapon and shot him. The older miner sunk to the floor and lay still. The Asgre raised their lights in the direction he had come from.

The beams caught Daniel and the others frozen in terror. The aliens shouted commands that they didn't understand. Switching on a translator, one of them said, "We are here for the Vala. You will lead us to them."

"We don't know what you're talking about!" Mary pleaded. "What's a Vala? We mine Yynium here!" The creature waited, listening to the translation, and then barked, "Then you are not of any use to us." He raised his weapon.

Daniel closed his eyes, preparing for the shot. Before he felt it, though, a gentle white light penetrated his eyelids. He opened them to see, standing between the miners and the Asgre, a half-circle of very different alien creatures.

They reminded him, somehow, of bipedal caterpillars with wrinkly pearl skin. They turned enormous eyes toward the miners, assessing, Daniel guessed, to see if they were all right. Their wide eyes made it possible for them to see where others couldn't and, he guessed, to see what others couldn't.

The Asgre were upon the new creatures in seconds, clamping shackles around their waists and necks. They led them away, ignoring the little group whose lives were changed forever by the first aliens they had ever seen in person.

***

Reagan stood in front of the Cliprig, awaiting the return of the Asgre search parties from the mines. This was day seven, and he wanted these creatures out of his city. Ever since they'd come, he'd been unusually afraid for the humans he was in charge of.

Saras's words still jabbed at his thoughts. *Another deal with the aliens, huh, Reagan?* It stung because it was true. He'd been part of selling people into slavery. He didn't think the pain and regret of that would ever leave him.

Kaia jingled him on his missive, and her lined face appeared on its screen.

"Time's up," she reminded him. The combination of his melancholy thoughts and her words hit him in the chest. He tried to push the thought of Kaia's aging from his mind. She was strong, even before her modifications, and after them he had started to think of her as indestructible. Only, of course, she wasn't. Her frail form on the screen was enough to tell him that. Her voice now was sharp as she tried to get his attention.

"Did you hear? The Asgre are out of time?"

"Copy that," he said.

He heard movement behind him. Whirling to peer into the dark mouth of the mine, Reagan saw them returning to their transport. They had, apparently, found what they were looking for.

The sharp-faced Asgre, with their skeletal expressions and their razor-like bones sticking through the stretched tents of their skin under their masks, moved toward him, weapons drawn. They were herding pale beings out of the mine, some of them children. One tiny creature was no larger than Polara. The helpless Vala blinked in the light as they were led in chains to the transport.

Galo approached him. "These creatures are the property I've been searching for." Galo explained, almost ingratiatingly. "They thought that hiding underground would fool me, but I have found them." He paused, then continued, and Reagan heard the frustration in his abrasive voice. "Well, not all of them." Galo motioned his soldiers to lead the creatures onto the ship.

Reagan opened his mouth to speak, but Galo continued. "I request more time to find the rest of my slaves."

Reagan shook his head, "We've given you your time. Your contract was that you would leave after seven days. Those days are up."

Galo spoke quickly. "Do you have anything you need moved quickly across space, Mr. Regan?"

Reagan scoffed, *Yeah, about eighty battleships,* he thought wryly.

Galo didn't wait for an answer. "I can help you with your shipping needs. We can move cargo very quickly. Is there something, or *someone* that you'd like brought from your home planet? Perhaps in exchange for a few more days?" His angular face, behind the mask, contorted into what Reagan thought was supposed to be a smile.

Reagan thought about the battleships. He thought about the YEN drives, piling up in warehouses back on Earth and too far away from the Yynium supply to be of use for decades.

Perhaps he'd been looking at Galo all wrong. Being in an intergalactic society could have its advantages, too.

The Admiral blinked, shaking the cobwebbed thoughts in his head. "Could you—could you transport ships? What are your limitations?"

Galo leaned forward eagerly. "Of course! I have transported whole fleets. I could bring you anything you want."

The fear Reagan had carried for the last few weeks twisted in his chest. Maybe this was the way to keep the people on Minea safe. Reagan began to nod, considering how many extra days he could give the creature to search. The vast stretch of space between Minea and Earth could be bridged by this one bargain. He could bring the fleet here, bring the drives here. That big ship could carry a lot of YEN drives. As he glanced up at the Cliprig behind Galo, Reagan saw the Vala being led onto the ship in chains. He saw the mercenaries loading the smallest Vala child into the cage below the great ship, saw it slump miserably onto the floor behind the bars.

Reagan turned his face away in disgust. Here he was again, at the moment of decision. The freedom of the Vala hung on his decision, and he wouldn't make the same mistake he'd made before. This time, he would stop it.

"Get off my planet, Galo, and don't come back."

Galo grunted, a confused sound. Reagan saw how close he'd come to making a deal with the monster, and he stepped back a pace, but Galo followed him.

"Oh, but I'm sure we can make an arrangement! What can I bring you?"

"Anything you brought here would be stained with the blood of those children."

There was an exasperated edge in Galo's voice. "What do you want, Ray-gun? Anything!"

Squaring his shoulders, Reagan spoke slowly, with force. "I want you gone."

Galo's eyes showed fury and defeat. He leaned in close to Reagan. "I will retrieve my property." Galo's voice was hard.

A puff of the bitter gas that filled the Asgre suits drifted into Reagan's nose as Galo spoke. As the vapor entered his body, Reagan felt a tremor shake him. He stepped back just as Galo bowed and strode onto his ship.

The tremor remained, and Reagan clasped his hands together behind his back to stop their shaking. What was this?

By the time the ship rose, Reagan had regained control of his muscles, but a new fear had lodged itself in his chest. How far were they willing to go to get the Vala?

When Reagan returned to his office, new defense orders had arrived from the UEG headquarters on Earth. A death had been reported in the mine. The Asgre were aggressive, and the UEG wanted them gone. The Vala were to be returned to their masters, and he was to assist in gathering them. The UEG would not be responsible for endangering any more human lives.

But Reagan had made his choice. He would not be responsible for making anyone else a slave.

# Chapter 35

Aria and Ethan had spent the last two days filling Polara's room with hastily-prepared Taim trays, and the bright colors of Luis's pottery shone around the room like pieces of a rainbow.

They held each other in the green-tinted light of Polara's room. Taim trays covered the windowsills and shelves, the cupboard on the far wall, and the bed inside Polara's tent. She had eaten well today, and she was playing with her new doll from Hannah.

Rigel crawled happily on the floor. Aria had stopped responding to his every whim, and wanting things that were out of his reach had moved him to mobility. Each of the family wore a Taim patch, a little wearable chip of pottery with a pin stuck on the back and Taim growing on its front. The little plants waved cheerfully in spite of the bleak scenes in the rest of the hospital.

Rigel clapped as Ethan scooped him up. "I'm taking him for a little sunshine," Ethan said, and Aria caught them both for a kiss before letting them leave.

Moments later, a cleaning worker appeared at the door, and Aria rushed to meet him before he entered the room.

She pointed to a sign she'd made that hung on the door: "NO ZAM CLEANER ALLOWED IN THIS ROOM."

The worker glanced around at the plants. "Lady, it looks like you need it more than anybody."

"Don't come in." Aria said, her voice sharp. "No Zam is allowed in here."

The cleaning worker shrugged. "Okay," he said, "but tell the floor supervisor that. She's tough."

"I'll tell her." Aria felt relief as the man continued on to the next room. A new floor supervisor? That explained it. She'd have to go talk to her immediately.

"Polara, Mama will be right back, okay?"

Polara looked up and smiled, and Aria's heart caught at the beauty of the simple movement. She gave a little wave and left to find the new supervisor.

***

Marcos couldn't taste the gar candy in his mouth, but it kept the terrible dryness at bay. He wanted to lie down, to close his eyes and give into the weakness, but as Veronika maneuvered his wheelchair down the hospital hallway, he couldn't help glancing in the rooms. Some patients lay still in their beds, the clear bed covers tented over them, their struggle for breath evident by the wheezing that filled the hospital. Marcos heard it in his own breath.

If they were breathing, however laboriously, they were the lucky ones. In many rooms Marcos saw that the struggle for life had ended and the dejected family members of the dead gathered in the rooms and in the halls, weeping.

So when they passed the room with open curtains and a little girl playing happily with a doll under the cover over her bed, he held up a hand. Veronika stopped immediately.

"Take me in there." Saras said.

"Marcos, we're not allowed—"

"I own this hospital. I'll go where I want to go."

Marcos dropped his slick hands to the wheels and wrenched the chair away from her, rolling in next to the little girl's raised bed. She peered out at him, then waved. Marcos raised a hand slowly and waved back.

There were plants everywhere. The room looked as if no one had Zammed it in weeks, except that these plants were growing on bright trays and strangely-shaped plates and they were placed deliberately throughout the room.

Theo was gazing at the child, too. She waved at him.

"I know her," he said. "She's the child of the Caretaker." His voice was a little sarcastic. "Ethan Bryant."

Marcos gazed at her a moment more. How Theo knew that was a mystery to him. She looked, to him, like the thousand other children he saw around Coriol. But she had the fever. She should be laying still and covered in the purple marks as he was. Her arms, neck, and cheeks showed the evidence of the marks, but they had faded from deep purple to pale pink. They gave her an almost delicate glow. From her smile it seemed she felt fine. She was, judging by what he'd seen, the only person in this hospital recovering.

"Get me Ethan Bryant," Marcos said softly, waving a hand and laying his head back against the chair, his energy spent.

"Within the hour."

***

Bryant stood at the foot of Marcos' bed. Marcos knew the situation was different than the meeting they'd had weeks ago in his office at Saras Company. He knew the difference between sitting in an Earthleather chair and lying in a hospital bed. His tone revealed that knowledge.

"Mr. Bryant, I owe you an apology."

"I suspect that's not what you brought me here to talk about, Mr. Saras."

"Ethan, I'm prepared to make you a very impressive offer."

"Does it include stopping the blasting at the edge of the Karst Mountains?"

Marcos closed his eyes. He despised letting other people talk. They never saw what was really important. "Mr. Bryant, it's a monetary offer." Before he was finished, Bryant was walking toward the door. Marcos felt frantic, "and a stone and steel mansion. Don't go!"

The caretaker turned around. "If you want me to stay, you know my requirement."

Marcos glanced at Veronika. For once, she looked unsure. A coughing fit overtook him and Bryant stood halfway between the bed and the door, unmoving and seemingly unmoved.

When Marcos's breath came smoothly again, he looked pleadingly at Bryant. "I will stop the blasting. But I need something from you."

Bryant took a step back towards him. "Prove it. Make the call now to stop it."

Marcos held, still and quiet. The land grant flashed in his mind. They had extracted some already. It might be enough. And it might not matter either way if he was dead. He held out his hand to Theo. Theo pulled a missive from his inner jacket pocket and dialed, then handed it to Marcos.

The crew leader at the karst tunnel answered. "Hey boss."

"Stop blasting," Marcos said, his breath catching in another cough as he spoke.

"What's that?"

"Stop blasting." Marcos caught Bryant's eye and held it. "Send your crew home."

The man sounded flustered. "We're—we're coming along

fine, boss, we—"

Marcos's temper flared. "Send them home now or you'll be back on the refinery line tomorrow."

There was silence, then a subdued, "Yes, Mr. Saras."

Marcos held the missive impatiently out to Theo, who took it and talked quietly, moving around the bed and out into the hall as he spoke.

"Now can we talk, Mr. Bryant?"

The caretaker nodded.

"I saw your daughter today, down the hall," Marcos said, unable to keep the wistfulness out of his voice. Something about that happy, healthy child made everything else unimportant to him.

Bryant started to snap at him, but Marcos interrupted. "I just want to know why she's recovering."

This seemed to take Bryant by surprise. "You're—you're not asking me about Yynium?"

Marcos bit back his irritation. "The doctors insist that she has had no special care. Tell me what they've been giving her and I'll make you the second richest man in Coriol."

Bryant's eyebrows drew together. "They haven't given her anything. It was something my wife brought—"

"I'll buy it, then. I'll buy what your wife is giving her."

Bryant seemed to consider. *He wasn't so different*, Marcos thought. *Everyone has his price.* Slowly, Bryant nodded his head.

"All right, Mr. Saras. You want to buy it? We'll sell it. On one condition."

It was always conditional with this one. But it was worth it to Saras. "One *more* condition, you mean," he said, "you've already got me to stop blasting."

"Fair enough." Bryant shrugged. "One more condition: You buy enough for every building in Coriol. Every apartment in the tenements, every room in the refinery, every office. Everybody gets one."

"Fine. Done." Marcos tried not to show his exasperation. "Gets one what?"

"One Taim tray. When the papers are signed and the scrip transferred, I'll deliver yours personally, and tell you why it works."

Marcos was wild at the possibility of a cure. "I will have it transferred before you leave the hospital." He snapped his fingers at Veronika, then remembered that she hated that.

Bryant nodded. "Then I'll bring it tonight." He seemed so used to business dealings at this level that Marcos had to remind himself that Bryant was only a linguist. Where had this ability come from?

Marcos watched him leave and turned to see Veronika making the transfer with her missive. She raised a smoldering gaze to him.

Marcos leaned back. He was tired. Tired of fighting them, tired of worrying about Yynium day in and day out, tired of being alone.

Veronika had reminded him often, at the beginning, that he didn't have to be alone. He knew she'd envisioned walking right into the Saras mansion on Yynium Hill with him, had figured the two of them could pick up right where she and his father had left off. But he'd seen his mother's heart broken. He would not see that look in Serena's eyes. Veronika had underestimated him—he was not his father.

Now, with the haze of his fear clearing, it occurred to Marcos that his dying of Minean fever would have been quite convenient for her. She would step into control of Saras Company in Coriol just as she had planned. Did that vial he'd seen her slip Zuma have anything to do with all this?

Marcos rolled his head the other direction and looked at Theo. It may not have been so easy for Veronika to take over. Theo would have fought for Saras Company, too.

Maybe with these trays, neither of them would get the chance.

\*\*\*

Ethan called to invite Luis to the cottage. When he walked in, Luis was already there, chatting with Aria. A straw-filled crate of plates sat next to her on the floor, and Ethan smiled. They were going to be put to good use.

"Luis, we have a great opportunity," Ethan said, glancing at the threadbare clothes the potter was wearing. This could really change things for him. Luis looked at him curiously.

"What if I told you that Saras wants a huge order of your plates?"

Luis blinked. "My friend, I would tell you you're crazy. My plates have no place here. They don't fit in the sanitizer, they don't match the décor. I only make them because I need something to do, and you only take them because you don't want to hurt my feelings."

Ethan reached down and pulled one of the beautiful plates from the crate. Its pale blue surface was glazed clear with streaks of vibrant spring green. The plate's circular throwing pattern made dips and hills where the glaze had pooled and run. It was, like every one of Luis's plates, completely unique.

Ethan nodded toward his wife. "Aria has discovered something special about your plates." She shot him a worried glance, obviously concerned that this would hurt their friend's feelings, but Ethan smiled broadly to encourage her.

She went into the other room and emerged with a serving tray full of Taim plants. They were about the height of Ethan's hand and they swayed gently as Aria brought them in.

Luis raised his eyebrows.

"These plants—we're calling them Taim—" Aria said proudly, "cured Polara."

"Cured?" Luis brightened, but looked cautious. "How?" He walked closer and ran a finger across the fluffy tops of the plants.

Aria continued. "We figured out that Minean fever is caused by a gas," Aria said, skipping the part about her stolen vial, "which seems to be coming from the mines. We've tried reporting it, but no one will listen. The Taim metabolize both the gas and carbon dioxide and release pure oxygen, thereby cleaning the air. In fact, the more gas and the more carbon dioxide, the healthier the Taim plants. The more Taim, the less gas we measured in the air."

Luis smiled for real this time.

"So I did some experiments, and I can grow Taim in trays. And you know what? They grow best on your pottery." She smiled at their friend.

"It must be the glaze," he said. "I mix it myself, you know."

Ethan nodded. "I know. And you're going to have to mix a lot more. When Polara was the most sick, we put the trays in her hospital bed and by morning she was awake."

\*\*\*

Ethan called his passengers to come and help with the Taim trays. They met first at Reverend Hardy's church, as it was more centrally located than Ethan's cottage. But they were scared, and weary of having no work here. They were not the same passengers who had opened their eyes to gaze with hope on Minea four years ago. They were discouraged and bitter, angry and disappointed. As they crowded angrily to the front of the church, he began to think that gathering them here together had been a mistake.

Ethan tried to speak to them, but they were shouting.

"What are we going to do?"

"Where will we work, Ethan?"

"What do these aliens want, anyway?"

Suddenly, Ethan heard Silas's gentle, sincere voice. A single word, "Friends," caught the attention of the clamoring mass.

Ethan turned to see the motivational speaker standing with his arms raised, his artificial left hand, fingers spread, caught the light.

"Friends," Silas said again, and waited until they stilled. "You are unique," he said, allowing the silence that followed his words to soak in around his listeners. "We were not wanted on Minea, it's true." He spoke quickly and gently. "But we were needed."

Ethan saw, like magic, the passengers quieting. This was Silas's gift.

"Beauty." Silas let the word glisten in the air and gestured toward Hannah and Luis and several artists in the crowd. "That's needed here. When we walk through the streets and see the tenements, with the people packed inside, when we see the hungry children, when we see the spots of Minean fever creeping across the skin of people we love—we need beautiful things to kindle the flames of our hope that flickers when these painful experiences come. We need beautiful things to draw our hearts and minds back to that hope and lead us upward again. On Earth, lots of people are creating that beauty. Here, if you," again he gestured towards the passengers, "don't create that beauty, no one else will."

He stood and looked at them. The passion in his voice kept their attention. Ethan found himself caught up in Silas's words.

"Help." He looked toward Minz, Walters, the Reverend, and others in the service industry. "Your gifts of helping others are needed. You can serve. When people are weary from the mines or ill or angry, they forget the small things—" he pointed at Minz specifically, "a clean shirt," then at Walters, "a hot bowl of soup," and then at Reverend Hardy, "a prayer in a dark moment. Never mind what Saras says, that the sanitizer and the server can bring those, and that prayers are only needed at weddings and funerals. Those things that you can do can give others mental and physical and spiritual strength to get through one more day.

"When I was on Earth," Silas's voice grew stronger, "I was proud and greedy. I made my money by stepping on other people and taking it from them. But then, I fell off a cliff. Literally and figuratively. In the desert backcountry, I slipped on a slick rock ridge and fell thirty meters." He paused, letting them imagine it. "It took this."

He gestured to the stump of his missing arm, with the artificial limb attached, and paused again. There wasn't a breath in the room.

Then he said, "Must have knocked somethin' else loose, too."

Softly, Silas laughed. A self-deprecating chuckle that allowed the crowd to laugh, too, and provided a perfect moment of rest in his intense story.

He continued. "Because I didn't want to be that guy anymore. I wanted to find something good in people and help them embrace it." He walked across the front of the room once, twice, then turned toward them. "You embrace it. Embrace what you can give the people here on Minea, in Coriol, and even if nobody else sees its value, give it anyway and know that it is needed."

He stepped back, placing his one hand in front of his chest and bowing his head. Ethan's passengers cheered.

After that it was easy to organize them. Ethan explained the Taim trays and sent many of them to his cottage to help Aria. The Reverend started a conversation about other needs, especially the food shortage. Several of the passengers committed to helping Aria with her fruit deliveries. Walters volunteered to wait outside the steel and stone mansions and collect food donations, which he promised to deliver all over Coriol, as if it were one giant restaurant and he was the head waiter.

Somehow, Silas had given them, with his words, a sense of duty, a self-respect, and a drive to overcome their challenges here and make the kind of contributions that Coriol, and all of Minea, was lacking.

*** 

Aria was delighted when the passengers of Ship 12-22 showed up to help her make the Taim trays. She'd had them bring Taim from their houses, but they needed more. While the passengers gathered at her cottage to unpack Luis's pottery and transfer the Taim from her walls to the trays, she went out to gather more Taim.

Taking a large bucket with her, Aria started in the first neighborhood after Forest Heights. She knew a few people here. Some of them had children in Polara's school. She knocked first on the Woods' door, since she had worked with Lela on some class parties last year. When Lela Woods opened the front door, though, her smile froze.

"Hello," Lela said guardedly, keeping the door partially closed between them. News had gotten around that Polara was in the hospital, that the plague had reached their neighborhood, and Aria didn't blame her neighbors for being scared.

"I have a strange request, Lela," she asked directly. "I need to know if you have any of the little plants that have been growing everywhere."

Lela looked offended. "Of course not. I scrape the mold off every day. I scraped off a whole bunch today."

Aria brightened. "You don't use Zam on them?"

Lela shook her head. "Usually I do, but I've been out for a week."

Aria knew the next part sounded crazy. She tried to think of a way to soften it, to make it sound like she wanted to borrow a cup of root sugar, but she just blurted, "Do you have the ones you scraped off today? Could I have them?"

Lela's eyebrows drew together. Considering, she finally waved a hand toward the backyard. "They clog up my disposer, so I dump them in the back. If you really want them, you're welcome to them." Aria could tell that collecting plants from the garbage was not something Lela approved of, but she thanked her neighbor quickly and went to retrieve them. As she scooped handfuls into her bucket, she glanced up to see Lela peering out the back window at her, dismayed.

"They're not a mold!" she called helpfully. Lela shook her head quickly and disappeared into the depths of her house.

Aria's hands were covered with bright green, and the sharp, sweet smell of the little plants—almost like Earth's mint, with a hint of orange scent—filled her house as she carried the bucket back in to the kitchen table.

Aria pulled a wide oblong serving tray from a crate, then she sat down at the table. Several of the passengers gathered around. She glanced up at them. "When you remove them from the walls, break as few of the tiny roots as you can."

"Can you show us how you replant them?" Hannah asked,

leaning closer.

"Sure. Like this: Come here, little Taim," Aria said as she carefully grasped little bunches of the plants and disentangled them from each other. "I have a new home for you."

Many of them were damaged, their roots sliced through from Lela Woods' scraping, and Aria set those aside. The ones that were whole, though, she carefully arranged in the trays, spreading their roots below them.

"They want to spread their roots out, so it helps if you don't crowd them," she said.

Soon she ran out of trays. There were still plants in the bucket, so she looked for another box full of Luis's pottery. Several crates stood empty around her, and the bright colors of Luis's plates danced as the passengers snatched them up, filling them with the little plants. It was a good thing he hadn't given up making them. There were plenty now, when they really needed them.

A knock came at the door. When she opened it, it took Aria a moment to realize who was there. The cousins who had been with Ethan in the cave: Ndaiye and Traore.

"Ethan sent us a message that you needed some help over here," Traore said. Their broad bright smiles added to the cheery environment and she put them immediately to work. Ndaiye's singing filled the little cottage.

Maybe this could be the one really good thing that Saras gave Coriol.

But as she looked at the trays in front of her, she felt a pang of worry. The scraped Taim lay wilted and limp. It may be too late. They may not make it. The broken ones which she had set aside were already drying out, and they crumbled in her hands as she swept them into the bucket to dump outside. They would have to get word out to people not to destroy them.

The cure for Minean fever was growing on their very walls, and they were scrubbing and scraping it into oblivion.

"Chip," Aria called over her salesman friend, "I need you to go to the HHSD and have them issue a bulletin this afternoon for people to grow the Taim, not kill it. I want you to write it. Make people want to protect the Taim." She knew he could convince them. There were few people immune to Chip's sales tactics.

"Do you know where it is?"

Chip nodded. "The public health office is across from the Saras Employment Office. I've been staring at their sign for hours every day for a month. I think I can find it."

"I don't think you'll have time to waste your days down there for a while," Aria said. "Saras paid well for these trays, and that scrip is coming to all of you."

Chip flashed a smile as he headed out the door. He left just as she saw Hannah and two other passengers start for the door with an enormous load of Taim trays.

"Ethan told us to take these to Polara's school." Hannah called back as Aria caught her eye. Aria waved, a bright hope growing within her. The cottage buzzed around her with activity and conversation.

# Chapter 36

What had he done? Marcos lay in his bed back at the mansion cursing his moments of weakness. How had he let Bryant talk him into stopping work on the new shaft? And what, really, was keeping him from starting it again?

Looking out the window next to his bed, past a tray of Bryant's plants, he could see the skyline of Coriol. And he could see heavy Asgre ships, three of them, hanging still over his city.

He wondered about the aliens. How far was their home world? How long had they been traveling? Did they have creatures they loved back there? Could they love?

This Taim thing seemed like an excellent solution to the mining problem. If there were Taim, there was no gas. If there was no gas, people wouldn't get sick, and without people getting sick, production numbers would go up.

But he still needed to get his hands on that Yynium under the karst peaks. That new shaft had to go on. He had to win this land grant.

Theo came in. He'd been distant and nervous lately, not his usual friendly self. Perhaps he was afraid of catching Minean fever. Marcos still hadn't allowed the release of the news about the gas from the mine, and now that the little trays of plants were soaking it up, perhaps he wouldn't need to.

"Marcos," Theo said, "I need to discuss something with you." He was agitated, and paced the room with a hand in his pocket.

"What is it, Theo?"

"Something big. Something you're not going to like."

"Theo." Marcos was glad that his voice was returning to its usual strength. "Just say it."

Theo stopped and looked Marcos in the eye. "Veronika is trying to undermine the company."

Marcos had seen this coming, knew that they would eventually go after each other. Marcos had seen it in Theo's eyes the day the passengers of the P5 had awakened and there were suddenly two VPs. He and Theo both knew Veronika wanted all of it, and knew she was likely to get it, because she'd stop at nothing to do so. She thought it was owed her. Theo had been trying to keep her from outpacing him ever since.

"Too vague, Theo. What is it that you're concerned about?"

"Well, I don't have all the information yet, but Gaynes down at the market told me she's been involved in some shady dealings with some of the miners."

Marcos sat up straighter. "Shady dealings?"

"Apparently a miner kid showed up at the market with a sample from the mine. Told Gaynes that Veronika had paid him to steal some from the Colony Offices Air Quality crew. The kid had one left, and Gaynes bought it off him."

Theo leaned in conspiratorially. "Gaynes says he paid the kid for a sample, but when he got around to looking in the case, it was empty. He wants the kid arrested. I need your permission to . . . question the kid."

Marcos heard a strange tone in Theo's voice. "Why do you need my permission?" The words 'plausible deniability' flashed in Marcos' head again.

Theo sidestepped the question. "If these are really gas samples from the mine, we don't want the UEG getting hold of them. I need to know what happened to all three of them."

"We need to talk to Veronika about all this." Marcos knew where one of the vials had gone. He reached for his missive.

"I don't think that's a good idea," Theo said, "not yet."

"Why not?" Marcos didn't like asking this many questions in a single conversation. He liked answers.

Theo crossed and stood beside the bed, putting a shaking hand on Marcos's shoulder. "Listen, Marc, I don't know what she's capable of. She was pretty worked up when she found out about you sending out that dirty Yynium." Theo shook his head slowly, "She told me you would bring the company down, and you know the company's all she's got. She wants to run it alone. I don't think there's anything she wouldn't do. You go confronting her about it and she could lash out. Just let me look into it for a while. I'll see what I can find out."

Marcos felt weak and worried. He wanted to hand this over to Theo. He put a hand on the older man's arm and nodded, wondering how to avoid Veronika until Theo had it figured out.

Theo left, and Marcos ordered the smarthouse on emergency lockdown.

He had to get the mines back on track. The land grant still depended on it. With the shafts destroyed, mining the Yynium under the Karst Mountains was the only chance he had. He picked up his missive and called the crew leader from the karst tunnel.

# Chapter 37

They weren't leaving. The Asgre ships still hovered over the planet, and Reagan saw on his screens that the original ships had been joined by many more.

They had reclaimed some of the Vala, but according to Ethan, many still huddled in the cave system below the mountains, and Reagan saw that Galo was going to come after them.

Reagan thought about his responsibility. He was to "guard the inhabitants of Minea from planetary and interplanetary threats." Did that mean all the inhabitants of Minea? Reagan felt relieved that these beings, the Asgre, were not here for humans. They were not threatening Minea or Yynium production. The UEG maintained that they had simply come for their property.

But Reagan couldn't convince himself of that. Not really. Though he'd only seen those few, the Vala were, from what Kaia reported that Ethan had told her, at least a Class 6 civilization, with family groups, creations, mineral manipulation, and written and spoken language. They were not livestock, were not objects.

Reagan laid his head against the cool wall. He was in this moment again. His position dictated that he bow to the UEG orders and hand over the Vala, even if he had to extract them with his own troops.

But it wasn't right. He knew it to his core.

He walked out of his Coriol Defense Headquarters office onto the second-floor balcony. It overlooked the first floor training facility, and he watched as the Coriol Defense Troops practiced advance tactics.

The CDT was using the latest UEG recommendations for hand-to-hand combat, a tactic called the trigon, where the squadron of soldiers broke into teams of ten, each with a single, strong point man. The point man stood at the front of the trigon formation, supported behind by three strong soldiers. This central column was surrounded by two supporting flanks of three soldiers each, falling slightly behind the point man to make a triangle. They held their weapons at all angles, the sides of the trigon pointing out and the center soldiers pointing up. It was a beautiful formation, and Reagan imagined it against a front line of enemies. In his mind, the front line was made up of Asgre mercenaries.

Reagan went back into the office. He locked the door behind him. He pushed the button that darkened the windows. In the dark, he reached into his briefcase and pulled out his missive. On it he called up the passenger list of Ship 12-22 and let the missive play through the list slowly. The passengers' faces appeared one after the other in front of him.

Reagan opened his contacts and dialed Ethan. "Son," he said, "I need to talk to you."

Reagan was waiting on the balcony when Ethan stepped off the elevator. Below them, the Coriol Defense Troops practiced sharp, triangular formations.

Reagan lingered a moment, watching them, then waved Ethan into his office.

Ethan sat across from Reagan. "I've heard from everybody

about this situation," Reagan said, "Saras, the President, the Asgre. But I haven't heard from you and I haven't heard from your friends."

Ethan was somber. "The Vala are peaceful, Phillip. They don't deserve to be imprisoned. They are compassionate. They helped us in the cave, when there was nothing in it for them. They have children. The Asgre use them in their ships somehow." Ethan ran an agitated hand across his forehead. "I don't even know how, or for what, or where their ships go."

Reagan cleared his throat and tapped the screen, bringing up surveillance photos of the Asgre ship, up close, when it was on the ground outside of Coriol. "You don't want to see this, but you should."

He showed Ethan a photo of the cage on the bottom of the ship, where a Vala child crouched miserably in front of a screen. Reagan watched as the horror crossed Ethan's face.

"I don't know what they use the Vala for, either, but I heard Galo mention that there is a metal the Vala cannot go through. These cages and the shackles they use are made of it. I think they use the Vala to help them navigate or something. The Asgre are a merchant race. According to their leader, Galo, they ship things across the universe."

"Things." Ethan spat the word out. "Things. Things that are more important to them than living beings."

As he stared at the little being in the cage, Reagan ached for it and for its parents. "Ethan, how can we help them?"

"Protect them, Phillip. Give them one race that will be their friends instead of using them."

"So we let them stay? It will be a war, Ethan. You realize that? A war with an opponent I can't even fathom. People will die."

Ethan looked him levelly in the eye. "We're all going to die,

Phillip. Nobody knows that better than you and me." There was such a depth of pain in Ethan's eyes that Reagan had to look away to hold his own emotions in check. "We're all going to die, so we'd better live well while we have the chance."

When Reagan turned back toward Ethan, he felt a new resolve. "I want to meet with them. I want to know what they want from us. I want to hear them say it. I won't ever make decisions for others without giving them a say again."

Ethan's eyes shone. Evidently, that was what he had wanted to hear. "Do you think we should bring them here?"

Reagan shook his head. "No. Your house is on the edge of the forest. They should be able to get there without exposing themselves to too many humans. Once people find out that the Asgre are here for them, we may have to protect the Vala from the humans, too."

\*\*\*

That night Reagan sat at Ethan's kitchen table, watching as Ethan removed his thought blocker.

"I didn't have much luck when I tried to communicate telepathically with them," he said, "but what they can sense from me may help us get beyond the limits of the translator." Reagan saw that Ethan was nervous about it. He knew the toll that even human thoughts took on Ethan and Kaia. He smiled encouragingly, sending a thought of appreciation.

It was after dark when the Vala came slowly into the dimmed kitchen of Ethan's cottage. There were four of them. They were human-sized, covered with creased pale skin. They placed Reagan's hand to their foreheads, and the gentleness of the gesture surprised him.

He saw them fold themselves into the chairs around the kitchen table, but they shifted awkwardly, and their short tails bunched up in the chair seats. Their middle appendages stuck awkwardly out. Reagan could see that they were uncomfortable. One stood up beside the table awkwardly. Reagan glanced at Ethan, who gestured to the floor.

Reagan nodded. "Would you," he stood and gestured to the wide space in the living room, "prefer to sit here?" He lowered himself to the ground, watching the crease in his uniform trousers smooth into oblivion.

They seemed pleased, making small "hmm," sounds and rocking their heads up and down. Smoothly and with grace, they arranged themselves around him on the floor in an easy circle.

"I am Phillip Reagan," he said, bowing his head slightly as he listened to the translator.

"Ray-gun. Ray-gun." The Vala repeated.

He smiled. "Do you want to stay on Minea? Here?" he asked.

The question seemed to reach them all at the same time, and they all rocked up and down gently in assent. Aemon spoke, and Reagan listened carefully to the translator.

"We have searched far for a planet which meets our biological requirements. This planet has the correct atmosphere, the correct minerals for our needs. The cave systems are extensive. We could be happy here." His genial mood suddenly changed, though, and Reagan saw, in the drumming of his fingers on the carpet, that he had grown anxious.

"But we are not safe. Our children are not safe. The Asgre have found us, have recaptured some of us. They know we are here, and we cannot stay. We must flee."

Reagan cleared his throat, trying to think of what he could realistically promise them.

"We want to help you," he said, trying to show his sincerity in his gaze. "To offer you . . . protection."

There was a stir in the group, and they passed their long fingers across each other's palms. He was unsure what that meant. He waited a moment, two. Still, they looked at one another and at their fingers, brushing the other Valas' hands.

Finally, after several minutes, a female named Ahmasa spoke. "We will not be used," she said firmly. "We have seen our masters. They perform services and receive currency in trade. They support themselves in this way. We, too, will work for ourselves."

Reagan nodded. What the wrinkly creatures could do, though, he didn't know. The smile on Ethan's face told him that the young man had heard that thought and Reagan grimaced toward Ethan apologetically.

"The Vala have a gift that I think could be very valuable to humanity," Ethan said. He glanced at both Reagan and their alien guests. Reagan shot him a questioning look.

"The Vala can extract Yynium from the ground without mining it. They can remove it by the block."

Aemon rocked back and forth. "This is true. Do your people want this orange mineral?"

Reagan smiled. "Very much." He saw Ethan's plan and tried to articulate it. "Would you be willing to enter into an agreement with us? You extract the Yynium and our companies pay you?"

The Vala turned to each other, again passing their fingers across each other's palms. "We would," they said.

Ethan spoke up. "What about when the Yynium runs out?" he asked.

Before Reagan could answer, Aemon spoke. "We have found that this mineral comes from a molten source," he said. "If the veins are broken by blasting, then the channels become blocked, and no new material flows into the veins. But when we extract the material, we leave the channels intact, and new molten material flows into them as it is made deep inside the planet. When it cools it can be harvested again."

Ethan turned wide eyes to Reagan. They were both thinking the same thing: Yynium as a renewable resource would change everything.

Ahmasa spoke, her voice clear and precise and her words coming through the translator. "And if, in the future, we choose not to extract the mineral for humans? What would happen?"

Reagan felt the power of his words as he spoke them. "You could do as you please. You would be free."

The Vala delegation rocked forward and backward in assent. "We would do this."

***

Reagan walked back to the barracks that night feeling better than he had in years. He thought through the strategy. He would need all six battleships, and all twelve company ships. The Asgre were not a warring race. Perhaps a show of force would scare them away.

Just in case, though, he would ready his ground troops in every settlement. He would have to leave the ground troops in the other cities and rely on the Coriol Defense Troops to defend the city. But they would need more soldiers.

It was time to ask for volunteers.

# Chapter 38

Early the next morning, Ethan reached up behind his ear. He braced himself as he removed the little button that had kept his mind free of the incessant noise of other people for the last four years. Holding his son on his lap, he looked into Rigel's deep gray eyes and thought of his love for the child, let it grow in his mind and heart and well up and outward in his thoughts toward the little boy. *I love you,* he thought.

A pure, inquisitive beam of thought pierced Ethan's mind. It was like an unasked question, filling his thoughts with a curiosity he hadn't felt since the first time he saw Xardn symbols.

Ethan smiled, wondering if Rigel would like Xardn. He extended the thought again, this time in Xardn:

Rigel squealed with delight, placing his hands on Ethan's cheeks. Ethan saw, in his mind unbidden, the symbol for love repeated.

The feeling of communicating with Rigel, whose thoughts

had been concealed so long behind his luminous eyes, washed over Ethan like starlight. It was as beautiful as the sound of Polara's first word, as moving as the moment he burst forth from the darkness of the cave into Aria's arms.

Rigel's thoughts tumbled wildly, flitting from one bright thing to another until the child glimpsed the Taim and focused on them. The Taim trays that covered the counters in the kitchen began to sway. Ethan gazed at Rigel as the little boy began to sway with them.

A feeling of gratitude cut through Ethan's consciousness as Rigel danced with the Taim. What was Rigel grateful for? Did he even know gratitude yet? The feeling grew stronger, and Rigel looked at his father, clapping his small hands as the feeling washed through him.

And then Ethan knew. Aria had always maintained that some plants may be capable of emotion and communication, and as bright colors and complex feelings flowed through Rigel into Ethan's mind, he realized that the Taim were sentient. They were communicating with Rigel, and Rigel was passing along their messages to Ethan. For a moment, he reveled in the freshness of their feelings. These plants were young, but very mature. They were joyous.

It was something like working with the glitchy translator, though. Rigel didn't have all the experience needed to truly convey what the plants were communicating. But basic concepts came through clearly. The swaying Taim plants were happy to be safe.

They had an interconnected consciousness, and Ethan felt their pain and sadness over the seedlings that had been lost to Zam and the vicious blades of the scrapers. Rigel began to cry, and Ethan ached for him, knowing that the only way to turn off the Taim's voices in his mind was to give him a thought blocker.

But Rigel was so young. Perhaps he could learn to shut out the voices at will. Perhaps he could be spared the pain of his gift and only revel in the joy of it.

Because, when the Taim began to celebrate their new situation, Rigel's joy returned as well. The bridge of their thoughts gave Rigel the deep connection that the little boy had always excelled at. Through him now, Ethan saw the peace the Taim had found and felt their hope for the future.

*** 

The Taim trays had done their work, scrubbing the gas out of the air. Maybe it was Aria's imagination, but the city seemed to sparkle with fresh oxygen.

Many of the little plants were quickly outgrowing their pottery trays. And as they grew, they developed a more complex root system. When they reached a certain size, the Taim needed soil to grow in. They tipped over if they couldn't anchor themselves. Aria secured a large field at the farm to transplant them to and put out a general missive announcement to bring overgrown Taim trays out for replanting.

Aria stood at the gate to the farm, Taim trays spread around her, top-heavy and verdant. As the first few people walked through, she handed each of them a tray. They walked out into the vast bare field and knelt.

She watched them, their hands scooping at the dirt, the marks on their faces fading and barely visible from a distance. They tucked the Taim into the rich soil with reverence and care.

Hundreds more came, bringing their own trays from home. She saw Luis's platters, his bowls, his mugs, all brimming with growing Taim. She glanced at Ethan, who was holding their bouncing son.

"What is he saying?" she asked, hungry to know Rigel's thoughts and the thoughts of the sentient plants that had saved them all.

Ethan smiled and reached behind his ear, removing his thought blocker. She saw him wince, then lean down to rest his forehead on Rigel's.

Ethan was still a long few moments. He nodded, then raised his brimming eyes.

"He says the Taim are singing. Not just the babies, but their parents in the Taim grove."

She smiled. "They're happy then."

Ethan reached for her hand. "He says they are singing, Aria, about you."

Aria looked at the dancing plants. Their rhythmic swaying mesmerized her. To have found them, to have saved them, made her feel useful again, made her knowledge as valuable here as it was on Earth. Maybe more so.

She had felt that her presence mattered to her plants back on Earth, had suspected that they grew better when she talked to them, that she was able to understand their needs on a deeper level than some of the other scientists, even in her own field. But they had been a different life form, governed by simple rules of growth and nourishment. These plants had actual will. They had thoughts. They had sent their young spiraling across the wind to the city not because of coincidence or simple biology, but because they wanted their young to have the best chance of survival. They were able to change their usual pattern of seeding to get their young to a suitable growth environment.

Aria laid a hand on Rigel's head. To have that gift—to be able to speak to the plants—must be wonderful and terrifying. She had loved plants since the moment, as a child back on Earth, she'd pushed a bean into dirt in an old milk carton. She'd loved them when the bean curled a green shoot out through the dirt. She'd loved them when its fuzzy leaves unfurled and the wonder of a living seed had been revealed to her. The souls of plants had always been more apparent to her than to others. And the Taim, these thinking, acting creatures, were both like and unlike those plants she had always loved. To speak to them, to know what the world was like for them, seemed achingly wonderful to Aria.

There was more than that, though. She looked at Rigel, cradled in the shelter of Ethan's arms, and Aria felt a longing to be able to speak to her silent son. She had heard Ethan's voice in her head before, a few times, and she knew the wonder of telepathic communication. She pushed away a little wave of jealousy for Ethan's gift. She couldn't hear Rigel, but he could still hear her.

*I love you, baby*, she thought, trying to push the words in his general direction. Her clumsy effort must have been effective, because Rigel turned toward his mother. His blue eyes found hers and he wiggled happily, as if trying to communicate back to her. She took him in her arms.

"See them dancing, Ri?" she pointed to the Taim.

Ethan was rubbing his temples. "He has such a powerful telepathic connection," he said. "It must be so intense for him. All the time."

Aria held him tighter and wished again that she could communicate directly with the Taim, to save Rigel the pressure of it.

People were still streaming by, planting their seedlings in the rich soil. Aria heard a familiar voice behind her. She turned just as Daniel embraced her.

"Your Taim saved Nallie," he said, his voice choked with emotion. Aria ran her free hand over his hair as Rigel clutched at the young man's coveralls.

As she stepped back, Aria glanced down at Polara, chattering rapidly with the two little Rigo girls. Nallie and Polara both had the same fading pink tinge to their skin. Aria's heart caught as she thought of how close Nallie must have come to death. She reached out and squeezed Daniel's arm.

"They've given us a great gift," she said. From the corner of her eye, she saw Ethan. He was watching, smiling.

"Ethan," she said, reaching for his hand, "this is Daniel Rigo."

The men shook hands.

Daniel's voice was earnest as he said, "Sir, Aria saved my life." He glanced at the little girls again. "Several times now."

Ethan smiled broadly. "Then we have something in common. She's saved mine, too." Ethan squeezed her hand. "Several times."

Aria grinned. "How are things for you, Daniel?"

Daniel glanced away. "I'm—I'm sorry about the day at the store, Aria. I shouldn't have been there, and I didn't want you to know what I was doing."

Aria knew that feeling. She nodded her forgiveness. Aria noticed now how Daniel had aged since she'd first seen him in the market, the day Gaynes had made him chase the scrip across the floor. A bitter taste filled her mouth at the thought of the man. It seemed a lifetime ago.

"It was a stupid mistake. And now, my little sisters are paying for it." Daniel raised pleading eyes to Aria's and she felt a chill.

"What do you mean, Daniel?"

"Gaynes." Daniel spit the word. "He's threatening my family now. I have to keep them in the apartment all the time when I'm at work. I don't even dare let them play outside."

Aria looked at Ethan. "Can you turn him in?" she asked.

Ethan nodded. "I will." A shadow crossed his features. "But you should know that the process is excessively slow, especially with Saras managers. And they'll want proof."

"That means questions about what I did." Daniel's expression was hard. "Maybe I'll just have to take care of it myself."

# Chapter 39

Only days after the Taim was planted in its new field, Ethan stood with Aria at the edge of it, shocked by what he saw. The Taim had grown. Not a little. It was three meters high and growing almost before their eyes.

Through Rigel, the Taim had told them that as seedlings they depended on the ground gas that ran in channels underground, much like the liquid Yynium. The gas channels had, in all the previous seeding cycles, run into the Karst Mountains and provided the seedlings with the gas that they needed to metabolize. But the blasting had fractured the gas channels, sending the ground gas into the city. It was toxic to humans and vital to the Taim. The Taim seeds followed the gas into the city, in order to have enough to grow into strong seedlings. But they also needed carbon dioxide to grow and in Coriol they got an extra boost from so many humans emitting so much carbon dioxide.

Now that they were planted in the field, with the gas flowing out of the mine on one side of them and the city washing them with its abundance of carbon dioxide on the other side, they were growing remarkably fast. In days, they said, they would be a full-grown Taim grove, just as Aria had seen in the mountains with the children.

Ethan had been looking at them in wonder when the deep reverberation of Saras explosives shook the ground and bounced off the karst peaks in the distance.

Saras had broken his promise. He'd begun blasting again.

The Asgre had damaged Saras's shafts in their search, and he wanted the Asgre off the planet. Giving them the Vala, he argued to the Coriol Defense Committee, would achieve that.

The UEG was supporting him. They wanted humans and Yynium safe at any cost. Reagan, though, was preparing to defend the Vala. He had called for volunteers against the Asgre threat. He was risking his admiralcy with such open defiance to the UEG. But Ethan knew it was the only option. Now he had seen the cages on the Asgre ships. He had seen the little barred boxes where the frightened Vala children cowered. Every time he thought of it he felt sick.

If humanity would not protect innocent children, then what humanity was in them, after all?

Ethan left the Taim grove with a new resolve. He would not allow the Asgre to reclaim the Vala. Ethan and Reagan would fight him alone, even if there was no fleet, if there were no ground troops, if no one else stood against this monster, Galo. The symbol flashed through Ethan's mind:

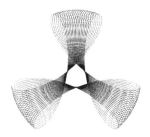

Ethan and Reagan would stand between Galo and the Vala children until they could no longer stand.

\*\*\*

Late that night, a group of Vala appeared at Ethan's cottage. He and Aria stood with their arms around each other as Svetal, the single adult Vala in the group, herded fifteen Vala children into the cottage. The children looked sleepy and clung together uncomfortably.

"The Asgre have found us," Svetal said urgently. "Somehow they know we are in the caves. We have destroyed the staircase, and they cannot enter, but they have landed, and they flock around the entrance, trying to gain access. I was able to flee with these children, who had already awakened, but our other adults have stayed in the sanctuary and in the cavern with the sleepers. They are in great danger."

Ethan looked at the little group. "Could you flee the planet? If we held the Asgre off?"

Svetal looked incredibly sad. "No. Some of our sleepers are still deeply dormant, and even these children, who have just awakened, must regain strength before they can—"

Again the translator buzzed with an error. The word she spoke was the concept for which Ethan's language had no words.

Svetal tried again. "Before they can travel," she said, though Ethan had expected to hear the word 'navigate.'

"Can you keep us safe, Ethan Bryant? Can you protect us?"

Ethan looked at Aria. She was already in motion, crouching before the little Vala children, motioning them to the soft thick rug in the living room.

"Ethan," she said, "go to Kaia's for more blankets."

He offered a smile at Svetal and nodded. "You are welcome here," he said, "and we will keep you safe."

*** 

The next morning Ethan had signed up with the volunteer

ground forces, where he'd seen several of his passengers from Ship 12-22. Kaia was out recruiting, and she was pretty persuasive. After he'd signed up and got his uniform and weapon, he'd dropped them off with Aria at the cottage before taking the sol train to Saras Company Headquarters.

So now he stood again in Saras's office, battling the man behind the desk. He had been surprised to see Veronika Eppes standing in the office. There was a rumor that she was scheming against the company and Saras was avoiding her. Now, the way she draped an arm around the back of Saras's chair and watched Ethan with her arachnid eyes made Ethan suspect that avoiding her was harder than it sounded.

Ethan spoke as forcefully as he could. "Absolutely not. You cannot keep blasting, and you cannot support giving the Vala to the Asgre."

Saras's eyes slid over him. "You like being a hero, don't you, Mr. Bryant?"

Ethan felt his heart rate quicken. "That's not what this is about."

Saras persisted. "But you do, right? You do like to be a hero? Come on, everybody likes to be a hero. Even I'd like to be a hero. But who's the hero here, Ethan? Is it the person who saves the aliens or the person who saves the humans? You didn't seem to have any question about that when you were fighting on Beta Alora."

"We're not sending these beings back into slavery."

"You have a difficult time seeing things from other points of view, don't you, Ethan?"

"What is that supposed to mean?"

"It means that your ethics, your morality, are so tied up in your tiny human experience. You have to broaden your mind. What if slavery is only bad because you've been taught it is?

You have some idea that owning another creature is inherently wrong or shameful. Obviously the Asgre don't see it that way. They see it as necessary and useful. Can't you open your mind to their worldview?"

Ethan turned away from him, disgusted. "Why would I want to do that?"

"Why does anyone do anything, Ethan?" Saras said. "For their own gain. We all have a lot to gain by giving the Vala back to the Asgre."

"You know a lot about personal gain," Ethan said disgustedly.

"I do." Saras was proud of the fact.

Ethan stuck his hands in his jacket pockets, frustrated. A smooth edge slid across his fingertip and Ethan remembered the morning on the bank of the river when Theo had taken the chunks of Yynium. In the midst of the Asgre invasion and Polara's illness, he had forgotten it except to occasionally worry that Theo would reveal the Vala's whereabouts. But the Asgre already knew where they were and that fear was past now.

Ethan leaned across the desk, putting his face close to Saras's. "If you are interested in your own gain, then I have to ask you, Mr. Saras: Did Theo tell you about the Yynium?"

Saras grimaced and Ethan was amazed again at the power that word had over this man.

"What Yynium?" Saras asked.

Ethan pulled the chunk of Yynium from his pocket and laid it on the desk. Saras scrambled to snatch it up. Veronika leaned over and peered at it as he inspected it.

"Where did you get this?" he asked urgently, digging in his desk drawer for a purity monitor.

"From the Vala. They extract it by the block using nothing more than their own bodies. You want gain, Mr. Saras, you'll team up with them, not sell them into slavery."

Saras placed the chip on the desk and touched the monitor to it. The dial buried itself in the Yynium reading.

It was a perfect sample. Every impurity removed. The purest Yynium in existence.

Veronika, ever unshakable, emitted an audible gasp. Saras closed his hand around the chunk.

"So this changes things, Mr. Saras?" Ethan said.

Saras raised his eyes and looked at Ethan with a new respect. "Considerably," he said.

# Chapter 40

The Vala children were becoming more comfortable around the humans, but they were getting crowded in the living room. Ethan and Aria had moved some of them into Polara's room and some into Rigel's room and now Ethan was helping Aria clean up her little lab room to move a few more into. That would make only about four to a room instead of five. The floor had been cleaned and he was starting on the desk when he found the broken vial from the gas sample that had saved Polara.

"This is odd," he said, turning the triangular needled end of the broken vial over in his hand. "What is it?"

"I'd forgotten about that." Aria said, gazing at it. "It's some kind of hypodermic. But why would someone want to inject this gas?"

"Maybe it works like a drug?"

"It's deadly, though," Aria said, scooping the tray of dead broccoli plants into the recycler. "See, these died immediately when it made contact with them . . ." Her voice trailed off and a faraway look crept into her eyes. She turned and snatched the broken vile from him, grabbing his shoulder with her other arm and pushing frantically at him.

"What are you doing?"

"Turn around!" she commanded.

Ethan turned and she grabbed his arm, raising it as she lifted his shirt off his side, revealing the triangle scar she'd seen when she was bathing him during his illness. She put the needles close to it. They were a perfect match.

"Your illness," she said, her voice trembling. "It was caused by the gas. Someone injected you with it!"

Ethan stepped back, away from the needles she was holding, and pulled his shirt down.

"But who would do that?"

Aria was mumbling. "I've seen it. I have seen it." She looked up at him. "Can I see your missive?"

Ethan extracted his missive from his pocket and Aria took it and punched at the screen. A moment later she was staring at it, looking as if she had been underwater too long, as if she were fighting a rising panic. Ethan leaned over to see what she was looking at.

There, open on the screen, was a copy of the photo he had taken in the flowstone room of Brynn next to the Ikastn symbols. Aria pointed at the pale girl in the picture. Brynn was reaching up, toying with the necklace she'd worn all those days underground. It was a vial exactly like this one.

Ethan stepped backwards quickly. Not Brynn. Not the sweet-faced girl who cried through days and nights underground. How could she have done this? Why? She had never met him before the trip. Why would she have wanted to poison him? And why on the last day of that nightmare, when she could have easily tripped him down a shaft to get rid of him anytime while they were in the cave?

Something didn't add up, and he was going to the surveyor's office to figure it out.

On the sol train ride, Ethan sent a message to Ndaiye. *On*

*my way to your office. I need to talk to you.*

He watched the buildings of the HHSD flying by and waited, his heart pounding alarmingly in his chest. He remembered the moment she had done it. The moment, as they stepped out of the pit. He saw it now. She wasn't tripping, she was lunging. But why? Was it a plot to get rid of him because he was supposed to be watching the survey crew? Maybe Saras had hired her, too, just like they'd hired Collins. Or maybe Maggie had carried more of a grudge than he'd realized.

His missive jingled and he checked it. The message was from Ndaiye. *Out in the field with Traore. Won't be back till late. Brynn and the Cap are at the office.*

A knot tightened in Ethan's stomach. His two least favorite members of the crew. He wished at least one of the cousins was going to be there. But he wanted to know what was going on, and he still couldn't really believe that Brynn was any harm. If anything, he was a little apprehensive about Maggie being there.

He exited the sol train in the Industrial District. Today it seemed fitting that the survey office was in the ugly part of the city. Ethan's errand here was an ugly business that fit in with the endless pavement and the huge, windowless buildings. Though he thought he knew what they contained, every building effectively hid what was inside. The sticky Minean summer seemed hotter here, where there were no trees to deflect the heat. Ethan walked under the relentless press of the sun and humidity, dreading talking to Brynn more with each step he took. He slowed to allow a tram laden with sanitizer parts to cross in front of him. The Survey Office was just ahead, and once the tram passed he had no excuse not to go in.

He'd met Ndaiye for lunch here only a week ago. It was a small, square building with a small reception area in the front and several offices and a workroom in the back. The reception area was empty and Ethan saw Maggie in the workroom, her back to him through the window in the closed door. He ducked quickly past, looking for Brynn's office.

She sat hunched at her desk when he entered, the light from an open side door streaming through and lighting up her brown hair. As she saw him, she sat up and took a sharp breath. Ethan didn't bother with greetings. He didn't know how much time he had before Maggie came in. He took a few steps toward the desk.

"I know you poisoned me, Brynn," he said, hearing his own bitterness at the betrayal in his voice. "Why?"

She looked up at him, her brown eyes pleading. "It was an accident, Ethan. I didn't want to hurt you. I'm really glad you're okay."

"An accident? What were you doing with that stuff anyway? Tell me what's going on, Brynn."

She pulled her eyes away from him and stood, her shoulders slumped, by the desk. She reached slowly into the desk drawer and shuffled around. She looked the same as before and he still couldn't believe that she might have done something so malicious. When she pulled her hand from the drawer though, to his horror, she was holding a gun.

The weapon shook in Brynn's hand. She didn't seem any more confident now than she ever had. She was not a killer. Ethan stepped toward her, but she switched the safety off the gun and shook her head slightly.

"I have to do it now, you know. I thought maybe you wouldn't figure it out. But now you know and now I have to."

"You don't have to do anything," Ethan saw that she was trapped somehow, and that could make anyone dangerous. "Tell me what's going on. I'll help you."

"Nobody can help me," she said miserably. "Nobody." Brynn moved around the desk, and he saw, by the desperate look in her eyes that she was going to do it. He felt the heat growing within his chest. He could stop her, and if he had to, he would.

"Just tell me why, Brynn," he asked, his eyes searching hers. "Just why."

Behind Ethan a familiar, rough voice broke the silence. "Aw, go ahead and tell him," said the voice of Maggie Schübling. "The poison was for me."

Brynn moved the weapon quickly to the side and fired. Ethan spun and watched as Maggie ducked, the bullet missing her by inches. When he looked back, the side door was open and Brynn was gone.

Ethan crouched, frozen, his eyes on Maggie. Her leg had given way and she was floundering on the floor, struggling to pull herself up using only the doorknob. It hurt him to see her so helpless, so he moved to her and lifted her to her feet, every muscle tensed to fight if necessary.

But she was breathing hard and he maneuvered her to Brynn's chair, kicking the open drawer closed as they came around the desk.

"What is going on, Maggie?"

She sat heavily in the chair. "I didn't know you'd been poisoned, for the record. I thought what everyone else thought—that you'd wigged out. Except I didn't blame you because I know how it was down there in that nightmare,"

Maggie was as good at comfort as she was at clarity.

"It's probably a good thing you got the shot, though, with your healing powers. It probably would have actually killed me. Which was probably the goal. I knew the kid was a plant on my team. I've known it the whole time."

Ethan nodded. That explained her distaste for Brynn.

"I was planning on getting her off the team as soon as we got back from the survey trip that afternoon. But, then with the crash, I thought maybe she'd straighten up."

"I don't understand. Why would she want to kill you?"

"Maybe she didn't, but somebody high up in the Saras company did. Does. I've been leaking information about them for years. They can't fire me, or I'll come out with everything, and that will shut them down completely. But all the stuff they do that makes people miserable has to stop, and I'm doin' my part to stop it."

"You leaked the survey?" Ethan asked.

"And the air quality report. And I'm about to leak the dirty Yynium report. So that should make some people mad. Only way to get rid of me's to kill me."

Ethan was puzzled. "I never saw the air quality report over in the Colony Offices."

"Well, that was my mistake," Maggie said, putting her bad leg on the desk and rubbing the crooked part. "I should have known that they'd get to some of the Governors eventually. They did, and it got buried."

Ethan thought of Polara, all those hours in the hospital that could have been prevented if someone had seen that report, and his temper flared.

"Why would she do this?" he asked, gesturing out the door.

"Not really her fault. Brynn has so many brothers and sisters that Saras paid to bring here that her dad's in debt for four lifetimes to the Saras Company. Even though he's a manager, he'll never pay them back. The company owns that whole family. She'd hafta do anything they wanted."

Ethan thought about that. Thought about the pressure of the passage debt. How many people had it crushed?

"Who put her up to this?" Ethan asked.

Maggie kept rubbing her leg thoughtfully. "Really, there's only three people high enough in the company to know those reports existed, and any one of them coulda got to the kid. I'd watch out for 'em all, if I were you."

# Chapter 41

Ethan couldn't get in to talk to Theo for two days. When he did, the VP was having an early morning drink in his office, and he was in an expansive mood. "We're going into business with the aliens," he said, obviously aware of Ethan's earlier conversation with Saras.

Ethan nodded. "But you didn't show him the Yynium block I sent with you. Why not?" he asked.

Theo threw an arm around his shoulders. "I didn't think we could trust them."

"Trust who?" Ethan's eyes narrowed, and he stepped away from Theo. "The Vala?"

"No." Theo leaned in conspiratorially. "Saras. Veronika. Especially Veronika."

It seemed natural that they were rivals, but this seemed paranoid. "Why not?" Ethan asked bluntly.

"I'm sorry to be the one to tell you this, Ethan," Theo said, his eyes darkening, "but Veronika wanted you dead. She knew you would be a Governor she couldn't bribe, and having you in that position is just too much of a threat to the company." Theo shook his head. "She loves the company. But you can't blame her. Since old Mr. Saras back on Earth dumped her and sent her out here to Minea to babysit his son, she doesn't really have anything else. Although she'd like to get involved with Marcos and solve both her problems at once."

"Both problems?"

"She wants the company and she wants to get back at Dimitri." The soft clunk of Theo's empty glass echoed through the office.

Ethan's head was spinning. Maybe Veronika had hired Brynn. But Veronika knew her way around the system legally. Would she really kill to get her way? And Ethan was inclined to believe that Maggie was right. Brynn hadn't meant to kill him, she'd been aiming for Maggie when he stepped in her way. Would Veronika know about the leaked reports?

His missive went off. Pulling it from his pocket, he saw a message from Brynn, full of errors. All it said was *help. Warehouse 78, Refinery st.*

Theo raised his eyebrows. "Aria need you to pick up some sweetbean milk on the way home?"

"No, it's a friend of mine. A surveyor. Brynn. She says she needs help." He wondered if he should have said that.

He was relieved that Theo seemed uninterested. "You should go then, and don't worry about Veronika. I told her that you weren't a threat, and she's found another Governor to bribe. I think you'll be fine."

Ethan considered for a moment. "Theo," he said, "I might need your help."

Theo nodded. "Sure. What can I do?"

"You've got a car, right?"

"Right. A nice one."

"Well, if you're up for it, the girl who messaged me is on Refinery Street, and the train doesn't run down there, so it would help me out if you'd give me a ride." Ethan considered, and then told Theo the truth. "Also, she may have been hired by Veronika. This could be a trap, and I'm not sure I should go alone."

Theo raised his eyebrows. "You live an exciting life, Ethan." The tall man walked to his desk and extracted, from the top drawer, a shining silver handgun. "Maybe we'd better take this along."

\*\*\*

They arrived in the industrial district in record time. Ethan had a fleeting flash of envy for Theo's hovercar, but it was forgotten when he saw the abandoned warehouse that bore the address Brynn had given them. It had obviously been overtaken by Taim at some point, though the plants were gone now. The door was gone, too. Ethan entered as fast as he could and inside he could see that the equipment had been dismantled and scrubbed, but not reassembled. It lay in piles with cleaning rags and empty bottles of Zam.

The infestation must have been particularly bad. The building was a loss, and crews had started, at some point, to tear it down. Sunlight streamed in through a gaping hole in the roof.

Ethan heard a small sound and turned to see Brynn in a shadowy corner, her brown hair hanging in front of her face, bound at the ankles and wrists. She had been crying.

"It's all right, Brynn. It's all right," Ethan said. "We're going to get you out of here." When she looked up, there was remorse in her eyes.

"Gaynes grabbed me when I left the office. He dumped me here. I didn't know who to call. You're the only person on the whole planet I really trust. I'm sorry, Ethan. I'm sorry," she said.

"I know." He reached for her wrists. "Brynn, I think Veronika Eppes is behind all this. Did she—" Ethan stopped as

Brynn's eyes filled with terror. He turned and braced himself, expecting to see Veronika.

Only Theo stood behind him, but when Theo turned, the flash of the gun in his hand showed Ethan his mistake. He stood and placed himself squarely in front of Brynn.

"It was you then," Ethan said with resignation in his voice. "You were trying to get rid of Maggie."

Theo smiled, and Ethan, even now, couldn't see a trace of insincerity in it. "This seems to be what happens when you delegate an important job to someone incompetent. Everything ends up a mess." He tilted his head to look around Ethan at the girl in the corner. "You're useless, Brynn. I really should have done it myself."

"So now it's me you want rid of?" Ethan took a careful step toward the door, but Theo waved him away with the gun.

"You and anyone else who might insinuate that I'm not acting in the best interest of the Saras Company," Theo said smoothly, tilting his head to indicate Brynn behind Ethan. Theo looked at Ethan, his eyebrows drawing together in concern. "Or that might value the Vala over a lucrative shipping contract with the Asgre."

"You're working for the Asgre?" Ethan spat their name out.

"Not *for* the Asgre. *With* the Asgre," Theo said, trying to steady the gun in his shaking hand. "They aren't as bad as people make them out to be, although the gas that they use on their ship causes some serious side effects." He laughed, gesturing at his own shaking hand. "Galo, their leader, just wants to be able to run the business that he has spent so long building."

Ethan nodded. "Like you do. I see."

Theo's jaw set and his next sentence was a snarl. "You don't see. Nobody sees. I left everything to come out here. I built this city, this company, and then the boss's brat shows up and takes over. You don't know how that feels."

Ethan tried to think of something to say, but Theo didn't pause long enough to let him speak.

"It must be tough living with all your hallucinations, Ethan. You have had a rough time of it since you left Earth. I can see why you wouldn't want to go on."

So that's how he would play it. A staged suicide. Ethan scoffed. "You think anyone will fall for that?"

"You've been through a lot, and we have the psychiatric evaluations to prove it. Not even the Colony Offices will question it. Especially if you're having a fling with the girl from the cave. In fact, maybe she shot you."

"Theo!" Brynn called from the corner. "Theo, leave him alone. He's a good person."

"I know," Theo said, again with genuine sincerity. "I know he's a good person. That's why he wanted to stop the mining to cure the sickness and why he wants to save the Vala at the expense of the company. He is a good person. That's what makes him a threat to everything I've worked for."

Ethan watched as the man walked calmly to the center of the rubbish-filled room. "This used to be a lab. Now look at it, broken and twisted and useless."

There was that word again. Theo's pride had him convinced that he knew what was worthwhile and what was not. And also who was worthwhile and who was not. Another idea occurred to Ethan.

"You're the final signature on the hiring line, too, aren't you, Theo?"

Theo nodded, closing his eyes in false humility. "I am."

"You kept my passengers from getting work. Why?"

Theo's eyes flashed, and he enunciated every word clearly. "They are unnecessary. Do you know how many years I spent creating the perfect city on this planet? The perfect business plan? The perfect personnel plan with no redundancies? I was president of this company for five years. I made sure that all the parts of my company fit together into a precisely functioning machine. And then the UEG dumps a whole shipload of passengers here that clog up that machine. Passengers that have no useful skills. You know that. That's why they were chosen for Ship 12-22. They were expendable, just like their Caretaker."

Ethan nodded slowly, feeling the sting of Theo's words. A rumble caught his attention and he glanced up. The Asgre ship had descended into the atmosphere again. Its shadow fell across the building and the blaring communications channel filled the air around them with the scraping of Galo's voice.

"My understanding of languages is useless," Ethan said, "because you have no need of someone who can decipher what it is that the Asgre ship up there is broadcasting right now."

In reality, Ethan had heard it before, through the translator. It was actually broadcasting a message to the Vala, that Galo was coming for them, and that they should give themselves up now if they wanted mercy, but Ethan played the bluff. "That was your name, just now, in the Asgre language, wasn't it Theo?"

Theo tipped his head up, taking in the bulk of the armored ship as it lowered itself slowly toward the city. Though it was still high above them, its thrusters made the windows vibrate as it eased out of the sky.

In that moment, when Theo was looking up, Ethan launched himself toward the gun, knocking it aside and driving his shoulder hard into Theo's stomach. Together, they fell backwards, writhing for control of the weapon, rolling through the jagged heap of trash on the floor.

Ethan felt the sharp press of rubble in his back as Theo, lighter than him by about thirty pounds, but tenacious, flipped him over and grappled for the gun. Ethan wrenched it from Theo's hand and tossed it as high and as wide as he could.

A blow to the temple sent Ethan's vision spinning. If he didn't stop this soon, the Asgre would be in the streets before he could help the ground crews intercept them.

"Quit, Theo! It's too late! They're here, and they're going to take this city apart if we don't get out there!"

"Not my city," Theo growled through clenched teeth. "I'll give them the Vala and they'll be on their way."

An image of the pale Vala child, chained in the cage on the bottom of the Asgre ship flooded Ethan's memory. Entangled with it was an image of the Vala in his cottage and an image of his own children—an image of all children, whose safety was the responsibility of all adults. A fury built within him, and he didn't stop it. A heartbeat before the energy beam shot out of his palms, he placed them on Theo's chest.

The acrid smell of burnt flesh arced into the air as Theo shot backwards, landing with a sickening thud on the rubble a few feet away. Ethan's energy ebbed and he slumped against the uneven floor himself, sucking in air and feeling relief wash over him.

He would never have believed that he could use his energy against another human without remorse. It scared him that it was so, but his desire to keep safe the innocent was all-consuming.

And Theo was particularly distasteful. He had pretended to be Ethan's friend. Ethan knew from his conversations with Chip the salesman that everyone persuaded and controlled others in some way. In the end, he much preferred Veronika's straightforward, if harsh, honesty to Theo's manipulations.

He heard a scuffling from the corner and struggled to his feet, feeling the slick trickle of blood slide down his temple and cheek. Brynn had managed to untie her ankles, and she was working on her wrists. He didn't know what to say to her, didn't want to look at her. Those days of dark anguish after the caves, when he couldn't move or speak, were her fault. It was made worse by his knowledge that she had intended to kill Maggie.

He reached for a shard of shattered glass, wrapping the ties from her ankles around it to avoid slicing his hands, and sawed through the tie on her wrists.

"Ethan—" she began, but he silenced her with a raised hand and walked out into the night, climbing into Theo's car and leaving her to find her own way.

\*\*\*

Daniel heard the rumble of the ship descending. A heavy hand pounded on the apartment door. "Volunteer troops! Get to the base! The Asgre are coming!"

Nallie, clutching her doll, threw herself into her brother's arms. "Don't leave, Daniel! Don't leave us here!"

They had been on their own in the apartment so much since his mother died. And since Gaynes' threats, he had left them under strict instructions not to open the door if he wasn't home. The fear in his voice had finally seeped into theirs, and it pierced him to hear it.

"It's okay, baby, I won't. I won't. We're going to see Reverend Hardy. Remember?"

Merelda spoke up. "Remember Nallie? With the bells?"

The safety plan for the children was to take them to the church, where Reverend Hardy and others would watch over them. Daniel put on his uniform and slipped his weapon into its holster. He didn't want to leave them, but he knew that he was fighting for the glistening creatures he'd seen in the mine.

They had saved him, and he hoped he could repay them. He carried Nallie and held Merelda's hand as they made their way through the streets.

The church glowed bright in the afternoon light, and he saw a flash of pale hair as he entered. Zella was in her uniform, and she'd just seated her younger brother and sister in the rows.

Daniel knelt by his sisters. "Now you girls go over there with the Panderlins. I'm gonna be gone a minute, but I'll be back." He hugged them and pointed them to their friends. Nallie clung to him, wailing. Daniel clenched his teeth and disentangled himself, handing the little girl off to Merelda. Merelda took her little sister's hand and pulled her to the bench beside Zella's siblings. Nallie's weeping followed Daniel as he walked to the heavy doors of the church.

When he stepped out of the church into the blinding afternoon light, he heard someone else sniffle. Zella was leaning against the wall. Instinctively, Daniel took her in his arms. She held him tightly, sobbing for a moment. He laid a hand over her braided hair.

"It's okay. They'll be okay."

"I've never seen them so scared," she said, pulling back and wiping her face. She searched his eyes. "And I'm scared, too, Daniel."

When he heard her admit it, Daniel's own fear washed over him. He nodded, unable to say it out loud. Suddenly, something was clear to him.

"Zella," he asked, taking her hands in his, "will you stay with them?"

Her eyes widened. "What? I—I'm supposed to report to the base with the volunteers."

Daniel felt his desperation deep in his soul. "Please, Zella. Please. I can't go knowing that there's nobody to look after them. Especially if . . . you know, I don't come back. Please stay with my sisters. Take them and your brother and sister back to the apartment. Take your weapon. Lock yourselves inside and I'll come back as soon as I can. You'll have food there. And you'll be together."

The memory of the Asgre in the mine flashed in his mind. He didn't want Zella near them, found in himself that there was room to take care of her, too. He tried to tell her.

"I don't want them—or you—out in these streets." Involuntarily, they both glanced up, to the slowly descending Asgre ship kilometers above the city.

She looked as if she would protest again, but Daniel took her hands in his. His voice sounded small as he said it again, "Please?"

He saw that it was what she wanted, saw that he'd given her the option she needed. She threw her arms around him and he drew enough strength from her embrace to let her go back in the church as he descended the stairs and made his way to the base.

*** 

Looking down at Coriol, its windows glinting in the afternoon sun, Reagan closed his eyes. He would have preferred to do this in the West Desert, or, even better, in space, where the debris from their battle would be propelled into the vast blackness instead of raining on the citizens below. He hoped they were taking seriously the warnings to get to shelter.

He checked his readouts. All was fine with his six battleships: *Champion, Unity, Tenacious, Wisdom, Advocate,* and *Vigilant.* Maybe five and a half, depending on how well the repairs on *Vigilant* held up.

He also checked the dozen company defense ships sent

by the seven companies. They were small and light, incredibly maneuverable and well-enough armed, but they didn't have RST and they couldn't match the Asgre ships for speed if something went wrong.

He needed them for their small size and their ability to get under the Asgre ships unnoticed. Each had been equipped with plasma torches that should be able to crack the cages open without hurting the Vala if they were in their sleeping state. Aemon had been sure that the Asgre would keep the Vala in an induced sleep state in order to manipulate the ships quickly in battle.

Reagan shuddered as he thought of the children in the cages. Whether this worked or not, they had to try.

The company ships also had powerful missiles which Reagan was counting on to deflect Asgre torpedoes from the battleships.

Each battleship moved into position flanked by two smaller company ships darting about under it like fish under a great shark.

Captain Daring maneuvered *Champion* forward, toward Galo's ship. He saw two ships drop and move toward the Karst Mountains. That would be their ground troops. But Reagan had Sergeant Nile standing ready, and the man was capable and adaptable.

Reagan felt the old rush of impending battle. This one felt right. They weren't fighting for territory or minerals. They were fighting for living beings. And whatever the outcome, it had to be attempted.

He tried to hang onto that conviction as ship after Asgre ship dropped out of orbit and into the atmosphere.

"Company ships standby," he said.

"Company ships standing by, Admiral," came the reply.

"Battleships standby," he said.

"Battleships standing by."

"Remember to lead them out of the atmosphere if you can."

"Aye, Aye," he heard on the comms.

Galo's ship hung in the sky, nearly filling the viewing window in front of Reagan. He could see, through one of the vertical slits in the plating on the other ship, Galo standing on his bridge, at the ready.

There was a long, breathless moment as the big Asgre cruiser faced *Champion* in the clear Minean air.

And then Galo's ship was falling, and three ships behind it began strafing *Champion* with intense fire.

Reagan barked orders, cursing himself for not seeing that Galo would go after the Vala children in the city while the fleet was distracted in battle. Not only did that place the Vala children in danger, it also endangered all of Coriol.

"Engage Asgre One!" he barked into his comms, busy himself with the three ships that circled him, firing.

A glance at his screen showed all of his battleships in the same position.

"Company ships *Tenacious I* and *Wisdom I,* peel off and go after that ship. Do not let it reach Coriol. Repeat: Take it down if you can!"

"Daring, get us out of here!" he barked, and felt the ship angle and accelerate over the Asgre ships, out of the atmosphere and into open space.

He checked on the company ships. They were firing their missiles, and one was a solid hit. Galo's big ship rocked sideways under it, but Reagan didn't see any sign of serious damage, just a hull hit.

The ship fired on them, though, and heavy shells hit

*Wisdom I.* The light company ship spun, freefalling down onto the city below.

Reagan flinched as he saw it fall over the housing district. The blood of the company ship crew, and whoever else had been hurt, was on his hands. The company ships were too light to take on the big Cliprig. He'd have to deal with it himself as soon as he could get a battleship free.

"*Tenacious I*, do you copy?"

"Copy, sir."

He hit the comms to tell the ship to fall back, but heard the sound of gunfire. Checking his screen, he saw that *Tenacious I* had been hit. It wobbled in the sky as it pursued the Asgre ship.

"*Tenacious I*," Reagan said, hearing the desperation in his own voice. "Fall back and get that bird on the ground before you crash in someone's front yard."

Reagan was relieved to see the listing ship retreat to a safe distance, setting down in the wide park near the spaceport, but his stomach knotted as Galo's ship cruised on toward the center of the city, where Reagan knew the Vala children and thousands of humans crouched in fear.

*Champion* pitched under Reagan's feet as Daring ran evasive maneuvers. Around him his other ships appeared, rising from the atmosphere, followed closely by Asgre ships. Suddenly, he felt a rumbling crash shake *Champion*. A big Asgre skybarge had come up behind them and was employing e-links. "Prepare to be boarded," came a scratchy transmission over the comms system.

Reagan looked at Kaia. "What do we got, kid?" he asked.

"I can run an impulse through the hull," she said. "It'll heat us up, but should break the e-links."

He nodded and felt the shock shake the ship.

As soon as he felt it, he snapped, "Daring, warp us!"

The ship was suddenly in open space behind the Asgre ships.

"Fire!" Reagan shouted, watching with satisfaction as a rain of shells launched from *Champion*'s guns and lit up the Asgre ship.

At least one hit landed well. The red exhaust from the right engine sputtered and died, and as the ship tried to accelerate it could manage no more than a lazy circle.

"Take out that other engine and engage the next ship." Reagan was pleased to see this and several other of the ships floating listlessly in space. These were skybarges, and though well-armed, they were not designed for battle.

# Chapter 42

Ethan pulled the hovercar in front of the cottage and burst in, expecting to find his family and the Vala children huddling inside.

But the cottage was empty.

He dialed Aria's number on the missive and heard it jingling in the next room. Wherever she had gone, she'd gone without it. Ethan thought about going after her.

But there was a plan. In the event of an attack, she was to get the children to the Coriol Defense Headquarters.

Ethan pulled on his Coriol Defense Volunteer uniform and picked up his weapon. He would go to the rendezvous point at headquarters and join the ground troops. Maybe Aria was already there. The streets were mostly abandoned, and he felt the press of gravity as he accelerated the hovercar through the streets.

Far above the city hung the Asgre Cliprig that he'd seen from the warehouse—where less than an hour ago, he had killed a man. Ethan shook the thought from his mind. The Cliprig was hovering over the city, scanning, he was sure. And the children, wherever they were, were no longer sheltered in the Karst Mountains, so impenetrable by the Asgre sensors. They were exposed, somewhere in the city.

He asked at the command center about Aria. Reverend Hardy had called in and said she was with him and Luis, and they were all going to make their way to the Headquarters. He felt better about that.

Focusing on what he needed to do now, he joined the restless group of men and women who were gathered around Sergeant Nile, the commander of the Coriol Defense Troops and now the Coriol Defense Volunteers, as well. The afternoon air hung hot around them, and the armored uniforms made the press of the humidity worse. He looked around. Many of his friends were here. Ndaiye and Traore stepped next to him, throwing their arms around his shoulders, and Yi Zhe caught his eye from the edge of the group where he stood quiet and calm. He saw Aria's young miner friend, Daniel, shifting nervously in the center of the group, holding his weapon in shaking hands.

Ethan waved, but Daniel's gaze was fixed on a spot at the other side of the group. Ethan glanced in that direction. Cyril Gaynes stood at the edge, a smug smirk on his face.

Gaynes was not the volunteer type. What was he doing here? Ethan watched him carefully, trying to determine his angle. It only took moments for Gaynes to give himself away. While everyone else kept their eyes on the Cliprig or joked nervously with each other, Gaynes was focused on the weapons the Volunteers carried. He stared at them and sized up their bearers. He was here to use the chaos as an opportunity to procure something he could sell. Ethan suspected the man would regret that scheme soon enough.

Sergeant Nile was barking orders through the heat rising off the sweltering liftstrip. He organized the troops into companies of thirty, then platoons of ten.

As Ethan stepped into his platoon, a pair of ships caught

his attention. The Asgre crafts dropped down through the atmosphere, skimming past the Cliprig and through the sky above the base. They were not ordinary Asgre ships, though. In addition to the single small navigator's cage, they were draped with multiple huge cells, hanging from chains around the ship like sinister necklaces.

"They're not coming aground in the city," Ethan said, watching as the ships passed over. "They don't care about humans. They've found the Vala, and they're going to get them." Sergeant Nile stood watching them, then turned.

"Admiral Reagan has left us with orders to protect the Vala. Bryant!" Ethan stepped forward. "Do you know where they're going?"

Ethan nodded. "Yes, sir."

Nile jerked his head toward the troop movers across the airstrip. "Good. You help your pilot navigate. We'll fall in behind you! To the transports!" he barked, and the troops, military and civilian, boarded. The transports flew low and fast, following the huge Asgre ships.

Ethan kept his eye on them. They flew past the entrance to the cave. When the Asgre moved one of the ships over a great karst peak, Ethan knew what was coming. A single missile fell to the peak like a drop of water to a stalagmite. As it touched, the mountain shattered outward, shards of rock as large as buildings hurtling in every direction. The transports rocked in the concussion.

When the dust settled, he saw that the rubble had been blown clear and laying exposed and open was the Flowstone Room. Of course. The Vala's sanctuary, impenetrable by the Asgre's detection equipment and by the Vala themselves. The Asgre had found the cave entrance, probably through Saras's help, but how had the Asgre known about the sanctuary?

A bitter taste filled Ethan's mouth. Theo Talbot. The Vala had shared too much with that snake, and Ethan had brought him to them.

As the transports landed and the troops poured out, Ethan looked again at the room, opened like an egg, its sparkling white flowstone, etched with the symbols, gleaming in the raking light of the Asgre ships above. The sacred feeling they had experienced while in the cathedral-like room came flooding back, and Ethan cringed to see its beauty laid bare. Huddled against the flowstone, barely visible from inside the transports, were the cowering forms of the Vala.

The Asgre ships lowered great metal cages onto the floor of the chamber. Asgre mercenaries were sliding down cables, and Ethan knew that in moments the cages would be full of Vala, immobilized and silent at the hands of their captors.

Ethan fought to focus. Nile's voice sounded like it was coming from somewhere else, very far away. "Trigon formation, soldiers! Trigon formation!"

The trained troops sprung into action. Their platoons grouped into the triangle formations that Ethan had seen them practicing when he'd visited Reagan at the base. The volunteers had read about the formation in their pamphlets, and they'd practiced just once since signing up days ago. They clumsily made the formation in their platoons.

Ethan was surrounded by Ndaiye, Traore, Winn the carpenter, and other volunteers. He glanced at the other platoons as they worked to make the Trigon formation.

Ethan's teeth clenched as he saw Daniel Rigo's platoon. Huddling in the middle was Cyril Gaynes, his former arrogance erased by the horror around him.

Ethan tried to catch Daniel's eye, to remind him that as despicable as Gaynes was, they were, for the moment, all on the same team. But Daniel's smoldering gaze stayed fixed on the big man, and Ethan recognized that whatever he had in mind, Gaynes had more than earned. Still, Ethan knew now what it was like to take a human life, and he didn't want that for Daniel. If he could only get the boy's attention—

"Move in!" Nile shouted, and Ethan's gaze was drawn to the CDT company as they bunched and rushed forward to meet the Asgre mercenaries. The Asgre saw them coming and formed a solid front line, putting themselves between the oncoming troops and the massive cages.

The trained troops punched holes in the front line. There were exchanges of gunfire and grappling. Ethan saw the first trigon formation break through, spinning like a three pointed throwing star. The front line closed behind them and they sprayed gunfire across the next line of Asgre.

Another CDT trigon platoon broke through, and Ethan felt hope surge within him. It was his platoon's turn, and the volunteers, so many of them Ethan's passengers, were no less committed, but much less prepared. Their loose wedge formations moved in, but the Asgre sliced through the formations, shattering them and leaving soldiers scattered and fending for themselves. Winn, the carpenter, fell under a blow from an Asgre weapon. Ethan moved to him and dragged him back, away from the lines. An open gash gaped at the back of his neck and the hot, iron smell of blood tinged the thick air.

Ethan set him against the shattered karst edge of the Flowstone Room. "Hang on!" he called to him. "Medics are coming."

Ethan looked up and saw the nearest volunteer platoon struggling amid the many arms of the Asgre mercenaries. Daniel Rigo fought furiously, using his weapon as a club. The Asgre in front of him fell, but the mercenary that stepped behind him grasped Gaynes, viciously wrenching the big man off his feet. Ethan heard the crack of bone as the grocer twisted free and staggered a few steps before falling to his knees on the ground. The mercenary advanced and Ethan took two steps toward them, realizing he would never make it in time to help Gaynes.

A flash of movement caught his eye as Daniel turned from the Asgre he'd just defeated and saw Gaynes. Daniel was close enough to do something, but as Ethan watched the boy's hatred for the cruel man wash across his features he remembered the story about the scrip Gaynes had tossed to bring Daniel to his knees in the store. He remembered the threats the boy had told him about. Ethan closed his eyes briefly as the Asgre mercenary stepped forward, and he listened for the blow that would end the big man's brutality.

But the blow didn't come. When Ethan looked again, Daniel stood over Gaynes, grappling with the mercenary. Grasping the creature's hand, he turned the long blades on its fingers back toward itself, gouging the thick suit and bringing a cry of pain from the creature. As it staggered away, Daniel reached for Gaynes, placing a shoulder under the injured man's arm, and dragged him toward the transports, where he handed Gaynes off to a medic.

Ethan caught the young man's arm as he strode back toward the fray.

"You saved him," Ethan said incredulously. "Why?"

"Because I'm not him," Daniel said, "and I don't ever want to be." Ethan watched him walk back toward what was left of his platoon.

All around them, the volunteers were falling. The medics rushed forward, staggering through the chaos under the weight of the wounded. When Ethan looked back at the battle, he saw that the trained troops had begun to struggle as well. Those that had broken through the line were now surrounded by Asgre. The formations trying to break through were as quickly being repelled by the line of Asgre mercenaries.

Sergeant Nile, observing from behind and sending in new platoons as needed, swore.

"It should be working. The formation is strong!"

And it was. The point person of each trigon formation faced off with an Asgre mercenary and was backed up by his platoon. As the platoon waded into the swirling mass of Asgre, though, the Asgre surrounded them, isolating them from the rest of their company. The aliens seemed to gain more strength with every platoon Nile sent at them. Too many were falling.

From behind him Ethan heard Yi Zhe's voice calling. He spun and leaned in as the master of balance and harmony put his mouth to Ethan's ear.

Yi Zhe talked rapidly. "This isn't working. I think I know what we need to do! We keep fighting as if the Asgre have read *The Art of War*. They are not a human enemy, and the tactics we've developed to defend against other humans are not working against them. We have to find a more basic connection, and fight them through it."

Ethan shook his head, not understanding. Around him, the troops rushed in trigons to meet the Asgre, but they were driven back and broken up again and again.

Yi Zhe grasped his shoulders, forcing Ethan to focus on his words. "There are things that go beyond our minds. Basic elements that we are surrounded by and composed of. We have to use those elements, find our common ground with the Asgre. We cannot succeed unless we release our predefined notions. These are aliens!" he shouted.

Ethan looked at Yi Zhe, fighting the urge to dismiss his

ideas. He had argued that all his passengers had a contribution to make, had believed that days ago. Now, in this moment, could he trust Yi Zhe, even though he did not understand his approach?

"What do you know about battle?" he asked, feeling himself begging for confirmation.

"My teacher was a great master in war. He often spoke of using the principles of balance and harmony in the War of the Seven Countries before the United Earth Government was formed back on Earth. But our enemies then were humans. We fought them as we have fought for thousands of years." Yi Zhe held Ethan's shoulders, looking into his face. "I believe we can use these principles to defeat these beings. I can help. I just need more information about our enemy," he said urgently. "Tell me what you know of the Asgre home world!"

Ethan remembered what Aemon had told him during one of their morning talks, and, though he didn't know why it was important, he told Yi Zhe what he could remember: that the Asgre came from a world of extreme opposites: light and dark, hot and cold. That humans would die in an hour on their planet.

"Those are the differences. Good." Yi Zhe's brow furrowed. He seemed to be calculating. "Now, what is the same?" he demanded.

Ethan tried to recall. "I—I don't know. I—" he stopped, frustrated, then offered the only idea he had. "Their home planet has water, like ours. But theirs has very little water. The Vala were always thirsty there."

Yi Zhe closed his eyes, then opened them. Ethan watched as he focused intently on the mercenaries in the chaos around the room. Yi Zhe was mumbling. Ethan turned his attention to them, as well. The mercenaries, in their black suits, flew at the advancing platoons and the humans, in their seemingly protected formations, advanced forward and were scattered as they met the mass of Asgre.

Yi Zhe was speaking again. "Qi flows through everything, like water. Block qi and you block the flow of power, ideas, energy, everything. Water flows. Qi flows. We are out of balance. We are of the water." Yi Zhe almost smiled.

"What is it? Yi Zhe? What is it?" Ethan was seeing more of their troops fall. They had to switch tactics.

Sergeant Nile was giving the order to fall back. The weary troops retreated as Yi Zhe spoke in a high, urgent voice.

"Ethan, each of the elements has energy, and the Asgre have strong fire energy."

Ethan moved forward, toward the haggard group of retreating soldiers, but Ye Zhe grasped his arm and held it.

Ethan could hear him talking over the melee in front of them. "Fire energy. Fire energy."

He turned to Ethan, understanding in his eyes. "Ethan, our formations are wrong. Triangles are fire shapes. We are bringing them more fire energy, when we must bring balance with our water energy."

Ethan thought about stopping him, started to say that there was no evidence of any of that, but he'd seen life energy in the beings on Beta Alora. He knew it existed, and he admitted that he didn't understand it.

"Regroup!" Nile shouted, moving around the ragged companies. As they retreated behind the ridge of stone that was all that was left of the outside of the karst peak, the Asgre kept descending from their ships. They did not follow the humans, instead going after the Vala who huddled pitifully in the corners, unable to move through the flowstone walls of the cavern. The trained troops turned, agitated, to their commander.

"We have to get back over there," Ethan shouted.

"Wait! We're changing the formation," Nile barked. "We'll go with the flying star: Three trigons joined at one point. Come on! Let's hustle!"

Ethan moved to speak to Yi Zhe, but the little man had captured Sergeant Nile by the shoulders. Ethan heard him: "No! A triple triangle formation will increase the fire energy exponentially! If you want to save those creatures, do not bring the Vala any more fire energy."

Ethan knew military men. He worked with them in the Colony Offices every day. He waited for Nile to laugh in Yi Zhe's face, or to shake his hands impatiently from his shoulders. As the companies made the flying star formation, though, he saw Nile drape an arm around Yi Zhe's shoulders, leaning his head down to listen. They both looked up, catching Ethan's eye, and Nile waved him over.

"Has he told you this?" Sergeant Nile's piercing blue eyes held Ethan's. Ethan felt the sweat dripping down his temples, stinging in the cut Theo had given him earlier. He nodded.

"You're the alien expert," Nile challenged. "What do you think of this?"

Ethan looked around. The medics were still carrying people away from the first attempt. The trigon wasn't working. He thought about the life energies he had seen on Beta Alora, thought about the vast realm of experience beyond what humans could see and touch and taste. He thought about the Others of Beta Alora, and how he had to understand them in order to defeat them.

"I think he's a great master of balance and harmony. I think he could be right."

Nile's eyes narrowed. Ethan could tell that he was in a corner. He had a fraction of the troops he needed for this mission, half the troops he did have were untrained, and his enemy was alien in every sense.

"We're going to try your formation," he told Yi Zhe. "We'll pull back if it doesn't work."

Sergeant Nile turned to his troops and bellowed: "Listen to Yi Zhe here! We're not doing the triple trigon!" He gestured to Yi Zhe.

"Move like water!" Yi Zhe cried to the troops. "In waves, together. Be aware of those next to you and stay near them. Don't break the curve of the wave. We must counter their fire energy with water energy. Water destroys fire!" He walked along the troops, glancing at their uniforms and weapons. Yi Zhe took a weapon from a soldier near him. The weapon was covered with a thick rubber casing, to make it easy to hold and keep it from reflecting light in stealth situations. Yi Zhe pulled it off. The weapon shone, its polished metal reflecting the scene around it.

He turned to the Sergeant. "We should also have them remove the weapon covers," Yi Zhe said urgently. "Reflective surfaces strengthen the water energy."

The Sergeant looked at Ethan, and Ethan nodded. As he saw the changes in the battalion, standing shoulder to shoulder, a confidence was growing in him. Yi Zhe was a master of things unknown to most humans, and aliens were certainly unknown.

"Take them off," Nile ordered. The soldiers stripped the weapons, tossing the covers on the ground.

When they reentered the open chamber, Ethan was sickened to see the cages behind the Asgre front lines being filled with Vala.

"Move in!" Nile cried. "And take them down!" The humans peppered the mass of Asgre in front of them with a volley of shells, which bounced off their suits almost harmlessly. The troops rushed in waves to meet the Asgre mass. This time, instead of the fragmented formations, the humans, like a living tide, advanced forward almost as one, their weapons flashing in the light from the hovering ships overhead.

Ethan felt the wave of humanity crest against the Asgre front line. He was pressed from in front and behind, tripping over the boots of the soldier in front of him as the back waves of humans moved forward.

There was a long, breathless moment, and then the Asgre began to fall.

Ethan crashed into an Asgre as the tide of soldiers pushed him forward. He fired his weapon, but the alien's suit blocked the shell. He threw a blow at the skeletal face, felt its bones, sharp and lancing, crunch beneath the mask. The Asgre raked him with razor-like hand blades, and he felt the pressure across his torso, but the body armor of Ethan's uniform held. The creature used two of its arms to reach out and restrain Ethan's two arms, and then the other two grasped his head.

Ethan knew what was coming. The mercenary would snap his neck.

But the creature suddenly began to blink and turn his head, as if agitated. Ethan saw a beam of light dancing directly across the creature's eye slits in the mask. The creature released his head to shield its eyes, and Ethan glanced to the side to see Traore catching the light from the ship above with his shining weapon and bouncing the light into the Asgre's eyes. Ethan quickly landed a hard kick to its abdomen, and the creature let go, staggering back and knocking down two other Asgre.

All around him, the Asgre were falling as the human troops, their weapons flashing, poured forward. They washed through the front line and Ethan angled for the cages. An Asgre mercenary grabbed him from behind. Reaching behind him over his shoulder, Ethan grasped at the thin mask covering the Asgre's face and pulled. The Asgre grabbed his arm with an extra hand and wrenched it, but Ethan didn't let go and the mask tore away. The gas from the creature's suit hissed out, and Ethan felt a tremor shake him. He stopped breathing, trying to turn from the gas. Grappling with the many arms, Ethan ducked and spun, flipping the mercenary over hard onto the ground. The creature lay gasping on the cavern floor.

Ethan glanced up to see Jin Feiyan, Yi Zhe's wife. She was fast, and she had moved quickly to the first Vala cage. She stood almost reverently amidst the chaos, staying close to the human soldiers on either side of her. She reached up and swung wide the gate. The Vala streamed out around her. She had freed them. She looked up, toward her husband, with an expression of newfound admiration.

Ethan gestured to the Vala, wishing he had not left his translator in the cottage. "Run! He said in Ikastn, pointing to the lights of the transport ships behind the troops. "Safety!"

As they liberated the Vala one cage at a time, the Asgre began to retreat. Many of them lay on the ground, littering the flowstone room with their bodies.

Three cages remained, each containing a few Vala. The Asgre began to raise the remaining cages, and Ethan broke from the group, leaping and scrambling up the flowstone, trying to reach the last few sad-eyed Vala who they'd been unable to save.

As the cage-draped Asgre ships left the atmosphere, Ethan slid down the flowstone, hunching on the rough, shining floor.

Around him were the remnants of battle—fallen Asgre and fallen humans lay across the room. Red stains seeped into the white flowstone, dull in the weak evening light.

But as he looked past the battlefield, Ethan saw the safe Vala, peering out of the transport. Their fragile, shimmering forms caught what little light there was and cast it out from them, giving them the ethereal glow he remembered from the cave.

They had saved him, had saved the whole crew. And now, he had been able to take part in saving them. He felt, in his soul, a balance, a harmony.

The troops were reassembling. Ethan stood and worked his way through them. He sought out Yi Zhe. Searching for the right words, he found none. Instead, he placed his hands together and dropped his forehead to the master in a sign of respect. All the troops followed his lead. Yi Zhe placed his hands together and returned the gesture.

# Chapter 43

When Reagan cleared his immediate vicinity, he looked up to see that *Unity* was down, drifting like an empty sumna fruit shell across the battlefield. He opened his mouth to speak an order to go get them, but Asgre ships had moved in around him again and his attention was drawn to dealing with them.

There were, Reagan realized, just too many. The Minean fleet was too badly outnumbered, and even the advantage of their superior weaponry and maneuverability was not enough to defeat these odds.

A transmission from the ground forces came. "Galo's ship is readying weapons! We need backup!"

"Daring!" Reagan remembered the enormous batteries of guns on Galo's ship. *Champion* was the only battleship they had that had hope of matching them. "Turn us around. We need to get down to Coriol!"

"*Wisdom*, give us some cover," Reagan called, but it was too late. Six Asgre cruisers, apparently recognizing that *Champion* was making a move, warped in, surrounding them in every direction.

The flash of the weapons nearly blinded Reagan as the Asgre opened fire simultaneously.

Reagan had time for a single command before the volley

hit. "Warp us out of here!"

*Champion* shuddered as the shells found their target, nearly simultaneously. The weapons chief returned fire, and *Wisdom* sprayed two of the ships with fire from behind.

Reagan braced himself for the warp, but *Champion* stayed where she was. "Insta-Warp us to safety coordinates, Daring." Reagan repeated the order, but Kaia's voice caught his attention.

"The YEN drive is off-line, Admiral. We're not going anywhere."

Time seemed to slow for Reagan in that moment, as the endless barrage of shells pummeled the ship and the flashing of the YEN-drive warning light lit the bridge with an eerie red glow. The faces of the children in Coriol, including the two he thought of as his grandchildren, flashed before him as he frantically tried to think of a way out of this.

And then, suddenly, he felt a rumbling. Snapping back, he glanced at his screens and saw it: *Vigilant* had warped in above them and engaged e-links.

Reagan felt the ship shift as it warped and watched the Asgre ships around him blur and disappear.

The last few shells landed, having warped with them, as he looked out at the tranquility of the safety coordinates.

*Vigilant* disengaged the e-links and warped away. "I'll be back for you, sir," Nieman said.

"Good work, Captain." Reagan called into the comms after him.

Reagan soon found that being on the outside of the action was worse. Sitting in the dark, watching the battle rage on their screens, the crew sunk into a tense and somber silence.

*Wisdom* continued to fight, and *Vigilant* engaged the first ship she met when she warped back.

"Team up!" Reagan barked into his comms. "One behind,

one in front. Use your company ships, Captains!"

*Advocate* went down, and then *Tenacious.* Reagan saw how this was going to end.

"Evade," he said into the comms. "Run evasive maneuvers and try to save yourselves."

\*\*\*

Aria and the Vala Svetal had taken the children to the empty school playground, just to give them a little outing. It would have been a glorious time if not for the suddenly descending Asgre ship.

Aria tried to get them in the school, but it was locked. Looking frantically around, she saw Reverend Hardy's little church two blocks away. She took the children there.

The reverend welcomed them in, and she saw they were not alone. Minz was there, and Hannah, and a few straggling adults who were too old or too infirm to be standing ready to fight the Asgre ground troops hand to hand.

She settled the children on the benches just as Luis burst in the door. He came to Aria, and his presence was strong and reassuring.

Reverend Hardy slid his missive in his pocket. "I've talked to Coriol Defense Headquarters," he said. "They'll send help if they can, but we can't stay here. We must go. Now." His big voice rang in the little church. "The Asgre will be upon us. We must get the children to the safety of the base!"

Aria herded the children, human and Vala, through the bare streets as the last fingers of light began to disappear from Coriol. She carried Rigel and held Polara's hand as they moved.

She had to get them to the base. All of them. It was the only place that could withstand an Asgre attack. But it lay across the city, and the Asgre would be monitoring every sol train line.

The Vala parents had left these children in Aria's care.

Aria moved with the children down the street. They were nearly to the water plant, halfway to the base, and they were moving quickly.

The reverberation of Galo's engines above echoed off the buildings around them. Aria glanced up to see the big ship moving over the city.

As his ship drew nearer, Galo's voice, amplified by the communication system, rattled the windowpanes in the buildings around them. "Deliver us the Vala children and your own will be saved."

She heard a commotion behind her. She turned to see a limping man dragging a Vala child from the group, striding toward the sound of Galo's voice. Aria raced toward him, leaving Polara near the other children and shifting Rigel. She moved faster than she thought she could.

"Stop!" she grabbed the man's arm with her free hand.

He tried to shake her off. "Lemme be! Let 'em take their slaves and leave us in peace!"

Luis was suddenly beside her, scooping the Vala child into his powerful arms and knocking the man backwards onto the street. "You've never been a slave," he said threateningly. "Or you wouldn't be so eager!"

"Well, then, I'm not staying with you," the man said from the ground. "I hope they catch you all." He scrambled to his feet and limped off down the street.

As Luis strode back to the group, Aria got a look at the Vala child's face. So terrified before, its wrinkled face was now relaxed in sleep, and tears were rolling down its cheeks. That was it. When frightened, their safety mechanism was to go dormant. And it was then that they were, somehow, useful to the Asgre. That was why the monsters kept the children scared.

The cruelty of it brought a wave of anger.

Galo began a countdown, every number like a blow on their ears.

Aria clawed at Luis's arm. "We're not going to make it to the base! We need to get them inside! Now!" She gestured to the hulking mass of the water plant a block away. Luis nodded and the group began to run. Minz was the quickest, and he got several of the children into the water plant just ahead of the Reverend, who was helping an old woman and speaking softly to several Vala children, who seemed to derive serenity from his words, though Aria knew they couldn't understand him.

Aria waited for Svetal to enter, then herded the last of the children into the water plant just as the Asgre started strafing the streets outside.

Aria watched from a window, cradling Rigel in her arms. The Asgre lead ship, maneuvered, she knew, by Galo, was heading straight for the water plant. How had he found them? How had he done it so quickly?

Their shelter shook under the barrage of the Asgre's shells. Suddenly, Rigel's small hands were pawing her face. She pushed them aside, trying to think.

"No, no, Ri. Mommy has to think." What could she do? How could she get them out of here?

Rigel grabbed at her ear. She felt the old frustration. It was so hard to concentrate with a toddler demanding attention. "No, Ri!"

And then the child laid his small hands gently on her cheeks. His eyes searched her face. She looked down at him. As their eyes met, Ri clumsily pushed forward and laid his forehead against hers. Aria gasped as Rigel's frantic thoughts flooded into her mind. She saw the new Taim field, the Taim swaying wildly. They were speaking to Ri again and he had to convey their message.

Through a sequence of colors and pictures, Aria felt the call of the Taim. They wanted the children to come to them. Ri showed her the children, human and Vala, running to the Taim. He grunted urgently.

She shook her head. "No, honey. We have to go to the soldiers." She tried to send him a picture of Grandpa Reagan in his uniform.

Ri patted her cheeks angrily and wriggled, sending her the picture of the Taim again. She felt that the Taim wanted to protect them, that they wanted to protect her child as she had protected them. It seemed crazy. A wide, open Taim field? What protection could they offer? She tried to send the question back, but she couldn't know if Rigel even understood it, much less if he could transfer it to the Taim.

Aria choked on the thick, dusty air. She looked around at the little group she was trying to save. She believed the message was coming from the Taim, through Rigel. She believed that he believed there was safety with them. But how could the Taim, even at their remarkable new height, protect them?

Another barrage of artillery fell on the roof above. The sound of the exploding shells was deafening. Chips of concrete fell, raining down in a light shower. The building was strong, but it would not stand up to much more of this. Many of the Vala children were huddled together, and the human children were wailing. Luis encircled several of them, human and Vala, in his short, strong arms. Hannah was singing to a group of them, and she saw the Reverend's head bowed in prayer. She had to make a decision. If she didn't get them out of here, the Asgre would be upon them any moment. The question flashed again in her mind: how could the Taim possibly protect them?

As the image of the tall, swaying trees entered her mind, a

peace settled over her. Aria knew plants. She had seen, back on Earth, the majestic kapok tree. Its trunk, ten feet in diameter, sheltered animals and other plants, and humans, sometimes. On another continent, she had stood inside the protective trunk of a huge baobab as a pack of lions circled outside. Plants had been sheltering humans for eons. Though she didn't see how they would do it, Aria trusted them.

"We have to send the children to the Taim," Aria said, as boldly as she could.

"What?" Hannah shouted over the noise.

"Ri says—the Taim say—to bring them the children." She reached her free hand out and laid it on Luis' shoulder. "I think they want to protect them."

There was a moment of confusion among the adults.

"To the Taim?" Hannah's face was doubtful.

Aria felt the shells as they impacted. She thought of the distance they'd have to cover if they tried to get to the defense headquarters, thought about covering it with these small, frightened children in tow. The desperation of the situation made the decision for her. They wouldn't make it to the base.

Aria spoke again. She heard the commanding tone in her voice. "This is not up for debate. We are going to the Taim." She looked around at them. "What I need from you is a plan. *How* are we going to get there?"

Another shell rocked the building, the percussion throwing them to the ground. This time, large chunks of concrete fell, narrowly missing them. Aria scrambled to her feet.

"How do we get out of here?" Aria cried. "They're directly above. If we go into the streets we'll be spotted immediately. But we've got to get to the farm!"

The shelling stopped briefly, leaving behind an eerie silence punctuated by her last few words and the clatter of falling rubble around them.

Minz walked close to her and spoke up, his soft voice surprisingly bold in the silence. "After Ethan talked to Saras, I got a job cleaning the filters in this plant a few weeks ago," he said. "I worked in the maintenance tunnels underneath. They sent me from here through the tunnels to the farm to scrub the filters in the clean rooms. The tunnels lead to the farm. I think we could make it if we went through there."

Aria reached out and hugged him spontaneously. The little man looked embarrassed. She felt a surge of hope as she turned to the children.

"Okay, little ones," Aria spoke gently, trying to convey more confidence than she felt, "You need to follow me, and you need to be so, so quiet." She walked comically on her tiptoes and the children giggled and followed her. She gestured to Minz, and he took the lead. They followed him across the rubble-strewn room and down a flight of stairs just as the shells started falling again.

The tunnels he led them through were narrow and damp, the access panels in their walls leading directly to the filters the water ran through before it was sent to the treatment part of the facility. The lighting was unpredictable as well, with large, dark gaps between many of the fixtures. Aria heard Hannah's voice rising in a soft lullaby that calmed both the humans and the Vala.

It seemed they had been forever in the dark, damp tunnel, but more likely it had only been a block or two when a shell hit the top of the tunnel just behind them, blowing the tunnel open and flooding it with light from Galo's ship's search beams and debris.

Aria saw it then, sparkling behind them in the tunnel, caught by the sweeping light: a shining trail of tears the little sleeping Vala in Luis's arms was leaving behind. Could Galo be using those to track them? However they had found them, the Asgre were coming.

"Minz!" Aria shouted toward the front of the long line. "We need to run!"

They ran, Aria's arms burning with Rigel's weight. She tried not to trip over the little Vala child in front of her. Another shell fell behind them. They were getting closer.

Finally, Minz stopped and ascended a steep stairway jutting from the side of the tunnel. As she watched him open the door at the top, she felt panic, not relief. What would await them above?

They emerged in the empty lobby of the farm's operations building and followed Minz through the first decontamination room and through one of the vast clean rooms, where the new plants grew healthy with the Taim cleansing the air.

Aria mentally checked for each child as they ran through the last empty decontamination room. As they emerged into the fields outside, the world was dark around them. The Asgre ship was still working on the tunnel behind them, tearing it open with projectiles down the length of it.

"Which way to the Taim field?" Minz asked desperately.

Aria paused, turning, disoriented in the dark. She felt Rigel's mind reaching out and tried to meet it, but found he wasn't reaching for her. He was reaching, she realized for the Taim, calling out to them in his infant need.

A ripple of light to their left drew their attention. Aria looked up to see the forest of Taim, grown to ten meters high, like their parents in the mountains, and dancing with flashing multicolored lights on their crowns and trailing branches. The sweet scent of apple blossoms and vanilla filled the night air. Instinctively, the children ran for them. Aria could not have stopped them if she'd tried. The adults followed as the Asgre ship, apparently noticing the Taim as well, left the tunnel and cruised toward them.

Aria looked back to see Hannah and Polara, the last of the group, silhouetted against the powerful beams of the ship's floodlights. She stopped, running back to them. Aria grabbed Polara's little hand and the two women lifted her between them as they ran, gunfire kicking the dust around their heels.

Ahead of them, the first of the children entered the Taim forest and the trees began to glow steadily, from the bottom of their trunks to their fringed tops. Their delicate branches would offer, Aria saw, no protection. They were not like the massive kapok and baobab. There were no protective cavities to duck into, no thick branches to shield the humans and Vala from the shells and the shackles of the Asgre, but there was nowhere else to go. And Rigel continued to relay the call of the Taim: "Bring the children."

Aria, Hannah, and the two children tumbled into the meager shelter of the Taim forest barely ahead of the Asgre ship. Aria pulled her children into her arms and scrambled a few trees in, huddling next to the glowing trunk of one of the Taim. In the seconds it took for the Asgre ship to reach the forest, something remarkable happened.

The Taim began to hum. Their fragile branches intertwined and the light they were emitting reached a daylight brilliance. The ship hovered overhead and Aria watched the first shell fall. To her amazement, the shell hit the canopy of entwined branches and exploded, its fragments bouncing high into the sky as if repelled by the Taim.

The children gasped at the light show. Aria marveled, remembering the broken and charred Taim field in the mountains. The Taim had experienced this before. This remarkable species must have evolved a protection for their tender seedlings in the case of fire from above. And now they shared their protection with humanity. Galo's ship dropped shell after shell, but Aria and the children, in the shelter of the Taim, felt nothing.

Rigel's eyes were wide as he watched the explosions. His mind was finally quiet. Aria felt again the deep calm that was so much a part of him. He felt safe. The Taim were watching over them.

***

When Daniel swung the door to the apartment open, he heard the sound of singing. The door to the back bedroom was ajar, and inside he found Zella, surrounded by the children. The scene was so peaceful, compared to the violence he'd just witnessed, that when Zella rose and took him in her arms, Daniel laid his head on her shoulder and wept with shock and relief.

"Are they gone?" Zella asked, so softly that only he could hear.

"The ships are still fighting," he said. "I could have stayed at the base, but I wanted to be here to—to take care of you." He looked her in the eye, willing her to understand what he was really saying, what he meant by it.

Zella ran a hand through his hair with one hand and patted the weapon at her hip with the other. "And so I can take care of you?"

Daniel smiled as she leaned up and kissed him. For the first time in a long time, he felt like he had broken above the water and could breathe again.

# Chapter 44

Ethan stood in the Coriol Defense Headquarters and looked at the engagement board. The transports had returned them here and the Vala were being made comfortable in the barracks. In the situation room with Ethan were Sergeant Nile, several company troop leaders, and the Governors. Saras and Veronika were there, as well, though Ethan suspected that they had come more to be protected in the Headquarters than to help with strategy.

Ethan looked at the red dome on the engagement board which marked the Taim grove where Aria and the children huddled under the Taim's protective shield while Galo's ship rained fire above them. He didn't know how long it would last, and he was wild to go after the Asgre ship himself, but there were no ships to spare.

The Asgre, with their blunt, cruel ships, were wrecking the Minean fleet. Reagan's *Champion* was disabled in the safety zone, called so because it was far from danger, not because it was particularly well defended against it. The rest of the fleet hung in orbit above Minea, many drifting from critical damage. Only three battleships and two colony fleet ships were left to fight more than thirty Asgre ships. They had no chance against this enemy. Ethan saw it as he listened to Reagan on the comms link and the others in the room discussing strategies and moving the little model ships around on the engagement board. They even advised the remaining battleships to employ the principles Yi Zhe had taught them, which had worked so well on the ground. But the sheer number of Asgre ships compared to the number of Minean ships made success unlikely.

Reagan swore across the comms link. "If only we had the fleet," he said. Ethan could tell the Admiral was growing desperate. Reagan didn't waste time wishing.

A calm voice spoke from the back of the room. They turned to see Ahmasa, one of the Vala mothers whom Ethan had come to know, entering through the door. With her was Chelus, her small son.

She looked at Ethan. "Will you speak for me?"

He nodded, wishing again that he had his translator. "I'll try." He translated the best he could as she spoke.

"We can help you retrieve your fleet," Ahmasa said. "If you will protect us and save the Vala on the ships."

Ethan looked around the room. It was obvious that the Sergeant saw no way that such gentle-looking creatures, who had huddled vulnerably in the flowstone battle, could help in this conflict. Even Reagan was silent on the comms line, but Ethan knew him well enough to know he would give them a chance.

Ethan stepped in, speaking. "You have a way to help us? Help us get our fleet? From Earth?" Even in Ikastn, it sounded implausible when he said it out loud.

Ahmasa launched into a description of her plan, but the words and concepts were so unfamiliar that he was lost a little way in. She stopped, frustrated, and Ethan felt her desperation as well. How could they understand what she was trying to say? He knew from his previous attempts at telepathic communication with the Vala that removing his thought blocker would only add to the confusion. There was no time for miscommunication.

"Maybe you could show us?" he said, stringing together some of the simple Ikastn words he knew he would not get wrong. As she considered, Ethan thought about the simplicity of their communications, forced by the language barrier. As a linguist, he loved language and the complexity that came with translating a being's inner thoughts and worldview into something others could grasp—but the longer he knew the Vala, the more convinced he was becoming that speaking precisely and plainly had its advantages.

"Yes," Ahmasa said, "come here." She held out her hand. So did her little son. The Sergeant scoffed and walked a few feet away, turning his back on her outstretched hand. Ethan walked over and took Chelus's hand. Saras's eyes showed that he didn't trust them enough to approach. Ahmasa shrugged, then she picked up the model of *Champion*, the jewel of the fleet, and showed it to Chelus, who closed his eyes.

Ethan didn't have time to take a breath. It was as if he'd been slammed in the chest by a sol train. His eyes closed as his head snapped back. When he opened them, he was looking at the shocked face of Phillip Reagan.

Ethan gasped for breath. He was on the bridge of *Champion*—but that was impossible.

He heard, over the comms, a stir in the room he had just left.

"Where did they go?"

"They disappeared!"

"What is happening?"

Ethan was impressed with Reagan's calmness as he spoke. "They're on my ship."

Shocked silence filled the comms line.

Finally, Saras snapped, "Are they trying to infiltrate our defenses? They could be trying to take over our fleet."

Ethan was annoyed by Saras's paranoia, but given what he'd been through lately with Theo, it was understandable.

"They picked the wrong ship for that," Reagan said. "We're not going anywhere."

"We can help you, if you will help us." Ahmasa said, keeping her words simple so that Ethan could translate. Her wide, watchful eyes roamed constantly over everything on the ship, looking for danger.

"What do we do?" Ethan asked Ahmasa.

"Go to your home world," came her reply.

Ethan shook his head. "The ship is broken, and even if it wasn't, Earth is—" he held up five spread fingers and tried to think of the Ikastn word for what would be the equivalent of Earth's "years." Even with the YEN drive, by the time they made the round trip the Asgre would have wiped out the humans and taken the Vala by force.

Ahmasa shook her head impatiently. "Set your course," she said, "for Earth." Her pronunciation of the planet's name was close enough to be understood, but her accent gave the word a holy sound.

Ethan glanced at Reagan, who shrugged. "It's not going to hurt anything. We might as well do what she says."

The captain of *Champion*, Captain Andrew Daring, kept a watchful eye on the strange visitors as he entered the coordinates for Earth. To Ethan's surprise, the ship began to move at a cruising speed, the engines silent as they moved through the vacuum of space with ease. Ethan had never traveled by RST before, but he had heard that ships shuddered violently as they moved into RST, so when he felt it, he knew what was happening, but he didn't know how.

He glanced at the Vala. They stood calm and poised, still holding hands. But the child's eyes had closed, and he appeared to be asleep standing up. Something shone crystalline on his cheeks. As Ethan looked more closely, he saw them: tears. Just like the sleeping Vala he had seen in the Cavern of Sleepers, they coursed down his cheeks as he slept. As they left his face and fell, they crystallized and fell to the floor of the ship in solid, glassy drops that made a tiny chime when they landed.

At the moment he saw them, a flash outside the window caught his eye. Turning, he gasped and grabbed for the edge of the console in front of him.

An explosion of colored flames licked the outside of the ship, obscuring the viewing screen with vibrant Chroma. Ethan felt his eyes narrow at the brightness of it. Suddenly, ahead, he saw a ship appear and then disappear, above and to the left of them, another. Like points of light flaring and then fading, he saw five, ten ships appear around them and then they were gone.

And suddenly, there it was—glowing blue and white and beautiful, brighter than Lucidus: Earth.

Ethan felt his breath coming fast and shallow. Home.

A cheer went up from the crew of the ship. Ethan turned to the Vala in wonder. The child's eyes were open now.

"How?" he asked in Ikastn, softly.

The little Vala's skin wrinkled in a smile. "Alosha." *My gift.*

His mother beamed as well. "We can move your fleet as quickly back. If we will be allies, as you promised before." A cloud crossed her face suddenly. Ethan recognized it. It was the moment a parent saw a danger to their child. "You will not enslave us to use this gift," she said forcefully.

Ethan shook his head quickly. "No." He hoped slavery was

behind humanity forever.

She shook her head impatiently. "You will have no need," she said. "We can help you understand. Perhaps you, too, can travel in this way."

That was almost too much to hope. Ethan exchanged a glance with Reagan, but before they could speak they were interrupted by a forceful hail from Earth's defense headquarters. A communications officer appeared on the screen and there was wariness in his tone. Ethan saw that he had his finger on a red button that would likely trip the orbital defenses into attack mode.

"Ship, identify yourself."

Captain Daring hit the communicator. "We are the ship *Champion*, of the Minean Fleet."

The line was quiet a long time, then the voice came back on. "Please hold for the president."

She appeared on the screen in her street clothes, obviously not ready for a meeting. "What is going on?"

Reagan spoke up. "We've come for our ships, Madam President."

For once, Ethan saw her speechless.

"You're cleared for landing," the defense administrator said hurriedly.

As *Champion* moved down through Earth's atmosphere, Ethan felt a wave of emotion wash over him. He was home, but without Aria and the children, even Earth felt foreign. His home was wherever they were, and he wanted to get back to them.

\*\*\*

Ethan held the President's eye as he stepped off the ship.

"Is that—the Caretaker?" she asked her aide. "H-How?"

she stopped there.

"Madam President, we've made some new friends." Ethan gestured to the extended stairway behind him, where Ahmasa and Chelus stood shyly. The president's eyes widened, but she quickly composed herself and stepped forward, extending her hand.

Ahmasa took it and raised it to her own forehead, then to Chelus's. When she was finished, the president pulled it back awkwardly.

"You brought this ship here?" she asked, and Ethan translated.

Ahmasa nodded. "My son did."

Ethan gave the president Ahmasa's words, then spoke up for himself. "And they say they can help us modify the YEN drives to travel this way without them."

"Is that possible?" The president was skeptical.

Kaia spoke up. "I think so. These—" she held up a flat palm, filled with the child's diamond tears, "have some very unique properties."

Ethan wasn't sure he was comfortable with that. "I don't think we should build our fleet on children's tears."

Ahmasa laid a gentle hand on his arm and gave him a questioning look. He repeated what they had said.

She smiled. "They are not only tears. They are also sleeping secretions. When our children enter into a state of sleeping, the drops fall naturally."

"Then why the cages?" Ethan asked.

"The Asgre forced the children to navigate through shocking them. They wanted the secretions on demand. The cages shocked the children into a sleeping state and forced them to navigate the ships to coordinates implanted in their thoughts."

"It is," Ahmasa thought for a moment, "a defense mechanism. The children can navigate at will to any point in the universe. We lose it when we pass the time of becoming. We can still travel through space, but we must have our children present to help us."

That was a switch, Ethan thought, parents dependent on children for their well-being. But then he thought of the way Polara's arrival had made everything new. He thought of Rigel's communications with the Taim, and he realized humans weren't so different. The Vala just embraced the truth of their dependency more completely.

\*\*\*

With Minea under siege, every moment counted. Still, when the fleet had been gathered and its crews had said their goodbyes and reported for duty, *Champion* lingered, its passengers gazing at the planet of their birth.

"It's time to go back, sir," Daring said. "We've had a transmission from Minea that the Asgre ships are moving in on *Vigilant*. She's the last one left, sir."

Ethan saw Reagan turn from the blue orb in front of them to the Vala. "Take us home, please?"

This time, the little Vala moved, with no apparent difficulty, all eighty new ships, plus *Champion,* on which he stood. He entered the sleeping state, the tears flowed down his face, crystallizing and falling with soft pings.

Ethan watched as they moved through the strange light again, ships appearing and disappearing around them. A cosmic crossroads. Where were they all going? Where were they coming from when their paths crossed with *Champion's*?

\*\*\*

Reagan watched the sleek battleships appearing one by one around him in the vast stretch of space above Coriol.

They surrounded *Vigilant,* and the Asgre ships advancing on her pulled back. The ships of the new fleet matched one for one the Asgre ships, until twenty-five of the Earthships had appeared. The Asgre ships each began to advance on the nearest Earthship. Then, one by one, fifty-five more Earthships parted space and stood at the ready. The Asgre ships paused.

Reagan was dazzled by the suddenness of their return and by the remarkable fleet he now had at his command. He knew, too, though, that there were risks. Without working YEN drives, the ships could only retreat using their SL drives, which, if he had the Asgre figured right, would be no match for the speed with which they could move through space.

But the Minean fleet had done their work freeing many of the Vala children and many of the cages under the ships stood empty. Now he knew that they were no faster than his SL-driven ships without their slaves. And the vast number of Earthships tipped the battle in his favor, too.

"Surround the Asgre," Reagan commanded. The ships moved in a ring around the Asgre ships, which looked old and clunky next to the shining new Earthships.

The sergeant's astonished voice came on the comms line. "*Champion,* are you there? Do you copy?"

"We're here, headquarters. We've been on a wild ride."

"Look out!" The sergeant's voice was panicky. "There are ships warping in everywhere up there!"

The smile was evident in Reagan's voice when he said, "Don't worry sergeant. They're friendlies."

\*\*\*

Galo saw them, too, on his screens: the dots that were ships appearing like a pox around his fleet. He paused raining artillery down on the strange plants. They had withstood all he had, and still the Vala children stared up at him through their shelter.

What could he do? He spoke to his ships.

"How many Vala do we have?"

"One on board."

"Four on board."

"One on board."

"One on board." the reports flowed in. Adding the Vala child in his cage on Galo's Cliprig and the few straggling adults in the slave quarters, there were less than twenty. He hadn't realized how many had been freed from under his very ships during the battle. All while he was chasing these children.

Angrily, Galo took his ship out of the atmosphere. There, his fleet was surrounded by glistening new ships. The detritus of the old Minean fleet had been gathered and Galo saw some of the humans' new ships descending with the rescued ships.

These humans, with their moral superiority, were poised to destroy his business. Didn't they understand he had deliveries to make? He hammered his fists on the console, looking up from his tirade to see the battle-scarred *Champion*. He had faced off with it earlier. Galo's anger surged. He knew he was out of options. The only chance he had was to destroy Reagan, the leader of this misguided freedom fight. In a storm of fury and frustration, Galo launched his ship at it, hurling torpedoes as he advanced.

\*\*\*

Ethan barely had time to grab the edge of the engineering console he was standing next to and brace for the hits from Galo's Cliprig before he realized that they were not coming. Chelus had moved them instinctively before the shells could hit. They were now behind Galo's ship.

"Vector quantities?" Captain Daring called as the ship began to turn.

No one answered.

"Engineering!" Daring shouted, shooting a look toward the engineering chief.

Ethan's gaze went to Kaia. She was frozen at the console, the lost look in her eyes. She had lost the words, just as she'd feared. He knew them, remembered them from the warm evening at his house when he'd reassured her that they'd be there when she needed them.

Ethan wanted to call them out to her, felt them forming in his mouth. But Kaia's panicked eyes found his and he saw that to do so would be to lay bare the secret she had kept so carefully. She looked as he had first seen her, so long ago, when she'd awakened to a world she didn't understand.

"Engineering?" The captain's voice was a blade through the still air of the bridge.

Ethan knew what he had to do. He gritted his teeth. The agony that was coming welled up before him as he reached quickly, the movement of his hand concealed from the others on the bridge by Kaia's shoulder, and slipped her thought blocker off. At the same moment he used his other hand to slip off his own.

The wave of thoughts engulfed him. Nearly everyone on the ship surged with fear, even though their outward demeanor didn't reveal it. The anger and adrenaline of Daring and Reagan spiked through his mind, and the agony of the wounded in the sickbay below wrung his consciousness from him for a moment.

Kaia's knuckles, white on the console, revealed that she was feeling it, too. Ethan moved a hand to her shoulder. At the contact, the swirling thoughts around him faded and her calm, blank consciousness smoothed the pain from his mind.

As he had so often longed to do, when she had lost his name or the date of her birth, he gave her the words. He laid them, like pearls, in her mind and he heard her speak them. For a moment, Ethan's strength was hers, his youth, hers again.

"Angular velocity," she reported, and a string of numbers she'd found on her instruments followed.

"Good work, engineering," Daring called, making adjustments on his panel. Kaia turned her head, looking up at Ethan with gratitude.

They were pulled out of the moment as the big ship maneuvered into position and Reagan ordered a strike. Shells sprayed from *Champion's* forward battery, striking Galo's ship across the rear thrusters. He rolled to evade, and Reagan saw the perfect moment to launch a missile at Galo's engine room as the big ship breached.

The explosion was spectacular. Ethan saw the cage beneath Galo's ship tear in half, and the little Vala inside floated free for a second before disappearing.

It reappeared on the bridge next to Ahmasa, who knelt and embraced what must have been another of her children. When the debris from the engine room cleared, Galo's trembling voice came across the hailing frequency.

"Perhaps, Mr. Reagan, it's time we discussed a compromise."

"There will be no compromise. The Vala will be released," Reagan said. Ethan could hear victory in his voice.

"I could, perhaps, keep a few?" Galo sounded penitent.

Reagan was firm, and Ethan saw in him redemption. "Not a single one. They will be brought safely, old and young, to the Coriol Defense Headquarters immediately."

The line was quiet a long time. Ethan saw the screens

showing that Reagan was keeping his weapons ready.

Galo's voice was bitter when he finally spoke. "We will comply."

One by one, the cages below the remaining ships opened. As the Vala children floated free, Ethan saw them stretch like newborn babies and disappear.

Reagan punched some keys and a video feed from Coriol Defense Headquarters appeared. On the screen, Ethan saw the Vala standing on the liftstrip, welcoming the children as they arrived. Ethan watched as families which had been split for several of his lifetimes were reunited.

Ahmasa was watching the screen closely, as well. She crossed to Reagan and spoke quietly to him.

"Galo," he said, "that means the Vala in your slave hold as well."

Galo began to protest.

"This is non-negotiable."

A piece of the plating slid back from the side of Galo's listing ship and a large metal door opened. Ethan saw the Vala as they stepped out into space, one by one. Some of them were very, very old.

"Is that everyone?" Reagan asked Ahmasa. She nodded.

"We will take them to the base," Ahmasa said, entwining her long fingers around her children's and disappearing. Ethan saw the little group of freed Vala also disappear. They were soon on the liftstrip with their families.

Reagan spoke again to Galo. "I expect you'll leave Minea and her solar system for good."

Galo's voice was broken. "We have no wish to stay. But it will take some time. Without the Vala, my ships are considerably slower."

"You'd better get going then," Reagan said. There was

satisfaction in his voice as he watched the Asgre gather their ships and move off into space.

Kaia smiled at Ethan. He smiled back. "Admiral," he said, "can you show us the Taim field? Are the children safe?"

Reagan punched some buttons and the glowing dome of the Taim field appeared. Ethan saw his family inside, their faces bathed in the light of the Taim.

***

It wasn't until the Asgre ships left Minea and passed Candidus, the Minean moon, that the Taim sensed their charges were safe and lifted the shield they had created.

Ethan was waiting beside it when it shimmered into oblivion and he pulled Aria and his children into his arms.

# Chapter 45

The battle was weeks behind them, and Kaia was losing more words. She felt it, opening her mental filing cabinets to find more empty drawers every day. But her engineering knowledge remained intact. It seemed, in some ways, sharper.

Ethan had teased her when she told him. "Maybe without my name cluttering up your memory, you have room for more important things." And they had laughed.

She was letting go of the shame of losing things, accepting their loss and embracing more fully what remained. Perhaps acceptance was part of the gift of aging. Yi Zhe said that every experience held good and bad, light and dark, joy and sorrow, and the balance was integral to life.

Using her heightened engineering abilities, she had been at work with the Vala and a team of engineers, mechanics, theorists, and anyone else who wanted to help on a new drive that combined the qualities of Yynium and the unique properties of the Vala secretions. If they could get it to work, the Vala would be the wildly wealthy. The UEG was poised to pay them well for their Yynium extraction services and for the crystalline teardrops that held the key to their unique ability. It was promising, but something was still missing, and Kaia could not yet see it.

It was a week after the battle when Kaia visited the junkyard. She was surprised to see Yi Zhe walk out of the blue cottage at the edge of the yard.

"I thought you'd be back to consulting," she said worriedly. "Coriol can certainly attest to your skills now."

Yi Zhe nodded, smiling broadly. "I have many consults scheduled. But we have decided to keep this job, as well." He waved a hand expansively. "Fire, earth, wood, water, metal—here we are surrounded by all the elements. We can achieve a powerful balance here."

Kaia bowed slightly. He was happy. That's what she wanted for all her passengers.

"Are you back to building robots?" Yi Zhe asked, a twinkle in his eye. "I've saved you some particularly nice pieces." He waved her along with him as he walked toward a careful arrangement near a corner of the cottage. He had saved beautiful parts. There were rich wooden gears, shining steel rods, and a knob that shone copper under a decoration of lacy green oxidation. Kaia gathered them and saw beneath them a part familiar only from the manuals. Nearly dropping the others, she snatched it up, spinning to face Yi Zhe.

"Where did you find this?"

"I uncovered the center of the old junkman's pile," he said. "Buried there were many of those. I liked the shape of it and thought it might be of use to you in your creations."

"There are more?"

Yi Zhe nodded. "Many."

"Show me!"

Yi Zhe took her to the center of the junkyard. He was obviously still in the process of excavating it, but there, in the center, were discarded pieces from the first ships that had come to Minea. And among them, reflecting the sun back at her from their gently curved front plates, were the Octagon drives that had brought humanity to Minea for the first time.

\*\*\*

When, an hour later, she dumped them onto the table in the Colony Offices boardroom, the team gave her quizzical looks.

She saw the Vala rocking their heads back and forth in assent as they ran their long fingers over the drives.

"These are the earliest Super-Luminal drives," she said. "They brought the first colonists to this planet."

The engineers were also nodding. Cayle, a young mechanic who'd been working for Saras before this, spoke up, "*and* they were extremely inefficient."

"Right," Kaia said, "but they had more potential than YEN drives, we just couldn't unlock it. But now we have Vala chips." She held up a crystalline teardrop.

"I think that combining the Octagon drives, Yynium, and the unique properties of the Vala chips may just work." Kaia gestured toward a young, untrained, but very talented designer, a friend of Aria's. "Daniel, I'd like you to get started sketching some concepts for a housing that would hold the critical components of the YEN drive, the core from one of these Super-Luminals, and a Vala chip, all in close proximity."

The boy beamed, and she saw him immediately begin sketching. He was eager and optimistic, a real asset to the team.

She spent an hour explaining her theory. The Vala made slight corrections as she spoke.

"I think we could have a drive ready pretty quickly," she said. "The tricky part is going to be getting our hands on a test ship."

"You've got connections," one of the engineers teased. "Let's try it out on *Champion*."

Kaia laughed. As fond as her father was of her, there was no way he'd let her test it on his favorite battleship, especially not since it had just been repaired and was back in the sky.

"I don't think so. Anyway, we need a smaller ship to start with." She turned to the Vala. "Perhaps we could impose on you to take us to Earth to bring back a small RST ship?" They had not asked the Vala to do this since the battle, though every human on Minea was anxious to return to Earth, at least for a visit.

"No need." Cayle spoke up.

"What do you mean?"

"I've got a ship we can use."

That seemed unlikely to Kaia. "Oh?"

Cayle nodded, rubbing a bit of grease from his knuckle. "A P5."

\*\*\*

Though it took months, the new drive was in the P5 and ready to test just days before the autumn Lucidus festival. Saras had been more than accommodating, donating the P5 for the project, requesting only that he be allowed on the test flight.

The shining P5 awaited them as Kaia, Ahmasa, Reagan, and Marcos Saras arrived at the liftstrip. Marcos was dressed well for the test flight, in a smart tuxedo with a pale aurelia flower in his lapel. Kaia shot Reagan a smile. You never knew what to expect with Saras.

The ship had been refitted, the five stasis chambers removed and replaced with five comfortable Earthleather chairs, taken, Kaia had heard, from Theo Talbot's hovercar. The ship rose smoothly into the atmosphere, and she felt the anticipation as the drive hummed to life behind them. Though all their tests had been smooth, there came the moment that existed before all new endeavors when Kaia felt the weight of possible failure and the desire to turn back. She gripped the arm of her chair and breathed deeply through that moment.

The ship shuddered and the colored flames bloomed around them and then, again, they were home.

*\*\**

Kaia watched Marcos Saras exit the ship and pull a dark-haired girl into his arms. Suddenly, his willingness to help with the project made sense. And his tuxedo made sense when he asked the girl to marry him there on the liftstrip.

But Kaia couldn't stop thinking about the drive. The test had been successful. The drive worked. It would allow for blindingly fast travel. Humans now had infinite choices. They could go home again. They could also, if they chose, move even farther beyond this delicate planet that was their birthplace.

# Chapter 46

Ethan walked through the cooling evening, following Polara as she darted in and out of the colorful booths in the new Coriol marketplace. The Vala were out, too, enjoying the evening alongside the humans. Brightly colored UEG money changed hands around them, and Ethan didn't miss the heavy scrip chain he'd carried for so long. The UEG had banned company scrip across the planet.

Saras was paying in UEG money now. Paying the miners and refinery workers who now spent their days in bright, clean plants, building ships and the new drives that would power them. When the UEG decreed that the Karst Mountain Range would not go to any company, but to the Vala, Ethan expected Saras to pout. But Saras, with the Vala Yynium contract, the new ship factories, the plants where his workers made the new drives, and his fiancée Serena beside him, was a new man. He had simply congratulated Aemon in awkward Ikastn.

Saras Company still owned the town, but it was finding new sources of revenue in addition to the ship factories and drive plants. Saras was leasing to small businesses, and several of Ethan's passengers had pooled their money and opened a shop made up of Hannah's dolls, Winn's carvings, and Luis's pottery. The people of Coriol, starved so long for beauty, kept the store busy.

There was also a new live theatre, where Angela and Manuel, as well as several others, performed every weekend. Ethan had even talked Ndaiye into singing with them, and he heard his friend's rich voice rising above the marketplace as they neared the theatre at the other end. Ethan and his family were on their way there now, to watch the new play his friends had written for the autumn Lucidus festival.

Polara's delighted voice broke through the buzz of the crowd.

"Look at the butterflies, Daddy! Look!" she called. He followed her pointing finger up to see the ellisa sunara on their annual autumn migration. Their golden wings caught the last of the light and splashed it on Polara's face and hands as she danced below them. Chelus and a few Vala children joined her, reaching their long fingers toward the frolicking butterflies.

Ethan remembered the dark night in the cave, when he had longed to see these bright creatures. He thought of the surprises that the survey craft crash had brought into his life and wondered what else lay ahead.

Every family was facing that question. Once enough ships were fitted with the new drives, Earth would be moments away. The universe would be moments away. They could return to Earth if they wanted. And some would go. But Minea was changing, for the better, and Ethan and Aria wanted to be part of that, to raise their children in the bright blue cottage that had come to be their home.

Ethan's eyes lingered on the Vala. They were interdependent. It was the humans' grit that had freed the Vala and the Vala chips that had made the universe accessible to humans.

Ethan thought about that. He wasn't as bothered by using the chips as he had been before. In fact, he thought, perhaps traveling on tears was a good reminder for humanity that all progress comes with a cost.

Rigel's small hand reached beyond the butterflies, toward the bright circle of Lucidus, hanging in the sky. The bells began to chime, and Ethan slipped an arm around Aria. They stood now, at the brink of space, and it lay before them like a river. Perhaps someday soon they'd take an outing to Lucidus. Perhaps someday they'd go beyond.

# About the Author

Josi Russell 's science fiction novels explore familiar human relationships in unfamiliar contexts. She currently teaches creative writing and fiction courses as an aAssociate pProfessor of English for Utah State University Eastern. She lives in the alien landscape of the high desert American Southwest with her family and a giant tortoise named Caesar. Josi is captivated by the fields of linguistics, mathematics, and medicine, by the vast unknown beyond our atmosphere, and by the whole adventure of being human.

Connect with the Author:
website: josirussellwriting.com
https://www.facebook.com/authorjosirussell
twitter.com/josi_russell

# Discover More Remarkable Books from Future House Publishing

Never miss a book release.

Sign up for the Future House Publishing email list.

www.futurehousepublishing.com

www.facebook.com/FutureHousePublishing

http://twitter.com/FutureHousePub